What can *you* feel in the dark?
How far are you willing to go beyond it?

Angela Knight does it . . . in the psychic realm of a woman attuned to the touch of strangers—and the powerful temptations of a seductive and mysterious protector.

Emma Holly does it . . . in the fantastic demon world where a powerful queen rules—until she commits the sin of falling in love with the handsome son of her worst enemy.

Lora Leigh does it . . . in the domain of a strange Breed, part man, part wolf, on the hunt for the woman he craves—and needs—to fulfill a hunger clawing at him from within.

Diane Whiteside does it . . . in an alternate universe of Regency magic where two lovers are threatened by a vicious mage and swept up in a turbulent war off the Cornish cliffs.

Beyond the Dark

Angela Knight
Emma Holly
Lora Leigh
Diane Whiteside

BERKLEY SENSATION, NEW YORK

THE BERKLEY PUBLISHING GROUP
Published by the Penguin Group
Penguin Group (USA) Inc.
375 Hudson Street, New York, New York 10014, USA
Penguin Group (Canada), 90 Eglinton Avenue East, Suite 700, Toronto, Ontario M4P 2Y3, Canada
(a division of Pearson Penguin Canada Inc.) • Penguin Books Ltd., 80 Strand, London WC2R 0RL,
England • Penguin Group Ireland, 25 St. Stephen's Green, Dublin 2, Ireland (a division of Penguin
Books Ltd.) • Penguin Group (Australia), 250 Camberwell Road, Camberwell, Victoria 3124, Australia
(a division of Pearson Australia Group Pty. Ltd.) • Penguin Books India Pvt. Ltd., 11 Community
Centre, Panchsheel Park, New Delhi—110 017, India • Penguin Group (NZ), 67 Apollo Drive,
Rosedale, North Shore 0632, New Zealand (a division of Pearson New Zealand Ltd.) • Penguin Books
(South Africa) (Pty.) Ltd., 24 Sturdee Avenue, Rosebank, Johannesburg 2196, South Africa

Penguin Books Ltd., Registered Offices: 80 Strand, London WC2R 0RL, England

This book is an original publication of The Berkley Publishing Group.

This is a work of fiction. Names, characters, places, and incidents either are the product of the author's
imagination or are used fictitiously, and any resemblance to actual persons, living or dead, business
establishments, events, or locales is entirely coincidental. The publisher does not have any control over
and does not assume any responsibility for author or third-party websites or their content.

First edition: December 2007

Library of Congress Cataloging-in-Publication Data

Knight, Angela.
    Beyond the dark / Angela Knight . . . [et al.]— 1st ed.
       p. cm. — (Berkley Sensation paranormal romance)
    ISBN 978-0-425-21876-1 (trade pbk.)
    I. Title.
    PS3611.N557B49 2007
    813'.6—dc22

                                    2007029889

PRINTED IN THE UNITED STATES OF AMERICA

10   9   8   7   6

CONTENTS

Dragon Dance

~

Angela Knight

CHAPTER ONE

Sergeant Arial Dean strode toward the command van, the beam of a flashlight bouncing ahead of her, illuminating dead brush and icy ground. For once she was grateful for the heavy weight of the bulletproof vest that provided extra warmth in the December cold. In summer, the vest quickly became a sodden, sweaty mini-sauna, tolerable only because it kept her from taking a round in the chest.

The white, blocky bulk of the RV loomed before her, emblazoned with the gold and blue James County Sheriff's Office shield that matched the badge on Arial's blue-jeaned waist. She hesitated at the narrow door and scanned the surrounding woods. Through the skeletal winter branches, a double-wide mobile home sat gleaming in the moonlight. White icicle lights hung from its eaves, their dim glow illuminating the beer cans lying in the patchy grass.

The patrol cars that were parked up and down the road weren't visible from the double-wide. Neither were the SWAT team members who'd surrounded the trailer in their black fatigues, lying belly-down and patient in the frosty leaves, rifles at the ready.

The sheriff was being extremely low key. Arial approved. The last thing they needed was to spook the asshole in the trailer into doing something stupid. They needed him to start using his pea brain before somebody got killed.

Like the little girls he'd taken hostage.

Arial slapped a hand on the RV's door. It opened with a creak and thump, and she scrambled up the narrow steps, nodding at the uniformed deputy in the driver's seat.

Sheriff Bill Davis looked up from his spot behind the bomb squad specialist. Davis was a tall, wiry man with a rawboned face who looked as if he should be riding the range. Like the bomb tech, he wore green fatigues and black combat boots. A green ball cap with an embroidered sheriff's star rode his thinning red hair. "Glad you're here, Dean. You gonna get this joker out of his hole for me?"

"I'm sure going to try, Sheriff." She made her way down the narrow passage between the RV's seats. "What have we got?"

"Tommy Phillips, thirty-five, white male. His wife is Charlotte. They've got two kids, Rebecca, who's three, and Mary, who's five." The sheriff pushed his ball cap up and leaned on the back of the bomb tech's padded seat. "Charlotte called 911 saying her husband was threatening to kill them all. When deputies arrived on the scene, Tommy informed them he was going to fry them *and* his wife and kids."

"*Fry?*" Arial frowned. "I don't like his choice of words. Do we know if he's armed?"

"No idea. He hasn't fired on anybody yet. Could be he's running a bluff . . ."

"Or he could have more weapons than Al Qaeda." And it was best to assume he did. This was the most dangerous kind of hostage incident. Unlike a cornered robber in a bank, a man who took his family hostage had no interest in negotiating with police. His objective was simply to kill his captives and probably himself. His wife and children weren't really hostages at all, but victims-to-be. "Have we made contact yet?"

"Nope. I've called him repeatedly, but our guys say they don't hear a phone ringing. Either he's just not answering—"

"Or he pulled it out of the wall. We need to get him a throw phone."

"Already on it." The bomb tech glanced up from the remote controls of the squad's robot and gave her a thin smile. His dark eyes glittered with an adrenalin junkie's intensity under his cap.

"I figured you were." Smiling grimly, Arial leaned over his shoulder to look at the black and white image on his laptop screen. The picture jounced, showing the view from the robot's camera as the little machine trundled toward the trailer on its caterpillar treads. It gripped a cell phone in one claw.

The department had bought the robot with Homeland Security funding a couple of years before to deal with suspicious packages, but it also did double duty in hostage situations. Sometimes subjects even surrendered to it, realizing that where the robot was, there were probably lots of cops with lots of guns.

Arial had a feeling Phillips wasn't going to be that accommodating.

The robot reached the trailer steps and stopped. The tech manipulated the joystick on his laptop to aim the camera at the door, then handed Arial a small microphone.

Her mouth went dry as she accepted it. She'd been a hostage negotiator for three years, but her first contact with a suspect never failed to tie her stomach in knots. She keyed the mike. "Tommy Phillips?" Her voice sounded steady and cool despite her nerves.

After a tense pause, the robot's microphone picked up Phillips's voice as he yelled through the trailer door. "What the hell do you want? And what the fuck is that thing?"

"It's a robot, Tommy. It's got a cell phone. We just want to talk to you. Nobody's been hurt, and we want to keep it that way." She hoped he picked up the subtext: *But if you get stupid, we're going to shoot you full of more holes than a hunk of deli Swiss.*

"Who are you?"

"Sergeant Arial Dean, Tommy. I'm the department's senior negotiator."

"Uh-huh." A short, calculating silence followed before Tommy said, "Okay, put the cell in front of the door and have Robbie back the fuck off."

Arial nodded at the bomb tech, who busied himself with the robot's joystick. The view from the camera jostled as the machine crept up the steps and extended its clawed arm, depositing the cell on the small wooden porch. That done, the robot headed back down the stairs and started off through the woods. Its camera was still pointed back at the trailer.

The door opened a few inches, and a man's hand appeared to grab the cell. He drew the phone inside, then extended his hand again, fingers spread wide. Arial tensed. "What the hell is he—"

A bright hot flare shot from the man's palm. The picture flared into static.

"Fuck!" yelped the deputy in the RV's driver's seat. "He just blew up the robot!"

As the tech cursed, Arial and the sheriff ran to the front of the RV to stare out the windshield. The robot burned like a torch, sixty thousand dollars in grant money going up in smoke.

"Oh, hell," Arial breathed, meeting the sheriff's wide-eyed stare. "Phillips is a Hyper!"

. . .

"MY team isn't equipped to deal with a Hyper." Captain Joe Gaines was a short, broad-shouldered, beefy man who'd commanded the SWAT unit for ten years. He was the kind of coolheaded commander who could be trusted not to overreact in even the worst situation, but he was visibly sweating now. "Especially not one who can do that." He gestured out the windshield, where a fire department brush truck was spraying the flaming robot with a deluge gun. None of the volunteer firefighters wanted to get out of the truck to attack the blaze with hoses.

Arial couldn't blame them. Hypers had first appeared five years before: seemingly ordinary people who abruptly developed abilities straight out of some kind of demented comic book. Flight, fantastic strength, the ability to control weather, telekinesis, other talents even more exotic. Abilities neither physics nor biology could explain. They weren't mutants, though that had been the initial theory. There was absolutely nothing about them that was genetically abnormal. They weren't angels or devils or witches, either, though those theories had gained proponents once science failed to offer anything better.

There was one thing everybody agreed on: Many of them were nuts. This wasn't the first time unlucky cops had found themselves in a standoff with a Hyper. Confrontations the cops tended to lose, with bloody results.

Yet somehow Arial was going to have to talk this particular lunatic out of his hole without getting anybody killed. Especially not his family or anybody in a uniform. She felt her palms start sweating at the thought.

Come on, Dean, she told herself. *This is what you've dedicated your whole life to: making sure no more innocents end up dead.*

Innocents like Jenny.

An image popped through Arial's mind: her best friend's pale, terrified face, huge blue eyes meeting hers. Jenny's father, the barrel of his gun shoved against the little girl's head. His slurred voice screaming threats at the cops.

The boom of his gun had sounded like the end of the world.

Arial thrust the memory away. She didn't have time for that. Not now. Not here.

Davis pulled off his cap and scratched his balding head. "Where the hell did this guy come from? We've never had a Hyper in this county. That's the kind of thing you get in New York or San Francisco, not James County, South Carolina."

"He may have picked Hyperism up somewhere else," Arial told him. "There's a theory that it's communicable."

Gaines stared at her. "So his wife and kids could catch it? My *guys* could catch it?"

She shrugged. "It's possible, but they don't think it spreads that easily. Otherwise there'd be a hell of a lot more Hyper humans than there are."

"Let's hope so. The one we've got now is more than enough." Davis glowered furiously, gnawing on his lower lip a moment. Finally he said, "I'm calling the Feds in on this. They've got agents on standby for shit like this. And we're going to need some means of containing this jackass once we take him down."

"It's going to take time for anybody like that to get here," Gaines pointed out. "The closest guy they've got is Tracker, and he's a couple hours away."

"I'll see if I can get Phillips on the phone," Arial told them. "Maybe I can keep him from killing anybody until Tracker can drive in from Charlotte."

· · ·

THE barbell was loaded with eight hundred pounds as Josiah Ridge pumped out another set of repetitions. It was cold as a bitch in the basement, and steam rose from his bare shoulders, tempting him to turn on the heat in the barren cement-block room. He didn't. Being cold was the whole idea of this little exercise in masochism. He was trying to discourage the aching hard-on in his sweats. The damn thing looked like a baseball bat.

Celibacy sucked.

Christ, sometimes he'd kill just to sit in a coffee shop and look into a woman's eyes. Listen to her talk about her day, her newest pair of pumps, anything. Unfortunately, he doubted he had the self-control to restrict himself to conversation. And he just couldn't take the chance.

Not with his Beast clawing for control.

To distract himself from his burning biceps and hungry dick, Josiah listened to the police scanner crackling on the weight bench behind him. If he got really lucky, the cops would need Tracker. A good fight would burn off a lot of frustration.

As if on cue, a series of high-pitched beeps sounded.

"Thank you, Jesus." Somehow he managed to resist the urge to drop the barbell and lunge for his beeper. Last time he'd done that, he'd cracked the concrete floor. Instead he forced himself to gently lower the weights to the ground before plucking the beeper off the bench.

His brows flew upward when he saw the number on the tiny screen. It was John Myers, his FBI contact.

This promised to be a hell of a lot more interesting than the convenience store robbery he'd expected. If John was calling, it meant there was Hyper trouble.

Which meant he was either going to get the fight he was spoiling for . . .

Or he was going to end up dead.

• • •

"SHE thinks she can leave me," Phillips snarled. In the background, a dog yapped furiously. The microphone planted in the throw phone picked up the sound clearly, just as it carried the sound of muffled sobbing. "Well, hell with that. I'm gonna fry the bitch. Her and her brats."

Arial's palm felt slick around the phone. Her sweat-damp T-shirt felt glued to her back under her Kevlar vest. Her throat was hoarse from trying to talk sense into him over the past two hours.

Groping for inspiration, she glanced down at the file that had been compiled by another negotiator, who'd been calling Phillips's friends and relatives. "Tommy, we've talked to your mother. She said this isn't like you—you love Charlotte, Rebecca, and Mary. They're great kids, beautiful kids. Charlotte's a good mother. If you do this, you're going to regret it the rest of your life. And think about the rest of your folks, your brothers, their kids. They'll never get over it." Arial certainly never had.

"This ain't my fucking fault!" Phillips yelled over the dog's high-pitched barks. "I didn't ask for this—becoming a Hyper. I was normal! Just fueling my rig in a truck stop in Mobile when this bitch came up and blasted me. For no reason!"

Arial frowned. "A woman *attacked* you? And that's how you became a Hyper?"

"Oh, yeah. I came to lyin' beside my truck, and the bitch was gone. The next day, fire starts shooting from my hands. I caught my own fucking rig on fire. Company canned me! It was an accident, but the bastards fired me anyway. Fuckers."

She winced. Lost job, wife walking out—it was the classic nightmare recipe guaranteed to push a control-freak male into killing somebody. "There's no doubt you got a raw deal, Tommy. But what you're doing now—"

"Now this bitch says she's gonna walk on me. Says I'm dangerous!" He lifted his voice and yelled at the animal, "Dammit, Pugly, shut the fuck up!"

"Don't kill him, Daddy!" one of the little girls screamed.

Arial tensed. If he went off on the dog, it could trigger him into attacking the rest of his family. She had to get him calmed down before the situation spiraled into murder. "Becoming a Hyper isn't your fault." *But taking your family hostage is, you selfish shit.* "But it's not your wife's either, or those pretty little kids'. Turn 'em loose, Tommy."

"Yeah, right. I do that, and you cops'll kill me."

"We're not going to hurt you. Not if you let your family go." *But if you kill them, I'll personally put a bullet between your eyes. Even if it's the last thing I ever do.*

Arial took a deep breath and fought to inject her voice with a calm she didn't feel. "Look, nobody's been injured. We can still help you. But if you let your anger run away with you, you're going to ruin everything for your children, your wife, and yourself. There won't be any going back."

"You think you can take me?" He'd reeled from fear back to defiance. "Did you see what I did to that robot?"

"I saw. But we're still not going to let you kill those people, Tommy. Let us help you."

He fell silent. Children sobbed softly. A woman's voice spoke. "Listen to her, Tommy! I won't leave you, I swear. Just don't hurt the kids—"

"You're lying," he roared. "You think I don't know what you're doing? You're trying to play me!"

The call cut off.

"Shit." Arial hit redial. The phone rang repeatedly, but there was no answer.

Sheriff Davis walked over to her, the captain of the SWAT team at his heels. Davis's normally ruddy face looked pale. "Are we out of time?"

She raked her hair back from her face. "Let me try to get him back on the phone. As long as I've got him talking, he's not cooking anybody." The fact that she'd kept him on the phone for two hours was actually a good sign. At least he was willing to talk. Too often in this kind of situation, the hostage taker wouldn't answer the phone at all.

"You think he's going to blow?"

Arial shrugged. "Blasting the robot was a bad sign. And from what I gather, new Hypers are emotionally unstable. Something about the brain chemistry . . ."

"So if I lead my guys in, we could end up like the robot." Gaines drummed his gloved fingers on his holster, a ferocious frown on his face. "But if we don't go in, the woman and the kids could end up crispy critters. I don't like either of those options."

"Neither do I. Let me get Phillips back on the phone. Maybe I can still talk him out." She hit redial again.

No answer.

Suddenly the radio crackled. "Hey, Sheriff? Tracker's here."

"Thank God!" Davis said. "Let him through."

Arial hit redial again. "Answer, dammit."

She was listening to the phone ring when the RV's door slid open. A man stepped onto the bus and strode down the aisle toward them. Arial looked up—and almost dropped her cell.

A long duster swung around his booted ankles, emphasizing the width of broad shoulders and powerful chest. He wore something black and gleaming beneath the coat, a one-piece suit constructed in jointed segments that suggested very expensive, very high-tech body armor. A black mask covered his head and the upper part of his face, its thickness obviously designed more to protect his skull than disguise his identity. Red lenses shielded his eyes, making it impossible to determine their color. The end result called attention to the broad line of his jaw and the sensuality of his mouth.

He sure as hell didn't look like any Fed she'd ever seen.

"Hello, Sheriff," he said in a deep male rumble. "I gather there's a problem."

"You could say that," Arial muttered, hitting redial.

"All right, bitch," Phillips growled, picking up at last. "Tell me again why I shouldn't blow this trailer to Kingdom Come—along with every cop for ten miles around."

"Yeah," Tracker said. "That does sound like a problem."

. . .

AFTER a less than encouraging briefing from Sheriff Davis, Josiah stepped outside the RV to sample the air and listen. With his Hyper senses, he could easily pick out the sounds of muffled sobbing coming from the trailer. It made his gut coil into a knot. Keeping Phillips's wife and little girls alive was going to take every bit of skill and strength he had. Not to mention sheer, dumb luck.

He wondered if the asshole had any other powers than the ability to melt robots into slag. He hated dealing with new Hypers. You never knew what they were capable of. Plus, they tended to be batshit crazy. It could be weeks before they regained enough judgment and experience to control their powers, and in the meantime, they could do a hell of a lot of damage.

Josiah's initial delight at getting the call from John Myers had vanished as soon as the agent started describing the situation. Unless he could get his ass to James County in a hurry, he was about to have a lot of dead cops and civilians on his hands.

Five minutes later, he'd hit I–85 with light and sirens screaming. He'd floored his black SUV all the way.

Though he wasn't technically an employee of the federal government, Josiah's quasi-official status made his life much simpler. For one thing, it meant he didn't have to worry about being arrested as an unlicensed Hyper vigilante.

The badge did come with strings, of course: the understanding that if he screwed up, he could go to jail. The Feds had his true identity on record, though it was kept secret to protect any family and friends from other Hypers who might be harboring a grudge. And of course, the deal also meant he had to answer midnight calls to risk his ass against nut jobs like Phillips.

His armor might be fire resistant, but he had the ugly feeling this new Hyper could dish out more than it could take. If he wasn't fast—and lucky—he could end up a crispy critter himself.

But better him than Phillips's wife and kids.

Josiah glanced back at the RV. The pretty hostage negotiator was still sweet-talking, which was why he hadn't already kicked in the trailer door. He'd rather give her the chance to get the bastard out peacefully than risk a confrontation that might end with dead bodies.

One of the dim interior lights spilled across the woman's face, illuminating her elegant profile. Her eyes were large, a deep, lustrous brown that precisely matched the long, straight sweep of her hair.

She had the kind of bone structure a supermodel would envy, and her mouth was full, sensual, and soft. The only flaw he could see was a small silver scar that sliced down her stubborn little chin. The contrast between the looks and the scar was intriguing. He wondered how she'd gotten it.

Her voice went with the face, a husky whiskey purr that gave a hint of phone sex to even the deadly serious conversation she was having with Phillips. No wonder the asshole was willing to stay on the line with her. That voice was a weapon all by itself.

Once Tracker would have taken one look and started making plans to seduce himself a pretty cop. But even if that had been an option now, his Hyper senses picked up a faint smoky blue glow surrounding her. He scratched his jaw and sighed. He'd have to warn her before she got herself into real trouble.

She glanced out the window at him. He gave her a smile, but she didn't smile back.

Great. She was one of those. A lot of people hated Hypers, even the good guys. He'd encountered that kind of bigotry more times than he could count in the five years since his transformation, but he'd never gotten used to it.

He looked back across the woods. The dog was yapping again, shrill and relentless. It was getting on his nerves.

As if on cue, a male voice rang through the trees. "Pugly, *shut the fuck up*!"

BOOM!

A single, agonized yelp. Three female voices began to scream.

Josiah's head jerked around, and he met the negotiator's horrified eyes. He could see in her face exactly what he was thinking. *The kids are next.*

. . .

ARIAL saw Tracker run for the trailer at a speed an Olympic sprinter would envy. She was up and running for the RV's exit before she even had time to process what she was going to do. "Sheriff, Tracker's going in!"

Someone cursed as she stopped at the door to jerk the fire extinguisher out of its rack. She slammed the door open and hit the ground running. Behind her, Davis bellowed, "Dean! What the hell are you doing?"

He was right. *I'm the hostage negotiator. I don't do this. This is SWAT's job.*

But there were little girls in that trailer. Little girls like Jenny. Somebody had to get them to safety, and Tracker was going to have his hands full with Phillips.

Swinging the fire extinguisher up on her shoulder, Arial ran faster. As she raced through the woods, she heard Gaines bellow behind her, "We're going in!"

The members of the SWAT team lunged from their concealment in the surrounding woods, vengeful black-clad ghosts. Brush crunched as they began to run, male voices rising in shouts. "Police!"

Just ahead, Tracker cleared the railing of the trailer's tiny porch and hit the door in midair. It crumpled like tin foil with a thunderous screech. Shrieks rang—the cry of the mother, the shriller screams of the children. Phillips howled obscenities.

Arial leaped up the steps after Tracker to find the minuscule den full of smoke. She coughed and squinted, barely making out the two male figures writhing on the floor in the thick black cloud.

Tracker was straddling his opponent face-down on the ground, holding Phillips's palms pinned against the back of his head. Smart. Phillips couldn't blast without incinerating himself. The agent's massive arms bulged as he fought to control the Hyper, who heaved and bucked in an effort to throw him off.

Beside them, an overturned coffee table blazed furiously, the flames licking at the surrounding carpet, edging dangerously close to the drapes. If they caught, the whole trailer would go up in five minutes flat.

Arial shouldered past the broken door and pointed the extinguisher at the fire. A stream of cold foam snuffed it with a hiss.

"Get the kids out!" she yelled at Phillips's wife, who huddled on the couch with her children, one of whom clutched a small, cowering dog.

What do you know, Phillips's potshot at the dog missed.

Jolted, the woman jerked her youngest into her arms, grabbed her five-year-old by the hand, and darted past Arial, dragging the child behind her. The dog fled after them, tail tucked. All four hesitated at the bent and broken door that blocked their escape.

Arial turned and kicked the door the rest of the way open. The woman scurried outside just as the SWAT team arrived at the front steps. One of the men swept the five-year-old into his arms, while two others hustled Mrs. Phillips and her daughter to safety, the dog yapping in pursuit.

Arial started to step back for the rest of the team. As she pivoted, she felt something clamp ferociously hard around her ankle. She looked down and realized, with a sense of sick horror, that Phillips had grabbed her leg.

The world went a sharp, electric blue. Pain smashed into her consciousness like a freight train.

And then she saw nothing at all.

CHAPTER TWO

Josiah watched in horror as a blue-white crackle of energy threw Phillips and the hostage negotiator in opposite directions. She slammed into the wall as the fire extinguisher went flying. Cursing himself, he pounced on Phillips.

Not only was the fucker a fire-caster, he was also strong as a bull. Which was how he'd managed to slam an elbow into Josiah's head and get away.

But he'd miscalculated badly in his choice of hostage. Phillips obviously hadn't realized the consequences of grabbing a Potential. The energy discharge had knocked him for a loop.

He was too stunned to resist as Josiah grabbed him and slammed a fist in his face. The Hyper's eyes rolled back in his head, and he slumped to the floor, unconscious.

Snarling a curse, Josiah straddled him and dragged his lax arms behind his back, then pulled a pair of blocker cuffs out of his coat pocket. He clamped them on the Hyper's thick wrists and sat back with a mental sigh of relief. The cuffs would nullify Phillips's powers until the Feds could get him into a cell.

Wearily, Josiah climbed to his feet and turned to see several members of the SWAT team gathered around the negotiator, who was out cold.

Well, Josiah thought grimly, *this sucks.*

• • •

INVISIBLE thanks to the slave by her side, Kali stared through the trailer doorway, thoroughly disgusted. If Tommy Phillips had held off his meltdown for one more day, she could have gotten to him before the cops did.

She'd spotted him at the truck stop the week before. The smoking glow around him told her Phillips was a Potential, so she'd touched him. It had been pure whim; she'd had no idea what he'd turn out to be.

Finding out was half the fun.

Kali did wish she'd been able to track Phillips down sooner—preferably before he attracted the attention of the cops. A fire-caster would have been a useful addition to her stable. And adding him would have been no problem, since from what she'd seen, Phillips's will would have been no match for her psi. She'd have put him under control with very little effort.

Unlike Tracker, who'd damn near ripped her head off when she'd tried that trick on him.

She was tempted to send a team in to recover Phillips anyway. Brute's strength was very nearly a match for Tracker's, and with Ghost making him invisible, he could keep the bastard busy while the others grabbed the fire-caster.

But that would have gotten the Feds involved. They could command a far larger stable of Hypers than Kali could, and she had no desire to end up wearing a pair of blocker cuffs. The minute she lost her powers, one of her slaves would probably kill her.

So, no. She had no choice except to write Phillips off as a loss.

Brooding, Kali watched as one of the SWAT team officers helped the female cop to her feet. Seen with Kali's Hyper senses, energy popped and flared around the woman, who staggered woozily.

Kali's eyes narrowed as she watched the play of developing forces surging through her aura. Phillips, the idiot, had Triggered the cop's powers when he'd grabbed her. Kali had a feeling her abilities would turn out to be really impressive, though it was impossible to tell exactly what they were this early.

Perhaps this little adventure hadn't been a total loss after all.

"Come on, boys," she murmured to the six slaves surrounding her. Together, they faded back into the woods to watch.

• • •

PALE blue lights flashed like fireflies in Arial's peripheral vision. Automatically, she waved a hand to shoo them away—and realized the sheriff was eyeing her as he drove. He'd insisted on taking her home from the hospital, despite her protests.

Pulling up in front of her apartment complex, he stopped the big unmarked Crown Vic and turned to her. She resisted the urge to squirm as he studied her in the light of a streetlamp. "I want you to take the next couple of days off, Sergeant."

"Thanks, Sheriff, but that's not necessary. You heard the ER doc. The X-rays and CT scan were fine."

"Yeah, I can tell that by the way you're batting at things that aren't there. Phillips blew your ass across the room, Dean, and you were out cold for fifteen minutes. I want you to make an appointment with your doctor. I don't like the look in your eyes."

She stiffened. "I'm fine."

"I'm sure you will be." The steely note in his voice told her it was time to stop arguing.

"Yes, sir. Thank you, sir." Arial swung open the car door and got out, somehow managing not to stagger as those damn blue lights darted around her head.

The sheriff frowned at her, his sharp eyes missing nothing. "You get some rest now."

She gave him a stiff nod and closed the car door. He flicked her a half-salute and pulled off.

Arial watched the Crown Vic rumble out of the parking lot. As soon as it was out of sight, she turned and limped for her building. The cold night air felt bracing, and she sighed in relief as the fuzziness in her head began to lift for the first time since Phillips had hit her.

Still, every muscle and joint she had ached from slamming into that wall. She needed a painkiller and bed.

Maybe those days off would be welcome after all.

Wearily, she started climbing the wooden steps to her third-floor apartment. The complex was relatively new, and most of the tenants were young professionals saving for their first homes. Glancing across the parking lot at the adjacent building, she noticed darkened Christmas trees in her neighbors' windows draped in swags of garland and hung with colorful ornaments.

Maybe she should use her days off to decorate her own apartment. Christmas was only a week away, but she'd been too busy to even think about it.

When she reached her floor, something glowing and gold attracted her attention. A tiger, reclining like the Sphinx on the wooden floor, striped in light and darkness. Apparently one of her neighbors had weird taste in Christmas decorations.

Then it looked at her and licked its chops.

Arial froze, her eyes widening in astonished fear.

A gloved hand flicked on the switch beside her front door. Blinding yellow light washed the tiger away, leaving Tracker standing in its place. "Sergeant Dean?"

She must have been imagining things. Fear made her voice sharp. "What the hell are you doing here?"

His masked head tilted. "We need to talk."

"Tracker, it's four in the morning, and I've had a rough night. It can wait." Her heels rang on the wooden floor as she headed for her door.

"No, actually. It can't." He took a step closer, tall and broad and imposing. She stopped warily as the awareness of him flooded her senses—his scent, his size, his warmth, radiating across the narrow space to envelop her.

Arial shook off the impression and dug her keys from the pocket of her jeans. "Fine. Come inside. No point in freezing our butts off out here."

But despite her crisp words, her hand was shaking too badly to get the key in the lock. Leather-clad fingers closed over hers. "Let me."

She released the key as if it burned and watched him turn it. He opened the door and stepped inside with the air of a man alert to possible threats. His back looked damn near as wide as the door. Deep inside her, something purred feminine approval.

Arial forced herself to ignore it and stepped inside after him. She flicked on the overhead light and watched him prowl around her living room like a cat. He looked big and dark surrounded by the sunny yellow walls and cheery orange furniture. All black leather and outrageous masculinity.

"Nice place."

"Thanks. Look, what's this about?"

He turned. Despite the stern mask that hid so much of his face, there was something compassionate in his expression. "Since Phillips touched you, you've been . . . seeing things. Colored lights. Glowing auras." For an instant, a tiger's eyes shimmered in the eye slits of his mask.

Unnerved, Arial jerked her gaze away and managed a shrug. "The doc thought it was a concussion, but the CT scan didn't show anything."

Tracker took a deep breath and blew it out, like a man about to impart unpleasant news. "When Phillips grabbed you, his powers Triggered yours. Those lights you're seeing are a symptom of the transformation."

Arial blinked at him, bewildered. "What are you talking about? What transformation? What powers?"

Even through the eye-slits of his mask, she could see the compassion in his gaze. "I hate to tell you this, Sergeant, but you've become a Hyper."

The room seemed to dip. Tracker took a long step toward her, reaching out as if to catch her if she fainted. "Maybe you should sit down."

Instinctively, she stepped away. "No. I can't be a Hyper—that's not possible."

"I'm afraid it is." He dropped his hand, pain and sympathy on his face. "For what it's worth, I know how you feel. I went through the same damn thing."

Blue light zipped around her like fireflies. She watched them numbly as goose bumps broke across her skin. "How? How could ..." She broke off, but her mind completed the thought. *How could my whole life disappear with a touch?*

He shrugged those impressive shoulders. "One theory is that somehow the Power jumps from Hyper to Potential, but not everybody is susceptible. Otherwise half the people on the planet would already be Hypers. A friend of mine thinks you have to have some kind of psi to begin with, and the energy jolt just intensifies it ..." Tracker trailed off, frowning as he eyed her. "You need to sit down. You look like you're about to pass out." He caught her by the upper arms and steered her over to the couch. They sank onto its orange upholstery together.

Snippets of memory flashed through her mind. Phillips's voice—*caught my own fucking rig on fire ... it was an accident, but the bastards canned me anyway!* Her own—*new Hypers are emotionally unstable.* Was she going to go nuts and start blowing people away? "This can't be happening."

She was going to lose her badge. Her apartment. Her car. Everything she'd worked for.

What if she hurt someone? Oh, God!

No. Tracker had to be mistaken. She—

An inquisitive golden muzzle thrust from the center of his chest. The tiger she thought she'd imagined earlier shoved its huge head over to sniff delicately at her. She recoiled. "What the hell is that?"

"What?" Tracker gave her an odd look. "What are you talking about?"

"Ummm. Nothing." *Great. She was hallucinating.*

Or was she? Golden eyes looked up into her face, calm and assessing. Somehow the tiger's stare steadied her, and she took a deep breath.

What if Tracker was right? What if she had become a Hyper?

One thing was for damned sure: Freaking out wasn't going to help. If eight years as a cop had taught her anything, it was that panic made everything worse. She had to calm down, think rationally, and figure out what to do.

Much as she hated the idea, it was logical to assume Tracker knew what he was talking about—she had indeed become a Hyper.

If he was wrong, it would become apparent when she didn't develop powers. But if he was right, she needed to be somewhere someone could keep an eye on her and make sure she didn't hurt anybody. The last thing she needed was to go nuts the way Phillips had.

Arial forced herself to meet Tracker's worried gaze. "All right. What do I do now?"

His head rocked back. "You believe me?"

"What, you'd rather I scream and run around the room?"

"I just expected a longer denial period." His lips twitched. She noticed absently how sensual they were.

"Cops are trained to be realists, Tracker. Denial just wastes time." And she'd learned how pointless it was when Jenny died. She grimaced. "Not that I couldn't use a stiff drink right about now."

Tracker's grin was almost boyish. "You and me both. Being the bearer of news this bad is never any fun."

She shrugged. "Could have been worse. Nobody's dead."

"Good point."

"I suppose I need to register with the Feds." Who'd tell the sheriff. He'd have to fire her. The public would go nuts if they learned a Hyper was a member of the Sheriff's Office.

She felt sick.

Tracker frowned. "I . . . wouldn't suggest it. Not right away."

Arial frowned back. "But according to federal law, Hypers have to register."

"And you should. Just not yet." He sighed. "Sergeant, they'd lock you up for at least six months while they test and poke you. The transition is hard enough as it is without the kind of treatment the federal camps tend to dish out. And if some shrink decided you were a danger, you wouldn't get out at all."

A chill crept over Arial. There'd been news reports that the Feds' treatment of new Hypers could be draconian in the extreme. There hadn't been much public outcry about it, though. Hypers like Phillips had made it painfully obvious that some of them were simply too dangerous to be allowed to run loose.

But it was a lot easier to ignore civil rights issues when you weren't facing the possibility of being locked up yourself. "So what *do* I do?"

"Come with me." He leaned toward her, bracing one powerful forearm on a muscular thigh. "A friend of mine has a place in the mountains. It's underground and really isolated—we won't have to worry about any innocent bystanders while you learn to manage your powers. If we can get you through the next two weeks, you'll probably stabilize enough to avoid the camps."

"Probably?"

Tracker shrugged his broad shoulders. "Nothing's ever certain. But I know a lawyer that specializes in Hyper cases. If we can demonstrate that you're in control—especially given your law enforcement history—he should be able to convince a judge that you don't need to be locked up for the public good."

Arial shook her head. "Those sound like some pretty big 'ifs.'"

He spread his gloved hands. "It's the only game in town, Sergeant."

She studied him, wishing he wasn't wearing that damned mask. "Why are you doing this for me?"

A grim expression flickered across his face. "I knew somebody once who went to one of those camps. I swore I wouldn't let it happen again if I could avoid it."

"I gather it didn't end well."

"No. It didn't." He shrugged. "Besides, I liked the way you handled yourself with Phillips."

"Yeah, right. Ending up a Hyper was a real smooth move."

"You couldn't have anticipated that. Besides, it took guts and quick thinking to grab that fire extinguisher and get the family out of there."

She lifted a brow at him. "Hey, I'm a cop. That's my job."

"And that attitude is why you'll make a good Hyper agent." He gave her a smile, though it looked a little forced. "All we have to do is get you through the next couple of weeks—and convince the Feds."

Arial sighed. "Yeah, that sounds like fun. Okay, I'll go pack a bag."

. . .

KALI hung in midair, one arm looped around the neck of the slave who held her in his arms. Her attention was focused on the apartment building below. Tracker and the female cop were inside.

She growled a curse. When the cop had gotten out of the car, Kali had been on the verge of descending to launch a psychic attack. Then she'd sensed Tracker's presence and instantly realized she didn't dare. Not without her powerhouse fighters, who were waiting back at the motel. Daedalus could carry only one passenger at a time, so she'd had to come alone.

Footsteps rang on wooden stairs, and she went on the alert. Tracker led the girl out of the building to a black SUV. Kali watched them get in. The truck started with a roar and pulled away.

"Follow them," she ordered Daedalus.

The slave stiffened against her. She felt him try to open his arms.

"No," Kali snapped coldly, slamming her will into his mind. Forcing him to tighten his grip. Forcing him to support her, instead of letting her fall ten stories to splatter on the ground.

Daedalus gritted his teeth in rage, fighting her. Kali jerked her head around and glared into his eyes. "You heard me."

"Yes, mistress." Gasping, he yielded and started after Tracker's SUV, Kali in his arms.

The wind whipped her face, cold and clean. She smiled in satisfaction and looked down to watch their prey.

Once they found out where Tracker was taking the cop, she'd bring the others in. They'd take care of the Fed once and for all.

After he was dead, Kali would add the cop to her stable of slaves.

All she needed was patience.

. . .

THE SUV sped through the night, houses and trees whipping silently past. Arial stared out the passenger side window, feeling as if she'd taken one too many head blows too close together—wrapped in a kind of throbbing silence.

Tracker shot her another concerned look, drawing her attention.

His big, gloved hands were skilled and competent on the wheel. Muscle leaped and played in his biceps as he steered the massive vehicle around curves.

A mildly shocking thought penetrated her fog. *It might be fun to find out what's underneath all that leather . . .*

It wasn't as if she had anything to lose, after all. Her life had been neatly derailed. Why not grab what pleasure she could?

It had been months since her relationship with Randy Evans had gone south. The detective had an ugly temper and a tendency to take the stress of his job out on her. He'd never gotten physical, probably because she'd made it clear she was willing to hit back. But she was also far too familiar with just how badly that particular syndrome could end up, so she'd broken it off. She'd been disinclined to try again since then. It seemed like too much hassle for too little reward.

But a little meaningless passion with Tracker the Wonder Stud might be just what the doctor ordered . . .

Oh, who am I kidding? My life is complicated enough as it is.

"How are you doing, Sergeant?" Tracker's voice was deep and rich in the darkness.

She lifted one shoulder in a shrug. "Fine."

He shot her a skeptical glance. She turned to look out the window again.

• • •

THEY'D ridden in heavy silence for another twenty minutes when a golden muzzle suddenly thrust from his side to give her an inquiring sniff. Without thinking, Arial reached out and stroked a hand over the ghostly tiger's broad head.

Sensation spilled over her, hot and somehow erotic.

Tracker inhaled sharply and stiffened, his gaze flying to her. "What did you just do?"

Arial jerked her hand away. "I . . . uh . . . just pet the tiger."

"*What* tiger?"

It was halfway in her lap now, its big weightless paws on her thighs as it examined her face with golden eyes. It wasn't as big as a real tiger—only about the size of a German shepherd, though broader and thickly muscled. Cautiously, she touched its jaw, felt thick, velvety fur against her fingers. Warmth spilled through her body. She felt her nipples harden, and swallowed. "You saying I'm hallucinating?"

"No. I *felt* that." Tracker's voice sounded strangled. He pulled onto the shoulder in a shower of gravel. His gaze locked on hers as he threw the car into park and jerked up the emergency brake. "And I've never felt anything like it."

"So it's real?" Arial stared at him as the tiger butted its big head against hers like a cat begging for an ear rub. A whipsawing purr filled the car, deep and rasping. She scratched him absently under the jaw—and almost purred herself at the sensation that flooded her. Ghostly fingers stroked her nipples, her clit, sent pleasure pouring along her nerves like a river of heated honey.

Was that amusement in those big golden eyes?

"Are you doing that?" she asked the tiger, and stroked a hand between his ears.

Even as another ripple of delight rolled over her, Tracker gasped. Arial glanced at him, startled. He sat rigidly, as if fighting the urge to writhe.

A thick bulge extended up his flat belly under the leather of his suit. She stared at it as her mouth went dry.

Somehow the thing with the tiger was affecting him, too. Instinctively, she jerked her hand away.

The tiger rumbled, the sound somehow disappointed. It butted its massive head against her hand, but Arial resisted the urge to touch it again.

Until a thought struck her. Was this her power? This thing she was doing to herself—to Tracker?

Not exactly in the same league as throwing fireballs, she thought, *but a hell of a lot more fun.*

Tracker was staring at her, lips parted, brawny shoulders pressed back into the seat. Somehow at her mercy.

Arial just couldn't resist. She reached out and touched the tiger again.

• • •

JOSIAH clenched his jaw and watched helplessly as Arial's graceful hands stroked over empty air, absently, like a woman petting a cat. It felt as if those long fingers were tracing over his naked cock, sliding between his thighs to caress his balls. Instinctively, he spread his legs, allowing her greater access.

Not that she seemed to need it.

Hunger boiled through him in a hot and savage tide. He sucked in a breath—and inhaled her scent, rich and spiced with feminine arousal. Deep inside him, something growled.

"Stop," he rasped, though he desperately wanted her to keep going. "Whatever you're doing, just stop."

She froze, looking at him with those huge brown eyes of hers. "Am I hurting you?"

"God, no. I'm afraid I'm going to hurt *you*." The Beast was too close to the surface. And when it came out, people got hurt.

Arial gave him a small, hot smile. "I'm not that fragile." There was hunger in those eyes now, hunger and excitement and a certain fevered recklessness.

He knew what she was thinking as clearly as if she'd shouted the words. Everything in her life had just come crashing down around her. Her career had gone up in smoke. Why shouldn't she walk on the wild side with a superman, when she so obviously had nothing left to lose?

"I haven't touched a woman in two years." The confession burst from him as a deep, tormented rasp.

Her grin flashed in the darkness, wicked and white. "Then I'd say you're due." She reached down at her side. The click of the seat belt was loud in the ticking silence of the car.

Normally fast and graceful, Josiah fumbled as he reached for his own seat belt. He had to get the hell out of the SUV before she . . .

Arial scrambled over the center console, agile as a cat. Just like that, his lap was full of warm woman, sandwiched between his body and the steering wheel. Her negligible weight came down across his desperate erection, and he groaned. Cool fingers spread over his jaw, tilting his head back.

She kissed him, her mouth warm and teasing and wet. The delightful smell of feminine desire flooded his head for the first time in two years. And he knew he was lost. With a vibrating growl of raw lust, he returned her kiss. He'd just have to control it. Somehow.

Somehow he'd keep her safe.

CHAPTER THREE

Tracker may have been living like a monk, but he certainly didn't kiss like one. His mouth was hot and skilled, his tongue stroking deep into hers in breathtaking mating thrusts. Big gloved hands came up to cup the back of her head, angling it for his possession.

Arial sighed in delight. He tasted of mint and man—and something feral, woodsy, like a dark forest on a moonlit night. She slid her arms around his neck. His hands traced down her back to cup her backside, and he growled against her mouth, sounding remarkably like the tiger. His hips rolled upward, and she moaned in pleasure at the feeling of his leather-clad erection pressing against her sex.

Big hands found her breasts through the fabric of her T-shirt. Teased and caressed until she writhed helplessly against him.

She wasn't the only one with magic hands.

He flipped the hem of her shirt up, hooked his gloved fingers into the cups of her bra, and tugged downward. Hard nipples sprang free.

Tracker's rumble of male hunger made her shudder in anticipation. His mouth covered her nipple, suckling the tight pink point. Pleasure spiked through her, and she threw her head back with a gasp, as she ground down on his impossibly delicious erection.

And her butt hit the steering wheel.

Arial laughed. To her own ears, the sound was strangled. "Houston, we have a problem."

Tracker grinned, more a baring of teeth than anything else. "The one nice thing about this gas guzzler is the rear seats flip down." He hit a button on the dashboard. Something hummed behind them. "Sometimes I transport prisoners."

"Kinky." As Arial watched over his shoulder, the seats disappeared into the carpeted deck with a thump, extending the cargo area. She gave him a mischievous grin. "Last one into the back eats the other one."

"Hey!"

Before he could grab her, she scrambled off his lap and slipped between the front seats. As Tracker cursed and laughed, Arial pounced on her suitcase. By the time he'd folded one of the seats back enough to accommodate his big body, she'd opened it and produced a little box with a flourish. "Condoms!"

Tracker grinned, his teeth flashing white. "Smart girl."

"Cops and Boy Scouts, always prepared." She ripped cheerfully into the box.

But even as she pulled out one of the plastic packets, Tracker hesitated. He looked deliciously big and broad in the dim light spilling in from the dashboard. "There's a reason I haven't made love to a woman in so long," he said in a low voice. "My strength—what if I hurt you?"

"You haven't yet. Just don't start now."

The tiger suddenly thrust its furry head from his chest to reach out a massive paw to her. Arial grinned and rubbed a hand over its head, and it shuttered its huge golden eyes in pleasure. "Besides, I don't think your friend will let you."

Tracker stiffened with a gasp. "I have no idea what the fuck you're doing, but I like it." As the cat disappeared back inside him, he shrugged out of the long leather duster and flipped it over her like a blanket. She clutched its heavy, fragrant warmth and watched as he jerked off his gloves and threw them aside, then grabbed the covered zipper that ran down the front of his suit.

The zipper hissed open, revealing an arrow of naked male flesh. Arial licked her lips in anticipation. Finally his cock spilled free, beautifully long and thick.

She dropped the box of condoms to wrap her fingers around it. It felt smooth, hot, simultaneously soft and hard at once, like velvet over a core of steel.

"Oh, God," he groaned. And pounced, pushing her gently down on the carpeted deck.

Tracker shoved aside the coat he'd used to cover her with, then dragged up her T-shirt. Her bra was still pulled down, giving him access to her pebbled nipples. His tongue swirled over one of them, as his right hand found the other. Thumb and forefinger squeezed and teased with exquisite care, sending molten delight spinning through her.

Arial rolled her head back, groaning. She loved the feel of him, the solid, muscular leather-clad weight. Loved the way his cock filled her hand with its silken heat.

Loved his mouth.

His teeth scraped deliciously across her nipple, a tiny pleasure-pain, before he began to suckle. Instinctively, she grabbed the back of his head—and felt only the mask that covered it.

It occurred to her she was making love to a man clad head to toe in leather. She laughed. "This is probably one of the kinkier things I've ever done."

He lifted his head, and she caught her breath at the golden glow shining through the lenses of his mask. His grin flashed. "You think this is kinky? Oh, darlin', I haven't even gotten started."

• • •

"WHAT the fuck are they doing?" Daedalus demanded, shivering against Kali as the two floated in midair.

Kali snorted. "I have a feeling 'fuck' is the operative word."

"Well, I'm getting tired, and I'm freezing my ass off. I'm not going to be able to support us both while Tracker gets his rocks off."

"And the son of a bitch can probably go forever. He looks like the type." And damn, wouldn't she love to taste his talents firsthand? Two bad his will was as strong as those delicious biceps. "All right, find someplace to land where we'll be concealed. We'll keep an eye on the truck and fly out when they move."

Whenever that was.

• • •

TRACKER had stripped Arial, but he was still fully dressed, except for that marvelous, jutting cock. She lay sprawled across the fragrant leather of his coat, her calves draped over his powerful shoulders, his head between her thighs. The thick material of his mask brushed her legs as he swirled his tongue over her most delicate inner flesh. Each pass, each skillful lick, each thoughtful nibble sent hot little jolts of delight through her body until the muscles in her thighs twitched. She could feel herself going slick and hot between the passion-swollen lips he teased so skillfully.

"Maybe you'd like to let me ... Oh, God! ... return the favor ..." Arial managed as her entire nervous system sparked and flamed like an erotic Fourth of July.

"Mmmm." He seemed to consider the question. Gave her a slow, leisurely lick. "No. No, I don't think so."

She squirmed. "You're ... AH! Turning down a blow job?"

Big hands reached up her torso to capture her breasts and pluck her nipples with sweet, relentless skill. He looked up over her body at her, his eyes glowing through the slits of his mask. "You like being in control, Sergeant." Deliberately, he closed his teeth gently over the flesh of her thigh in a slow bite. "But so do I. And I get what *I* want."

He reached between her thighs, stroked. Found her slick opening. Slid a forefinger deep, tearing a gasp of pleasure from her mouth. "You're ready." It was a deep, rasping growl. "Are you ready for me, Arial?"

She rolled her head back into the leather of his coat, gasping. "God, yes!"

"Hmmm. That *is* too bad." Another hot lick. "Because I'm not ready for you."

Arial arched in need even as she laughed. "Judging by the condition of that horse-choking cock, I'd say that's a damned lie."

His chuckle gusted warmly over her sex. "Maybe I should rephrase—I'm not ready to stop teasing you."

"Sadist . . ." Biting her lip, she dug her bare heel into Tracker's back as one of his big hands twirled her nipple and the other plundered her sex.

"Oh, yeah." He bent his head and danced his tongue over her clit. "I'm a real bastard."

. . .

HER legs were long and endless, her pretty pink sex creamy and slick, her hips pumping against his face. Her lovely breasts filled his hands perfectly, white and soft, except for those hard, rosy little nipples.

Josiah could feel himself skidding out of control. His Beast was out and growling, demanding he drive into her, take her hard and fast and ruthlessly. It had been so damned long since he'd even let himself touch a woman. He shouldn't be touching Arial now.

But she'd done—whatever the hell she'd done, and he'd been on her before he'd known it. Fortunately, the Beast liked teasing her as much as he did, so he'd been able to slow down, regain some control.

He gave her pussy a long, slow lick and felt her jolt against him. The Beast growled in pleasure. Maybe, God help him, it was going to be okay. Maybe he could do this without losing it . . .

The problem was going to be actually fucking her. The Beast wanted *in* her. And so did he.

Now. He'd do it now, while his control was still good. While he could go slowly and carefully.

Josiah reared off her and sat back on his heels. Arial blinked up at him. To his delight, those big brown eyes looked more than a little dazed, and her lips were swollen with passion. Her gorgeous breasts heaved and danced with her hard breathing, and the soft delta between her thighs was slick from her arousal and his mouth.

The Beast growled.

He wanted to jerk her against him, ram inside. It took every ounce of his control to open one of the rubbers and slide it onto his aching cock.

Then, carefully, he palmed her thighs and drew her close. Leaning down, he pressed his sheathed cock against her tight, creamy entrance. And began, slowly, so slowly, to work his way inside.

The pleasure had him grinding his teeth as his Beast fought to ride her hard.

. . .

ARIAL gasped at the searing delight of Tracker's thick cock sliding inside her, inch by torturous, luscious inch. She dug her nails into the thick, tough armor covering his shoulders and stared up into his eyes. They were fierce with concentration, and glowed behind his mask, so bright they cast shadows. His teeth clenched as if he were in pain.

She lifted her head and found his mouth. At first, he held it tight against her, but Arial wanted none of that. She licked his lips slowly, teasing him even as he drove in and out of her with that maddening control. He groaned. His lips parted and softened for her, as he began kissing her back. She growled in triumph and hooked both calves over his muscular backside, using the strong grip of her thighs to pull him closer.

Still he pumped in and out, slow and relentless, each thrust packing delight up her spine. Almost fast enough to tip her over the edge into orgasm, but not quite. Holding back. Driving her insane.

Arial caught his head between her hands and looked up into that glowing gaze. "More." She licked his mouth, gently bit his plump lower lip. "Faster."

His eyes narrowed. A muscle in his jaw flexed. "No."

He drew back, braced his massive arms beside her head, and kept pumping. Slowly.

Arial ground her teeth.

Just as a glowing feline head thrust from his chest, eyes feral and hot. She released Tracker's masked head and grabbed it.

And the tiger roared without sound.

Tracker stiffened, his eyes going wide and blazing, his lips peeling back from his teeth.

Then he began to fuck her. In furious, driving thrusts that had her arching against him in delight. His cock felt a yard long, impossibly thick, each stroke ruthlessly deep. Too deep. Pain shafted through her. Arial writhed, her fingers still wrapped around the tiger's ghost head, and his thrusts gentled, moderated. Just enough. Pleasure blazed through her like a comet, and she came, screaming her delight.

Tracker and the tiger roared together. And for a moment, it seemed Arial could feel all three of them, caught in a burning tsunami of a climax, searing and delicious and endless.

. . .

JOSIAH collapsed over her, drained and panting. God, he'd never come like that in his life.

Arial lay sprawled under him. She groaned softly.

Fear stabbed him, and he jerked off her. She lay still, her dark lashes fanning her cheeks. "Arial! Did I hurt you?"

Her eyes opened, and she gave him a slow, lazy smile. "Hell, no."

He rolled off her and fell on his back, weak with relief. "Shit, don't scare me like that."

Arial rolled over on top of his chest. She felt no heavier than a scarf. "You should be scared. Now that I've had you, I'm going to want more." Her smile was feline.

He frowned. "That was dangerous."

"It didn't feel dangerous." Her lids lowered over those dark eyes. Flecks of amber seemed to glow in their depths. "It felt good."

He cupped her face in his hands. He had to make her understand. "Arial, the last woman I lost it with like that went to the hospital."

Dark brows lifted. "Why?"

"When I came, I broke three of her ribs. I had an arm around her waist, and I'm so fucking strong . . ." He shuddered, remembering

Sharon's cry of agony. Remembered the doctor's condemning stare after he'd rushed her to the hospital.

A cool, soft hand touched his cheek, drawing his gaze. "You didn't hurt me, Tracker. It was wonderful."

A memory flashed through his mind—the way she'd released him to grab at empty air. Pleasure had blasted through him like a lightning bolt, and the Beast had taken control. The next thing he knew, he'd been riding her like a madman. "There at the end— what did you do?"

"I don't know." She gave him a cocky little smile, but it looked a little forced. "Maybe making superheroes come is my Hyper power."

"Well, don't do it again. I could have hurt you."

Her smile broadened into a grin. "Hey, it's a risk I'm willing to take."

He didn't grin back. "I'm not."

. . .

THE silence that fell between them as they dressed and got back on the road was more than a little cool. Arial was surprised when Tracker broke it. "I probably sound like an old maid with all this 'sex is dangerous' stuff."

She eyed him. "Does seem a bit out of character."

He grimaced. "Yeah, sometimes I can't believe I'm saying it either. Thing is, I did a lot of damage during my Transition. If I hadn't been one of the first Hypers, I'd probably still be doing time in a Fed camp somewhere. So I'm a little paranoid about letting go."

"What happened?"

He didn't answer for so long, she was starting to think he wouldn't. "You've got to understand, I've always been a big guy. My mama raised me to be really careful about not throwing my weight around with people weaker than me. Especially women. 'Boy, you save it for the football field. Big ol' bull like you could kill somebody.'"

"You were a jock?"

"Played ball in high school and college. Quarterback. Did pretty well. I was hoping to go pro until I blew out my knee. So I started coaching instead. Got a job at this little high school." The hard line of his mouth softened. "God, I loved that job. My kids . . . Half the time, they'd start out as little pricks, all balls and testosterone. But if you were patient and worked with them long enough, you'd start seeing the man come out."

Fascinated, she said softly, "That must have felt really good."

"Oh, yeah. A couple of them went pro. One guy, everybody said he was a sure bet for prison, but he turned his life around. Got married. Has three kids and a good job now." His grin was proud.

Arial grinned back, only to see his smile freeze and fade.

"Then at practice one afternoon, this little redhead walks up to me on the sidelines. I turned around, figuring she was somebody's trailer park mama, judging by the makeup and Daisy Duke shorts. But it was Kali." He growled the word, his eyes slitted as he glared at the road ahead.

"The Hyper?"

"Yeah. She touched me." Tracker shrugged. "You know what happened next."

Arial remembered the arching blue light, the explosion of pain. "Boom."

"She ran before my assistant coaches could stop her. But that night, she showed up at my house. She enslaves Hypers, makes them do her dirty work."

"And she tried to take you."

"Yeah. And she damn near succeeded. When she grabbed my face—I'd never really believed in evil, you know? It sounds corny, but . . ."

Arial remembered looking into Carl Logan's mad black eyes the moment before he'd blown his daughter's head off. "It doesn't sound corny to me. What happened then?"

"My Beast came out, and I went nuts. I wrecked the house, damn near killed her. She ran. Then the cops showed, and everything went straight to hell."

"Ow." Arial winced.

"It was like being an animal. I couldn't think. Didn't understand anything, didn't even realize I wasn't supposed to kick the nice policemen's collective ass. I totaled a patrol car with my fists. Just beat the crap out of it. I didn't kill anybody, but a couple guys went to the hospital. Then I ran. And kept going."

She stared at him in horror, trying to imagine what it must have been like. "No wonder you're paranoid about losing control."

"Yeah. If Psych hadn't come after me, I don't know what would have happened."

"Psych," Arial said slowly. She'd heard of him. "He's the telepathic, telekinetic guy, right?"

"Right. He was able to use his telekinesis to trap me without hurting me. Then he spent the next two months helping me get sane again. I owe him my life." Tracker shot her a look. "That's where we're going. He's agreed to help me teach you how to manage your powers."

"If I've got any."

He turned his attention on the road. "Oh, you've got 'em. It's only a question of what they are."

• • •

ARIAL woke to the sight of black granite cliffs flashing past the SUV's passenger window. She blinked sleepily and lifted her head. The sun was coming up, pinkening the indigo sky beyond the tree-covered mountains that lay like dozing animals around them. She couldn't have been asleep long.

Tracker turned off the main road and sent the SUV climbing up a steep gravel drive. Stones spat beneath the tires as the big truck jounced up the incline.

A listing wooden shed waited at the top, looking as if it was going to collapse any minute. Its double doors swung silently wide at the truck's approach, and he drove inside. The SUV's headlights illuminated rusting tools hanging from the walls, festooned with cobwebs. Arial shot them a jaundiced look. "Where the . . ."

The floor began to sink under the truck. She yelped, as the big vehicle descended into a spill of florescent light. Craning her neck to see below them, Arial realized the truck rested on some kind of hydraulic platform that was lowering them into a huge underground garage.

When the platform stopped, Tracker pulled the SUV forward into a parking space between a delivery van and a Porsche. He turned off the engine and gave her a tight smile. "We're here."

"But where the hell *is* here—the Batcave?"

His mouth curled into a dry smile as he opened the driver's side door and went around to the back to get out her suitcase. "Something like that."

Arial scrambled out herself, watching the hydraulic lift rumble back up to the shed. "Interesting camouflage method. You really like your privacy, don't you?"

"Oh, this isn't mine." He started off across the garage, the bag in hand. He handled the big case as if it were weightless. "I wish I could afford a setup half this good."

"Don't we all?" She hurried in his wake, eyeing their surroundings. A quick count revealed ten vehicles ranging from a nondescript sedan to a low-slung black sports car that looked like something James Bond would drive.

They stepped out into a concrete corridor—and almost ran into a tall, broad-shouldered man. "There you are!" He gave them a charming smile and reached out to pump Tracker's gloved hand. "You made good time."

"I figured we'd better, before something else went wrong." He turned to her. "Arial, this is Psych, my best friend and the guy who saved my ass when I was in your shoes. Psych, this is Sergeant Arial Dean of the James County Sheriff's Office."

They murmured greetings and shook hands, as Arial studied her host. Like Tracker, he wore a one-piece armored suit, though his was in a dark blue synthetic material that had a faint, metallic sheen. His mask was a bit more streamlined than his friend's, not quite as suggestive of a snarling animal. Though tall, he wasn't quite as broad as Tracker, built more like a swimmer than a heavy-weight boxer. "I didn't know you lived around here."

"That's the idea." His smile was warm and friendly, his jawline and cheekbones angular and strong. He was probably handsome underneath that mask. "I understand you're one of us now."

"That's what Tracker tells me, but—"

A high, sweet female voice interrupted. "Keep your distance, witch."

Another chimed in. "He's ours. Do not interfere, or you will regret it."

As Arial jolted back in surprise, two ghostly women emerged from Psych's shoulders, slim, lithe, trailing floating, transparent streamers. Their faces were pointed, dominated by huge dark eyes that should have looked vaguely childlike.

But the expression in them was anything but childish.

"Get away from us," one said in a voice like chiming bells. Her hair floated around her face in a shimmering mane, as if she were underwater.

Arial licked dry lips and took another instinctive step back. "Look, what's the problem? I don't mean you any harm."

"You had best not, little witch . . ."

"Or you will certainly pay the price." Their twin gazes were so malevolent, a chill stole over Arial's skin.

Psych's head came up. "What? What are you talking about?" He shot Tracker a look. The big man shrugged, his expression profoundly uneasy. He lowered the suitcase to the ground as if to free his hands.

Great. Now they thought she was crazy. And maybe they were right.

The two women were swirling around her now, a pair of pro-foundly pissed-off ghosts. Both had upswept pointed ears, thin, straight noses, and pouting mouths. When they hissed, their lifted upper lips revealed tiny fangs.

One of them swiped at her with knifelike claws. With a startled yelp, Arial touched her face. There was blood on her fingers. "Hey! Cut it out!"

"Leave!"

"Go now, or we will *make* you go!" They darted close again, claws flashing toward her face. "We will not have you telling our secrets! He is ours, and we will not give him up!"

"What secrets?" Arial swung at them, but her hand shot through both narrow torsos as if they were mist. "*Dammit, back off!*"

Big black eyes narrowed and flared red as stoplights. "You know what secrets, thief!"

They whirled around her, faster and faster, tighter and tighter, their passage whipping up some kind of psychic wind. Arial yelped as her feet left the ground. Bobbing in midair like a balloon, she kicked out furiously. Her booted foot cut right through a ghostly shoulder, which re-formed behind it. Claws raked her thigh in stinging retaliation.

Great. Just great. She couldn't hurt them, but they could sure as hell hurt her.

"Look, I have no idea what you're talking about!" Arial swung at them again anyway, refusing to give up. "Just tell me what you think I'm going to do!"

"Let's take the little interloper for a ride, sister!"

"High!" the other agreed. "Very, very high!"

"And then we'll drop her!"

"SPLAT!" With bell-like laughter, they bore her off down the corridor as if she weighed no more than a soap bubble.

"Stop!" Arial yelled. "Why won't you listen to me? Tracker, do something! They're going to kill me!"

Over the sound of high-pitched laughter, she heard Tracker's furious bellow. "What the hell's going on?"

"I've lost control of my powers!" Psych's voice was tight with strain as the two men charged down the corridor after Arial and her captors. "I can't stop it!"

"Well, you'd better damn well regain control! You're tearing her apart!" Tracker leaped forward and wrapped both massive arms around her waist, then curled himself around her, trying to shield her body with his. For a moment, Arial thought his weight was going to pull them both to the floor, but the ghost women swirled faster, dragging them higher.

He hissed in pain as a set of claws opened a gash across his right arm. "Jesus! Bloody hell, Psych, *stop it*!"

"I'm trying!" Psych yelled back.

One of the women darted in, malice distorting her lovely features, as she drew back a hand. Arial instinctively threw an arm up to shield Tracker's face from those flashing claws.

Abruptly the tiger's head thrust from his, jaws snapping. The ghost ducked and glared at it. "This is none of your affair, Beast! She threatens what is ours!"

"You're nuts, lady!" Arial yelled over the tiger's outraged roar. "I'm no threat to you!"

"Liar!" the ghost spat, dodging the big cat's swiping paw. "You will tell him of us, and he will try to drive us away!"

Tracker yelped as ghostly claws scored his back. Instead of letting go, he curled tighter around Arial, tucking his head against hers. The tiger struck out with glowing claws, as the second spirit flashed too close. The creature spun away, laughing that chiming laugh before darting in again.

Frustrated rage poured through Arial. These two harpies were going to claw Tracker into hamburger, and there wasn't a damn thing he could do to defend himself. He couldn't even see what was attacking them.

Arial flung out an arm, teeth bared. "ENOUGH!" The roar tore her own throat like ground glass, it was so deep and inhuman.

A dragon poured from her hand.

Sinuous, iridescent, flaming scarlet, it slammed into the two spirits like a tornado, blowing them backward. Screeching curses all the way, they flew down the corridor to vanish into Psych's chest. The impact knocked him off his booted feet and sent him reeling into a wall.

Arial and Tracker hit the cement floor like a bag of bricks. He took the brunt of the fall, but the impact still rattled her teeth. She yelped.

For a long moment, there was no sound except the desperate rasp of breathing.

When Arial dared lift her head at last, she found herself face to snout with the dragon. He wasn't the classic winged reptile of

English myth, but a Chinese dragon, with a long, elegant head, huge, intelligent eyes, and a square muzzle full of impressive teeth. A green mane surrounded his head, matching the long tendrils that waved around his snout and marched down his sinuous back. "Hello," she said softly, stretching a hand toward him.

He gave her a dragon smile and arced upward, then flowed into the center of her chest. Warmth burst there like an explosion of sunlight, then poured through her veins at the contact. She drew in a breath in wonder.

If this was what being a Hyper was like, maybe it wasn't so bad after all . . .

Well, except for the homicidal ghosts. Those, she could have done without.

CHAPTER FOUR

"Are you okay?" Tracker's deep voice asked in her ear.

Arial shook off her astonishment. "I think so. A few cuts, but that's all." Rolling gingerly off him, she landed on her hands and knees and turned to study him. "You?"

"The same." He grimaced and rose to his feet, then reached a hand down to help her up. "But I'm going to be sore tomorrow. Psych?"

His friend was sitting on the floor, his back braced against one concrete wall of the corridor. He raised a shaking hand to his head. "My skull feels like it's about to split wide open. I haven't lost control of my powers like that since my Transition. What the fuck happened?"

"That's a good question." Tracker gave Arial a searching look. "You were talking to someone . . ."

"More like screaming." Psych climbed slowly to his feet, moving as if he felt just as battered as Arial did. His gaze sharpened as he eyed her. "Who was it?"

Arial sighed. "You're not going to believe me."

"Try us." Tracker's inflexible tone didn't invite argument.

She raked a hand through her tangled hair and decided it was best just to spit the whole thing out. "They looked like ghosts.

Spirits. Or, hell, for all I know, fairies. They came pouring out of Psych and attacked me."

"Like this tiger you keep talking about."

"Tiger? Spirits?" Psych threw Tracker that *are-we-dealing-with-a-nutbar* look.

"I know this is hard to believe, but I'm telling you what I saw." Arial told him. "Two women who looked like escapees from a *Lord of the Rings* movie just . . . *flowed* out of your body. They had claws, and they did this." She pointed at the raking wounds across her cheek, then at the similar injuries on Tracker's body.

Psych moved cautiously closer and examined the cuts. "My power has always produced marks like that. I don't know why." He looked up at her, a frown on his face. "You said they looked like ghosts? Could you describe them in more detail?"

She shrugged. "Pointed ears, delicate bodies. They had this kind of Tinkerbell thing going on, but really pale. Except for the eyes. Big, black eyes that flashed red when they got pissed—which they pretty well were the whole time. They seemed to think I was going to tell you something they don't want you to know."

"Like what?"

"How the hell should I know? They didn't say."

An expression of profound unease crossed Psych's face. "This doesn't make any sense."

"This entire night hasn't made any sense."

A comforting hand came to rest on her shoulder. "Maybe it will become a little more clear after we all sleep on it." Tracker gave her a smile that seemed to indicate he, at least, didn't think she was crazy.

That was something, anyway.

• • •

"WHERE the fuck did they go?" Kali screeched. "One minute they were there, then they rounded a curve and disappeared!"

"I don't know, but I'm freezing my ass off." Daedalus shivered against her. "I can't feel my fucking feet. We've been over this damn mountain a dozen times, and there's no sign of them. Can we go back to the hotel now?"

"Might as well." She snarled at the steadily climbing sun. "Somebody's going to spot us if we hang up here much longer. We'll bring the others back tonight and conduct another search. Maybe Cerberus can pick up the scent."

"Kali, they're in a car."

"I don't give a shit. Tracker's here—I can almost feel him." She curled her upper lip into a snarl. "And he's not getting away from me again."

• • •

PSYCH showed Arial and Josiah to a suite of rooms that Josiah recognized.

"This is where you put me the first time I was here. Once I was a little more sane, anyway." Josiah carried Arial's suitcase and put it on top of a familiar king-sized, cherry sleigh bed with a dark blue coverlet. The crystal lamp sitting on the bedside table was new, though. He'd broken the last one.

"Sane?" Arial's delicate brows arched.

"He had a rough Transition," Psych said with admirable restraint. Changing the subject, he gestured at a connecting door. "Bathroom's through there. Tracker, you can use the bedroom across the hall if you like."

Close enough that he could keep an eye on their guest, just as Psych had once watched over him. And he'd needed it. "Thanks, Psych."

"It's my pleasure." Turning to Arial, his friend added, "I can't tell you how sorry I am for hurting you. I don't understand how it could have happened."

"It wasn't your fault," Arial said in that luscious whiskey and velvet voice, giving Psych a smile that sent a stinging stab through Josiah.

Jealousy? He frowned.

"Yeah, I know—it was the killer fairies." Psych's tone was light, faintly mocking, but there was strain in the line of his mouth.

"Well, something sure as hell did this." Arial gestured impatiently at the five raking scratches across her cheek. Marks that did look as if they'd been inflicted by a female hand.

With claws.

"Good point." That was definitely unease on Psych's face. "I'll see what I can find out. Maybe some meditation . . ."

"Meditate later." Josiah clapped him lightly on the shoulder. "Sleep now."

"Sure." He gave them a troubled wave and started off down the corridor. "I really am sorry."

Tracker watched Psych go with mingled feelings of affection and frustration. "He'll be up for hours staring at his belly button." Catching Arial by one shoulder, he steered her through the door to the utilitarian bathroom. "Let's get you patched up. I don't like the look of those scratches."

"I'm not the only one who needs a box of Band-Aids, tough guy."

"So I'll patch us both up."

She scanned the small room, taking in the simple white porcelain sink, toilet, and bath. The white vinyl flooring was scattered with tiny roses, and the shower curtain was clear plastic. Everything was so spotless, it shone. "Nice. A bit Spartan, but nice."

"Decorating has never been high on Psych's list of priorities. At least not down here." He gestured to her to sit down on the toilet while he raided the medicine cabinet.

"Down here?" He wasn't surprised she picked up on the implications. "As opposed to up where?"

"Afraid that's classified."

"Figures."

When he turned around with his supplies, Josiah found Arial sitting slumped against the back of the toilet, a weary line to her delicate shoulders. The sight sent a shaft of tenderness through him. Between Phillips, him, and Psych, she'd had one hell of a night.

"Psych isn't the only one who's sorry." He wet a washcloth in warm water and dropped to his knees in front of her.

She tilted her chin and let him blot the blood from the cuts on one high cheekbone. Brown eyes studied him, flecks of golden amber in their depths. "What do you have to be sorry about?"

"Letting Phillips nail you. If he hadn't gotten away from me, you wouldn't be in this mess."

Arial snorted. "One thing I've learned over eight years as a cop—you do what you can do. You're good, Tracker, but you're not Superman." He blotted at the cut again, and she closed her eyes, long dark lashes fanning against her cheek.

Josiah remembered the way she'd felt, her lithe little body cradled against his as invisible energies buffeted them. Remembered the ferocity in her gaze as she'd thrown out one hand and done—*something*. She had only a fraction of his strength, but he knew she'd been trying to defend him. He'd seen it in her eyes, in that moment when those claws had raked him.

And she'd succeeded. Somehow, she'd stopped Psych's involuntary assault when neither man had been unable to do a damn thing about it.

Josiah wasn't used to being defended. He was the one everybody expected to save the day. Yet she'd come through for him.

Before he knew what he intended to do, he was leaning forward. He had to taste that sweet mouth again.

Arial's eyes flew wide as he kissed her, then slowly drifted closed. Her lips felt like damp satin, tasted of ripe, erotic heat. Unable to resist, he edged his tongue along the seam of her mouth until she opened for him with a sigh.

God, she really did taste exquisite.

Arial lifted a hand, rested it against his cheek. Her skin felt cool and silken against his.

It took an effort to pull back, but he knew it was best. He could feel his Beast rising again, fierce and hot. It seemed that having had her, the need had become even harder to resist.

"We need to finish getting you patched up." Josiah forced himself to rise to his feet and step to the sink. Drawing in a deep breath, he turned on the tap and started washing out the cloth.

· · ·

ARIAL watched Tracker, heat running molten through her body. She'd never felt the punch of a simple kiss with such intensity. Not even when he'd kissed her before.

What was it about him? It was more than the powers, more even than the impressive body. Something about the man himself called to her in a way that struck her as simultaneously dangerous and irresistible.

Tracker turned back to her and bent to blot at the scratches on her forearm. His hands were exquisitely gentle, his eyes intent through the eye slits of his mask. His scent was intoxicating. Leather. Masculinity. Honest sweat from his efforts to protect her.

She watched him as he worked, feeling breathless at the way his big body dominated the small space of the bathroom. There was no sound except the slow drip of the faucet, the rustle of leather. The soft tread of his boots on the ceramic tile.

She hadn't even seen his face. She didn't know his real name. Yet she could feel her nipples hardening. Heat gathered between her thighs, liquid and sweet.

Arial stirred, realizing she was unconsciously pressing her thighs together in an effort to soothe the ache.

"Bend forward. Something's bleeding through your shirt." Tracker's deep voice seemed to vibrate in her body's hidden places. She obeyed, dry-mouthed, and closed her eyes as he pulled her shirt up to clean a cut on her back. As he pressed on a bandage, he told her, "You were lucky. I don't think any of these need stitches."

"That's good." Arial opened her eyes to see blood running down his leg from a set of vicious scratches in his thigh. The ghost's claws had ripped right through his tough armor. She frowned, eyeing it as she stood. "Your turn."

He took a hasty step back. "That's not necessary." The tip of his tongue wet his lip. "I can take care of it."

"Don't be such a baby. Sit."

He obeyed with visible reluctance. Glad to have something to do with her hands, Arial turned and busied herself getting another washcloth out of the drawer he'd pulled his from. "Pull down that suit. I can't work on you if you're covered in leather."

She glanced around just in time to see heat leap in his eyes. "I don't think that's such a good idea."

"I can withstand the sight of your abs without being overcome by lust."

"You're not the one I'm worried about." He smiled, slowly, almost reluctantly. There was more than desire in that smile—there was a wry humor, a certain self-deprecation. She found herself smiling back.

His zipper hissed, loud in the stillness of the room. Arial watched him shrug one powerful shoulder out of the suit, then the other, before tugging it down to his waist.

Muscle flexed and rolled all up and down that gorgeous chest. His shoulders looked even wider out of the suit, all smooth, tanned skin. A luscious little ruff of chest hair spread from nipple to nipple, then narrowed to dive down past his navel. Luring her eye to the prominent bulge under his suit.

Maybe she shouldn't have been so quick to promise not to attack him.

As if reading her mind, Tracker stood in a restless rush. "This is really not a good idea."

She shook off her desire and gave him an impatient frown. "Neither of us is a virgin, Tracker. And considering what happened earlier tonight . . ."

"We got lucky. And I've learned not to push my luck." Before she quite knew what was happening, he jerked up his suit again and stalked out of the bathroom, zipping it as he went.

Arial hurried after him. "Tracker, you still need those cuts tended."

"I've been tending myself for years." He strode across the bedroom and out into the hall without breaking step. "And I'll keep on doing it."

"Dammit, Tracker!"

Before she could say anything more, he closed the door in her face.

• • •

INSTEAD of heading across the hall to the bedroom Psych had given him, Josiah strode down the corridor. He knew good and damned well he wouldn't be getting any sleep for a couple of hours at least.

And unless he missed his guess, Richard was in the same boat.

He stepped into the elevator around the corner, keyed in the code Psych hadn't bothered to change, and took it down two levels to his friend's penthouse-in-reverse.

The elevator doors slid open on the smell of turpentine and oil paint. Richard had been indulging in his hobby again. One of them, anyway. Along with genetics, physics, computers. And fuck, rocket science for all Josiah knew.

"Tracker?" Richard called.

"It's me." Josiah walked through the library, his boots barely silenced by the worn Persian carpet. Unlike the rest of the underground complex—Arial was right; it was spartan—Psych decorated his personal quarters in castoffs from upstairs. Some truly ugly Victoriana had found its way down here. A footstool shaped like an elephant, gaudy lamps, a bust of Napoleon with a broken nose—everything Richard either hoped to restore or simply couldn't bear to throw away. "I sent Arial to bed."

"Why aren't you in it with her?" Ice clinked. "You two were throwing off so much heat, you damn near singed off my eyebrows."

"I'm celibate, remember?" He followed the rattle of ice through a doorway hung with a moth-eaten fringed curtain.

"Yeah, right." Richard snorted as Josiah stepped into the room. "Save it for someone who's not psychic."

"You can't read Hypers."

"After what we've been through, who needs telepathy?" His friend stood surrounded by canvases standing on easels or propped against the wall. His blond hair was still wet from a recent shower, and he wore a pair of loose cotton pants and a faded MIT T-shirt. Ice clinked again as he tipped up a crystal glass of aged bourbon, his green eyes locked on the painting in front of him.

Getting a look at the canvas, Josiah stopped dead with a soundless whistle. Two ghostly women with pointed ears, immense black eyes, and shimmering pale skin swirled around a naked male figure. It wasn't clear whether he writhed in pain or pleasure. "Fuck."

"Exactly. I've been dreaming about them for years. I painted this six months ago." Richard took another deep slug of his drink. "How did she know, Jos? Is she psychic, too? Did she see this in my thoughts—can *she* read Hypers?"

"Maybe." He headed for the crystal decanter on the scarred sideboard. Poured himself two fingers, no ice. "Or maybe she really did see them just the way she said. Just like she saw the tiger."

"What tiger?" Richard moved over to a distinctly hideous pink settee and flopped onto it with that boneless grace Josiah had always admired.

Settling into a clashing orange armchair, Josiah described the moment in the SUV when Arial had seemed to touch something that wasn't there. "I *felt* it, Rich. Every time she touched that tiger she kept talking about, I felt it. And it drove me crazy. Me—and my Beast."

Perceptive green eyes studied his. "You think it was your Beast she saw."

"I'm starting to wonder." He leaned forward, bracing his elbows on his knees. "What if she's right? What if our powers aren't psi, but some kind of possession?"

Richard curled a well-shaped lip. "You suggesting we've been taken over by devils, Jos?"

"What, like those nuts who think we're in league with the Antichrist?" He made a dismissive gesture. "Hell no. But if there is some kind of power inside us, and we could get rid of it . . ."

"You mean have a priest perform an exorcism so you can pretend the last five years never happened?" Anger flashed in Richard's eyes. "Hell, if you're really lucky, maybe you can go back to coaching high school football."

Josiah ignored the stab of longing. To get his life back . . . "Give me credit for a little sense, Rich. I know that ship has sailed."

"Exactly. We are what we are, and there's not a damn thing we can do about it."

"That's easy for you to say," he growled as his own temper ignited. "You've got all this. I sit in that barren little house in Charlotte, waiting for the cops to call so I can go kick some poor prick's ass. Not daring to even talk to a woman for fear of starting something I'll want to finish. I'm sick of this shit, Rich. I want a fucking life!"

"And you think I don't?" Richard snapped back. "You think you've got it bad? At least you can't hear every woman you meet wonder how big your bank account is. I just love listening to some bimbo speculate about how much she could get in the divorce settlement before we've even gone out once." He stood up and stalked to the sideboard to splash more whiskey into his glass. "Hypers are the only people I can't read, and half of them want to kill my ass. What's more, I want to kill them right back."

Silence ticked past, almost ringing with emotion. Finally Josiah asked softly, "So if I'm right—if we've been possessed by some kind of spirit—you saying you wouldn't get rid of it if you could?"

Rich's eyes drifted to the canvas with its swirling ghostly women. "I'd give my left nut to get rid of this." He swallowed half the contents of his glass in one gulp. "But there's some shit you just can't undo."

• • •

ARIAL took a shower, reapplied the Band-Aids that had washed off in the process, and made use of the hair dryer and toothbrush she'd packed. Then she slipped into her favorite white silk nightgown.

She might have to dress in jeans, suits, or uniforms during the day, but at night, she liked something a little more girly.

Weary and battered as she was, she was asleep five minutes after her head hit the pillow. Which was why she didn't see the dragon emerge from her chest and consider her with mild regret.

"You're not going to enjoy this," he said. "But it is necessary."

• • •

IN the dream, Arial was twelve years old again. She'd had to do some fast talking to convince Mom it was okay for her to sleep over at Jenny Logan's house. Jenny's dad gave Mom the creeps, but

Arial had pointed out Jenny's dad had moved out. Anyway, it was the last summer night before school started, so Mom had, reluctantly, given in.

Now Arial and Jenny were curled up on the bed in pajamas and bunny slippers, munching on popcorn. It had been a busy night. They'd put each other's hair in ribbons, painted their fingernails pink, and donned makeup from Jenny's Barbie kit.

"So Sherri Rice said Bobby Miller has, like, this huge crush on you," Jenny announced, crunching her popcorn with gusto. "He's really cute."

Though she could feel her cheeks getting hot, Arial shrugged. Bobby had big brown eyes and killer dimples. "I dunno. I guess he's okay."

"Hey, this is me you're talking to," Jenny scoffed. "I saw you drop your books when he smiled at you in the hall."

"It's the dimples," Arial confessed, scooping a fistful of popcorn. "The dimples get me every time."

"Yeah, he . . ."

"Marion, you bitch!" The savage roar was followed by a furious pounding. "You open this fucking door and take what's coming to you!"

Jenny jumped, sending the bowl of popcorn flying. "Oh, no, it's Daddy! He's not supposed to be here!" She scrambled off the bed and raced down the hall.

Arial jumped up and ran after her, her heart in her throat.

This was bad. This was really bad.

They charged into the living room to find Jenny's mother yelling through the front door. "Go away, Carl! I've called the cops!"

"You think I care, bitch?"

"Oh, no," Jenny moaned, twisting her hands together. She was as pale as the popcorn as she looked at Arial with wild blue eyes. "He's drunk!"

The last time he'd gotten drunk, he'd choked Mrs. Logan. She'd had to go to the hospital, which was why she'd finally told him to move out.

"Maybe we'd better . . ."

Sirens sounded in the distance. "Hear that, Carl?" Jenny's mother yelled. "It's the cops. Go away and sober up, you bastard."

"Go to hell, cunt!"

The boom of the gun was shockingly loud. Arial screamed, the sound blending with Jenny's cry. A hole appeared in the front door, smoke and flashing blue light flooding through it.

For a moment, Mrs. Logan just stood there, staring at it with her back to them. Then she slowly toppled over and flopped bonelessly onto her back.

"Mom!" Screaming, Jenny leaped for her mother. *"Daddy, what did you do?"*

The front of Mrs. Logan's pretty yellow shirt was all red and wet. It didn't look real.

This can't be happening, Arial thought, staring numbly, as Jenny bent over her mother howling in grief. Then, distantly, *I should do something. I should help.*

The air was filled with shrill police sirens that sounded just like a television show. The door burst open with a rending crash as Jenny's dad kicked it in. His face twisted like a monster's, he dove for his daughter, a huge black gun in his hand.

"Jenny!" Arial jolted forward and grabbed for her friend just as the girl reeled to her feet and tried to run.

But it was too late.

"Come here, you little brat!" Mr. Logan grabbed Jenny's arm, jerked her away from Arial, as two cops charged through the broken door.

For an instant, Jenny's terrified eyes met hers. Then her father whirled, dragging her between him and the cops, his gun to her chin. "Get back!"

The boom of his gun sounded like the end of the world.

• • •

ARIAL moaned in her sleep, flinging out her arms in protest, a single tear running down her cheek. Even as she fought to wake, she heard a distant dream voice say, *I'm sorry, my dear. We're not done. Not yet.*

The colorful dragon flowed down the street to the sound of firecrackers, undulating in the hands of the team of dancers who carried it. Drums boomed and cymbals crashed as the watching crowd applauded. Arial, standing with her parents, watched in numb silence.

To distract her from her grief for Jenny, her parents had taken her to see the Chinese lunar New Year celebration in New York's Chinatown. She knew they were trying to cheer her up, but all she could think about was what a coward she was.

The dragon danced closer, shaking its great head. Its big, long-lashed eyes met hers. "Why do you think yourself a coward?" Its voice was deep, lightly accented with music.

This had to be a dream.

"I didn't do anything. She was my best friend, and I let her die."

"What could you have done?" Fireworks exploded around them, flooding the street with smoke. When it dissipated, the dragon dancers were gone. A real dragon stood in their place, towering over her, horned head cocked, as it studied her with wise, golden eyes. "You were only a little girl."

"Doesn't matter. I should have made her run away, but I just stood there." It was her secret, the shame she'd hidden all these years. Even from herself.

"Look again." The dragon coiled himself around her. His scales felt surprisingly warm and smooth against her skin. "And see."

Suddenly she was an adult again, standing in Jenny's living room. A small, dark-haired girl stood watching as a balding man with a mustache kicked in the door. Gazing into the child's face, Arial recognized the shell-shocked expression she'd seen so often on other witnesses of sudden violent crime.

"Now look at him, Arial. What could you have done?"

Her experienced cop's eye told her the man was six-two, with the muscle-and-beer-belly build of a construction worker and part-time drunk. "Nothing," she said in amazement. "There was nothing I could have done. I never realized that before. Or I did, but . . ."

"But you never believed it."

"I spent all those years torturing myself." She shook her head. "I've been an idiot."

"No." The dragon smiled as the room faded away around them. "You experienced tragedy, but you didn't let it break you. You made yourself strong so you could defend those who are weak. That's why I chose you, of everyone I could have had."

"Chose me for what?"

But the dragon had faded away, too.

CHAPTER FIVE

Arial opened her eyes. In the dim light spilling in from the bathroom, she recognized the room Psych had given her. "Oh, man," she groaned, rubbing her hands over her face. "I can't have been asleep more than an hour."

"Forty-five minutes, actually," a familiar accented voice said.

She yelped and sat straight up to find the Chinese dragon coiled on the pillow next to her, an expression of amusement in its ancient eyes.

"Jesus!" Arial rolled off the bed, landing with a thump. "You're real!"

"Of course. You did see me earlier."

"And you can talk."

The creature tilted his regal head. "It would be difficult to communicate otherwise."

She scrubbed her hands over her face and tried to cudgel her brain into something approaching working order. "Tracker's tiger didn't."

"He could if he chose to." Sharp teeth flashed slyly. "As it is, he seems to get his needs across."

"Good point." She watched the dragon launch itself from the pillow and start snaking around the room, exploring, moving like a

wave in the air. "Why can't the others see you? They think I'm crazy."
On a mutter, she added, "And I'm beginning to wonder, myself."

Coiling around a brass bedside lamp, the beast smiled at her.
"Oh, you're not crazy."

"Considering you may be a delusion, you're not exactly a reliable source."

"Did a delusion claw that pretty face?"

"Why did they attack me, anyway?" She grimaced. "Assum-
ing they're real."

"They told you why, Arial. They don't want Psych to know
they exist."

"Why not?"

"He might find a way to force them from his mind. His will is
powerful."

She considered him. "Could we do that?"

"Oh, I suppose you could learn—if you wish to kill us. We
could not survive without you." He cocked his head, a teasing
smile on his snout. "But there are many more interesting things I
could teach you."

"Like what?" She shook her head, frustrated. "Look, do you
have a name?"

He considered that a moment. "You may call me Shen-Lung."

Even in the depths of her grief, Arial had been fascinated by the
dragon dance she'd seen in Chinatown. As a teenager, she'd done a
research paper on Eastern dragons; she still owned a collection of
ceramic dragon figurines. "In Chinese mythology, Shen-Lung controls wind and rain. Are you saying you're some kind of god?"

"No, but if you'd like a warm breeze or a nice white Christmas, I could certainly oblige." As she blinked, the creature undulated closer. "Come. It's time you learned to fly."

"I can fly?" She'd heard that some Hypers could.

"With a bit of instruction."

Once Arial had dreamed of flying with a Chinese dragon. Just
leaving all her guilt behind . . .

"Oh, hell, why not?" She felt a reckless smile spread across her
face. "What do I do first?"

"Relax." And the dragon dove into her chest, igniting another delicious surge of warmth. "I'll carry you until you learn the trick of it."

Arial gasped, as power rolled through her, heady and intoxicating, literally sweeping her off her feet. As Shen-Lung carried her out into the hall, she found herself laughing like a child.

• • •

JOSIAH lay rigidly in the bedroom across the hall from Arial's, trying not to remember the way she'd tasted. Unfortunately, his dick had a mind of its own, and it was preoccupied with her silken skin and heady scent. He gritted his teeth against the temptation to cross the hall and take up where they'd left off.

He held temptation off with the memory of the pain and anguish in Sharon's eyes, and the crushing guilt in his own heart.

Frankly, he'd rather jerk off.

Josiah eyed the tent in the sweats he'd donned in an effort to defeat lust. Maybe if he took care of business, he could get a little sleep. He started to snake a hand down his waistband . . .

Feminine laughter rang in the corridor, a sweet peal of delight.

He lifted his head, frowning. "Arial?" Rolling out of bed, he strode toward the door and opened it.

Just in time to see the hem of a white silk gown whip past at eye level. "Hey!"

Josiah stepped out into the hall and watched in astonishment as Arial literally flew down the hall, soaring along six feet above the floor. Her body undulated, feet together, hands at her side, as if she were swimming underwater. Her hair streamed behind her like a chestnut flag. The skirts of the white nightgown whipped around her, showing glimpses of bare, toned legs.

"Arial, what the hell?" He started after her. "Where do you think you're going?"

She didn't appear to hear, moving with such speed he was forced to break into a sprint. A fierce wind blew in her wake, gusting into his face. Yet despite its force, the wind was warm, smelling of exotic spices and femininity. His body responded with a silent growl of hunger.

"Arial, dammit! Come back!"

But she kept going. He lengthened his stride, running hard. By rights, he should have caught her, but she stayed just ahead. He reached one hand toward a slim ankle . . .

She arched upward, heading for a hatch in the ceiling. The heavy iron door blew open, and she zipped inside.

With a growl, he leaped upward, caught the steel ladder inside the tube, and scrambled after her.

"Arial!"

Had the Transition driven her over the edge, the way it once had him? Remembering the nightmare of his madness, fear clutched at him.

Arial lost in that kind of hell . . .

Josiah leaped upward, clearing three rungs to catch a fourth in his desperation. *"Arial!"*

• • •

THE wind whipped Arial's face, surprisingly warm and sweet scented. Flying was exhilarating, a hot rush that fed her adrenalin junkie's soul. And with Shen-Lung within her, it was surprisingly effortless. She need only think, and the wind answered her whims.

It was like being a goddess.

Another hatch lay at the end of the access tube. A flick of her fingers sent a blast of wind against it, and the door flew open. She shot out into the open air and headed skyward.

The sun had risen, spilling pools of flame and gold across the horizon. She spun as she arched upward, savoring the sun on her face, the warm wind that supported her, despite the winter chill all around. Looking downward, she gaped in surprise.

Below her feet lay a sprawling castle of cream stone she instantly recognized. It was Bayfield House, a nineteenth-century mansion built by Michael Bay, the eccentric heir to one of America's greatest fortunes.

Psych's headquarters lay beneath Bayfield House?

Arial's eyes widened as she put two and two together. Psych must be Richard Bay, Michael's great-great-grandson. Her joke about the Batcave had been closer to the mark than she'd dreamed.

Damn. One of the most powerful men in the South was a Hyper. How the hell had he managed to keep *that* secret?

Telepaths can always find blackmail material, Shen-Lung's voice said in her mind. *But at the moment, we have a more immediate problem. You must learn to call the power.*

But it isn't my power—it's yours.

No, I'm only the power source. Yours is the will that shapes it. That's the arrangement.

What arrangement?

You give me life. I give you power.

Arial blinked. *I don't remember making that particular deal.*

My people have a slightly different conception of these things than yours.

No shit. But it was hard to quibble with the elegant sweep of Bayfield House below, surrounded by its grape arbors and gardens, the Blue Ridge Mountains rolling all around it like ocean waves. What a view it would be in the spring . . .

Concentrate, girl. You need to feel the patterns of energy around you, if you want to influence them.

She frowned as she stopped her rise and hovered, feeling weightless as a soap bubble. The wind swirled around her, warm as springtime. *How am I supposed to do that?*

What's your body made of?

Arial shrugged. *Skin, blood. Bones.*

Deeper than that. Look. An image of herself floating in the air flashed into her mind. It grew, drew closer and closer, like a camera zooming in, the view tightening on her arm, her hand, her fingertip, until she could see the swirls and ridges of her own fingerprint, then the tiny pores. And then even closer, down to the cellular level, from cell structures to chains of molecules, then impossibly even closer to the dance of atoms, the fuzzy glowing zip of electrons swirling around atomic nuclei. Deeper and deeper to the smear of quarks.

The image blurred outward again with a speed that was almost nauseating, but all she could see now were darting flashes of energy. It was no longer possible to tell where her body ended and the air around her began. *Because it's all the same,* Shen-Lung said. *The barriers between one and the other are illusion. Concentrate now, and you can feel it.*

He was right. She could see the swirls and eddies of energy, of heat. The fat, dancing molecules of water, oxygen, carbon dioxide, and countless others. Wonder rose in her—the kind of emotion she hadn't felt since the day she'd watched a little girl die. "Ohhhh," she breathed softly.

That's it, Shen-Lung said. *Now fly.*

And he dropped her.

Arial yelped, as lines of force snapped tight around her body and jerked her downward. Instinctively, she reached out and sent power surging outward, countering gravity.

She shot upward like a rocket, her teeth snapping together so hard she bit her tongue.

Too much power, Shen-Lung observed.

Arial growled a curse and tried again, easing back on the energy that flowed from her, slowing her flight to a hover. "You might have warned me!"

And what would you have learned from that?

Yeah, well, if I'd killed myself, I wouldn't have learned a damn thing.

Would I have allowed that, when I've worked so hard to find you? The dragon thrust his scaly head from her body and glanced downward. *Speaking of those who are looking for you . . .*

Arial automatically followed his gaze, her sight returning to normal. Beneath her, a familiar figure stood looking up. He wasn't wearing his armor or mask, but somehow she knew him anyway.

"Tracker," she breathed.

• • •

JOSIAH stared upward, his heart pounding furiously. When Arial had dropped, he'd instinctively lunged to catch her, even knowing it was worse than futile. The impact would have killed her anyway—and probably him, too. In that moment, he'd known that if she died, he might as well die, too.

It was completely irrational. He didn't even know her, for God's sake.

Then she'd caught herself at the last moment, and hope and relief had bloomed in his chest, so intense they'd dizzied him.

He watched her float to earth, her long dark hair whipping in the wind, energy sparking and snapping around her. The glow illuminated her delicate face, the lush line of her mouth, the gold in her dark eyes. The white nightgown with its thin spaghetti straps hugged her torso, even as its full skirt danced around her thighs. She looked more like a goddess than anything human.

She descended, weightless as a dream, until her slender hands touched his shoulders. Josiah reached up and took her waist in his hands, drawing her close.

She let him take her weight at the same time as he took her mouth. He supported her easily as they kissed, deep and slow. She tasted of power and desire and clean spring wind. "Tracker," Arial breathed.

"Josiah," he corrected roughly, catching her under her knees to cradle her in his arms. "My name is Josiah Ridge." He started back toward the hatch with her. "And you scared the hell out of me."

"Maybe it's time you stop being scared," she said softly, combing a hand through his dark hair. "I'm not that fragile."

Josiah looked down into those goddess eyes. "I'm beginning to figure that out."

Then he gave her a grin, flipped her over his shoulder, and carried her down the hatch to the sound of her laughter.

• • •

WITHOUT the mask, he was a little more rough-hewn than she'd expected, with thick dark brows over deep-set hazel eyes. His Roman nose was a bit off-line, as if it had been broken a time or two. His jaw was a bit too broad and square for *GQ* beauty, an effect heightened by the ruthlessly short brush cut of his sable hair. Somehow, that lush mouth looked even more seductive against all that aggressive masculinity. She couldn't wait to taste it again.

Arial got her chance when he carried her back to his bedroom. She'd half-expected to have to coax him again, but the moment her backside hit the mattress, he was peeling her out of her nightgown, dragging its silky hem over her head and tossing it aside. Leaving her clad only in a pair of tiny lace panties.

Then he stepped back. And simply stared. For a moment, his hazel eyes flared tiger gold, pupils turning to slits. Arial caught her breath as every muscle in his body coiled as if he were about to spring. He was so big, so broad, muscle lying in sculpted ridges under his tanned skin. She swallowed, feeling her nipples tighten.

Those eyes flicked to the pink tips and flared even brighter. He licked his lips.

Then he caught the waistband of his sweats and pushed them down, as if he couldn't stand to have his body covered another instant. Straightening to his full height, he paused, his gaze challenging.

The full effect of his nudity was stunning. He was so erect, his cock angled slightly upward in an elegant male curve, his balls hanging full between powerful thighs.

His was not the shaved and airbrushed perfection of a male model. There was hair on his chest, calves, and forearms; veins snaking along his big hands; a couple of ugly scars framing one knee that suggested surgery some time in his past.

He was not, after all, some comic book fantasy man. Powers or not, ghost tiger notwithstanding, he was flesh and blood.

And she wanted him more than she'd ever wanted a man in her life.

Arial slid her fingertips into the waist of her panties, and tugged them down over her legs. His eyes flared hot gold as she tossed them aside.

"God, Arial . . ." And then he was on her, kissing her with a stark hunger that left her boneless, his tongue sliding deep in conquest, his teeth gently scoring her lower lip. She dug her nails into his powerful bare back, loving the feel of his skin under her hands.

When his strong, warm hands palmed her breasts, Arial could only close her eyes in delight.

He growled, the sound not quite human, and bit his way softly down the tendons of her throat. He paused at her collarbone to taste and lick, as his fingers plucked her nipples, twisting with a wicked, breath-stealing skill.

By the time he pulled his head away, she was gasping, her heart hammering in her chest. He gave her a feral, slit-pupiled look and covered her breast with his mouth. Suckled, pulling fiercely, giving her no mercy as he played with her. Driving her insane.

The rake of his teeth made her back arch. "Tracker!"

"Josiah." He growled it, fierce and animal, as he punctuated each word with a gently stinging bite. "My name. Is. Josiah."

"Josiah." She wrapped her hands around his head. "Josiah, Josiah. Keep doing that, and I'll call you whatever you want."

"Betterrrrr." He reached down the length of her body to quest between her thighs. Strong fingers strummed over her clit, making her writhe. Then slid slowly, carefully deep. Pumped. He looked up with those glowing eyes. "You're *wet*."

Arial laughed, the sound strangled. "Hell, yeah."

"You're going to be even wetter." He bent his head and went back to licking and suckling her nipples even as he pumped his finger within her. In. Out. Inexorably. Mercilessly.

Until she was writhing, half out of her mind. "God, Josiah! You're driving me insane!"

"Not yet." He grabbed her by the hips and flung himself down on his back. Before she knew what was happening, he'd spread her over his face.

For a moment she instinctively tried to pull away, but his big hands tightened, forcing her down onto his ruthless mouth. With a whimper of surrender, Arial grabbed the headboard. His tongue lapped and danced over her clit, the sensation so furiously intense, Arial flung back her head, yowling, dimly aware of her hair whipping her bare back.

He growled at her like the tiger, working her with teeth and lips and tongue, licking at her clit, her inner lips, thrusting into her. Until she shook on top of him, blinded by heat.

The orgasm rose in a fountain of flame, pouring up her core, ripping a scream from her throat.

Somewhere in the distance, she heard a tiger's deep-throated roar.

. . .

JOSIAH listened to Arial's helpless gasps of pleasure, as his cock jerked in lust. In some distant part of his mind, he knew he was out of control, but he didn't care.

He could trust Arial not to let him go too far. His goddess could stop him whenever she wanted.

Her cry of pleasure made him grin. *Not that she's going to stop me anytime soon.*

He drove her to a second orgasm, then a third. Until, gasping, she dragged herself from his hands and collapsed on her back. Those beautiful breasts rose and fell, quivering sweetly.

"And where," he asked in a silken voice, "do you think you're going?"

Arial gave him a wild-eyed look. "Josiah, wait . . ."

"Nope." He flipped her over onto her belly, dragged her beautiful ass into the air. "My turn."

Then he drove his cock into her in one hard, delicious thrust. They both froze, shuddering at the sensation.

"Well," she said at last, her voice strangled, "if you insist."

Josiah laughed, the sound a little ragged, and began to work his way in and out of her hot, tight clasp. She felt so deliciously snug, so wet, he knew he'd never last. "God," he gritted, "you're sweet."

She flung her head back, grinding her lushly curving backside against his hips. "I'm not sure . . . *sweet* is quite the word."

He shuttered his eyes and fought to hold on against the clawing delight. "Yeah," he panted. "Good point. Ahh! *Sweet* doesn't do you justice at all."

Arial hunched back, taking him in to the balls, milking him hard. Josiah could feel the tiny pulses as she began to come. With a growl, he let go, pounding into her in deep, ferocious thrusts that drew his balls tight as his cock jerked, then pumped jet after jet. He opened his mouth to bellow in pleasure . . .

Before the sound even left his mouth, energy shot from Arial, a hot blue crackle that arced into the center of his chest. The impact threw him backward just as an answering electric jolt shot from him. Just before he hit the back wall, he saw it strike her, heard her strangled shout.

And then he saw nothing at all.

. . .

SOMETHING was wrong.

Richard wasn't sure what. Hell, he didn't even know why he was so sure. But five years as Psych had taught him to listen to that little voice in the back of his head.

And it was definitely yammering now.

He went still, eyeing the entrance to the garage. The buzz of his instincts grew more frantic. For a moment, he could have sworn he heard female voices whispering, but he couldn't quite make out what they were saying.

Maybe he should beat a quick retreat and get Josiah. He'd feel a lot better with Tracker's superpowered muscle at his back.

Thing was, when he'd walked past Jos's room earlier, his friend had sounded . . . busy. Besides, he was Psych. He'd handled more than his share of pissed-off Hypers before without Tracker's help. Including, come to think of it, Jos himself.

And what a memorable fight *that* had been.

He flattened his back against the wall, then sent the door rolling open with a flick of power.

Nothing. No ball of fire, no rampaging Hyper storming his way into the hall, no nothing. Richard darted a look around the door frame, but the room appeared empty of everything except a whole lot of expensive engineering.

Cautiously, he made his way inside. Not for the first time, he cursed the fact that other Hypers seemed to have a natural shielding against his telepathy. He'd have been able to sense an ordinary human hiding in the garage.

BOOOOOM!

The ear-splitting crash of rending metal made him jump.

BOOOM!

"What the fu—"

BOOOM!

It was coming from overhead. It sounded as if something was being slammed repeatedly into the hydraulic lift in the barn above.

Hay drifted lazily downward.

"Oh, hell." The metal platform that formed the floor of the barn was actually bending, spilling the hay that disguised it into the garage.

BOOOM! He glimpsed what looked like the hood of a car, hammering one side of the platform until it bent like a foil pie plate.

A female head thrust through the opening, red hair spilling around a wickedly smiling face. "Why, it's Psych! Hi, there, honey!"

"Shit," Richard breathed. Then he lifted his voice into a desperate bellow. *"Tracker! It's Kali!"*

CHAPTER SIX

Arial dreamed of a world with no trees, no grass, nothing but tearing winds and forking lightning and stifling, brutal heat. Merciless heat that whipped the winds to speeds they'd never known before, convulsed the world into hurricanes. It was the heat that somehow frightened her most.

Something was wrong with the sun.

She couldn't see it, but she could feel it out there, could sense it with the alien perceptions of her kind.

Some part of her recognized she was not human. In fact, she had no body at all. There were those who thought the race had physical forms once, but that was uncounted millennia ago. They were creatures of power now. Pure energy, riding the alien wind, drinking the lightning.

But all of their power could not save them from their swelling sun, as it grew and grew and licked greedily toward their world. They all knew they had at most a few more years before the sun engulfed the planet completely. Then Arial and all her kind would die.

But perhaps there was hope. One of the Wisest Ones had found another world within the range of a single Passage jump, an alien place yes, but around a comfortably stable sun. A world inhabited by beings of the flesh and blood they'd need in order to survive.

Humans, the aliens called themselves.

Without such bodies, the People would never be able to live on a planet so alien, with such a thin atmosphere and infrequent life-giving lightning.

The one problem was that so few of the humans were compatible hosts. Most had minds that were impenetrable to the People. For a time, all despaired.

Then the Wisest One identified a compatible human host and managed, with great effort, to open a Passage into his mind. Then he sought a second host for another of their kind. It was easier this time, requiring only a touch for the symbiote to make her Passage.

And so, one by one, the People fled their dying world.

Now it was Arial's turn. She'd found the one she wanted, a big male, healthy and strong. Optimism singing in her heart, she leaped through the Passage into his mind.

And everything went wrong.

The host's world was too alien, and so were his thoughts. She couldn't make contact with his consciousness, no matter how she tried. She even took the form of the symbol she'd found in his mind—a *tiger*, it was called. To no avail.

Still, she tried to give him the use of her power in return for her life, though she soon realized he found it more burden than blessing.

That would have been bad enough, but she quickly discovered that some of those who'd made the Passage had been corrupted by their hosts. The one who'd found Josiah for her was one of those. What was worse, his host, Kali, was stalking Josiah.

Arial did not understand why until Kali caught up to them. She touched him—and her symbiote surged into his mind, trying to enslave him.

Arial did the only thing she could do. She took over, protecting Josiah's mind as she attacked Kali, driving the other symbiote back into the woman.

And then they ran.

• • •

"FUCK." Josiah's voice rasped from the other side of the room. "We always thought my Transition had driven me crazy with a little help from Kali. Instead, it was that damned alien's idea of saving my ass."

Arial opened her eyes and found herself staring at a fringed bedspread. Blinking, she realized she was lying on the floor. "What the hell happened?"

"E. T. threw us for a loop."

"Oh, yeah." Arial sat up, groaning, as bruised muscles protested. "That power jolt just as we climaxed." It had tossed them around the room like dice in a cup.

"Are you okay?" Josiah staggered to his feet and walked around the bed to help her up.

She cleared her throat. "A little singed, but I'll live. I gather you saw the same . . . dream? Vision?"

"Alien gas giant inhabited by whatever-the-fuck-they-are?" He grimaced and lowered himself to sit on the edge of the mattress. "I saw it. I don't know why I saw it in the middle of the best climax of my life."

"In your pleasure, your consciousness finally opened to me," a purring voice said. The tiger thrust its head out of his side. "I saw my chance and took it."

"Ahh!" Josiah leaped to his feet in surprise. The tiger's ghostly shape sat down on the bed and flicked an ear at him.

"I gather you can see him now," Arial said dryly.

"Yeah. Jesus!" He eyed the cat a moment before his brows suddenly shot up. "I'll be damned—it's the Tillman High tiger."

"What?"

"The mascot of that school where I taught football—it was a tiger. All this time you kept talking about a tiger, and I never put it together until . . ." He stiffened, alarm widening his eyes. "Wait a minute. Did you hear that?"

Arial frowned at him. "What?

He lunged off the bed. "Somebody just let loose an energy blast. And Psych doesn't do energy blasts!"

. . .

JOSIAH ran so fast, Arial was forced to fly to keep up with him. Even then, he reached the scene of the battle ahead of her.

She rounded the corner to find him standing frozen, staring at what had once been the door of the garage. It had been blown off its hinges. The crumpled hood of Tracker's SUV stuck halfway through the wall, as if something had picked the big vehicle up and thrown it.

From somewhere beyond the wreckage, a male voice groaned in pain. Mocking laughter answered.

"Not so tough now, huh, Psych?"

"He's definitely a little worse for wear," a woman agreed. "Feeling a little bit more submissive yet, darling?"

"Kali." Josiah jolted forward, but Arial grabbed his shoulder with a strength born of pure desperation.

"Wait a minute," she hissed. "We can't just charge in there without a plan of attack!"

He threw her an agonized look and whispered hoarsely, "Arial, *I can smell his blood.*"

"And he won't be the only one bleeding, if we don't keep our heads. It sounds like they've got us outnumbered in there."

For a moment he hesitated, visibly torn. Then he growled a curse and grabbed her by the shoulder, pulling her backward down the hall. "If she's got her full crew with her, they probably do."

"How many are in her crew?"

"Six. Judging from my truck sticking out of the wall, she's definitely got Brute. It would have taken Cerberus's Hyper senses to find this place. And if those two are here, the other four are, too. And you're right—there's no way in hell we can take all seven of them. That team of hers has some serious firepower."

Arial swallowed, fighting the sick sensation of rising fear. "So what do we do?"

"A little hostage negotiation." His smile was bitter. "There's one thing Kali really wants—and that's me. I'm the one that got away. I get her to hand Psych over, and you fly him the hell out of here and call the Feds. They'll have a team here before Kali finishes celebrating."

"What?" She stared at him in horror. For a moment, Jenny's wide blue eyes flashed through her memory. "Fuck that."

"Arial . . ."

"I'm not handing you over to have your mind raped by that sick bitch," Arial spat. "That's not the way it works, Jos. You don't give the good guys to the bad guys."

Josiah's expression turned stony. "It's not your choice." He turned away.

She stared at his broad back helplessly. With his strength, there was no way she could stop him.

Sensations spun through her memory: the heat and hunger in his kiss, the warmth of his hands, the exquisite way he'd made love to her. The sound of pride in his voice when he talked about his students. The tenderness in his eyes when he'd looked at her.

Oh, hell, Arial thought, *I'm falling in love with him.*

He was going to end up dead, and she wouldn't be able to save him. She was helpless. Just as powerless as she'd been when Jenny died.

Haven't we already been through this? Shen-Lung growled in her mind. *You know better.*

Arial froze, suddenly remembering his voice in that morning's lesson. *It's all the same. The barriers between one and the other are illusion.*

She focused on Josiah's broad back, looking hard. Zooming in just as Shen-Lung had taught her. Until she could see the cells in his body. The molecules. The swirling energy that made them up. Until she could no longer see the barriers between him and the air around him.

Or between him and herself.

Josiah.

She *heard* her thought ring in his mind. And it stopped him.

He turned to look at her, stunned amazement filling his mind. *Hypers can't read Hypers!*

Psych can't. I'm not Psych.

His lips twitched. *I noticed.*

Have you noticed this? She took a deep breath—and opened herself to him.

. . .

THE love Arial felt was delicate, as fragile with new growth as a shoot of spring grass forcing its way through the snow. Yet Josiah could sense the promise of warmth and budding strength in it.

It staggered him.

And in that moment, he also realized how familiar the feeling was.

Because he felt the same. *I'm falling for her.* Joy filled him with such intensity, a broad grin spread across his face. *Damn.* He took a step back toward her—

Just as Psych screamed.

Josiah froze in midstep, anguish ripping through his momentary joy. He could feel its reverberation echoing through Arial. She gasped softly in pain.

In that instant, he remembered Rich had worked to save him when he'd scarcely been human. *I can't let him die, Arial. Not even for you.*

No. He could feel the grief in her. *No, it would destroy you.*

Before he could turn away, Shen-Lung's voice spoke in his mind. *There is, however, another option.*

The tiger rumbled a purr of approval.

. . .

RICHARD lay in a blood-soaked heap, as Josiah walked into the garage. He'd been right: Kali had brought all six of her slaves: Brute and Cerberus; Ghost—who could turn invisible—the flyer,

Daedalus; Firecracker—who could cause small explosions with a thought—and Breaker, who controlled electricity.

If this doesn't work, Josiah thought, *God help me. They'll tear me apart.*

"I think he should be softened up enough by now," Kali said cheerfully. "Let's try this again. Psych, you stubborn bastard."

"Let him go, Kali."

Her head jerked up, red hair dancing around her shoulders, as an incredulous smile of delight spread across her face. "Tracker! There you are. What did you do with the pretty cop? I've got such plans for her."

"Forget her," he said roughly. "We both know who you really want. Let Psych go, and I'll give myself up."

Kali went still, her green eyes narrowing. "Now, why would I do a thing like that when I can just have the boys kick your ass? Then I'll have both of you—*and* the cop."

The thought sickened him, but he folded his arms and gave her a cool smile. "I think we've already established that you can't take me, Kali. On the other hand, if you let Arial get Psych out of here, I won't put up a fight."

Kali whirled toward Cerberus. "Is he lying?"

Squat and fiercely homely, the little man breathed deep to draw in Josiah's scent. "Don't seem so."

Brute flexed his massive hands. Jealousy gleamed in his small black eyes. "I don't trust the bastard. Let me work him over a little first."

Kali snorted, her gaze fixed on Josiah with eager greed. "And batter that pretty face? I don't think so." She licked her lips. "Swear you'll surrender yourself."

Josiah didn't let his eyes waver. "If you let them go."

"Fine," she snapped. "The cop can have him. He's too stubborn for me anyway."

Meaning she hadn't been able to break him. *Good for you, Rich.*

Arial stepped into the room and gestured. Richard's body rose into the air and floated toward her. Her teeth clenched as she struggled with his considerable weight.

He lifted his head and looked blearily around. "Wha?" Both eyes were so swollen, it was obvious he could barely see. Blood smeared his mouth and nose, and the knuckles of one hand were grotesquely swollen, as if his fingers had been methodically broken. "Jo—Tracker?"

"Shhh," Arial whispered. "We're leaving."

"A telekinetic," Kali said, staring at her with sharpened interest. "And a pretty damn strong one, at that."

"Do you want me or not?" Josiah snapped, drawing her attention.

"Oh, I want you, big boy." Her green eyes narrowed. "In fact, come here. Now."

He moved toward her, putting an arrogant roll in his walk and a taunting smile on his face.

"That's it." Kali grinned and purred, "Good boy."

His skin crawled as he stopped just within her reach. He lifted a brow. "Well?"

She rammed her hand hard against his chest. Josiah drew in a hard breath as her mind slammed into his.

And Arial's dragon and his tiger shot from his chest, right into hers. Kali stiffened with a cry of shock. She began to shake, eyes rolling back in her head.

A moment later, Shen-Lung and the tiger emerged again, dragging—*something*. Something bloody red, with curving horns, a misshapen face, and a whipping forked tail. It looked like a medieval woodcut of a demon, and it hissed in rage as it struggled. But the tiger had buried its fangs deep in the thing's throat, and Shen-Lung coiled around its barrel chest, all four sets of claws dug in.

Behind Josiah, female voices rose in a chorus of rage. He jerked his head around just in time to see two ghostly forms shoot from Rich's body. Together, the twin spirits flew at the demon and began to slash at it with their claws. It howled in pain and desperation.

Until an inhuman roar drowned it out. Suddenly the air was full of savage, glowing shapes, pouring from the six slave Hypers to surround Kali's demon in a swirling mob. Hiding it from view. Its screams grew shriller, more desperate.

"Jesus," Josiah whispered, feeling a bit sickened. They were tearing the demon spirit apart, feeding on its energy as they'd once fed on the lightning of their home world.

And with the creature dead . . .

"What?" Kali gasped, staggering backward. All the blood left her face, leaving it milk pale under the fire of her hair. "What's happening?"

He gave her a feral grin. "Looks like your slaves' spirits are getting a little payback."

"What the *fuck* are you talking about?"

"You'll figure it out."

There was a last choked cry . . . And nothing.

The spirits swirled away back to their hosts in a flurry of light and energy. Josiah gasped as his tiger dove back into his chest with a satisfied rumble. *Well, that was a pretty chilling display.*

But necessary. His host had driven Gerot mad. There was no other way to stop him from enslaving others to feed her lust for power.

"She's gone," Daedalus breathed, his eyes wide in his round face. "She's not in my mind anymore."

"Holy hell, you're right!" Ghost whispered. "I'm free!"

Brute turned a chilling grin on Kali. "We're all free."

She took a step back, her eyes widening with the cold terror of a woman who was seeing her worst fears realized. "No. No, I'll just . . . I'll just . . ."

"You'll do nothing, bitch!" Firecracker lifted his hands, obviously preparing to throw a blast.

A cold blast of wind slammed through the room, followed by a deafening clap of thunder. "That's enough!" Arial barked. "Kali, you're under arrest. The rest of you back the fuck off—unless you want to lose your powers too."

Brute lifted his big hands and flexed them menacingly. "You sure you can take us all, cop?"

She lifted an elegant brow. "Are you sure I can't?"

Josiah stepped between the two of them and curled his own hands into fists. "And if she can't, I can. Somehow I doubt you're quite as good a team without Kali pulling your strings."

Brute licked his thick lips with an expression of profound un-ease. He apparently remembered their last fight as vividly as Josiah. "I got no problem with you, Tracker. You just put that bitch in a cage where she belongs."

As Arial and Josiah watched, he whirled around, stalked to the opening left by the broken hydraulic lift, and leaped skyward.

Grumbling and casting dark looks at their former mistress, his teammates followed.

Arial watched them go. *Damn, I hate to let those bastards get away,* she said in Josiah's mind.

I know, but we don't have the firepower to take them out now. Don't worry—none of them can stand the others. They'll scatter and we'll be able to pick them off later.

Kali suddenly whirled on Josiah, an expression of helpless fury on her face. "What did you do to me, you son of a bitch?"

Josiah walked toward her, pulling a pair of cuffs from his belt as he gave her a toothy grin. "Pulled your plug."

"Come on, Kali," Arial purred. "Resist arrest."

She took one look at them and slumped in defeat.

EPILOGUE

One month later

Arial walked into the bedroom she was sharing with Josiah—
and stopped, staring at her own black-clad reflection in the
mirror over the bureau. She was still getting used to the sight of herself in Hyper armor. The suit was the same basic design as Tracker's, except for the small white stylized Chinese dragon that swirled
across her right eye and halfway down the cheek of the mask.

It had been a busy month. First she'd handed in her resignation
to the James County Sheriff's Office. It hadn't hurt nearly as much
as she'd expected. After that had come two weeks of federal psy-
chological and physical testing to become a Hyper agent. The Feds
decided to waive the law enforcement training requirement because
of her background.

All in all, it was a good thing Arial was a cop. The federal
medical specialists all agreed she was one of the most powerful
Hypers they'd ever seen, between her telekinesis and ability to ma-
nipulate the weather, not to mention her talent for seeing other
people's aliens. That last little bombshell had definitely set the
medical establishment back on its heels, not least because it was
conclusive proof of life on other planets.

Somebody probably would have been tempted to lock her
up for further study, if it hadn't been for the fact that she was so

obviously needed to hunt down the rest of Kali's gang. She was finally allowed to go to work on a provisional basis with Tracker and Psych.

Having spent a week in the hospital, Rich had been in the mood to kick ass. Arial and Jos had been happy to help him do it.

It had crossed her mind to wonder if any of the gang had been innocent, forced into criminal behavior by Kali's powers. After all, the bitch had intended to enslave the three of them, too.

But a scan of each thug as he was caught revealed that none of them were exactly choirboys. And as Rich had pointed out, they'd certainly enjoyed beating the hell out of him.

Today they'd caught the last one, Brute, who'd barely put up a fight before he surrendered with a certain amount of resignation. Apparently he'd heard how thoroughly they'd defeated his former teammates and wanted to save himself the hospitalization.

Arial gave her reflection a smile of satisfaction—which broadened as Josiah slipped up behind her and wrapped his brawny arms around her waist.

"I do love a woman in leather," he purred in her ear, then added, "Tempest."

She rolled her eyes. "God, I hate that name." The FBI had assigned her the handle, over her protests.

He caught the tab of her zipper and started sliding it down. "Well, nobody ever accused bureaucrats of having imagination."

She gave him a mock pout. "I really wanted Phoenix."

"Copyrighted. Comic book character." The zipper's tab reached the top of her breastbone. "We'd get sued."

"Yeah, well, in Chinese mythology, the Phoenix is the mate of the dragon."

"Yeah, but you're the mate of *me*."

She let her head fall back against his broad chest. "I'm not sure that sentence is grammatically correct."

"Darlin', I don't give a damn." He started tugging her armored coat down her arms. "And anyway, I used to read that comic, and Phoenix went evil and ate a planet. A billion poor broccoli people, dead."

"You geekboy, you." Arial smiled, shuttering her eyes as he pulled the edges of her suit apart. "Besides, I'm starting to feel kind of evil myself."

"Do tell." He slid his gloved hands down to cover her bared breasts. "How evil are we talking?"

Arial's smile grew into a smirk. "Evil enough to put Velveeta on the broccoli people."

"That's pretty evil." Strong fingers rolled her nipples, tugging sweetly. "In fact, I think you need to be punished."

"What have you got in mind?"

In one blurring movement, he grabbed the edges of her suit and jerked it down around her thighs, then dropped to his knees. "A spanking." His teeth closed over one cheek in a wicked little nip.

"AHH!" Startled, she lost her balance, but he caught her and tumbled her to the floor. "No fair!"

He reared over her, a sly grin on his masked face. "Who said anything about fighting fair?"

She sniffed. "I thought you were one of the good guys."

"Oh, I am." Josiah lowered his head. "Very, very good."

The kiss was slow, thorough, and so hot her toes curled in her armored boots. His tongue dipped and swirled, as his teeth raked across her lower lip, then tugged softly. By the time he lifted his head again, she was breathing hard.

So was he.

"Mmmm." Arial smiled lazily. "You *are* good."

He rested his forehead against hers. "You're not bad yourself."

"Trouble is, you're also covered in leather."

"Yeah." He started working his way down her torso, tasting her skin, dealing out licks and tiny bites to every part of her body he paused at.

"That was a hint." She sucked in a gasp as he discovered her nipples. "Get naked."

Josiah raised his head, laughing. "Yes, mistress."

He bounced to his feet with that weightless strength and started to hum a bump and grind as he shimmied out of his coat.

Arial snickered, but her laughter faded when he unzipped his suit and started working it down his broad torso. He turned his back, giving her a good look at his tightly muscled ass in the snug black armor. By the time he spun around to liberate his cock with a teasing grind of his hips, she was all but panting.

"I take it back." She watched him unzip his boots and kick them across the room. "You are definitely not a good guy. You're bad all the way to the boner."

He stopped and looked at her. "That was awful."

"Yeah, I know." She bared her teeth. "But what do you expect? I'm evil."

"You are that." He pounced. Before she knew what hit her, he'd swept her off the floor, sat down on the mattress, draped her across his knee, and landed a light swat on her ass.

"Hey!"

"You had that coming." Josiah spilled her onto the bed and grabbed her boots, tugging them and the suit the rest of the way off.

"Laugh now, geekboy. My vengeance will be terrible to behold."

Josiah straightened to survey her sprawled, naked body. "I'm shaking." His cock jerked once. He lifted a brow. "And do I look like a 'boy' anything?"

"I dunno." She rolled onto her knees and grabbed the thick shaft. Her fingers barely closed around it. "Let me get a closer look."

"If you insist . . ." He sucked in a hard breath as she engulfed him in one long swoop.

He was far more than a mouthful—smooth, salty, flavored with a hint of leather and Josiah's own seductive scent. Arial sighed in pleasure and settled down to suckle him in earnest.

• • •

HER mouth was breathtaking. Hot, fierce, wickedly skilled, her clever little tongue painting heat over the head of his shaft and along its snaking veins. Cool fingers cuddled his balls, rolled and caressed them as he shuddered.

Arial. His sweet Arial. Insanely brave, funny, wickedly smart. And she gave one hell of a blow job.

His own personal goddess.

And there was no way in hell he could take any more of this. "Arial," he gasped, threading his hands through her silken hair.

"Mmmm?" A snaking lick along the vein running the length of his cock.

Josiah shivered. "If you don't back off, you're gonna be really, really frustrated."

"I'll risk it." She nibbled mercilessly on the head.

"Oh, *God*!" It felt like the top of his own head was about to blow off. "Arial . . ." He was begging now and didn't care in the least.

She pulled reluctantly away from his cock with a pronounced popping sound, like a kid letting go of a sucker. "Oh, all right. Spoilsport."

"Wench."

He swooped down, grabbed her shoulders, and tossed her on the bed. Then he was on her and *in* her.

She was, thank God, deliciously wet—apparently teasing him had turned her on as much as it had him. He had to freeze after the first thrust, fighting desperately not to come as her delicate inner muscles milked him.

Arial coiled those exquisite legs around his back and dug one heel into his left ass cheek, a not-so-subtle hint.

"Giddyap," she breathed.

"Neigh." Biting his lip, he began to thrust, slowly, clawing for control.

• • •

NO matter how many times he'd taken her over the last month, the first really hard thrust never failed to make Arial's eyes roll back in her head.

She had to blink a couple of times before she managed to focus.

He was braced in her favorite position now, arms stiff, head thrown back so that corded muscle worked all up and down his powerful neck, chest, and arms. When she looked down the line of their bodies, she could see the tight lacing brawn of his abdominal muscles, as he slid that meaty cock in and out of her hungry body.

But what she really loved to watch was his face.

With her own climax shivering closer and closer, the sight of him fighting his off never failed to drive her crazy. His eyes were tightly closed, one muscle in his jaw flexing as he bared his teeth in effort. A bead of sweat worked its way down his temple from his short hair.

Arial hunched up at him just to watch him gasp. Deliberately, she circled her hips, clamping down hard on the thickness buried so far within her.

"Arial!" he roared, and came.

And that was the part she loved best of all.

Her own white-hot climax took her by surprise.

• • •

THEY lay in a tangled heap, panting. Long moments ticked by before Josiah spoke. "I've been thinking . . ."

"Congratulations," Arial groaned. "That's more than I'm capable of at the moment."

"Marry me."

She jerked her head up and stared at him. He looked perfectly serious—and damn near serene. She gaped. *"What?"*

His dark brows lowered with a trace of annoyance. "Don't look so stunned. I've told you I love you."

She licked her dry lips. "And I love you, but . . ."

"But what?"

"We've only known each other a month."

"Maybe, but it's been a really *busy* month." He smiled slightly. "And we knew we were falling for each other from day one. Literally."

"But . . ."

Hazel eyes locked with hers, sure and calm. "You're everything I want. Everything I've ever wanted. Marry me. Stay with me."

She looked up at him, feeling the dazed smile spread across her face. "Yes. God, yes!"

As she flung her arms around him, she heard a dragon voice say, *I told you he'd propose before the month was out. You owe me five bucks.*

Fine. Sounding disgruntled, the tiger added, *Where am I supposed to catch these "bucks"?*

Shen-Lung groaned.

Are they very quick?

Idiot.

The tiger snickered.

Caught by the Tides

~

Diane Whiteside

CHAPTER ONE

Northern coast of France, April 1803

The full moon lit the incoming tide like a pathway to Avalon. The waves lapped at the beach, filling the small cove with a gentle music which the greatest harpist might have envied. Beyond the headland, the English Channel was dark and touched with silver, as empty of ships to the naked eye as any highway to Paris.

Owen Bentham might have smiled at this evidence of a very great spell, but he was too busy finding the strength to stand upright. He'd just ridden for two and a half days to reach Normandy from Strasbourg, the great French and Alsatian city on the Rhine.

Now his legs were so numb they could have sunk into the sand before he noticed, while his back had become a jolting flame spiraling through his ribs and neck. He could map every fold in his neckcloth by his sweat's caked dirt and salt. He hadn't changed his buckskin breeches, or the rest of his clothes. He was badly unshaven, a sight his father's wife would have crowed over and cited as proof of his inability to be a gentleman.

But his knives were sharp, his powder dry, with all of his weapons in their places, ready for use at a moment's notice.

He listened again, straining every sense to search for pursuers.

Another set of waves came in, spilling higher across the sand, until it washed across the tip of his boots.

Where the devil were Bonaparte's men? He'd hidden his tracks, and he'd ridden fast. He'd chosen to be taken off near Le Havre, not Calais, making for a longer passage back to England but a more unexpected departure point.

All the time, he'd abjured the use of magick, lest its use be traced back to him. One of his great strengths as a courier was his ability to avoid magick in even the smallest details. His saddle was balanced on his shoulder, removing his few possessions from his final mount. He'd borrowed horses from other Britons whenever he could, leaving no traces of magecraft to be tracked by. Some had even ridden with him and tied him in the saddle while he slept.

The only sound was the tide singing to itself and to the land.

A muscle twitched in Owen's jaw. As a former sergeant in His Majesty's dragoons, he was far happier on land than aboard ship. But only the Navy could cross the Channel and carry him back to England. The French knew it, too, and would be watching for him, since it was the last place they could catch him—making that leg the most dangerous part of his journey. Still, there was no other route.

He shrugged and lifted his right hand, palm outward to the sea.

The moon struck crimson fire from his signet, sending a single beam of light dancing deep into the water.

Owen clenched his fist, turning the beam into a short pulse—once, twice, thrice. Then he held his hand open, letting the light shine uninterrupted for the count of ten.

A minute later, a cutter glided out from behind the headland, its crew rowing with the quiet precision of men who'd been trained under a cat-o'-nine-tails. Behind it, a bit of the moon's reflection rearranged itself into a naval sloop, skimming the water under a single sail. As he'd expected, they'd been concealed by an excellent cloaking spell.

Owen surveyed the silent cove once more, while waiting for the cutter to pick him up. Surely he'd have time to take a brief nap before offering to stand watch aboard the sloop . . .

Trethledan Cove, the next night

EMMA Sinclair braced her back against the cliff and scrabbled for a hold among the crumbling rock. Rain crashed over her head, hungry to knock her off her feet. Lightning ripped across the sky and showed the world around her—the ravenous English Channel battering at her ancestral lands, as if it would devour all of Cornwall tonight. Below her, waves pounded over the dark, jagged rocks of Trethledan Bay, little more than a shallow beach now with the high tide coming in.

She raised her eyes to the ocean beyond, looking for the sight that had summoned her during the worst storm for ten years or more. Earlier this afternoon, when the weather had been warm and sunny, she'd watched a sloop sailing far offshore on a very unusual course. She'd even thought she'd heard cannons firing—but shrugged it off as loneliness for her long-dead naval husband.

Then this storm had arrived, so hard and fast it had to have been built by a mage, and she couldn't sleep.

The wind caught her cloak's deep hood, whipping it back off her face. But she saw it again, as she'd seen it from her bedroom—a small bright spark of red, glimmering on the beach. A naval mage-light, which her husband had said meant someone living needed rescue.

Emma let go of the cliff and started scrambling down. In ten minutes or less, high tide would cover the sand, and anyone there would drown. She had to lead the mage to the hidden path before he drowned.

A stone turned under her half-boot, sending her sliding a good yard down the steep trail. Her heart stopped for a moment, and she gulped, almost inhaling salt spray from the crashing waves. She closed her eyes for a moment, forcing calm back into her veins.

There was, after all, no one else to do this. Emma's usual companion, Aunt Mary, was visiting Lydia, overseeing Emma's sister's first lying-in. She'd given all the servants leave to attend the great fair at Whitmore Hall—everyone except Nurse and Jem Keverne, Nurse's husband. And Grandfather, for all that he'd been a great general with the knighthood and honors to prove it, was well past eighty and very close to joining his beloved Deborah on the other side of Death's door.

The storm had come so quickly that the Gwythias had covered the bridge below the Morthol castle before any of the servants could return, thus isolating the four of them at Trethledan House. Grandfather, Nurse, and Keverne were sound asleep now, exhausted by age. She was the only one who hadn't completely collapsed after tending the animals.

Emma pushed her foot forward and took off again, not allowing herself to think of everyone who'd met their deaths on these cliffs.

She leaped onto the sand, searching for that red glimmer. Water roiled across the flat expanse, marked by greedy leaps of white foam.

Was that lump too rounded to be a rock?

Lightning shot across the sky, its trail laced with wickedly green phosphorescence. Another bolt crashed into the headland, sending a great mass of rock and boulders into the greedy ocean.

Emma swayed, almost falling to her knees. The wind clutched at her stout boat cloak, trying to rip it away from her body. But the deep folds, originally designed and made for the Royal Navy, stayed close.

Hunched over, fighting for every step, she staggered to the unknown form and stooped down.

It was a man, most definitely a man, and a large example of the species, at that. Brilliant red light glowed at his right shoulder, like a single candle. His chest was barely moving, and he had several days' growth of beard, obscuring his features. He wore riding clothes—buckskin coat and breeches, knee boots, white shirt. Crimson pulsed sluggishly out of his side, tinting the water in the fitful light. The ocean washed over and around him, ripping and tearing at the sand under him, as if hungry to suck him back into the Channel's maelstrom.

A ruby shone in the heavy gold signet on his right hand. It was a gryphon's ring, the mark of a King's Messenger. For him to be here, in a brutal storm and clearly close to death, meant an act of war—or treason—had been committed.

Emma growled, deep and low. Bonaparte's fleet had killed her husband at the Battle of the Nile five years ago. It might be 1803, England and France might be technically at peace, thanks to that idiotic Treaty of Amiens—but she would not abandon this castaway and let the French tyrant destroy anyone else, no matter what it cost her.

She gripped him under his shoulders, set her feet, and tugged.

Nothing happened.

She took a very deep breath and tried again, pouring her entire strength into it, until every muscle in her back screamed and her legs nearly crumpled under her.

He didn't stir an inch. But the ocean washed completely over his chest, leaving only his nose and mouth free.

Emma gasped for air, glaring at the seas in frustration.

If she had just a little bit of help, she could haul him over to the path and up it, just far enough to be out of the tide's reach.

How on earth could she move him? There wasn't time to run for help.

If only he weighed less. She could have carried a young boy.

Well, there was the old country charm that Nurse had taught her to make burdens lighter. She was no mage, certainly not enough to light the candle which would have gained her entrance into a competition for mage school. But she could work some of the truly ancient charms, like the one to make a bushel of apples feel light as a feather on the long walk back from the west orchard.

Another wave raced forward.

Emma gulped. She clasped the man's face in her hands and quickly said the charm, using Cornish as she'd been taught. Then she caught his shoulders again and heaved.

He came free easily, gliding across the sands like a swan, until he almost knocked her down. The red light at his shoulder blinked twice and went out, as if thanking her for beginning his rescue.

The charm had never worked so well before—but she'd no time to think about that.

She stepped backward, glancing over her shoulder to judge where she was going.

The ocean followed them, lashing and frothing at him. The water was alive with sand and gravel, slipping under her feet like quicksand. Rocks moved in it, tumbling at the edges of waves, always aimed at the two of them. Her hand slipped out from under him once, but she quickly grabbed him, biting her lip.

If she'd doubted before this was a mage-built storm, she didn't now, not when the ocean was clearly trying to catch them both.

She was chilled to the bone, colder than the wind and waves could account for, even with saltwater and sand slipping into her boots.

She had to take him up the path before the tide came in, but there wasn't time enough to drag him.

What other options did she have?

She could try another charm—the one she'd overheard Nurse using when her husband had drunk one too many pints. Supposedly it made anyone who was unconscious walk as lightly and easily as a small puppet.

But it was a very strong charm, more of a spell from a mage's arsenal. Nurse could work it, because she was a magick worker who'd competed for mage school, although she hadn't been selected. Emma didn't have any such strength, and the mage was too close to death to help. But perhaps the gryphon ring could help a little, although she'd never heard of such a thing in the old stories. Still, it was the only chance.

Squatting once again, she wrapped her arm under the man's shoulder and quickly chanted the puppeteer's charm. Then she straightened up, keeping his arm over her shoulder and her arm around his waist, hoping at least part of his body would come out of the surf.

To her vast shock, he stood up with her, his eyes shut. He was lightweight, unresisting—and wholly unable to steady himself.

Thunder cracked, as if hurling a curse. Waves crashed against the headland, and boulders tumbled into the ravaging sea.

Emma gulped, locked her hand into his leather braces to hold him, and ran for the path, her hip and leg rubbing against him with every stride.

The longer she held on to him, the more she brushed against him—and the easier it became to move him.

CHAPTER TWO

Emma shoved open the kitchen door and staggered across the threshold, her companion's head lolling against his shoulders, and his feet dragging across the broad planks. It was odd how her strength had come rushing back as soon as she'd stepped within the garden walls. Now she was barely winded. But she wasn't about to inquire into such details now.

She booted the heavy panel shut, a trick learned from a scullery maid, and something she hadn't used in years. Her mother had punished her severely back then, saying no lady behaved in such a fashion. But this was not a night when ladylike manners held sway.

Through the windows, lightning bursts reflected off copper and brass pots and pans. Water drummed against the walls and windows like an army demanding entry. Heavy bars to hold pots and pans lunged out of the deep hearth like dragons' snouts. The extremely modern and massive iron kitchen range, Cook's pride and joy, loomed against the creamy walls. By daylight, this would be a warm and welcoming place, but now it was a web of shadows and hidden threats, as heavy with remembered threats as the breathing of the man beside her.

Emma refused to sway, no matter how heavy and large he was, especially in comparison to any of the chairs. Or her chances of lifting him up onto the kitchen table alone.

The door into the hallway burst open, and Nurse rushed through, her mob cap awry and iron gray curls springing in every direction. "Miss Emma! Where have you been?"

"Who is that fellow?" demanded Nurse's husband, eyeing the unconscious stranger, as if the fellow could start firing a pistol at any moment. He held a candle high, showing the man's ragged beard, with water and blood streaming down over his shoulders.

"I found him washed up in the cove. Help me put him up on the table, Keverne," Emma snapped.

The head groom muttered something in Cornish, which his mistress ignored, before handing his candle to his wife. He took the stranger's legs and hips, somehow levering most of the man's bulk onto the sturdy table. Emma heaved the fellow's head and shoulders up, settling him reliably onto the long stretch of wood.

She caught her first true glimpse of him in the light—and her breath stopped.

If he'd been standing, he'd have easily mustered six feet or more in height. He had broad shoulders, heavy with muscle under his waistcoat and shirt, which almost filled the table. Like the rest of him, his buckskin breeches were sodden, displaying horseman's thighs above high cavalry boots. His hair streamed saltwater and blood over features bold enough to be labeled *arrogant*, and possibly *handsome*, despite a nose that had clearly been broken more than once.

Perhaps even *magnificent*? No, surely not. He was simply a traveler who needed help.

She shook off the fancy and stepped back to begin fetching him aid, sending his right hand dangling off the table.

For a moment, the floor gleamed crimson like banked embers. Wings flashed bright as flame above a lion's body crouched protectively over the man. A pair of fierce eagle eyes surveyed everyone in the room, its beak snapping the air over the unconscious man. Its furred torso reared up, challenging all comers with razor-tipped paws, while its great tail thrashed. It settled back down, and two piercing ruby eyes surveyed its watchers, its golden talons flexing.

A living *gryphon*? One of Britain's elemental spirits?

Yet it almost seemed as fragile as a morning mist, since she could dimly see the hearth and kitchen walls through it.

Desperately trying not to gape, Emma sank into a full court curtsy, the same homage she'd give a member of the royal family. Beside her, Nurse folded herself into the same curtsy and Keverne bent his knee, their gasps hanging on the air, despite the thunderstorm outside.

The great beast nodded slightly and lifted a single paw in salute. An instant later, it had spiraled back into the stranger's gold ring and disappeared.

Emma's heart started to beat again. She stood up shakily, her mind whirling with implications.

"A gryphon?" Nurse choked out and reached out to steady herself on the big wooden dresser. Keverne walked around her and began to silently light the fire, laid ready and waiting in the hearth.

"Standing watch over a King's Mage," an old man's voice confirmed, still sharp with authority. Emma's grandfather glared at them from the threshold, erect and commanding, despite the toll of four-score years. He began to limp toward a chair, his heavy cane marking time to his words. "His business is the King's business. Who aids him aids the King. Who delays him delays the King. And who injures him deliberately . . ."

"Damages the Realm and thereby commits treason," Emma finished the ancient maxim, staring at her still unconscious companion. For the first time since she'd found him, she was more than an arm's length away from him. "But here in Cornwall, so far from London or any of the great roads or ports? And so badly injured when we're at peace with France?"

The stranger sighed, the sound quickly turning into a harsh rattle. The death rattle.

No!

Emma ran to him and grabbed his hand, clutching it to her chest. "Don't you dare leave me!"

The rattle turned into a gasp, then a cough. A moment later, he was breathing softly again, his fingers curled around hers.

"Lady bright," muttered Nurse and considered the younger woman thoughtfully. She handed Emma some folded linen towels from the dresser.

Emma ignored that slip into the old ways. It had been a most unsettling night, after all. "I can see several nasty gashes on his head, which should be stitched. But what else?"

Nurse and her husband studied the newcomer, mob cap and grizzled queue leaned together. The storm raging outside obliterated any comments they made.

Emma watched them, her heart in her throat, desperate for reassurance that he could be saved. She'd heard too many stories and been in too many naval hospitals while growing up to have any false illusions about his chances. Her hands moved over his forehead, cleaning off the worst of the saltwater and blood.

"There's something wrong with his right shoulder, too," she babbled, unable to stop herself from fussing. "It hangs very limply, and there's a great deal of blood."

"Did you empty his lungs of water?" Grandfather asked, prodding a fire into full life on the hearth, his expression intent and appearing a few years younger.

"Yes, he coughed it up very neatly," she answered readily, still cleaning blood away. "In fact, he seemed to improve the moment we came through the gate."

Nurse shot her a long, considering stare, her braid falling to one side.

Keverne harrumphed, drawing everyone's attention. "Aye, he's been stabbed by something big, the size of a dirk, maybe." The spluttering flames made his swarthy face look like an apprentice demon. But he was the best horse doctor for miles around. "Probably a wood splinter that went clean through."

"Should we send for the surgeon?" Emma asked. Her unknown companion's hand was a little warmer under hers.

Keverne shook his head and went back to examining his patient. "After a storm like this? The Gwythias must have already flooded every bridge leading to the village, Mrs. Sinclair."

"We'll be lucky to have any of the other servants back before dawn." Emma's heart was in her boots, together with their prospects for aid. "There's no chance of bringing Mr. Miller here before noon."

"And the storm is unnatural," Nurse announced flatly.

Emma went cold at the confirmation of her suspicions, staring at her oldest confidante. High magick had been worked here, close to their little village? Still . . . "You lit the candle, and you competed for mage school. You'd know when there's magick afoot."

Nurse nodded grimly and began to pump water at the sink.

"The gryphon has shown himself to the four of us, granting us his trust—and giving me liberty to speak of what I learned from working with King's Mages during my army days," Grandfather announced from the great armchair by the hearth.

Emma twisted around to stare at him. She'd always thought he knew more about mage craft than he'd openly say, given how comfortable he was with the old Cornish ways. But to discuss military secrets with the three of them? Dear heavens, what was at stake to have wrought such changes?

"Two mages must have built it, one at sea and one on land, to obtain such a large storm." Grandfather's voice rang with every bit of his former authority as a general. "I saw no storm of any significance, except toward France."

A deliberate assassination attempt on her King's Mage by someone local? A growl built in Emma's throat, and she pressed a fresh towel rather more firmly against the worst gash.

"In that event, we'll have to hide him," she said flatly.

Grandfather's eyebrow elevated. "How so?"

"If there's a mage close enough to create a storm, then he'd probably be close enough to create some sort of hunting spell, correct? I don't know how the mechanisms would operate but . . ."

Grandfather and Nurse glanced at each other, two old tricksters considering options.

"Mages never willingly speak to ordinary folk of how they work magick," Grandfather pointed out. "So we've no way of knowing exactly what to guard against, except he must be very powerful."

Emma frowned, thinking fast. "He must be exhausted after creating the storm, which will buy us a little time."

"The other King's Mages will be searching for our fellow, too," Nurse put in, setting an iron kettle of water over the fire. "They may not be able to easily find him, since he's so weak."

Emma picked up the argument's thread. "But the traitor won't want to draw their attention, so he'll keep his spells less powerful."

"Limiting his search to a small area." Grandfather drummed his fingers on his cane. "It may buy us some time to see our fellow healed."

"Can we send a message for help?" Emma asked hopefully.

Grandfather's expression shuttered, turning as ancient as The Morthol's stones. "The traitor will likely have watchers on every road, watching every post, every express—every mode of communication, even carrier pigeon. If so, sending a message to Whitehall would brutally destroy the letter and the messenger."

Emma shivered at the memories running through his voice. "Have you seen it happen before?" she asked, hoping against hope.

"Often." His voice didn't invite further questions. "I'll see if one of Taylor's carrier pigeons can reach Falmouth with a message. That way, if the mage is watching all the routes, we won't lose any of the men."

Emma nodded, keeping her head high. Blast all traitorous mages—and Napoleon Bonaparte for his greed and stubbornness, which paid them and killed good men like her husband. She was damned if she'd let another Englishman die in Bonaparte's war.

She refolded the towel, refusing to flinch at its now crimson color, and mopped saltwater from her mage's temple. She lingered a moment to kiss his hair, silently promising him he would live.

His breathing hesitated a moment before steadying and deepening. Color almost touched his cheeks.

Someone would have to nurse him and give him the strength to heal. Someone young and strong. He was her catch, salvaged from the ravaging sea, giving her the first responsibility.

"Our guest has lost a great deal of blood. He'll need warmth and nursing during the night for healing. What bedroom should we prepare for him?"

Three appalled old faces snapped around to stare at her. Even though Trethledan House was large and comfortable, Emma and her grandfather were the only family members currently living there. So only two bedrooms had fires built in them and their beds warmed for sleeping. Preparing another bedroom would take time and precious energy, of which Nurse and Keverne had little to spare.

Emma hid a wry smile. "Surely something in the family wing?" she prodded gently. "Perhaps Mrs. Bennett's room? My sister's room is next to mine, so it may be a little warmer."

Nurse nodded grimly. "I'll go up once we have enough hot water here."

"He can wear my grandsons' clothing, especially once he starts moving about," the master of the house announced. "He looks to be fairly much of a size with them."

Now for the difficult part, the scandalous hurdle. Emma stealthily crossed her fingers.

"When we're done here, I will sleep with him," she announced softly.

"You will not!" Grandfather's cane slammed against the floor for emphasis.

"You've seen how he gathers strength from me, more than anyone else here. He'll need freely given companionship during the night to strengthen his heart, according to the old tales."

"Emma . . ." Grandfather growled. "Regardless of how much he takes to you, I'll not have you ruin yourself for a stranger."

"What scandal? I've been widowed for five years, so I don't have to watch every move like a young girl."

"I will not have you subjected to scandal!"

"A King's Mage has been attacked. It is our duty to succor him in any way necessary." She met the old general's glare steadily. At four-and-twenty, she was the only one here young enough to give the castaway any strength. "There are only four of us. I will share his bed."

"All she'd need is a day or two, perhaps three, until he's well enough to contact his own people," Nurse urged. "The other servants would never say a word."

"Are you so lost to all propriety, woman, as to suggest that your mistress lose her good name for a stranger?!"

"It is our duty to protect him, as we would the King," Emma hurled back. "To do anything less would risk killing a King's Mage. *And I will not lose another man to Bonaparte's murderers, no matter what I have to do or what it costs me.*"

An angry silence fell. Keverne began to cut her gentleman's clothes off.

Grandfather glowered at her. "You are the granddaughter of a general, the daughter of an admiral, and the widow of a naval lieutenant. I cannot deny you the opportunity to do your duty to your King and Country. But I do not like it, and it will not last a minute longer than necessary, do you understand me, girl?"

"Yes, sir." She dropped him a curtsy.

CHAPTER THREE

Owen stirred, his brain as uncoordinated as his limbs.
He ached damnably in every muscle with a sheer concentrated fury that would barely let him draw breath. His head pounded as if every Bavarian troll was trying to drill a spike through his temple. And his shoulder . . . Good Lord, it burned like all of Hades's nine circles.

Where was he? Instinct commanded him not to betray his wakefulness.

Cloth was very, very soft under his cheek. And his back, and his hips, and his legs. Everywhere, in fact. Whatever lay underneath cradled his body easily, unlike his shipboard hammock.

The universe was steady, with no storm throwing everything and everyone about, nor sending bursts of magefire and cannon fire to shatter solid wood. No screams of dying men in seas tinted with crimson—and his vows of revenge. No, here there was only peace.

He snatched at his slippery thoughts, since experience offered no guide. It must be a very fine bed, with smooth sheets caressing his skin and a feather bed for warmth. Someone had washed him up, so he didn't reek of saltwater and blood. They'd clothed him in a fine cambric nightshirt, which felt like a garment his father's wife would have crowed over. The only item he recognized was his gold signet's hard edges.

He shifted his vision, trying to use his mage's sight. His head immediately threatened to explode with pain, a million more trolls quickly slamming their hammers and picks into his skull and making his stomach roil in agony. He stopped searching and tried to relax, determined not to heave whatever small amounts of food lay in his stomach.

So all he knew of his surroundings' magickal qualities was what they chose to tell him. The room was uncommonly comfortable, with a strong protective glow underlying everything. It didn't seem to have been shaped and formed by a mage, though, at least not that he could tell. And, irritatingly, when he studied its powers for too long, he'd start to grow sleepy. It only deepened the puzzle.

Why was he here, in a natural fortress with strong healing powers? Why had they tended his wounds, bathed him, and clothed him?

No French prison would treat him this well. If he was in Britain, the mages' castles offered luxuries only for high-ranking mages, not those who'd chosen to walk alone.

He shifted, trying to find a position that didn't send a fiery mass of swords jabbing into his shoulder. He said a healing spell under his breath, wishing he had the strength to completely cure himself. For a moment, his ribs stopped aching.

A woman mumbled something.

Owen froze immediately. Was she friend or foe?

A slender hand, with long, tapering fingers, alighted gently on his bare hand. His shoulder's agony melted into a heavy ache, while the blazing knot in his skull became a steady pounding.

A chalice, someone who could store magick within themselves for later use in powering a spell? But there was no sign she'd worked her own spell to effect his cure, only provided the magick to aid his own.

Had the French put one here to try to make him talk? But surely even those cunning bastards wouldn't have a chalice, especially one so very deep, to spare for games of trickery.

He fought to lift his eyelids.

The room beyond was almost completely dark. A cheerful little fire burned, showing a gracious room with elegant furniture, pale walls, and crisply painted trim. Portraits were scattered around the walls like friends, while a rich Persian carpet gave life to the floor. Colorful draperies rippled across the windows.

A gryphon drowsed by the hearth, its head tucked under one wing. It was, as ever, as insubstantial as smoke, befitting the elemental spirit which guarded a mage who hadn't even learned the basics of how to link with other mages.

He didn't need to do that again—he'd done it once before in April 1794, during the otherwise disastrous Flanders campaign. He'd been a young trooper in the 15th Dragoons, the only true home he'd ever known. He'd always done his duty well, skilled with horses and weapons—and concealing his ability to light a match, no matter how foul the weather. He'd no desire to be plucked out of the army and sent to mage school, which would have meant meeting the mother who'd abandoned him at birth.

He'd also enjoyed dallying with the Prussian general's mistress. He'd been too damn green to realize she was a mage.

They caught the French column at Villers-en-Cauchies early in the morning. The bitch had been insatiable the night before, and he'd still been abed with her when the trumpets sounded the alert.

Would he ever forget how her long fingers shackled his wrist when he tried to leap out of bed? How her nails dug into his skin, drawing blood? How she'd laughed at his objections that he needed to ride into battle with his regiment?

Instead, she'd informed him he'd been sent to her bed by his general, as a potential mage. He still loathed army officers for having prostituted him.

She'd announced he'd provide the magick for the spell, since he'd inherited his mother's magick as her heir.

He'd sworn he would fight; she could grab her damn magick from some other fool. He did, too, resisting every wheedling reminder of the joys they'd shared together, every spell tearing into his brains and guts like a hussar's saber. She ripped him apart, fighting to reach the magick in his every fiber, shredding him until he rolled on the ground, howling in agony and bleeding from every orifice.

She took all of it from him in the end and threw his magick into her spell.

Villers-en-Cauchies was a glorious victory, where over thirty thousand French troops fled in terror from cavalry—an incredible feat of arms, one to be retold for decades to come.

Owen had been carried unconscious to mage school, never to serve in the army again. He'd used his studies there to ensure a similar experience would never happen to him again.

Now he turned his head very cautiously to see the woman beside him.

The raven-haired beauty slept in an armchair beside his bed, an intricate paisley shawl covering her shoulders and much of her simple white dress. Velvety lashes curved over her cheeks, and soft curls tumbled down her neck from under her lace-trimmed cap. A stray beam of firelight touched the bed curtains beside her, highlighting her features—the high forehead, the straight little nose, the graceful swan's neck, the very stubborn chin . . .

She stirred, and her elegant fingers clasped his wrist more closely, half-slipping under his sleeve. Energy flowed into him, golden and sweet as a summer day.

His legs stretched, able to move without stiffness for the first time.

Dammit, she definitely was a chalice!

He growled softly, disliking his need for her. He'd come this far in life without any attachments; surely he could heal without help.

Tsk, tsk.

Owen swung his head back and glared at the gryphon.

It clacked its beak at him again, *Tsk, tsk.* Its immense golden eyes were visibly amused above its crossed paws. *How much time do you have to waste, foolish boy? Can you send for help yet?*

No. He glared, too angry to add that the simple healing spell had left him so weak he couldn't even sit up.

The message shifted in his skull, its protective spell briefly glinting gold and green—and reminding him of the people who'd died to give it to him. He had the only copy of this spell, the one that would stop Bonaparte from finding the key to Britain's harbors. Britain, the only country with the resources and the will to fight Bonaparte to the death.

He closed his mouth, unwilling to admit he'd been about to argue with a gryphon. Reluctantly, fighting the habits of a lifetime every inch of the way, he curled his fingers around the woman's—strengthening their contact.

There was a soft rush of wings before the gryphon stood beside them on his bed, now barely the size of his fist but no less deadly than before. It sniffed delicately at her hand, rubbed its head against her wrist, and stepped neatly back into Owen's signet.

Owen angrily threw his head back against the pillows. If a gryphon enjoyed her company, then he could trust her to the death. At least with his life.

He could not possibly be interested in anything else, let alone gentler pursuits.

But how much time would the French grant him to regain his strength?

• • •

CHARLES Trevelyan swung back to face the silver scrying bowl, his banyan's crimson silk skirts slapping against his breeches. "I already gave you the storm, and it destroyed the mages' sloop, something no other land-based mage has accomplished in almost two decades. The King's Mage aboard must also be dead; no one could have survived."

The water lapped against the bowl's edges, but the image remained clear. The French officer there glared at Trevelyan, his blue uniform laden with decorations which marked him as having served since the Reign of Terror.

"*M'sieu*, the British spy was in my milieu, the water. Do me the courtesy, please, of acknowledging my expertise and agreeing I would have known if he was dead. The British spy is still alive and must therefore be killed."

Trevelyan made a rude gesture and knocked back the rest of his cognac, furious at his unwelcome caller. The Frenchman's brilliant eyes, smooth skin, and easy gestures showed no signs of strain from powering the gale of two days ago, which had ripped apart the Royal Navy sloop. He must be traveling with a coterie of other mages to power his magick. He probably hadn't needed to spend the intervening time sleeping, as Trevelyan had done to regain his strength.

Thank God he'd warded the roads against messengers while he slept, to keep any King's Mages from coming to investigate. Otherwise, he'd have been arrested for a reckless expenditure of the local land's magickal resources. And quite possibly hauled off to the White Tower for questioning, since he'd been schooled in France and had never registered himself as a mage in Britain.

Trevelyan forebore to spit, which would have disturbed the scrying and possibly betrayed his hidden chamber.

Above him, Whitmore Hall slept in these last few hours before the servants would rise again, to polish his estate and build his reputation in the county. Four generations of his family had owned this property—yet the damned locals still couldn't forget that his money came from the sugar trade.

He conceded the obvious. "Very well, the British spy still breathes—but changing that situation is in your hands."

The Frenchman leaned forward, determination marking his face like a hatchet. "He must be in Cornwall, close to you. It will be very simple for you to find and kill him, especially since my curse still stops him from sending for help. You, too, have reason to see him buried here, before he helps his masters to solve the mystery of who caused the storm."

Trevelyan tensed, his mind racing through scenarios he hadn't previously considered. A King's Mage loose in London, seeking vengeance for his lost shipmates? Even if he wasn't a seagoing mage, it would take very little time for him to meet with experts and piece together enough of the attack to trace it back to Trevelyan.

If that happened, Trevelyan would have to run for France, if he were to have any hope of surviving. And completely abandon

Whitmore Hall, all of the warehouses and ships that had made him and his family the wealthiest sugar importers in England, together with any chance at obtaining Emma Sinclair, the greatest prize of all.

"If I kill a King's Mage, here on British soil, the *magnum concilium* would know immediately," he protested instinctively, trying not to openly cringe at being discovered by Britain's greatest council of mages. "Every King's Mage would be after my head, and I'd need to depart immediately. Your First Consul would lose his most loyal mage inside Britain—at exactly the moment when he's planning an invasion."

The French officer hesitated, those ancient eyes in his young face turning thoughtful for the first time.

Trevelyan hid his sigh of relief; he might not need to immediately hunt for that missing courier.

"Ten thousand of your gold guineas," the Frenchman said finally.

Trevelyan blinked. So much? Good Lord, what message was that courier carrying? "Thirty thousand," he countered automatically.

"Twenty thousand, ten thousand now and another ten thousand when he's dead." The other mage lifted a quelling hand, a fiery lizard lifting from his palm. "And don't speak to me of any hardship from abruptly starting a new life."

The lizard hissed at Trevelyan, its heat touching him through the scrying bowl.

Trevelyan flinched, startled at the casual display of national powers. Good Lord, he hadn't thought that a mage serving Republican France—that his master, Bonaparte, the First Consul!—could claim so much of the old monarchical French strength so soon. An invasion would indeed be very possible.

The French officer chuckled dryly and tossed a mocking salute. "I look forward to hearing from you very soon, my dear English *friend*."

He waved his hand, and the water turned blank, instantly returning to clear liquid.

Trevelyan shuddered slightly, more relieved than he'd care to admit by the other's departure.

No matter what the Frenchman said, the storm must have almost killed the King's Mage. He'd have to find him quickly before the fellow died of injuries, losing Trevelyan any chance of claiming the full twenty thousand guineas. He'd do it after he recovered from this session.

He stood up to pace, kicking his chair out of the way.

He'd also have to redouble his efforts to court Emma and gain the use of her magick. It was a pity she'd used her grandfather's illness to excuse herself from attending the fair at Whitmore Hall on the day of the storm. He'd had such strong trap spells set to catch her the moment she crossed his threshold.

Of course, if she wouldn't willingly become his partner, he could always frighten her into doing so. Or simply kidnap her and sell her for the highest price in France. Bonaparte would undoubtedly pay very, very well for her.

Trevelyan began to chuckle, his teeth sharp-edged against his lips.

CHAPTER FOUR

Emma eased Mr. Bentham carefully into the big armchair in his bedroom. It was only his second time sitting up out of the bed since his arrival. She couldn't imagine why he should be healing so fast, given his nasty injuries.

He tossed the skirts of his sapphire blue banyan around his knees and leaned his head back, white lines around his mouth. Seen close-up like this, he was a remarkably handsome man, despite his features' rather Roman arrogance.

His face was most notable perhaps for that arrogant nose. Yet she couldn't help looking at the high cheekbones and the wide mouth held so firmly, and his lower lip was undoubtedly intended for more sensual pursuits. They were features meant to be carved onto a knight's bier, betokening a life spent serving duty. Or into the memory of the lucky woman who enjoyed his affections.

A frisson teased her, whispering of passion to be enjoyed again in a man's arms.

She busied herself with the tea tray, firmly ignoring her guest's attractions. The sea whispered from outside, quiet on a clear day.

Mr. Bentham shifted in his chair.

"You've seen the gryphon, correct?"

"Oh yes—Grandfather, Nurse, Keverne, and I all did. But nobody else." She handed him a cup of tea and sat down facing him, fascinated by his broaching of usually unmentionable topics.

"Can you work any magick, Mrs. Sinclair?"

"I can lighten a pail of berries or a basket of apples. Sometimes Nurse and I have shoved a recalcitrant gate back into place. But that's all."

"And you alone, completely unaided, brought me out of the ocean and up the cliffs. I will always thank you for that."

She blushed and kept doggedly to the conversation's main tack. "I don't know why I could rescue you. I knew some useful old charms, but they'd never worked before on anything as heavy as you are."

He steepled his fingers, contemplating her. A decision passed through his eyes and something warmer, something masculine and hungry.

Her lungs caught, and her breasts stirred.

"Do you know why you could do so little magick in Mrs. Keverne's presence but so much in mine?"

"No. Can you speak so openly of magick to me?"

"The gryphon has vouched for your trustworthiness. Besides, I've warded this room to keep our conversation private."

"Oh." She'd heard of magick like that, but to hear it mentioned so casually, as she'd say she'd locked the door! She shivered with delight, feeling ancient stories coming to life.

He chuckled dryly, stirring milk into his tea.

"You're a chalice, Mrs. Sinclair, someone who can collect and hold magickal power for mages to draw upon."

"You mean I have magick of my own?" Her head was spinning.

"A very great deal, else you couldn't have plucked me from the tides which were determined to kill me." His expression was deadly serious.

"How can I have magick and not work spells?" she demanded.

"You can work spells but only very small spells on your own. Otherwise, you must link with a mage: He creates the spell's intent and form, while you provide its impact."

"Two of us, acting together? The mage needs me, as much as I need him?"

"Correct." A shadow flitted across his face, gone before she could name it. "Your strength is apparent in proportion to the mage's ability to provide channels to use it."

She turned that over in her head.

"Nurse can't use it very well, so I'm very insignificant around her. But you're a King's Mage, which makes me . . ."

"Much more powerful, yes—since you're an incredibly deep chalice." His sapphire eyes approved of her. "Your participation would likely guarantee victory in a naval battle."

She smiled and straightened, tilting her chin up. A magick worker, by God, and a rare one at that. Sister Lydia would be both jealous and hopeful her infant would inherit the talent.

"One caution."

She looked her question.

"We know there's a villain in the neighborhood who's a mage. Any mage who works magick near you will know immediately by its increased strength you're a chalice—and will do anything to gain possession of you, since you're not bound to any one magickal source."

"That's nonsense. I'd never agree to being grabbed like a cow." She sniffed and took a sip of her tea.

"You're lucky. Chalices are so fragile that links can only be formed with your full consent. So enemies will court you first."

"And I tell you again, I'll refuse." She set her cup down. "Any other warnings?"

"Like any other magick worker, if you try to go beyond your capacity, you risk death. Unlike most, because your strength is so great but your ability to form spells is so small." He hesitated.

"If I try to work a great spell on my own, I could be greatly weakened. Or die." Her skin chilled. "Correct?"

He caught her hands, rubbing them with his thumbs. "Please don't worry. It's highly unlikely it will ever happen, dear Mrs. Sinclair."

She produced a smile, and he kissed her fingers, startling both of them.

He rose and paced to the window, moving much more easily than he had an hour ago. She eyed him, considering—for only the purest purposes!—his supple grace, his long stride, his erect carriage . . .

"Does my presence help you heal?"

He turned, a careless lock of hair tumbling over his forehead. How she longed to comb it back with her finger . . .

"Yes, very much so. You help me with every spell I cast."

"What if I aided you to send a message? Shouldn't the two of us together be able to send one to London?"

His eyes came alight before shuttering.

"I cannot ask it of you. You would have to open your magick fully to me, since I would not be opening my channels to you. We might have to use physical affection to form a strong enough link."

"Affection?" Why did her pulses leap at the thought and the look in his eyes?

"I only know a few techniques. But one of the most reliable is standing together with the mage's arms around the chalice, so they are pressed together at all points."

It sounded delightful.

"In these circumstances, we must do whatever is necessary," Emma said briskly, reminding herself that he was a stranger. And a King's Mage at that, sworn to travel wherever duty took him. He was not someone to find a home and children with. "What do we need?"

"Mrs. Keverne has already provided everything."

He swept everything off the round game table and set Grandmother's best silver punch bowl on it. (Emma gawked at its presence but said nothing, realizing that her best sterling silver was as dedicated to the King's service in this as anything else.) He filled it with colored sand and wrote a brief message on a small strip of parchment, which he rolled into a tight twist.

"Ready?"

She nodded, shaken by how much this man who looked like a warrior was so completely in command of such fine magickal details.

"Stand by the table—here—and try to relax. You'd better call me Owen, too, to promote an atmosphere of intimacy."

She stared at him over her shoulder. *"Owen?"* Her voice was a strangled squeak.

"Do you object?" He frowned.

Far too little. She shook her head hastily and reminded herself she was a widow of five years standing, far too sensible to be thrown into a tizzy by one very handsome man. "You may call me Emma, if you'd like."

"Thank you, Emma." His breath caressed her neck, and she shivered.

"You're very welcome—Owen."

His arms came around her, one arm wrapping her waist, and his other hand stretching over the table.

"Put both hands on my sleeve and lean back."

She obeyed and closed her eyes. But that was far too dangerous to her pulses, since it increased the heat sweeping through her skin and her veins. She cracked one eye open.

He swirled his hand over the bowl, chanting something. The sand dissolved into a fine golden mist, simmering at the base of the punch bowl. The tiny scroll rose and pointed northeast, toward London.

Owen tightened behind her, his breathing deepening. Emma moved closer to him, rubbing his hands and trying to lend him her strength.

The mist abruptly whipped upward. The scroll spun crazily in place like a top, losing all track of direction.

Another mist exploded into position and solidified into a shell surrounding the first.

The scroll reversed direction and spun to a stop. It sank to the base of the bowl, pointing directly at Owen.

The colored mist swirled briefly and steadied into a clear gold, immovable against the wall.

Owen snarled.

Emma turned around in his arms and grabbed his shoulders. "What is it? What does it mean?"

He wrapped his arms around her waist and tried to smile.

"We did better than I've been able to do on my own, but not well enough. The enemy is out there, and he's placed guards on every road, both magickal and nonmagickal. Any message I try to send will simply bounce back to me."

"What about the gold mist and the wall?" She leaned up against him, trying to see his expression better.

"My wards, combined with this house's natural shields, are strong enough to keep out the enemy's attacks. But I'm not strong enough to escape!"

Her heart ached for him. On impulse she reached up to kiss him on his cheek, but his head turned, and their mouths met. Their lips brushed, lingered, and clung. She sighed and pressed closer, their breaths meeting.

It was sweeter than sweet and over far too soon.

• • •

TREVELYAN glared at his favorite scrying bowl. It had taken him less than an hour to learn the damned King's Mage was hidden behind wards of unprecedented power, far too strong to simply show where he was to Trevelyan's spells.

Instead, he'd been forced to quarter the county for hours, looking for the bastard. If the scrying spell showed the usual small amounts of magick, all well and good. But if it mirrored his probe, he knew the British mage's wards were blocking his spell.

There was only one answer for where he was hiding: Trethledan House, with Emma Sinclair. Only with the aid of her astonishing depth as a chalice could that blasted mage have healed fast enough to power those wards.

He'd have to go in after them both, dammit, and trap her first, since he couldn't take her by force without destroying her.

Once the chalice was gone, the weakened King's Mage should be easy prey.

CHAPTER FIVE

Owen waved off Willis and took up the morning coat for himself. The old general's equally ancient valet stepped back, but stayed within arms' reach of Owen, his expression impassive. He and Emma had borne the brunt of nursing Owen these past four days, with Willis providing discreet and skillful care for Owen's more private needs.

Yesterday Owen had managed to sit up and walk around the bedroom. Today he was determined to go farther.

He shrugged into the blue morning coat and flexed his shoulders slightly, testing its fit. Behind him, Willis gave every twitch of fabric an expert's hawkeyed stare.

It needed to be loose enough not to pinch his bandages or to hinder his movement, should he need to fight. But it was four days after the storm, his wounds were almost completely healed, and the first time he'd dared to try becoming fully dressed. Or had been away from Emma Sinclair for longer than ten minutes. Not, of course, that he was listening to the clock toll the minutes.

Now a stranger studied him from the mirror, clad in fashionable broadcloth and breeches, with a striped waistcoat and a blindingly white neckcloth. Its crisp starch stroked his throat, a subtle reminder of the casual acceptance of money and power behind it.

Given the high value placed on a crisp, vividly white neckcloth, dandies only wore one once, since laundering it was very expensive. They signaled money as certainly as a snugly fitting coat, given that only aristocrats and rich men could pay a servant every time they needed to dress.

He turned, surveying himself from all possible angles.

These clothes were not the hallmark of the tradesman he'd pretended to be for so long, or of a King's Messenger. The only items that a King's Messenger might have used were the brightly polished boots.

In all honesty, this ensemble was far too stylish for a mage school, where student apparel echoed the wardrobe of Cromwell's time. It also bore no semblance to his old dark blue dragoon's uniform with the scarlet facings and white lace or the scarlet and gold brilliance of the King's Mages' uniforms. It was closer to that of a mage or a councilor's brat, not that he'd ever be one to flaunt such ancestry, especially after a lifetime spent avoiding any mention of it.

Still, there was something to be said for looking smartly turned out. At least the clothes were loose enough that he could don them alone, even if doing so stamped him as not being an aristocrat.

Faded blue eyes swept over him, missing nothing.

"Very good, sir," Willis murmured, echoing his own thoughts. "I have always said elegance is the true hallmark of a gentleman. Your neckcloth's simplicity, combined with using your signet as your sole jewelry, betokens a most superior style, which your inferiors would do well to copy." He coughed slightly. "If I may?"

"Oh yes, of course." Owen managed not to blink. He'd tied the blasted strip of starched muslin in the only knot he knew.

Willis circled him, his wrinkled hands expertly twitching folds into order and flicking off lint before he stood back, beaming. "Sir Henry's clothes fit you very well, very well indeed with Mr. Fitzwilliam's boots as the finishing touch. I shall be happy to inform the General that his instructions were carried out so successfully."

"My thanks to the General for the loan of his grandsons' clothing." Owen inclined his head slightly and turned toward the door.

Willis bowed, offering a heavy, gold-headed cane.

Owen shrugged it off, his mouth tightening. Dammit, he didn't need to use an old man's crutch, despite a bit of lightheadedness. Give him a bit of ale and some cheese, and he'd be right as rain.

He stepped out into the hallway, still grumbling silently, and stopped cold. Emma Sinclair was standing by a window a few feet away, talking to her old nurse. She wore a simple white dress resembling a Roman goddess's tunic, tied with ribbons under her beautiful breasts. Sunlight poured over her, silhouetting her slender figure through the few layers of delicate cloth.

His mouth dried. Heat danced through his bones and into his veins, yet he couldn't catch his breath. Without a second thought, he flicked his fingers and corrected his clothes' fit into a fashionable snugness, using power he'd meant to save for a signaling attempt.

· · ·

EMMA glanced sideways at Owen Bentham. Lord, he looked handsome! His coat's color was delightful, a perfect match for his vivid blue eyes, which were the same color as the summer sea. His hair had been cut into a fashionable style, the thick locks shorn so closely yet still seeming desperate to curl. She wouldn't have thought Henry's clothing would fit him so well. But it lovingly clung to his body as if it had been made for him, emphasizing the depth of his chest and the strength of his legs.

Despite those temptations, her glance kept returning to what she'd studied since she'd pulled him from the sea.

He should be painted by a great master in a single spectacular moment of passion. That strong neck arched back, muscles and tendons taut. His mouth stretched to kiss and kiss again, lips curled over white teeth. His blue eyes heavy-lidded with desire . . .

Her pulse leaped at the image, and she totally lost track of Nurse's discourse on early spring cleaning, while Owen prowled down the corridor toward her.

Mages were rare and valuable, especially to the Crown. They were also more powerful than ordinary mortals, so it was difficult to punish them by typical rules and regulations. Accordingly, mages lived under their own code of laws, most of which ordinary mortals didn't know about. Brehon Law was the ancient code which governed their interaction with others, and it was strictly enforced by both mages and the Crown.

Since magickal ability was inherited, one of Brehon Law's greatest priorities was to protect mages' children. Thus, if a mortal woman had a child by a mage out of wedlock, the union was treated similarly to a Scottish handfasting. This made the child entirely legitimate, giving it full protection under mortal law. The father had whatever role he chose in rearing the child—usually none, since mages were not inclined to spend long periods of time with mortals. More importantly, polite society now treated the child's mother as a widow and accepted the child.

Equally, if a mortal man sired a child on a female mage, the mortal man could be the one to rear the child, usually because the mage was disinclined to be saddled with a child for decades to come. It was an extraordinarily rare occurrence, since female mages loathed their inability to work magick during pregnancy, and all mages controlled their own fertility.

Did she want to have an affaire with Owen? But he was the first man she'd considered doing more than kissing in the last five years. And his face and form were so very tempting. He had such big, strong hands with calloused fingers. Would he take his lover firmly or stroke her slowly, teasing her with the contrast between his blunt fingertips and her smooth skin?

Emma quivered, frissons rippling down her spine.

Nurse coughed significantly and not at all softly.

Emma blinked down at her, composing herself with an effort.

"Very well then, Mrs. Sinclair," Nurse announced, fixing her with a gimlet stare. "I'll tell them to do it just the way we discussed."

Emma flushed. Owen was waiting patiently only a few feet away. "Thank you, Nurse," she managed to utter. "I'm sure you'll know exactly how to explain everything."

Nurse's mouth twitched briefly before she dropped a curtsy. She curtsied again to Owen, who nodded very politely, and she was gone, disappearing within seconds through a doorway concealed in the paneling.

He watched her go, his eyebrows flying up. "Do you have many such hidden doorways?"

Emma shrugged, more flustered than she should be by a man's arrival. She might be only twenty-four, but she truly did know how to handle herself, as befitted a naval captain's daughter. At least she'd always thought she did. "My grandfather enjoyed hiding the servants' passages when he rebuilt Trethledan House. But the older portion does have a few true secrets, such as a priest's hole. Would you like to see?"

"Certainly." He offered her his arm, and she accepted it gratefully, twining her hand around his forearm until she was leaning against him. His woolen coat rubbed her skin, while his breath caressed her hair.

They walked the hallway together, step for step as they had on the beach. Yet this time, he was so very much alive. His warmth stole through her, easing her worries about his health—and teasing her with reminders of pleasures last enjoyed years ago. Their destination came all too soon, when they reached the end of the hall and stepped over the threshold into another room.

"The Long Gallery," she announced, watching his face for reactions to her favorite room. It came by its name honestly, as any builder would affirm. Bronze and porcelain statues and vases the size of grown men stood next to surprisingly comfortable sofas, while carved tables offered beauty and efficiency. Oriental carpets swirled across the floor like flower beds. Banks of windows in the walls and ceilings flooded the room with light, even on cloudy days.

The walls were lined with paintings and other works of art collected by her family over the centuries, centered on her grandfather and grandmother's portraits. Her grandfather looked extremely martial in his magnificent scarlet regimentals, his sword at his side and hordes of vanquished adversaries in the background. But the true key to his attention seemed to be his beautiful wife, Emma's near-double, and their hands reached for each other across their portraits' frames. Below the carved and gilded wood hung the superb saber Clive of India had given Emma's grandfather in gratitude for saving his life, its golden hilt and jewels blazing as if eager to go to war.

Her wedding portrait hung here as well, both she and dearest Edward shining with joy.

"Your grandparents?" Owen paused before it.

"Yes. There's a similar one of my grandmother which he keeps in his bedroom."

"You must be very proud of him. He's still famous in the Army for his consideration of the common soldiers." An oddly approving note lurked in Owen's voice before he moved on. "The walls record a great many happy marriages, including yours. My condolences on your loss."

Somehow she could not let him linger under a misapprehension.

"I married Edward Sinclair when I was seventeen. Some thought I was too young to marry a naval lieutenant, but I was determined to snatch every day we could." It was a simple tale, one she'd spoken before without hesitation. "We were married for two years, most of which he spent serving with Nelson. He was killed at the Battle of the Nile, five years ago."

"Dearest Emma, I'm so very sorry."

"My only regret is that we spent so little time together." She patted his hand. "What of your family?"

There was an awkward silence. She'd started to smooth it over by offering a different conversational gambit, when he spoke.

"My father was a magistrate in Leicestershire, famous throughout the Midlands for his horse breeding farm. While selling one of his horses in another county, he spent the night with a lady not his wife and promptly forgot her."

Emma couldn't imagine what to say.

"The lady arrived on his doorstep nine months later and shoved a squalling brat into his arms—myself—demanding that he raise it. She was a member of the *magnum conciliorum*, the mages' high council, and refused to be burdened with a child. His wife promptly had hysterics, but he fulfilled his obligations under Brehon

Law, as befitted a magistrate." Owen's voice was completely emotionless, as if looking through a spyglass at someone else's life.

"How?" Emma's voice could scarcely be heard, even by herself.

"Brehon Law does not specify how much must be provided to the child. I was raised in the stables, and my wet nurse was a scullery maid of poor reputation. I was taught my letters, as the son of a learned man—"

"And as required by Brehon Law," Emma muttered. "They should have been shot!"

"You come from a very congenial family, my dear. I stayed there until I was twelve, when I enlisted in the cavalry."

"I'll wager you were welcome there, since you knew horses so well."

His expression softened for the first time.

"Yes, oh yes, it was the first time I'd found a home. Until Villers-en-Cauchies, that is."

"The great victory?" She blinked at him.

"Powered by my magick, ripped out of me by someone I'd trusted." His eyes looked into the distance at a past which made her shudder, before they returned to her. "I've never linked to anyone since then. Instead, I've built up very strong walls against it."

Dratted, greedy fools for having used him like a plow horse. She said nothing, afraid her voice would break.

He surveyed the room, deliberately considering the arched beams and heavy paneling, the architectural elements which spoke of times gone by.

"Do any strong spells survive here from the old days? Or are they charms, just little bits of magick or old folks' stories to make life easier?" He was extremely intent, far too much so for such a casual tone of voice.

But she could give him an immediate answer to this. "Oh, it's certainly common for folks hereabouts to work small magicks. But that's true for much of Cornwall and the West Country."

"How many spells and charms do you know?"

"Everything that Nurse does. She made certain I knew all the ones used on this land, even those that don't work for her." Emma arched an eyebrow at him. "Is it too soon to ask about your abilities?"

His fists opened and shut. "They're back but not at full strength."

"Can we seek aid from whatever built the house's shields?" she asked. He looked willing to flay someone alive.

"Perhaps, but it would be difficult and time-consuming," he all but growled. "Strong natural confluences always have their own protections, mainly because it's arduous for anyone not attuned to them to tap into their magickal powers. Trethledan House is built on such a confluence."

But if he couldn't tap Trethledan House's natural power since he wasn't attuned to it . . .

"Are you safe?" she whispered, forcing the words out through a suddenly tight throat.

"Almost certainly—as long as I stay within its boundaries." His mouth twisted.

CHAPTER SIX

Emma's mind whirled in a thousand directions. Trethledan House contained enough power to keep a mage safe? But if he couldn't leave, or send a message with his magick, what could they do? Two of Grandfather's carrier pigeons had died before he'd called off any more such attempts. Clearly, Owen would need to try again, but how?

He was pacing the carpet, as if it represented a prison's boundaries. She shivered slightly, hoping his magick would return soon before he battered himself to death trying to escape.

A brisk knock sounded, and one of the youngest maids entered, twisting her hands in her apron. "Mrs. Sinclair?"

Emma frowned slightly. Why did she look so nervous? "Yes, Simpson, what is it?" she asked, keeping her voice as gentle as possible.

Emma glanced sideways at Owen. His gaze met hers briefly—wary, calculating—before returning to the little maid, looking lost in her starched uniform.

"Mr. Trevelyan has come to call. Mr. Carey put him in the morning room and said I was to bring you immediately." She curtsied again, her eyes enormous in her white face.

Emma's jaw fell open. Why was her very well-trained butler treating Trevelyan like a dear friend of the family, instead of a regrettably close neighbor? He'd always helped her fend off Trevelyan's advances before, but this arrangement would provide an intimate atmosphere to their encounter. To say nothing of having Simpson ask her to come *immediately*!

"Tell Carey that Mrs. Sinclair and Mr. Bentham will follow you down," Owen purred, steel shimmering through the polite words. "And instruct him to serve tea in—fifteen minutes?"

Emma raised an eyebrow at him but nodded. "Yes, fifteen minutes."

"Yes, ma'am. Sir." Simpson bobbed again and fled, her apron's long ties rippling behind her.

"You shouldn't come!" Emma snapped at Owen, turning for the door. She could have slapped him.

He firmly placed her hand on his arm. "His arrival means danger."

"For you! What if he tells whoever the other mage is that you're here?"

"Do you have any idea who the treasonous mage may be?" His expression was as calm as if they were strolling in a garden.

"No," she snarled, "and don't try to change the subject."

Owen shrugged, still maintaining a relaxed facade. "He shouldn't be able to tell I'm a mage. There's more than enough power loose here for me to maintain a glamour, which will hide my magick from anyone except another mage."

"Owen!" Who cared about whether he could wear a disguise, when there was someone around who would prattle about strangers?

"I won't allow you to be alone with anyone who might be strong enough to set an attack spell in this house." He looked at her sternly, his blue eyes brilliant in his harsh face. "Do you understand?"

Her throat worked, but no words formed. Aches and sorrows, piled up responsibilities from years of caring for her grandfather alone, while the rest of her family built their lives elsewhere—

shifted and shattered at the first offering of protection from some-one else.

She smacked her hand into her fist, but reluctantly nodded and leaned on his arm, settling instinctively into a posture of deep trust and affection. "Of course. But I'll do my best to protect you, too."

He made a noise somewhere between a snicker and a snort. They arrived in the blue drawing room, still in perfect harmony—at least for the moment. His obstinacy probably wouldn't permit that to last.

• • •

THE morning room was obviously a gathering place for ladies, its few pieces of fragile furniture designed to encourage intimate con-versation. A single table held pride of place, adorned in the fash-ionable Egyptian style and ready to offer meals, cards, or any other diversion to the lady of the house and a few friends. A settee, a few chairs, and some tables offered opportunities for more casual chats. Elegant silk draperies framed the superb view of the Channel, while delicate wallpaper and superb wainscoting covered the walls. It sang of comfort, money, and a matchless style, all the more superb because it came without effort. It was exactly the sort of room that Owen's father's social-climbing wife would have given her entire wardrobe to enter just once—and that Owen had spent a lifetime avoiding.

Now he saw almost none of its beauties, since his skin was crawling with a thousand, tiny worms at the sight of its occupant. His personal wards had gone on high alert.

"Mr. Charles Trevelyan," Carey announced.

A dark-haired man, well-limbed, of average height with regular features, turned to face them from beyond the table. His attire was ostentatious enough for London's fancier clubs, with his gaudy waist-coat and intricately tied neckcloth. But his eyes, which had originally been warm, turned flat and cold as soon as they met Owen's.

A *French*-trained mage, one of the two who'd authored the gale, and almost certainly the bastard who'd built the land-based portion, damn him. Powerful, too—far more so than Owen.

He stiffened, eyeing Owen with as much warmth as one stallion would survey another sniffing around the gate to the stable.

Without any hesitation, Owen bespelled Carey, blasting through the few remnants of Trevelyan's original spell.

"Mr. John Smith," Carey announced and withdrew immediately, as ordered by Owen, not Trevelyan.

Owen nodded very slightly, never taking his eyes off the newcomer. If he'd had a magickal knife handy, he'd have used it. Thankfully, the house loathed Trevelyan, slowing its magickal currents around the traitor until they looked like a swamp to Owen's magesight.

"Mr. Trevelyan." Emma curtsied, with a remarkably false smile pasted on her face.

Owen ignored her reactions. As long as he was between her and Trevelyan, he was more worried about the traitor. He could explain matters to her another day.

"Do you mean to stay long in Cornwall?" Trevelyan asked rudely, circling the table to free himself for a move on Owen.

"I'm an old friend of the General's, if it's any of your affair," Owen drawled coldly, closely watching his enemy.

Damn it to hell, why hadn't he studied advanced magicks at school, including the use of coteries and coalitions, instead of demanding immediate service to the Crown? If he'd claimed more of his blasted mother's magick, he'd be better able to protect Emma.

The gryphon's shadowy feathers brushed his palm but didn't take shape. He bit back his disappointment, recognizing that this was yet another occasion when he'd be the first to take action, not look to an elemental spirit for help.

Emma circled behind him, her skirts rustling against his legs. She settled herself at the table, beside a package cleverly wrapped in crimson silk, and folded her hands, looking extraordinarily civilized.

"Did you travel here from London?" Owen fenced.

The other laughed, the sound coiling through the air.

"Paris, by way of Calais, keeping my boots dry the entire time. Did you travel as comfortably, Bentham—or did your wardrobe suffer through an untimely accident? Such a pity, isn't it, when ill-managed ships go down in storms." He took a pinch of snuff, his voice as silky as his words were barbed.

He dared refer to the deliberate destruction of a Royal Navy ship as an *untimely accident*?

Owen narrowed his eyes, his fingers curling into the first phrases of an attack spell. That settled it: Trevelyan recognized him and had challenged him to open war.

"No, you will finish dashed to pieces on the rocks, Trevelyan. Or should I say—*M'sieu* Trevelyan?"

The other glared at the open mention of treason. He made a short, jerky wave, and every candle suddenly burst into life, making the room as bright as a midsummer high noon.

Owen's mouth tightened. It had been a simple spell, yet Trevelyan had needed considerable strength to act against Emma's home's hostility to him. Power that Owen couldn't match, because of his recently healed injuries. Couldn't have matched on his best day, because he'd never allowed himself to work with other mages. Damn his foolish arrogance and hatred of any connection to his mother.

"Mrs. Sinclair is a charming lady, whom I have had the honor of escorting for some time," Trevelyan retorted, shifting the basis for combat, with his tones edged in steel.

Owen went cold, his fingers flexing in preparation for spell-casting. Like hell would he allow that damned traitor to announce that she belonged to him!

"Mrs. Sinclair is a remarkable *British* lady, whose grace and charm must be treated with respect. If she is treated with anything less than courtesy, her gift will disappear." *If you're arrogant enough to anger and frighten a chalice, especially one of her depth, you'll never be able to draw from her, you fool.*

"Until it is charmed back into life again." Trevelyan smirked.

Good God, was that the bastard's game? Did he mean to steal her, even knowing that he wouldn't be able to personally draw from her magickal reserves? Then sell Emma later, letting the highest bidder seduce her and bring her gifts back to life? Why, that—

"Mr. Trevelyan," Mrs. Sinclair interrupted. "It is very good of you to give me such a generous gift, but you must understand . . ." Her voice trailed off.

Owen whipped around and found the embodiment of a foul nightmare.

Emma Sinclair was staring down at a square of crimson silk on the table. An ornate Chinese fan lay in the center, with bejeweled ivory sticks and richly painted silks. The image was of entwined salamanders, bowing to each other and writhing together lasciviously. The French elemental spirits in their mating dance, dammit.

She was completely ensorcelled—and as a chalice, she lacked the means to break free.

She stroked the fan tentatively, and the painted salamanders seemed to reach out to her, the black brush strokes ready to glide up her slender fingers onto her wrist.

Good God, Emma, don't look at it!

"Mr. Trevelyan," she choked, still staring at the fan, "it's very beautiful."

Owen instantly formed every bit of power he possessed into a dart and hurled it at Trevelyan's heart.

An instant before it arrived, the traitor languidly waved his hand. A great mirror immediately dropped into place before Trevelyan, which reflected Owen and everything else in the room perfectly— including Emma, where she sat haplessly gazing at the silken lure.

Owen's dart pushed into the mirror, compressed, and sped back out—toward Emma.

Dear God, no! Owen immediately leaped into its path and gathered it close to his chest. It detonated in his arms, shattering the world into dark shards lit with occasional flames and ripping away his ability to breathe.

He gasped helplessly and rolled on the ground, aching in every bone. If he didn't protect her, nobody would.

Trevelyan shot Owen a look of pure triumph and almost chortled. "The fan suits you splendidly, my dear Mrs. Sinclair, especially its scarlet and gold."

"But—but it's very expensive." Her voice strengthened slightly on a lady's instinctive refusal. A little thread of hope slipped into Owen's heart. His lungs started to work on a more regular schedule.

"It's quite improper, I'm afraid." She gulped but didn't push the fan aside.

Owen was no longer seeing stars. He managed to pull himself up to his knees, using an empty chair.

"Don't you want to use it the first time you go to a very grand ball?" Trevelyan's voice tightened with malice, and the painted salamanders slipped onto her fingers.

"I, ah, I," she gasped, staring helplessly at the fan.

"Damn you, let her go, Trevelyan!" Owen tried to issue an order—but it came out as more of a croak.

"You can't stop me, now that she's willingly touched the fan," Trevelyan snapped back. "I'll march her out of here, and then I'll come back for you."

Hell and damnation! Trevelyan was too well protected by the mirror spell for Owen to attack him, lest any stray shots hurt her. After being blasted like that, Owen had the stamina of a first-year student.

What else could be done? Think, man, think.

"Mrs. Sinclair," Owen coaxed, racking his brain for what she'd told him. She might not be able to work *much* magick on her own, but she could still work *some*.

She paid no attention to him. The fiery lizards slithered up her hands.

"Emma!" He called her by her oldest name, the one her intimates used.

Her fingers stilled on the fan, but she didn't look at him.

"Be silent, fool," Trevelyan ordered.

Owen ignored him. His deeds weren't a direct attack, so the other couldn't use that nasty shield. But if he tried any offensive magicks, the house's own defenses should protect Owen. God willing . . .

"Emma, remember the spell Nurse taught you, the one for true sight of any danger?" He called her, using the magickal command voice seldom uttered by independent mages, lest its tones shatter every cell in their bodies.

She hesitated, her teeth gnawing at her lower lip. The lizards' tails reached toward her wrists like manacles.

"No!" roared Trevelyan. "You will not break the spell."

"She has a right to choose," retorted Owen. "The land here will back me in this."

A deep hum sounded, below anything his ears could have heard. God help them all, the land had heard him and would do battle for her. But he lacked the magick to be its master; only Emma could perform that role.

Its deep war cry echoed through his bones and lifted him to his feet. Staggering a little, he made his way to behind Emma's chair.

Trevelyan stiffened, glancing rapidly around the room. Did he have enough magick to tame the ungoverned land?

"I say she has already chosen!" Trevelyan gestured violently. The house acted, pouring more of its delays like a viscous liquid over the intruder, until he seemed to be moving slower and slower.

Owen's mouth thinned, and he turned his full attention to Emma. God alone knew how much time he still had to dissuade her. At least her true name had reached her through Trevelyan's spell.

"It's a very simple spell," Owen crooned, disciplining himself not to shout at her. They had very little time to act before Trevelyan succeeded in pushing aside the house's objections.

Emma nodded slowly, still enraptured by the writhing lizards.

"Say it for me, Emma." Because he couldn't speak it for her, lest the change in her vision be considered unwilling and therefore not break the spell. "Emma, please." His voice broke on the last word.

She shuddered slightly, but it was enough to make the lizards hesitate for an instant.

"Goddess bright," she began and went on, her voice growing more confident with every syllable.

And every word brought more power into the air, until all of Owen's hair was standing on end. Sparks began to float off the tables and swirl across the room. The house seemed to be holding its breath . . .

She confidently finished the request for white light and leaned back into his arms.

A blinding flash of brilliant light immediately washed over her hands and the fan, revealing the malicious snakes in all their writhing ugliness. A bitter scent swept across the room, borne on a river of fiery sparks.

Emma screamed and stood up, flinging the fan away from her. It tumbled over the floor to Trevelyan's feet, the sticks clattering like angry demons.

She collapsed back against Owen. He promptly caught her, his heart pounding at her safety and her proximity. She smelled of lavender and rosemary, of freedom and new beginnings.

"Mrs. Sinclair! How dare you break my beautiful offering?" Trevelyan snarled, his coat awry and murder in his eyes. "Do you have any idea how much it cost me to create that?"

Owen glared at him, his arms wrapped around the shaking woman. He lifted his hand to strike—and Trevelyan immediately countered with the same move, his mirrored shield springing into life above and around his palm. Damn, damn, damn—he couldn't break through that bastard's strength alone.

He forced the bitter taste of failure back and returned to what could be done without risking injury to her.

"You can demand that he leave, Emma," Owen encouraged her. At least she could move directly. "Emma, you know the spell."

Her throat worked for a moment before she found the words. "Depart, foul intruder!" she snapped.

Trevelyan finished sliding the fan into the pocket in his coat's tails and stood up, his ugly expression quickly smoothing into guilelessness. "But, my dear Mrs. Sinclair—"

She came erect, without Owen's assistance, and her voice rang with determination—and generations of magick-wielders.

The formal chant filled the room, lifting every hair on Owen's body and sending icy needles dancing across his skin. How the devil was she managing to control so much power? She was a chalice, not a mage trained to work spells. Even adepts might find themselves burned out—or even dead—after an exertion like this.

She flung her hands out and pushed Trevelyan away on the final syllables, her face as stark as any battle goddess's.

The house howled, echoes of its deep voice ringing through the halls. "Leave, Trevelyan, and never set foot on Trethledan property again."

Dear lord, the land's very roots were marching to war for her. Owen fought the instinct to duck and remained upright behind her, lending her all the mage craft he could, hoping against hope it would be enough to keep her alive.

The door to the hallway promptly swung open, untouched by human hands.

Trevelyan glared at it and deliberately turned back to Emma, his hair streaming back from his face.

She was shaking badly, her face white. Owen clasped her by the waist—and fire surged into him. He arched back onto his toes, his teeth clenched, but managed to maintain his hold. *My darling, hold on a little longer . . .*

She shooed her attacker away.

The floor rippled under Trevelyn, forcing him to lurch out of the morning room on a run and through the hall. The curtains swung forward violently, wind hissing in their folds, and snapped at his heels. Candles extinguished themselves around him, making a trail of smoke to mark his departure. The paneling groaned like a bull-baiting crowd booing a loser. Carey and the maids held fast to the staircase's balustrades, their clothing billowing around them.

The massive front door flew open, and Trevelyan rushed out, tumbling across the portico and down the stairs. The ground heaved and cracked, then snapped together again. His horses reared in alarm and bolted for the gate, his coachman barely able to hold on to his perch as the coach jounced wildly down the drive.

Trevelyan managed to reach his feet, one hand bracing himself on the ground and a great bruise rising on his forehead. He glared at them down the hallway.

"Do not think we're through, Emma Sinclair," he shouted, the words echoing through the house. "Or you, Owen Bentham! You belong to me, and this land will bend the knee to Bonaparte."

She shrank in on herself but didn't flinch. Her gallantry nearly broke Owen's heart. She had to maintain this until Trevelyan had left Trethledan House's land, thereby closing the spell. Otherwise, the magick would recoil on her and probably kill her.

Risking his own life by completely entering the circle of power around a mage working a great spell, he wrapped his arms around her waist, giving her all the knowledge of magick contained in his mind, bones, and blood. If he'd only taken those damn classes, he'd know exactly how to help her, instead of having to use animal instinct. *I am here for you, sweetheart.*

She leaned against Owen, her curls brushing his chin.

"You have outstayed my patience, Mr. Trevelyan," she commented and brought her hand down in a quick chopping motion.

A storm of gravel shot up from the drive and pelted him. He screeched furiously—only to be cut off when the ground heaved under him, tossing him toward the gate. He came to his feet half-running, half-limping, and cursing at the top of his lungs, all the while chasing his departing carriage.

The door slammed shut on him, cutting off sight or sound of his tirade. Carey and the maids straightened themselves cautiously.

Emma collapsed, sliding through Owen's arms like water.

He caught her up against him.

Her heartbeat was almost too faint to be heard.

CHAPTER SEVEN

Owen kicked the door open into Emma's bedroom, caring for none of its feminine elegancies, not with his fragile lady barely breathing in his arms. The only thing that had kept her alive this long was wrenching his blasted coat and shirt open, so her fingers could touch his bare skin and gain his heartbeat.

Now she needed to be restored to full health. God help them both, only a mage could do that.

Where would be best? A rosewood bed hung with linens that matched the window draperies faced the door. A graceful chaise longue, gilded and carved in the Egyptian style, offered a resting place near the French windows.

Owen sniffed the air, silently checking for the strongest confluence of magick—and found it coming through the windows. He set Emma gently down on the chaise longue, forcing his hands to remain steady.

Stepping back, he began to yank his neckcloth off, cursing every iota of his ignorance.

Mrs. Keverne cleared her throat from the door. Even the curls under her cap seemed to bristle with indignation. "May I inquire as to your intent here, *sir*?"

She hurled the last word at him like a sharpshooter's bullet, before crossing to Emma's side.

Owen flung the neckcloth aside and went to work on his waistcoat's buttons, ignoring the first two's loud pops and hasty retreats under furniture. He gave Emma's oldest friend the truth. "A mage's lifespan is determined by her loved ones' strength."

Emma's old nurse went still, stark terror running across her face. Her hands fell away from Emma's skirts, where she'd been smoothing them into respectability. "Is she that close to death?"

Owen nodded once, sharply, and jerked off his waistcoat.

"She should be tended by those who love her!"

"She walks now at the far edge of any path. Do you have the strength to bring her back?" he countered ruthlessly, cursing all ruffles which camouflaged buttons. God knows, if he didn't have to rip his life's foundations apart to save Emma, he'd be far happier. Even a courtship would be simpler.

Mrs. Keverne flinched, her face turning white. But she recovered as quickly as any dragoon wrenching his saber free to face a new enemy.

"Do you have the love to save her?" she challenged him.

Owen stiffened at hearing his choices presented so starkly, caught with his braces halfway down his arms. He would have died before he'd have done this to keep himself alive—linked with another mage, yielded all his magick, risked forming a permanent bond.

But for Emma? Dear gallant, generous, adorable Emma?

If anything happened to her, he would not be able to face life without her, God help him.

His world shifted into a new pattern, and he shoved his braces off. "Yes."

Mrs. Keverne studied him, clearly seeing more of his motives than he knew himself. "I'll inform the General you're tending Mrs. Sinclair," she said finally. "He may ask for you both in the morning."

Owen inclined his head and went back to his damn buttons. Emma's recovery would come faster with the fewest barriers between them.

Mrs. Keverne bobbed a curtsy. "Sir."

Startled by her respectful tone, Owen lifted an eyebrow. "Good afternoon, Mrs. Keverne."

She closed the door softly behind her.

What had happened to evoke that reaction? He had no knowledge of the fairer sex to decipher it with. He'd always avoided close ties with women and had never kept company with one for any amount of time. But that would change now with Emma—or he wouldn't live to see the next day.

He yanked off his shoes and socks.

Her chaise longue might be a "long chair," but it had been so extended and curved that it was shaped more like a flattened *S*. It rolled gracefully up from the floor, stretched smoothly to a pillowed slope, canted perfectly for a lady to recline against. Lion's feet upheld it, while a wooden armrest, upheld by carved Egyptian goddesses, stood along one side. Its tufted silk upholstery was enriched with tassels and fringe worked in gold and Nile green silks.

It was a throne fit for Cleopatra. But Emma lay silent and still on it, with only the faint rise and fall of her breasts giving her life. His gallant lady, who'd somehow brought him out of the storm and off the beach. Who'd risked her life to save them all, as valiantly as any dragoon on a battlefield. His dear, beautiful lady.

Owen prayed for strength to the god he no longer entirely believed in, before sinking down onto the chaise beside her.

He'd never taken the classes at mage school on how to link and share magick. He had only instinct and the merest fundamentals of magick theory. Emma had to believe in every iota of her being that he loved her, if he was to pour his magick into her and keep her alive. But how to build a bridge strong enough and to do it quickly? The fastest and most certain way was through intense physical contact. In other words, carnal relations. If they'd already been bonded, they'd have only needed eye contact.

It had to happen now, or she'd die, her life slipping farther and farther away the longer her magick was gone.

He lifted Emma's hand to his lips and brushed his lips over her knuckles. Her pulse was almost invisible. "Emma, dear heart."

His voice broke, and he pressed a kiss into her palm, unable to speak.

Her fingers fluttered for an instant against his cheek.

• • •

WARM skin rubbed against her hand, with hard bone underneath. Emma instinctively fanned her fingers to explore further and found a man's cheek, roughened by the first touch of late day stubble and built upon the strength of a stubborn jaw.

He choked and went quite still under her touch.

She stretched a little farther, her fingertips gliding over his cheekbones and her thumb touching the corner of his mouth. A warm, curving—sensual?—mouth.

"Emma," he breathed and lightly kissed her thumb.

Warmth crept over her skin. "Owen," she sighed, recognizing him instantly.

"Dearest Emma," he answered, catching her hand in his and kissing it tenderly.

Something deep inside her fluttered happily.

Her eyelids lifted slowly, fighting against gravity, to survey him. Amazingly, he was dressed only in a shirt and breeches, without so much as a neckcloth or a waistcoat, or even a banyan for respectability. They were in her bedroom, but she lacked the energy to inquire about that. More importantly, he was making a poor attempt at a smile.

She patted him on the arm. "Steady there, Owen. Steady . . ."

She was so very tired that her eyes were slipping shut.

"Emma!" He caught her by the shoulders. "Sweetheart, stay with me."

She blinked at him in surprise but didn't struggle. Why wouldn't he let her go to sleep? "Owen, it's been a very long afternoon," she began. "Surely a nap . . ."

He shifted his hold, lifting her up and sliding one arm around her waist. "Remember how we watched each other in the Long Gallery?"

Fireflies of light and heat danced along her skin and into her bones from where they touched. She could have sat up on her own, but she didn't, happy to feel his warmth enveloping her.

She nodded, bemused. She was pressed against him from her chest to her hips, acutely aware of his iron-hard body and his lack of respectable clothing.

Hunger curled through her, bringing both the eagerness and the ability to satisfy it. She slid her hand up his arm to his shoulder, fascinated by how her slightest touch could make him shudder.

"If we become lovers," he whispered, "you'll regain your strength."

Logic was slipping away every time his heartbeat increased its pace to match hers. "Lovers? Truly?" she muttered, heat sparking into her veins.

She lightly stroked his neck, exploring the hard juncture between throat and shoulder, which had always been hidden under his shirt.

He tilted his head to offer himself more openly to her caress, his eyes slitting with pleasure. "I promise. And any danger will be mine, if our magick isn't properly connected," he murmured.

"Yes to anything and everything," she murmured, not much interested in risk at a time like this, and slid her hand over his shoulder. Her breasts were tightening, her nipples hard and rubbing against her stiff corset. If only she had the energy to seize him and demand he take action to fulfill them both . . .

He kissed her, tenderness and passion swirling through his touch. She moaned and pressed against him. Fire leaped and sparked between them, danced off their clothes, dived into their veins, and delved into their bones.

"Beloved Emma," he whispered and pressed her closer, his hand stroking her back restlessly. She fondled him, his every aching gasp and ragged pulse thudding through her and filling her like spring rain into an estuary. His hair was the finest silk in her hands, while he greedily filled his fingers with her curls.

He kissed her throat, making her arch off the chaise longue to encourage him. It took him but a moment to shove down her sleeves and lift her breasts out of her dress, freeing them from her stays.

She blinked, startled at his disregard for the niceties of ritual undressing.

His golden head bent low and he tasted her, circling his tongue around and around her areola, until she thought she'd go insane with lust. She clutched his head close and moaned, cream gliding over her thighs. How could such frantic need and the strength to support it arise every time he suckled her? Surely his mouth should be outlawed for making a lady so desperate she'd curse and claw a man's back, when he insisted on keeping to oral ministrations!

She bucked against him again and again, on fire for his possession. Her skin was taut, almost crackling over her bones. The room seemed to swim around her, and the curtains fluttered, as if it too danced with hunger.

"Emma, my dearest," he crooned, rubbing his cheek against her hip through her thin dress.

She tensed at Edward's favorite endearment. Could she yield herself to the risk of loving again—to a near stranger, especially when losing Edward had nearly shattered her?

"My angel," Owen murmured. He teased her skirt and the shift underneath upward, his calloused fingers a delicious contrast to her aching flesh. Cream glided to meet him, her core softening and melting in welcome.

Her man, her lover.

Higher her skirts rose, their fragile folds easily managed by his big hands. Yet still he stroked and fondled her legs, his thumb sweeping over the long muscle, paying knowing attentions to the sensitive points behind her knees—why hadn't she realized before that spot could become a source of so much arousal?—always moving closer and closer to her aching center.

He kissed her thigh at the junction, nuzzling her dark curls as if she alone meant homecoming. He slipped a single finger between her writhing, tightly clamped legs and ruffled her folds. "Darling, I will do anything to keep you alive."

He turned his head, his hair sweeping over her and sending a hot pulse jolting through her womb and into her breasts. Need spun through her, for love and life—again, with this man, no matter what she risked.

Her fingers sank into his scalp and pulled him closer, demanding more—insisting on completion of his promise.

He choked, half laughter and half grunt of answering lust.

His fingers delved between her legs, teasing and petting her private flesh. He found her pearl with a single, talented finger—and she arched harder against him, almost sending him off the chaise longue. "Hurry, please hurry, Owen."

He chuckled, his face a mask of desperation. He was sweating and his breathing was a ragged, hoarse echo of its previous smoothness. His cock was a burning brand barely restrained by his breeches. Yet his iron will kept both of them to the tempo he chose. Two years of marriage—and most of that with her husband at sea—hadn't given her the experience to break through Owen's discipline.

"How much do you want this?"

She gasped, fighting for breath—and logic—enough to answer him. She writhed, driving herself down on his skilled hand—but he still wouldn't take her over the precipice.

"How much do you want *me*?" His fierce blue eyes watched her, as if worlds waited on her reply.

"With all my heart." She didn't need any additional reasoning to answer that question, not when she knew it in her bones. She'd taken him from the tides, and he belonged to her.

Owen's eyes flared, light sparking between them. He shifted—and only an instant later, knelt over her, her skirts tossed up, and his breeches undone.

She licked her lips in anticipation, thankful and impatient to welcome a mage of his talents. Eagerness and energy raced through her, her exhaustion long since forgotten in her hunger for this man.

Owen came into her smoothly, like the fast, hard sweep of a tide's first wave. She shuddered, her channel rippling and clenching him in welcome, lust pulsing through her spine and swirling through her veins.

His brilliant blue gaze caught hers, edged with desperation and pure willingness to give her anything and everything she wanted.

He thrust again slowly. She tightened herself around him with everything she had, her channel, her legs around his hips, her arms around his neck—and her eyes locked on his. "Please, Owen. Come to me."

His eyes flared. He moved faster and faster, still holding her with his gaze. She yielded utterly to him, always letting him see how much he meant to her and how much her strength grew. Everything in the world was narrowed to just the two of them—the harsh, wet sounds of their intimate flesh slapping against each other, their groans and sighs, his sweat-slicked hair hanging over his forehead, and his broad shoulders straining under her fingers, while he fought to ratchet her excitement up another notch. Her lungs, her loins, every inch was an impossibly tight knot, soaking wet and fiery hot in readiness.

She was incredibly alive, as if all the world existed only to help the two of them enjoy this moment.

She clawed his back, desperate for another position, another touch, anything to bring them both to the pinnacle—and shifted, bringing his cock deeper into her.

He shouted her name, startled, and climaxed, flooding her with his hot cream. His eyes turned molten gold, infinitely irresistible.

She shouted for joy and spun into orgasm with him in a fury of joy. It tumbled her end over end, like leaping into a waterfall, golden magick blasting through her in a fiery effervescence, carving her into a new person.

CHAPTER EIGHT

Owen tightened his arms around Emma, gasping for breath. Magick danced behind his eyes in brilliant cascades of light, like shooting stars transformed into waterfalls. He'd opened himself to Emma, allowing her ancestral lands' power to pour through them both. It still flooded his blood and bones.

Her heart thudded against his chest. She sighed and pressed closer, her curls teasing his throat, and her leg sliding between his. She delicately caressed the nape of his neck. "If this is the aftermath of one visit from Mr. Trevelyan, perhaps we should invite him back tomorrow."

Owen gave a rough snort of laughter before rolling over, freeing her from his weight, and drew the sheet up over her shoulders to keep her warm. She lifted an eyebrow at him quizzically.

He smoothed back a tempting lock from her forehead, wishing they could linger like this.

"Relax, sweetheart, while I try to send a message. There's a better chance now, with so much magick still running between us." Surely he had enough magick now to slip a few words through Trevelyan's wall. Heaven forbid it require more than what they had just shared, which was far more than Caroline Spencer had taken from him at Villers-en-Cauchies. Because if it did, he'd need to rip open his heart and soul to Emma—and he didn't think he could refuse her.

Emma nodded, heavy-lidded with satiation. "Of course." She slid her hand into his and laid her cheek against his shoulder.

Owen's heart skipped a beat at her complete trust in him. He forced himself not to consider other ways to enjoy it, such as kissing his way down her spine and between her legs until she was begging him for completion.

He deliberately reminded himself of the King's Mages' hall in London, with its ancient stonework and ever-vigilant sentries. He whispered the message spell, as familiar to him as breathing, and visualized his words appearing on the great silver message board, one by one. "Alive at Trethledan House in Cornwall. Traitor mage at Whitmore Hall."

Mist gathered thickly in front of Emma's window and trembled, fighting to shape his vision.

Emma tightened her hand around Owen's, watching it with him.

The mist thinned until it showed hints of stones, with a great rectangular board hanging in front. The message board! He was closer than he'd ever been before.

Owen focused harder, demanding that his dispatch go through. Emma's nails dug into his skin, sending a surge of magick into him like fine wine.

If he could just write the words, letter by letter . . .

The immense tablet clouded, as if someone had breathed on it. Flecks of light circled the board and gradually joined together.

He was starting to write, and the sentries had noticed. Just a little more effort, and he'd have a true message.

Owen pictured his words brushstroke by brushstroke.

The word *alive* shimmered in the air above it and was slowly etched in pale crimson on the silver . . .

Someone shouted in the distance.

A howling wind abruptly slammed shut Emma's window. The mist congealed into solid gray, erasing all sight of the message board.

Owen cursed under his breath and dismissed the vision. He needed no reminder of another failure.

Emma sniffed and lifted her head. She blinked down at him, all soft, inquisitive, dark brown eyes. "You fed the land's magick into me before to save me, correct? Did any portion of your message reach London, with my magick's help?"

A muscle ticked in his jaw. If only he could keep her out of this—but he couldn't. There was no time left to do anything except take advantage of her and anything else that came to hand. "Yes, that's what happened. The first word might have made it through but nothing more. Trevelyan's wall feels a good deal thinner, but it still stops me."

"Damn."

He cocked an eyebrow at her for having so perfectly captured his own sentiments. And with profanity, too. This must have greatly overset her usual patterns of thought, if she was uttering those terms.

"What if we fed more of the land's power into you?" She nibbled thoughtfully on a slender fingertip, her expression abstracted.

Hope trickled into his veins before he blocked it. After all, she'd nearly died only a few minutes ago.

"Are you strong enough? We will have to be completely united for me to tap into it."

She waved off his concerns. "Truly, I have never felt better. Your attentions"—she blushed sweetly—"gave me more joy and strength than I can express."

He gave her a quick kiss. Still . . .

"Where could we find a better link to the magickal confluence than here in the house?"

"At the Druid's Mount. It's a small hilltop surrounded by ancient standing stones, where Grandfather built a small Grecian temple at Grandmother's request. Legend says it was a place of power, long before the druids or King Arthur came here." She paused for a moment, her expression abstracted, before she continued. "Grandmother could light a candle with magick and she entered the mage school trials. She never said whether she failed them or not, only that Grandfather was her destiny."

Owen frowned at the odd phrasing, wondering if Emma's grandmother had had the gift of foretelling. He cupped Emma's face in his hands, seeing the small temple through her eyes. A very feminine structure, it was round and built of white marble, with a private room in the center.

He delicately probed further, using his magesight to see below the marble surface and the gardens around it. Something ancient and immensely wise looked back at him, uncoiling itself like a great serpent to inspect him. It was the confluence itself, part of a river of magick which flowed through all of Cornwall and, beyond that, England and Britain.

Owen stiffened his spine, fighting not to tremble. After all, adepts occasionally saw confluences, and councilors knew how to seek them. But confluences had their own will and ways of acting, including the ability to be easily offended for no apparent reason. Making a mistake at this point, or even showing fear, had destroyed more than one mage.

Emma's hands wrapped themselves around his wrists, offering her family's ancient connections to the confluence as comfort.

Calm flowed back into him. Inside his head, Owen bowed, offering his duty to the King and his link to Emma as *bona fides*.

The confluence reared up in consideration, before nodding to him. It shimmered briefly, like hands making a magickal pass.

A breath later, Owen and Emma stood within the Grecian temple. Fluted white columns circled them, while a white ceiling etched in gold rose high above them to form an elegant pavilion. The furniture was equally simple, primarily a carved ebony and rosewood bed raised on a dais, with a white gauze panel sweeping down from the ceiling at each corner. It was made up with the finest white linens, while white and red roses floated in bowls.

Emma moved to the temple's edge, where its white marble steps began, and looked out. More accustomed to magick's workings, Owen stepped up behind her, enjoying the scent of warm, well-pleased woman. If he had to rip himself open to allow another mage entrance to his magick and his heart, at least it would be Emma, someone whose motives he trusted and who he found infinitely attractive.

Broad meadows and ancient woods flowed into the distances beyond the temple, and a brook sang softly to itself. The Channel glimmered under the moonlight to the south, caressing the land's edge. The view was slightly cut off by Trethledan House, to the southeast.

Three ancient stones, rough-edged yet unmistakably created by men, stood in the herb garden just below the temple. Four other stones, equally old, marked each corner of the compass. An immense, ruined castle looked back at the temple from atop a ridge which ran east of Trethledan House. As obviously as the temple was the center of the confluence, the castle and the marker stones indicated its boundaries.

Under the land's surface, his magesight showed golden magick shimmering and pulsing, rising toward the moonlight. It was the land's pure strength running through the temple and leaping exuberantly across it in fiery chains. It twined itself through the marble, too.

Moonlight's silver gilded the temple's roof and the trees. It clung to his shoulders and sparkled across his skin before diving into his signet. It was the magick that could reshape men, as the moon itself was reformed. Joining himself with Emma meant opening himself utterly to the land's magick and every possible change that could follow.

"How did we come here?" Emma asked, spreading her hands to encompass the world beyond. Her eyes, however, lingered overlong on him, noting the breadth of his shoulders and the rise and fall of his chest.

"The confluence brought us," Owen answered, heat whispering through his veins where her gaze touched him. "It must greatly want to be rid of Trevelyan and sees this as the best step."

"Enough to act directly?"

Owen nodded, stepped behind her, and pulled her close, seeking contact with warm flesh and blood rather than insubstantial webs of power. "What are those stones out there?" he queried and kissed the top of her head.

"The Morthol, or hammer." She melted against him, her heart beating against his arm in the irregular pulse of desire. "The Gwythias, which means guardian, flows at the base of the cliff on the other side."

"They were built to guard the confluence. Can you see the power beginning to gather?" Owen cupped her breast, teasing her gently through the fine cotton. His pulse thudded ridiculously hard in his throat, sending an answering surge into his loins.

"Mm-hmm." She wriggled against him.

She wasn't speaking in complete sentences now, he noted with considerable satisfaction. She had the most responsive nipples he'd ever had the pleasure of teasing. "How old is the castle?"

"The site is—oh, Owen!—supposedly from Arthur's time. But it hasn't been inhabited since Tudor times." She managed to put her hand on his hip, pulling him forward, and rubbed her exquisite derriere against his cock through her thin skirts.

He grunted something encouraging, sparks skittering through his veins, and nuzzled her neck. All around him, magick pulsed in the land and sang through the air, foreshadowing its hot ripeness at harvest time.

Emma shivered and threw her head back against his shoulder enthusiastically. "There's still a—ah!—Druid stone altar where the southwest tower overlooks the Channel and the Gwythias, though. Grandmother always said that tower was why the Morthol was originally built."

She undulated against him, moaning happily under his hands.

A thought trembled in Owen's head and was gone before he could grasp it. But it was distant and insignificant next to her eagerness and the blood throbbing in his veins. Magick skittered up the columns and across the roof's etchings.

Owen gathered her skirts up in his hands, teasing their fullness over her legs. His cock swelled desperately against his breeches.

Emma trembled and tried to hook one slender leg back around his ankle. "I'm wearing too many clothes," she muttered crossly. Her stockings slipped down, one embroidered garter coming delightfully undone.

He snorted, half in laughter and half in disgust at his own tendency to torture himself. He tossed her up onto the bed, sending her skirts tumbling around her. Magick gathered deep within the temple's marble, suffusing every stone vein with gold and silver.

Emma blinked up at him, her brown eyes fathomless pools of desire. He kissed the inside of her knee, exposed by the sliding stocking, and she blushed hotly.

"Dearest, dearest Emma." He caressed her lightly, smoothing his thumb over her, savoring the hot leap of her pulse at his slightest touch. Magick poured deeper into his veins, matching every beat of her heart, every catch in her breath, every bead of cream gliding down her thigh.

He slipped her shoes off and drew her stockings down, revealing more of her exquisite limbs to him.

She threaded her fingers through his hair and pulled him closer, moaning his name.

Hunger sank deeper into his bones and his cock, tightening his lungs, until breathing was necessary only to bring him closer to her. Heat prowled through him, his magick coming alive in every cell of his body.

He drew her sleeves over her shoulders and grimaced at her stays. Removing them—sweetly seducing her out of them—would necessitate changing their position and losing her passionate hold on him. No and no and no.

A single spell later, Emma's clothes lay precisely folded on the temple's floor.

Her breasts were taut and flushed, her nipples ripe as springtime berries. Her narrow waist was perfectly formed for his hands to grasp while he rode her. And, oh dear heavens, the curve of her hips and the dark feminine mysteries between her thighs . . .

His mouth went completely dry, and he tried to decide what part of her to taste first.

Fire sparked across the ceiling, forming itself into ropes of flames that ran from column to column. Flashes of crimson and gold flickered against him and Emma, his magick answering hers.

"Your shirt," Emma sighed. "I need to touch your skin."

Owen snapped his fingers, and his clothing immediately removed itself, settling onto the floor in a neatly folded pile together with Emma's.

"My Owen." She kneaded his shoulders, her fingers digging into his muscles, and her nails scratching his skin.

He growled, his senses leaping at the heightened, more precise contact. She was his, dammit, his. No matter what else happened, he would claim her completely.

He kissed her breasts, swirling his tongue over her fine skin and tasting her plump nipple. Again and again and again, he suckled her, light arising wherever he touched.

She moaned his name, cream rippling over her thigh, and her musk enriched the air.

His cock hardened against her. Pre-come slipped forth, hot and eager as the flames dancing around them through the temple and the gardens beyond.

She writhed, twisting herself against him. He teased her pearl, circling it, toying with her folds, stroking her directly, ruffling her folds again—until she was sobbing with passion and his own cock was screaming in desperation.

Every breath rasped his throat. Hunger stabbed through his balls, locking them high and achingly tight against his cock. Silver poured over and through him, until he was barely recognizable to himself, yet he paid no recognition. Only Emma and the pleasure they found together meant anything now.

He gathered her up and lifted her hips to meet him.

Her eyes opened, and she smiled slowly. "Finally," she purred and arched to meet his thrust.

He growled and pulled her down onto him, gloving himself in her hot cream. She moaned happily, eagerly fondling his hips and waist—any part of him she could reach.

He bent his knees and brought her up into a sitting position, keeping them joined. She gasped at the changing sensations, a thousand flavors of delight passing across her face.

Owen kissed her, tasting her pleasure, as if it were his own, bringing her breasts against his chest. Their breaths swirled between their mouths, echoing every thrust of his cock, every eager pulse of her loins.

Magick ripped up from the confluence and through the pavilion, filling every stone and seam. It poured down from the ceiling and across the bed, setting the air alight more brilliantly than any royal display of fireworks. It surged into him, more dizzying and exhilarating than a wild weekend in a wine shop.

His own magick blazed up to meet up it, deeper and stronger, demanding everything his blood and bones had to give as fuel. Madness or ecstasy was the unknown destination . . .

Yet Emma was his anchor and his reality, from the taste of her on his lips, to her sweat gliding over his skin as if it were his own. They flowed together as smoothly as water and wine, completely unlike what he'd found before with any other mage.

He thrust again more slowly, and she twisted slightly, sending a stab of delight across his hips, through his balls, and up his cock. Her channel caressed him and clung. They moved together as one flesh, with even their breathing united.

He closed his eyes, groaning in ecstasy. Emma, dearest, dearest Emma . . .

Gold spun through him from wherever they touched, while silver rippled deeper and deeper into his skin—carving away his inhibitions and pouring new life into his veins.

They began to move together, faster and faster, in a dance whose pleasures only they fully understood, highlighted by their moans of delight, punctuated by harsh gasps and the fierce smack of flesh meeting flesh.

She arched, flinging her head back in a paroxysm of joy. Orgasm tumbled through her—and snatched him, vaulting him into ecstasy through their link. It blasted through his balls and out of his cock, erasing everything he'd ever thought he'd known about his own magick.

He howled, moonlight pouring over him, and became one with her and the land in delight. Crimson and gold surged through his magick, bright and strong as their pleasure, remaking his vision of what passing magick to another mage could mean.

CHAPTER NINE

Owen considered the lacing to Emma's stays, decided they would do well enough, and briskly tied them off.

Dawn shimmered in the east, barely disturbing a heavy bank of clouds. Dew gleamed on the grass, a silver reminder of the magick locked in the land. A few birds chirped awkwardly, as if practicing for the coming day, while a breeze rattled the heavy grass briefly and retired.

His experience with women was not enough for him to gauge how well he'd performed as a lady's maid, especially in this more intimate arena. Husbands helped ladies with their stays, not occasional lovers—a terrifying and exciting prospect.

But even if he was now admitted to all the boudoir's secrets, at least he'd still kept command of his own most essential elements. They'd never linked as adepts, naked to each other's minds while they passed magick and worked a spell. Lust blinded a mage too much to make him similarly vulnerable, unlike a conscious lowering of barriers. If the magick was worked without physical contact, it would mean that the union was truly without any barriers.

"Since you managed to reach London this time," Emma poked her head out of her dress like a tortoise to address him, "how soon do you think someone will come?"

"Since Trevelyan is allied with a French mage, who has a coterie and several warships, they're sending a party of adepts and some frigates." He began to button her. "They want us to lie low until they arrive."

"Noon, perhaps?" She bent her head forward for the last few buttons, muffling her voice.

"Or sooner. The Navy will be very eager to catch that French mage, since he destroyed one of their sloops."

She pursed her mouth, considering that strategy. "They're so certain of finding him here? Why would the Frenchman still be hunting you? Surely you've already delivered your dispatch."

"*I* am the message, sweetheart." He handed her a pair of half-boots, glad the confluence had provided a complete set of clothing. "I cannot speak or write it until I reach Whitehall."

"For safety's sake?"

"Yes. Courier bags can be stolen or destroyed. A courier is much more difficult to erase from the scene. It's why the French must kill me rather than simply destroy my pouch, which they've already done."

"What could be so important that a King's Mage's life would be risked for it?" Emma gaped at him.

A muscle ticked in his jaw. If Trevelyan attacked before the adepts arrived, he'd need her help—and she deserved to know why they fought, even though it stuck in his craw to risk her life again. At least the gryphon had approved of her loyalty by showing himself to her.

"Bonaparte plans to declare war and invade England." He gave her the unvarnished truth, as befitted the descendant of military men.

"So? The Navy will hurl him back to France!" She sniffed haughtily. He could almost see her father glaring at him.

"What navy? We have been at peace for almost two years and have only a fraction of the ships we once did. It's only twenty-two miles from Calais to Dover, less than a day's ride by Bonaparte's reckoning. As matters stand today, we couldn't mount a defense that could stop the French fishing fleet from crossing the Channel."

She opened her mouth and shut it, visibly fuming.

He crossed his arms over his chest and waited for the admiral's daughter to find Bonaparte's true difficulty.

"Even if he did make it over the water, he'd still have to land his troops. The French pilots know only the large ports, like Dover and Portsmouth, which are all heavily armed."

"But he can select a small port, which would give him the advantage of surprise. Someplace with difficult tides or a twisting channel but good roads, once he's ashore," Owen suggested mildly.

She raised a haughty eyebrow. "He'd need an English pilot, which he'll *never* have."

"Never?"

She stared at him. He allowed the silence to lengthen between them.

"After all these years of war, no English pilots have gone over to the French. At least not in sufficient numbers to guide an invasion fleet," Emma whispered, color draining from her face.

"Not willingly, no. But have you ever heard of the Lorelei?"

She shook her head, curls tumbling over her shoulders.

"They're faerie maidens who live in and around the Rhine, and their song has the ability to enthrall sailors. A small group of French mages have been working in Strasbourg for years on a spell, which could do the same thing. They succeeded late last year."

"If they stole our pilots or sailors . . ." Emma shuddered. "Bonaparte could invade where and when he chose, and his fleet would always be victorious."

Owen nodded, refusing to show any of his own fears. "Thankfully for us, many in Strasbourg loathe him."

"Why? Most of Europe's intellectuals welcomed the French revolutionaries, and he's their heir."

"Strasbourg was neutral before it was seized by Louis XIV. Even after that, it remained a free city until a few years ago, when the French revolutionaries revoked its traditional religious and academic liberties. Now Bonaparte's mages constantly hunt Strasbourg's few remaining magick workers."

"Will its mages help us?"

"Very cautiously. One of them locked the counterspell to the Lorelei's song into my head, before he died."

"Do the French know that's what you're carrying?" she whispered.

"Oh yes." Owen looked back at her, allowing his knowledge of how that Strasbourg mage had been torn apart to show, along with his white-hot hunger for revenge burning behind it.

She gasped, her face turning ashen. "What won't they do to stop you?"

"Nothing. But a chalice like you is just as great a prize, sweetheart." He shrugged. "We must stand together or be destroyed."

"If they attack, we won't be able to join ourselves as we, as we did last night." She blushed hotly, but bravely kept her eyes on him. "Won't that be necessary if you're to draw magick from me?"

"No. According to all the books, now that we've shared breath, we can simply look at each other and pass magick without physical contact." He hoped, by all the patron saints of mages, that that was true.

"Are you certain?"

"Yes." He pushed his doubts aside. He'd have to drop all of his self-made walls to pull it off, too. God help them.

"I'm glad." She leaned up to kiss him on the cheek.

He was silent much of the way back to the house thinking about how best to accomplish linking with her for battle—drawing up half-forgotten texts, remembering how Villers-en-Cauchies had begun, although that seemed so distant now. Would the binding be a spell primarily of intent or of word? Would Emma's incredible depth as a chalice affect the creation of a spell in any way? Her strength might want to join the linkage—or it might be hesitant, after all. Would he need to set wards around her, or would the confluence protect her as one of its own?

Emma spread her fingers over Owen's wrist, from where her hand rested in the crook of his arm, wondering if he felt the same shiver of possession and pride at her nearness. His heat and strength were as palpable now as his magick had been last night. She should feel safe, yet his expression was abstracted and harsh. They'd shared magick—oh dear heavens, had they made magick!—but she wasn't certain if he'd be able to drop his shields to let her help him.

God willing her love would be strong enough to carry them both through it. It was strange that her second love should come this way, for a stranger washed up by the tides. Still, her heart had known him from the first, and she'd follow him wherever he went.

Owen held the garden gate open for her, and she entered, instinctively listening for any watchers. She'd never come back to the house moments after dawn with a lover before.

She paused at the rose garden's edge, stung by the utter lack of familiar voices. Where was the under-gardener, picking the first berries of the day? Where were the grooms, crooning to the horses? Shouldn't coal scuttles be clanging from inside the house?

"Where is Grandfather?" She swung toward the terrace, looking for the most beloved face of all. "He's always out here on sunny days to drink his tea."

Owen sniffed hard, his countenance turning harsh.

"Trevelyan?" she whispered.

Owen deftly drew a complicated sign in the air. It hung for a moment in colored smoke before flaring crimson with a disgusting stench of sulphur. The blackened remains whirled rapidly, leaning onto one side, and pointed toward the cove.

"He came from the ocean. The French must be back, hiding in that early morning mist."

"Grandfather." A tear ran down her cheek, but she bit her lip until the blood came, forcing herself to stand still. She wouldn't risk Owen's life and his precious message, if this was a trap.

"He's no longer here, and there's no spell set on the house itself. He probably couldn't do so, even if he wanted to." Owen caught her hand, and they ran for the house.

They burst into the kitchen, slamming the heavy door back against the wall, only to find a horrific sight. Keverne, Cook, and the youngest scullery maid all sat immobile on chairs and stools, staring straight ahead like giant wooden puppets. And Nurse—Nurse hung from the great iron cooking crane by her best apron, her skin and clothes blackened, and her eyes staring. Her chest was barely moving.

Emma gagged, her legs turning to water under her.

"Trevelyan couldn't touch the land or the house but the bastard could savage the people." Owen's tone was a bitter indictment. "I should have guessed he'd do something like this."

He reached up to Nurse, chanting softly. As soon as he touched her, a crimson flare flashed over her and the kitchen. A piece of parchment drifted down, rapidly burning on every edge.

Owen caught it, ignoring the fire, and Emma gasped. If she lost him, too . . .

"You may exchange Sir George for Mrs. Sinclair at the Morthol in one hour. Otherwise, I will use him as blood magick against her." Trevelyan's voice dripped acid.

A muscle ticked in Owen's jaw but he said nothing.

"Come alone, Bentham. It's warded against all other magick wielders. Trevelyan."

Owen's fingers flickered, and the parchment evaporated into a single puff of smoke, taking Trevelyan's last syllables with it.

"What does he mean to do?" She shook his shoulder.

"You're a very powerful chalice, and your grandfather comes from the same blood. If he makes your grandfather into a blood sacrifice on the land that you draw your power from, it would be enough to bind you. And probably do unspeakable things with your power, as well."

Her skin crawled at the memories walking through his voice.

"Aye, it's enough to make me risk my message." He smiled wryly at her. "Help me take her down, sweetheart."

"Can we?" She gulped and came forward cautiously. "Should we fetch the surgeon, or . . ."

"Her injuries are purely magickal, like those of everyone else in this house." He lifted her hand and kissed it, his warm lips lingering on her knuckles. "With your aid, I can heal them all."

She couldn't stop staring at Nurse. All the happy years, all the laughter, the shared confidences, the tears when Edward had died—to have everything end like this.

"Emma!"

Her heart jolted against her ribs, and she stared at Owen.

"You must focus on me—or Trevelyan has already won." He rubbed his cheek against both her hands, watching her with those irresistible sapphire eyes. "You must give me the strength to heal them. I cannot do it alone."

He'd never lied to her. She nodded slowly.

"Now draw the power from the confluence for me, dear heart."

"How?"

"Simply ask for it."

She frowned at him. Everything else in magick happened with words and gestures and spectacle. How could she do so much so easily?

"I don't understand why it works, only that's what the books say—and you've gained it before without effort. Quickly, Emma, we haven't much time."

She pulled a face and closed her eyes, silently making her request to whoever was listening. Perhaps that big guardian spirit she'd always felt watching over her in the rose garden?

Something surged into her, stuffing her every pore and spilling out. Her dress crackled, and its ribbons snapped against her arms.

"Now give me your hand, Emma." Owen's blue eyes were confident enough to be a lifeline.

She obeyed, trusting him completely.

He chanted something complicated and harsh, finishing with a strong chopping motion of their hands.

A brilliant white light flashed throughout the kitchen and farther, illuminating every inch—even beyond what was covered by cloth. For a moment, Emma could see the bones in her hand and the window's iron frame behind the curtains. The house shuddered, surging upward and settling back down with a groan almost of relief.

Nurse dropped into Owen's arms, all signs of burns gone. The other servants gasped, almost a dry rattle, before they began to breathe smoothly.

Emma buried her face against Owen's back and prayed the confrontation with Trevelyan would take place as easily.

CHAPTER TEN

Owen led their way into the Morthol, every sense alive for the slightest sign of treachery. It had been a very beautiful castle once, with its finely fitted gray stonework, Gothic arches and pierced windows, and twisting bridges over the pounding surf.

Even in its decline, after centuries of abandonment to storms and landslides, it still maintained its ancient sense of power and brooding majesty. It stared across the meadows and forests to Trethledan House, as if it still kept watch over the confluence. The Gwythias ran fast and hard along its eastern edge, as if guarding it from the saccharine opulence of Whitmore Hall.

But a French frigate arrogantly prowled the waters to the south. Sails could be seen farther east—probably the promised fleet. The French, damn their eyes, had the weather gauge, meaning the wind came to their sails first. The British ships would have to tack back and forth to make any headway against that, adding hours—perhaps days!—to their time. Possession of such an advantage by the French was damned suspicious, but not Owen's first concern.

Emma was. Heaven forbid Trevelyan should take her, either directly or by sacrificing her grandfather. His fist clenched briefly, and he forced it to relax, finger by finger.

She was nattily attired in a crisp dark-blue wool riding habit, looking every inch the aristocratic lady. Even her top hat's ribbons and plumes jauntily announced her superiority and long ties to this neighborhood.

He'd chosen to wear his uniform as a King's Mage, all scarlet and gold silk, with lashings of gold braid across his chest and intricate lace on his forearms. An equally magnificent bearskin-lined jacket hung from his left shoulder, proclaiming his disdain for ordinary soldiers' miniscule wardrobes. His bearskin cap was crowned with a gryphon's feather, and gold tassels decorated his crimson sash and his knee boots. Her grandfather's saber rode at his hip, thumping his leg arrogantly with every step.

Bonaparte's hussars wore a blurred copy of the same uniform, condemned as mere mortals to wear wool instead of spider silk magickally capable of keeping its wearer warm in the winter, cool in the summer, dry in all weathers, and clean despite any adversity.

It was the first time he'd willingly donned full regimentals since Villers-en-Cauchies. It had seemed fitting to wear it when he was going into battle again.

He was escorting her in the most formal style, with only her hand resting on his. Neither of them wore gloves, maintaining physical contact for as long as possible.

They'd crossed over an arched bridge, along winding paths, under frowning battlements, to reach this final stone wall. They passed through an ancient room, only dimly lit from high-set, dusty windows.

They emerged into daylight, heavy with the scent of age and dankness, of old stone and green grass. Salt air teased the nose, carried by a stiff breeze which blew out of the west toward Plymouth and the other naval bases.

Before them lay the inner bailey, a large enclosed courtyard covered in grass and nothing else. Gray stone walls rose all around, pierced by narrow windows as formal as jurors. One side had been torn away to reveal the ocean, sparkling like a seductive jewel. Waves pounded at the rocks, roaring their desire to swallow the land.

High tide would arrive within the hour.

The French frigate hovered insolently less than a mile away, within easy reach by long boat or cannon fire. Farther away, small white triangles—little more than flecks—marked where British warships fought the wind.

Trevelyan turned to face them from the greensward, one eyebrow superciliously elevated. He was very fashionably dressed from his black, superfine dress coat to his highly polished Hessian boots. A saber hung at his side, its hilt the matte-black of a mage's weapon guided by magesight, not sunlight.

The hair on the nape of Owen's neck rose at its sight. Such weapons had a wicked taste for blood.

But Owen's borrowed saber was sworn to this land's defense, giving it some advantage in this battle.

Behind Trevelyan, the grass rose to a slight mound near the central wall before falling away.

Emma's grandfather was tied to a chair in the colonnade on the far side, his cane carelessly propped against it. Above his gag, the old gentleman's eyes were narrowed and deadly, like a cobra considering his first move.

"Bentham."

The ice-edged spell in Trevelyan's voice touched Owen and melted into a puddle on the grass. It was a very old test of another mage's shields.

Trevelyan's eyes narrowed. Yesterday—before Emma had healed him—that spell would have left Owen badly frostbitten.

"Trevelyan." Owen waited, not showing his triumph—and not bothering to waste his own magick to probe the other.

"Mrs. Sinclair." Trevelyan's voice was considerably warmer. "What a great pleasure it is—"

"Save your breath, and pay compliments to those who'd believe them," she snapped and gave Owen's fingers a quick squeeze. "I'll see to my grandfather now."

Trevelyan's mouth tightened. "Of course. You'll want to say good-bye to him before we leave for France."

"Harrumph." She leaned up and kissed Owen's cheek, an affectionate display which raised a hum of pleasure through his bones.

He smiled, knowing his face softened for her.

Something very ancient stirred behind the Morthol's stones, too deep for even his magesight to clearly see. A welcome warmth brushed the soles of his boots.

Trevelyan hissed angrily and opened his mouth.

Emma gave Owen's hand another squeeze, curtsied to him, and calmly walked toward her grandfather, for all the world as if they were in a formal drawing room and Trevelyan nowhere to be seen. Owen couldn't have been prouder if she'd been a raw recruit saddling up to go into battle.

"Have you prepared your statement for the mages at the White Tower?" he drawled, turning back to his enemy. "They'll be very curious about how a British subject managed to learn magery and serve a French tyrant so well."

"You're the one who needs to plan," Trevelyan retorted. "Your few ships won't save you, not while I control the wind."

Damn. He'd hoped Trevelyan wouldn't have enough magick to control both the weather and fight a duel. The traitor had probably arranged a standing spell so that the breeze would continually keep the British Navy away from the Morthol. If so, the fastest counter would be to break his concentration. But how?

He paced, coming out onto the green and making Trevelyan turn to face him. The closer he came to the mound, the faster the dew melted from the grass and the warmer his feet became, until he was as comfortable as on an early summer day. It must be where the old magick was centered, that Emma's grandmother had spoken of.

From the corner of his eye, he watched his lady.

Emma sliced through her grandfather's bonds with her pocket-knife, which she'd hidden in her riding habit, and began to rub the circulation back into his hands.

"Never you mind me, girl!" the old warrior ordered angrily, just above a whisper. "I'll do very well now. You go see how you can help your soldier."

Owen stopped below the inner wall, the highest and thickest mass of all. Once this had been the keep, the center of the castle's life, the place to be defended above all else. Now it surveyed the greensward—with its small mound only a few paces from the keep—and the ocean beyond, with the lurking French warship.

Even as Owen looked, a great drum roll sounded across the water. Bonaparte's frigate was clearing for action, ready to support the French mage and his coterie in Trevelyan's duel.

Would the bastard use magickal weapons or nonmagickal? Mages typically shielded themselves against only magickal weapons during duels. If the French mage chose to hurl nonmagickal weapons, everyone inside the Morthol could be injured—including Emma and the General.

Trevelyan drew his saber and tossed his sword belt aside. Owen did likewise, sending his into the colonnade near the General. They began to circle, gauging each other and their surroundings for every possible advantage.

Coolness washed over Owen, the old calm he'd known before so many battles as a dragoon.

His signet was light on his finger and no hindrance at all to his sword grip. Gryphon wings brushed him once and were gone, a reminder that the elemental spirit was aiding him enough to remove the signet's metal as a distraction. It also meant that no gryphon would personally appear unless he could open a channel for it, which was beyond the capability of any one mage.

"If you surrender now, you'll live," Trevelyan offered, never lowering his saber's tip. His smile didn't reach his eyes. "All Bonaparte wants is surety the spell doesn't reach London."

Owen snickered, keeping one eye open for his lady. "You'll need to lie more smoothly next time, Trevelyan. Even your saber blushed at those words' falseness."

Trevelyan clenched his teeth. He must have already sent most of his magick into his sword, including the ability to discern lies—the fool.

Emma stepped out of the shadows onto the grass. It came alive, standing upright and waving softly. She took a few steps more, reaching the edge of the mound.

Fire erupted in a thin line from the ground and raced through the grass, twisting and turning around the mound in an ancient, interlocking pattern like a labyrinth. Another line leaped up and echoed its pattern around the mound's other side.

Emma gasped and stood still, the flames leaping and dancing around her feet. Yet no matter how close they came, her clothing never caught on fire.

The two flames hurtled onto the mound's crest and entwined, leaping into the sky until they towered beyond the keep's roof. They exploded into an enormous scarlet and gold cloud before evaporating into the bright blue sky, leaving behind only charred black lines through the grass.

The old general let loose a string of foreign words, probably a curse. He was free from magickal compulsions since he wasn't a magick worker.

Owen swallowed hard, his magick awestruck and frozen in the face of a far greater power.

The flames had drawn an altar at the mound's center, with a labyrinth around it like a walking spell to approach and protect its worshippers. Owen would have wagered his signet only Emma could see the spell's full details, granted that grace since she stood at its origins.

He'd also wager that the spell only protected her from magickal dangers, not nonmagickal threats.

Emma was shaking softly, but her gaze met his steadily. She blew him a kiss, and he inclined his head, the only movement permitted by the resident magick.

Trevelyan growled, the animalistic sound turning into the first words of an attack spell.

She put one foot forward onto the charred grass, then another, and another. She'd be safe now, protected by the Morthol's ancient magick.

Owen came on guard, his own battle spells long since said and committed to his saber.

Trevelyan matched him, his blade flashing in the morning light. He swung, and their blades rang against each other, singing with bloodlust. Flames ran the swords' length and flared up, scarlet against taller indigo.

Dear God in heaven, the traitor did have a blade that hungered for blood . . .

At least Owen's nonmagickal blade hadn't broken.

Their eyes met above the steel. Trevelyan's mouth quirked, he parried, and disengaged. "Surrender now, and I may let you live."

"I'll see you in hell first."

Owen reached deep within, opening himself to every drop of his mother's blood. She'd been sworn to King and Country as he was, as his blade was. He'd never used all of her magick before, but he needed to now. A whispered spell and a quick kiss of his blade sent it into the steel.

Trevelyan lunged—and he parried, flinging the other back. Thank God he'd gained strength from his mother. Would it be enough?

Boom! Boom! Boom! Wheeeeee!

They looked up to the sky. Several balls were shooting through the sky toward the castle. They crashed into the outer bailey's wall, shaking it slightly, and fell into the ocean in a shower of rock chips.

The third cannonball smashed through the wooden gallery atop the battlements and bounced into the inner bailey, stopping against a wall. The ancient timber high above burst into flames, crackling with white-hot heat and sending off clouds of smoke.

A salamander, the French national elemental spirit, couldn't have caused more damage.

The damned French were shelling the Morthol with white-hot cannonballs, a nonmagickal weapon. It could kill either him or Trevelyan—or Emma or her grandfather, as well as burn down the entire castle.

If only the British fleet were here with an admiral's guard of gryphons to catch those cannonballs!

"They'll gladly kill you to see me dead, Trevelyan," he warned, trying to distract his enemy.

"They'll love any man who brings them a chalice." Trevelyan

underlined his retort with a nasty and very skillful flurry of sword-work, which sent crimson and indigo sparks flying high—and left Owen bleeding from a cut high on his arm.

He'd suffered worse, but this was only the first wound from a sword whose cuts would grow deeper and deeper.

God willing he'd last until the adepts came.

CHAPTER ELEVEN

Emma took another step, sliding one foot into position in front of the other, moving as fast as she dared. The scarlet and gold lines were so intricate that her feet had to touch each other—and tracing them allowed her no leisure to think of anything else, such as the appalling cannonballs whizzing past. More than one had come close enough to brush her skirts, yet she'd never been so much as singed.

Waves pounded the land, roaring like hungry tigers as the tide came closer and closer.

None of that made her pulses hammer as much as the glimpses she caught of Owen. He and Trevelyan were hammering at each other with those swords, moving in clouds of fire which seemed to fight each other as much as the men did. Both men were bloody, but Owen—dear, brave Owen was bleeding from a wicked cut on his cheek. Another dreadful slice seemed to have cost him the use of his right arm. He was fighting with the dogged, stubborn brilliance of a man who has nothing left to lose.

If she managed to reach the center of the mound, where the altar stood, surely she could summon the ancient magick there and give it to him. Surely she could help him.

She simply had to ignore the pesky cannonballs, no matter whether they were flying overhead or bouncing over the grass.

Somehow Emma managed to take the next step a little faster. And the next and the next . . .

She burst out onto the open expanse of grass and faced the ancient altar.

Now what?

Owen had said it would be very easy for her to claim the land's magick, since she was attuned to it by blood.

The altar wasn't stone, so she couldn't climb onto it. Perhaps . . .

She curtsied politely to it, asking permission—of what she wasn't quite sure—to join its company, and walked into the ancient enclosure, which was barely large enough to stand in.

Something instantly shimmered in the air around her and hummed through her bones, making her ache with awareness and strength. Was it magick? The Morthol?

Aye, you have finally succeeded in reaching me, a deep voice answered. *My power is yours to command in this battle against traitors.*

Emma gulped. *My deepest thanks, sir.*

She looked out across the grassy courtyard. God help them all, the British fleet was still trying to beat its way against the wind toward the French frigate. They were so far away, even their cannonballs made little impression on the brazen foreigner.

Protecting the Realm—saving Owen and his vital message—would have to be done by those within the Morthol. Somehow.

• • •

OWEN was bleeding from a small cut on his left hand, his sword hand. He ignored it grimly, focusing on Trevelyan's dislike of having his pretty face carved up. Owen had learned a few tricks on his travels about how to do that, and the old general's sword danced through many—but not all—of Trevelyan's shields.

Unfortunately, the bastard's sword was far better at reaching him. At this rate, he'd be on his knees within the next quarter hour at the most—or five minutes, more likely. He was now using the last dregs of his own magick simply to stand upright, while barely powering his shields or flaming his saber against Trevelyan's blade.

Any gryphon was a distant memory.

Trevelyan chuckled, tasting the end's approach as well as Owen could. He was almost lasciviously watching every move Owen made, as if the most delightful act he could imagine would be delivering the coup de grâce.

Another cannonball screamed overhead and smashed a corner of the keep. Trevelyan never blinked.

"Bonaparte promised a title for the man who brings him your head," he cooed.

A shadow glided along the high stone wall behind him, unaffected by Trevelyan's shields against magickal entities.

"I had thought to do so in the classic fashion, with magick. But perhaps a more mundane solution would be better. A keg of brandy or—"

Whack! Thunder clapped in the blue sky, and the air grew still, as if gathering itself.

The shadow stumbled back toward the wall, chortling. The General had rapped Trevelyan very hard across the back of his knees, breaking his concentration—and his control over the weather.

Trevelyan stumbled and almost fell, cursing violently.

Owen took a step sideways, keeping a wary eye on the sky.

The few birds still within hearing, although beyond the cannons, squawked and dove for cover into the trees and cliffs.

With a whoosh and a roar, the wind rose up from the ground and formed itself again, hurtling out of the east toward the Morthol and sweeping the British ships toward the French frigate.

The British Navy now had the weather gauge and the advantage in battle. The French mage would have to fight them, rather than simply shell unarmed civilians.

But Trevelyan would be stronger, since he didn't have to maintain the weather spell.

Owen reached deep for more magick—and found none of his own. Beyond that were the craggy walls he'd erected at Villers-en-Cauchies so long ago, when he'd vowed never to be destroyed by linking with another mage. Block after weary block, embedded deeply in his channels . . .

"You fool! You doddering, dim-witted ass! Do you know what you just did?" Trevelyan whirled. "By all the elementals, I'll destroy you for that!"

He advanced on the old man, his sword at the ready and his shadow rising up behind him with every step.

"Hah! I'm still a King's man, foolish puppy!" The General twisted his cane, revealing a swordstick, and flourished it. "I'll prove to you who has the right to live in this Realm."

"Grandfather!" Emma cried.

Owen fumbled through his resources. He threw a fireball, that simplest of mage school tricks. A puff of smoke the size of an apple wafted from his fingers and faded within a yard.

"Owen, please, please look at me," Emma gasped, her voice breaking. "Please let me give you the magick."

He spun back to face her, and their eyes locked, equally anguished.

He didn't know if he could—but Trevelyan was only a few steps away from the old general. Owen had no strength of his own to stop him, let alone save himself or Emma.

He had to trust Emma—and his love for her.

Love, the most dangerous and overwhelming emotion of all.

He was so weak magickally that, even if she gave him all her magick, he wasn't sure he could defeat Trevelyan. But he was entirely sure he didn't want to live without his beloved Emma by his side.

A mage's lifespan depends on his loved one's strength.

Gritting his teeth, he ripped out his old walls, an effort that left him pale and sweating.

"Owen, darling," she sobbed, her breath catching on his name. She took a step toward him but stopped before she left the altar precinct.

Her grandfather yelped—and hurled another, weaker insult at Trevelyan.

The last block broke free and disappeared from Owen's magickal channels.

Emma's gaze swept over him, bathing him in trust and approval. She offered him her cupped hands, as if she was giving him a drink of water.

He smiled at the childlike imagery—and a flood of magick burst into and through him. He was everywhere and everything in the Morthol, as aware of the ocean as the winds or the grains of sand.

Owen twisted his free hand with the signet in a mage's instinctive gesture to shape magick. Sparks danced and gathered in his palm—and burst upward into a pillar of light. Wings swept past him, and an eagle shrieked a war cry overhead. The eagle called again, sending echoes through the castle and the cliffs.

A gryphon swooped down like a javelin from the sky above the keep. Its golden-furred body was half again as long as a man, and its wings filled the ancient courtyard, beating the air louder than any division's cavalry charge. Its gilded feathers were like molten gold, blindingly bright in the morning sun. Its cruel beak was large enough to rip through timbers. Its intelligent dark eyes saw everything in a single pitiless glance, which spared no one's emotion or thought.

A gryphon had come in the flesh, the elemental spirit of Britain—master of the land and the air.

A white mist whirled up around Emma from the ancient altar, marking her innocence.

Owen instinctively prostrated himself. He'd summoned a gryphon, something only a party of adepts could do. He'd never imagined his potential was so great, and he knew he'd only reached it thanks to Emma.

Trevelyan spun away from the General, his expression appalled. But he was no coward, and his sword came up, fire running along the tip.

Emma's grandfather bent his head in homage to the elemental.

The gryphon shrieked its disdain of traitors to the skies and snatched Trevelyan up in two knife-taloned forepaws. The man screamed, the sound muffled by burbling blood.

The gryphon sprang into the air, the downdraft from its wings battering the humans like a great storm. It circled high above the castle, displaying its judgment and its victim to everyone nearby— including the rapidly departing French mage in his frigate.

It swooped upon the Morthol, the ancient hammer of protection for the confluence, and tossed the traitor onto the keep's roof, removing his body from sight. It pounced upon him, ripping and tearing in a flurry of razor-sharp edges and beating wings, whose details were mercifully hidden from those on the ground. Trevelyan wailed once, a hideous cry cut abruptly short.

Owen shuddered and signed himself. He'd never seen a gryphon take physical form, rather than mist, but he'd heard the stories. Trevelyan would never again be seen in this world, nor would his saber.

He ran toward Emma's grandfather, glad the Morthol's magick was still floating within him.

The old man lay facedown on the grass, groaning.

Owen patted him down quickly and carefully, checking for broken bones or cuts. He heaved a sigh of relief when he found none and rolled him over gingerly, just as Emma joined them. "Sir? How do you feel?"

Faded blue eyes blinked at him. The General coughed and tried to sit up. "Never better, sir. I believe that when the gryphon destroyed that traitor, he removed the wounds the wretch had caused—both yours and mine."

Owen had to agree with that description. Even his unmentionables seemed to have been returned to their previous immaculate condition.

• • •

MINUTES later, all of them were seated at the small table and chairs Owen had conjured and looking out to the sea, resting until her grandfather was well enough to return home.

A talented landscape painter would have enjoyed memorializing the scene, framed as it was by the Morthol's stone walls with their gothic arches. The ocean's roar was almost hypnotically relaxing, marking high tide on the rocks below. The French frigate was now a small blur fading into the distance, while three British warships grew larger and larger as they chased her. Overhead, the gryphon amused himself with lazy spirals, his feathers flashing in the sun, while he waited for the adepts to arrive.

Emma savored the peace, like a gardener enjoying a fragile flower. Mages had their own rules and way of life. No matter how Owen wanted to manage their affair, she'd still love him. But times like this, when everything seemed simple and ordinary, she'd cherish all the more.

She had no intention of thinking about Trevelyan a moment longer than necessary. The memory of Owen's battered body and that brute charging her grandfather with a drawn sword—well, she only wished the gryphon could have shredded the traitor into far smaller pieces.

Owen flicked his fingers. Crumpets and tea settled gently onto the table, complete with all the trimmings and served on the finest china.

Emma lifted an eyebrow at the arrival of her grandfather's favorite meal, but said nothing. Owen had always preferred meats in the morning.

"Splendid, lad, splendid. How did you know the wretch destroyed my breakfast?" The old man began to load his plate, his eyes still more than keen enough to find his favorite treats.

Owen rose and marched around the table.

Emma's hand froze on the teapot.

He snapped to attention before her grandfather. "Sir, may I have your permission to speak?"

The General frowned at him, set his plate down extremely carefully, and attained a remarkably formal stance in his chair. "You may, sir."

Owen dropped to one knee.

Emma gasped.

"Sir, your granddaughter, Mrs. Sinclair, is a lady of unparalleled beauty and intelligence. She captured my heart from the moment we first met. While I have no significant personal fortune at this time, I can safely promise that she will never know want."

"Young man, are you asking for my granddaughter's hand after only five days' acquaintance?" Her grandfather's tone would have sent an artillery regiment and their guns running.

Owen didn't flinch.

"Yes, sir. Additionally, Mrs. Sinclair has unique talents which are vital to the realm in these dangerous times. She needs schooling so they can best be used."

"Not only do you want to marry her—you mean to carry her off immediately. I say, sir, you have a great deal of effrontery asking for her hand in this fashion!"

"But you see, sir, I love her with all my heart—and I believe she loves me, too." Owen's eyes met hers across the table.

Emma flew out of her chair and ran to him. She dropped to her knees beside her dear, stubborn mage, sliding her arm around his waist. Her throat was tight with tears of joy.

He hugged her close, a reassurance which somehow turned into a passionate kiss.

The General coughed very loudly.

They broke apart, blushing, and held hands.

"You have my permission, not that you need it." He sniffed, but his expression was amused. "But in exchange for my politeness, I want a church wedding for my best girl, not some Brehon Law entanglement, d'you hear, young man? She brought you back to land, and you're to stay ashore with her now."

Emma stiffened, a little nervously. Her courier of a King's Mage would stay ashore with her?

"I'll do that, sir, and gladly. For the rest of my life, I'll only go where she walks with me." Owen lifted her hand and kissed it.

His brilliant sapphire eyes met hers—and she believed him. He'd come ashore to stay, for love of her.

Queen of All She Surveys

Emma Holly

The Yama are an ancient civilization, their
origins lost in the mists before recorded history.
No one knows how much of their early technology has
been lost—or where it ended up . . .

CHAPTER ONE

The sound of clashing metal and grunting men rang out from the practice yard behind King Ravna's palace. Three bouts were in progress, each man striving against his partner with the traditional hand-to-hand fighting tools of short sword, dagger, and small bronze shield. Sweat gleamed on their hard-hewn bodies, streaked with dust where they'd dropped to the ground to escape blows. None of the men wore more than an oxhide loin protector, the heat of the seventh month being too oppressive for armor.

Given the house guards' scanty dress, it was no accident that the female servants wandered to the nearby gardens every chance they got. Their gazes turned most often to King Ravna's son, though he was far from the most beautiful of the men.

But perhaps this was not surprising. Prince Memnon impressed by other means than comeliness. He was taller than his companions by at least a hand span, his body an amazing union of thick and lean muscle. His thirty odd years rested lightly on his warrior's frame, and more than one gaze lingered on the fit of his thick loin guard. Everyone had heard the stories of his prodigious sexual appetite, now as legendary as his god-king father's.

Unlike his father, who rarely met a female he didn't fuck, Memnon's restraint was honed. Rather than engaging in nightly orgies, once a month the prince would seduce a woman and seclude her in his chamber for the day upon day it took to sate his desires. Usually his partner was a soldier's widow or a village girl. As a result, few among his father's servants had tasted him—which only whetted their interest in watching him. The smiles his exhausted lovers wore on emerging from his chambers were the stuff of myth. What would it be like, the female servants wondered, to bed a god-touched male who actually cared that they were pleasured?

They had plenty of time to speculate today. As captain of the household guard, Memnon was fighting his twelfth match of the morning. The prince liked to train new recruits himself, but even with his extraordinary strength—another legacy from his father—the strain had begun to tell in the shortening of his temper.

"Watch your eyes," he snapped at his opponent, a young man named Ashok. The boy was strong, but as inexperienced a fighter as Memnon had ever seen. "You're warning me where you're going to strike before you do."

Ashok's jaw clenched as he tried to use his peripheral vision instead.

"Better," Memnon said, easily countering another wild windmill of blows. "Now stop attacking me straight on like you've been doing. Queen Tou's troops are street fighters. They're as liable to roll between your legs and slice off your prick as come at you on two feet."

Ashok promptly dropped his weapons and lowered his head like a charging bull. The move showed courage but no sense at all. Memnon had only to sidestep and stick out his foot to have the boy face first in the dust. Another breath and Ashok's spine was under Memnon's knee, with his arm bent and twisted painfully behind his back. When Ashok cursed, Memnon gave his head a sharp and ringing rap with his small bronze shield.

"No," he said. "*Not* like that." He removed his weight from the boy, sighing. "I'm sending you back to basic training. I don't want to see you again until I'm convinced you'd last past the sounding of the horn in a real battle. And, no, I don't give a damn how much your father paid to get you in the guards."

Ashok pushed up, spitting dust as a prelude to protest, but Memnon was already striding away. His father's favorite eunuch advisor stood behind the low stone wall that circled the practice yard. A large man with skin the color of oiled teak, Paneb was someone Memnon respected warily. Despite his secretive nature, Paneb was one of very few who could steady the king's volatile passions. As he waited for the prince, his round, solemn face gave nothing of his aims away.

Memnon found himself thinking the eunuch had more self-possession than many of the guards and was probably as handy with a blade. Secure in his position, Paneb inclined his head the minimum required for deference to Memnon's status as prince and heir.

"Forgive me for interrupting your practice," he said in his smooth light voice. "Your father wishes to see you immediately."

Memnon looked down at the sweat and grime that covered him. In addition to an impulsive temper, his father had an obsession with cleanliness. One of Paneb's duties, and probably not his favorite, was scrubbing down the king's nightly partners. One dirty fingernail could stir a towering rage. That being so, he wasn't going to welcome how Memnon smelled.

"Yes," Paneb agreed, reading his expression, "but it can't be helped. News has come from Kemet."

Not good news, apparently.

Dread clenched Memnon's belly as he fell into step beside the eunuch. His father's grounds were lush: soft, Memnon sometimes thought, with avenues of towering palms and water gardens brimming with fish and birds. The clamor of fighting struck up again behind them, as Memnon's second-in-command took over the guards' training. Even when the sound diminished, Memnon didn't ask Paneb to explain. The eunuch would only evade Memnon's questions—and probably enjoy doing it.

It didn't matter anyway. Memnon could guess what the problem was.

From east to west, the Indypt River cut Southland in two, with the small town of Kemet at its strategic heart. Above Kemet, the Indypt was a silver snake, its floodwaters feeding a rich green stripe between seas of sand. Below Kemet, the sacred river split into a thousand arms that turned the delta emerald. The king who controlled Kemet could, theoretically, unite Upper and Lower Southland under his crown. Consequently, kings had been trying to launch campaigns from and for it for centuries.

Memnon could hardly blame his father for the ambition, though it was, as yet, unfulfilled. Kemet might be his, but Queen Tou gripped Upper Southland in a fist as unrelenting as the desert sun. Her troops were as hard as she was and more loyal than his father's. King Ravna's men fought for plunder and prestige. Hers fought for love. Memnon might not have much experience with that emotion, but on the battlefield he knew how powerful it was.

Fortunately, none of this showed on his face when he and Paneb reached his father's audience chamber.

The king was pacing between the huge lotus-headed columns, his strides as vigorous as his son's. His features were more refined than Memnon's, but their bodies could have passed for brothers—one draped in fine gold and linen, the other in little more than his sweaty skin. Both were stronger and more vital than other men, enough that Ravna liked to boast a god's blood ran in their veins.

Apart from the sexual madness Memnon suffered from once a month, he rarely felt divine himself. Still, he could not deny his father was unique. The Bull of the Delta had ruled for four decades, with no apparent dimming of his powers. Those who'd been with him from the beginning claimed that he had not aged. They were old men now, ready to retire. Not so King Ravna. While no one could predict how long the king would live, Memnon's friends liked to tease that he'd be too decrepit to govern by the time his father loosed his grip on the crook and flail.

Some of his friends weren't teasing, of course. Some would have been happy to see their king step down at dagger point.

"There you are," Ravna said now, his pacing having taken him toward his son. His lip curled briefly at his sweaty state, but for once he pushed off his distaste. He raked one hand through his thick black hair, the other clenching a papyrus scroll tightly enough to strangle it. "I suppose Paneb shared the news."

"Only that there is trouble at Kemet Fort."

"Trouble." His father barked out a laugh. "Kemet has fallen to the witch-whore's army, with half our men dead or captive."

"Half." The news struck him nearly breathless. "That isn't good."

"No, not good at all. Especially since our mercenaries have switched sides. I don't know how they expect she'll pay the fortune they were bleeding me for. Her treasury isn't half as flush as mine. But maybe they don't like gold anymore. Maybe they'd rather kiss the witch-whore's ass."

King Ravna sank into his throne, his knuckles whitening with fury on the gilded arms. The wood beneath the fancy surface began to crack. Memnon had never seen his father this angry, though if there was anyone he hated it was the so-called Witch of Hhamoun.

Taking what might be his only chance to plead his case, Memnon fell to one knee.

"Send me to Kemet," he begged in his humblest tone. "With a hundred hand-picked men, I can at least win back the mercenaries. Maybe even pry Queen Tou from the fort. We can't let her get a foothold. Before you know it, we'll be paying tribute to her, too."

Memnon knew his father would be reluctant. His son was a bit too popular for comfort. The army had as good as raised him after his mother's death, and following the prince was like following one of their own. To allow Memnon even the chance of such an important victory would, in some quarters, invite a coup.

Despite this, he didn't expect to be greeted with quite so leaden a silence.

"By my mother's eternal soul!" Memnon burst out, surrendering caution in his impatience. "I have never given you cause to doubt my loyalty. I serve you, Father, and the throne. I wish only to see Lower Southland regain her own."

Memnon had forgotten Paneb watched this little drama; the eunuch was as silent as a cat when he wished to be. Now he cleared his throat delicately. "My prince, you mistake your father's hesitation.

The queen is already demanding tribute, and you will indeed be traveling to Kemet."

Ravna had the decency to look embarrassed. "I'm sorry, son. It's too late for heroics, much as I appreciate your willingness. The best we can hope for now is time to lick our wounds."

"But—"

"I told you it is too late!" The throne's heavy arms splintered like kindling at the smack of his father's palms. "Tou has proposed an alliance, and I'm accepting it. The bitch may refuse to take a king as any proper woman would, but you are going to be her next husband."

For a moment, Memnon could not catch his breath. "Don't you mean her next harem slave? By the gods, Father, whatever you think of me, I am the son of six generations of rulers!"

His father simply shook the scroll he'd been strangling. "Do you want to hear what she says?" He unrolled the message with an angry snap. "'Kemet is mine,' she has the gall to tell me. 'By right of the blood I shed there when I was young. If you wish even one of your soldiers returned alive, you will pay for my blood with your own. Gods willing, the self-styled Bull of the Delta's son is not as bereft of honor as his sire.'"

"That is a childish insult, not a reason to—"

His father leaned into his face and hissed. "You will ransom these soldiers' lives, Memnon. And, who knows, maybe you will get the barren bitch with child. One way or another, our blood will sit on both thrones."

Memnon felt his spine stiffen. "It is not my nature to fight our people's battles from a bed."

"Your pride is overscrupulous, my son. Just fuck her senseless and make her yours. Better women than she have softened beneath the labors of a good hard cock."

Memnon could see a number of problems with this approach, the primary being that Tou was no breathless maid to swoon at a prince's kiss. His own partners, appreciative though they were of his sexual powers, had shown no signs of giving up their will.

"Tou is nearing her sixth decade," he objected, with little hope of success. However lowering he regarded serving the queen in bed, he couldn't deny the value of getting back their troops. "Surely no one expects her to have children now."

King Ravna's handsome features darkened, his eyes sparking with a rancor Memnon didn't understand. "You will find the witch-whore younger than you think, and as pleasing to your eyes as to that hungry cock you inherited from me. You may have to pray for strength, my son, or she will make you her slave in truth."

You know her, Memnon thought but had just enough control not to say out loud. *You call her witch because she seduced you.*

The encounter must have happened long ago. King Ravna had not been in Kemet since he'd served as the area's governor for his own father. It had been a sleepy outpost then, held but not exploited by a king who valued creature comforts above conquest.

That flaw, at least, could not be laid at his father's door.

Memnon rocked his weight off his knee and stood, uncomfortable with the knowledge that his father's hatred for his rival might have no nobler basis than being spurned.

"I will do as you ask," he said. "To save our men."

His father waved his hand in vague acknowledgment, accepting his capitulation as if it were nothing. "The men are everything, of course. Tou has agreed to allow you an honor guard for the trip. Paneb's man, Zahi, can stay on to serve you there. At least you'll have someone to watch your back in that nest of asps."

Zahi was the last man Memnon would have chosen to watch his back. Paneb's protégé was no coward, but he was as sly as the snakes he'd be protecting Memnon from.

Lords of Sky and Darkness, Memnon swore to himself, knowing there was no point in arguing. His father had made up his mind. While Memnon shared his unusual physical strength, he did not share his ruthlessness. Short of turning to patricide and tearing their realm apart, he did not see a way out of this.

And maybe the king was right. Maybe an alliance with the witch-whore was the best solution. He doubted the common people were his father's priority, but they didn't care how many thrones his father sat on; they only wanted peace.

Wanting peace himself, for as long as it could be his, Memnon bowed and withdrew. He didn't expect the words that echoed through his mind: not of asps or ransomed soldiers, but a promise that his cock would find the queen pleasing.

In spite of all he wished would never come to be, a man with needs like his could not help but be stirred by that.

CHAPTER TWO

Queen Tou stood before the narrow window in her private office, watching the sun god's disk sink like beaten copper into the sand. A woman with needs like hers could only rejoice at the approach of darkness, but a mysterious restlessness held her where she was. Her harem would be waiting, hard already in anticipation of the pleasure she would bring.

How many of those beautiful men would it take to sate her desires tonight?

Her body heated at the question, a flush riding up her skin from thigh to brow. The little slave girls who sat on the floor behind her quickened their fanning.

Over the years, she'd discovered her body slaves had to be female. Boys grew into men too fast and began to want her. As slowly as Tou was aging, she didn't always notice when that happened—and it could be awkward. She was like a cat in heat, she sometimes thought, drawing all the toms to her door.

She rolled her eyes to herself. The gods had blessed her strangely on that long-ago fateful day, shaping who she was as much as what had come before.

She'd been a fifteen-year-old orphan before those divinities intervened: friendless, hopeless, cast out from her village for stealing bread. The exalted elders of her tribe had raped her first, just to make sure she understood how wrong her attempt at avoiding starvation was. Escaping into the desert had been her only choice, and she'd done it with every expectation that she would die. Instead, she'd found a chamber beneath the burning sand: the secret temple of her personal gods.

Even now, she couldn't guess why they'd chosen her.

She'd stumbled into that ink-black hollow in ignorance, hoping only for a scrap of shelter from the sun. When its walls had melted and embraced her, she'd thought she was dreaming. When it called her "goddess," she knew she was. Strange visions had speared through her, lights and colors and whirling stars. She was promised children, heirs who would guarantee that her strong blood lived on. Her mind had been sharpened, her body changed. When she crawled out, gasping, after the transformation, she'd been more than healed.

She'd been a queen-to-be, if only in her mind.

As she'd sworn, she'd built her palace around the chamber, its entrance hidden from all eyes but hers.

She'd sworn revenge as well, the final fruit of which was almost in her grasp. That coward, Ravna—"the King's Justice" he'd been called then—would pay for overseeing the violation that was done to her. He'd pay for sending the others off so he could rape her one last time himself. *Forgive me,* he'd mewled as he tore his way into her battered young body. *I cannot help myself.*

Tou was happy to help him earn forgiveness. She'd make him forfeit the one reward the gods had given him and denied her.

"Blessed by the gods," she murmured. "With everything but a child."

Truly, those who ruled human fates were more capricious than the wisest could comprehend.

"My queen," said a voice she knew and loved, one of few with the right to enter her presence unannounced.

Tou turned and smiled at Deir, her dark thoughts evaporating at the sight of the long-time master of her harem. Deir's hair hung long and silver down his broad shoulders, and she couldn't help but recall when it had been black.

Yesterday, she thought with a tinge of sadness for what the gods' blessings sometimes brought. She took Deir to bed only rarely now. Pleasuring Hhamoun's queen was a young man's game, dangerous to those who'd left the strength of their prime behind.

"Old friend." The warmth of her greeting called color into his face, a gratification she was pleased to give. "What can your adoring queen do for you?"

"Would that you did adore me," he quipped back. "I would have no need to give you my message. The men are wondering when you might visit. They heard you dismissed your council early."

"Ravna's delegation was sighted on the river this afternoon. They may make camp on the plain south of Bhamjran village, but I thought I'd wait to see if they arrived tonight."

Deir's silver eyebrows rose. "You thought you'd wait?"

Tou shifted in her sandals, aware that his skepticism was justified. As a rule, nightfall was as long as she delayed, her body's demands being too distracting after that.

"I've been waiting many years for this victory."

"Prince or not, Ravna's son will only be another man."

"Will he?" Tou stroked the golden pectoral that draped her neck. It was inlaid with a line of rubies, a match to the cuffs on her forearms and the circlet on her brow. She had dressed as a queen tonight, her finery on display. Out of nervousness, she wondered, or authority? "The stories people tell of Ravna are as wondrous as the tales they tell of me."

"Ravna is not your equal, my queen. If he were, you could not have defeated him at Kemet."

"Perhaps." Her mouth curved at the quickness of Deir's defense. She had more reasons than most to know how true wondrous tales could be.

"Ravna's son will not come tonight," the master of her harem said. "He will want to rest and present himself in good looks."

That made Tou smile again. "He is a warrior," she teased, "not a beauty like yourself. I think he will come as soon as he can, if only to get his humiliation over with."

Hurt flicked shadowlike behind Deir's eyes. Tou had forgotten he'd been a soldier once himself. She put her hand on his shoulder, meaning to soothe his pride. Before she could, one of the slave girls leaped to her feet and squealed.

"I see torches!" she cried. "Dozens and dozens coming up the avenue. They are here, your highness. Your new husband has arrived!"

Chills like schools of minnows chased along her spine, different from any she'd experienced at the arrival of previous consorts. Her body tingled with a fervor that was like a touch.

He is *only a man,* she promised herself. He would bow before her just as readily as the rest.

• • •

TO Memnon's mind, Queen Tou's palace was oddly situated, the land surrounding it too far from the Indypt's floodplain to cultivate on a useful scale. Odder yet, it wasn't built on a promontory or carved into a cliff, either of which would have been more defendable. Still, Memnon knew Tou's men controlled the wadis that led to it. He'd spotted enough of them on the sandstone ramparts, silently watching him and his guard traverse the old riverbed.

Memnon's men had touched their weapons as they walked, though none had drawn so much as an inch of blade. The prince appreciated the discipline that had demanded. To walk peaceably beneath enemy eyes had made the back of his neck crawl.

Not just enemy eyes, he reminded himself. Those eyes belonged to his captors.

The final approach to the palace was lined not with palms but with obelisks two times the height of a man. The moon spilled like water down their highly polished sides. Red granite, he thought, the color hard to discern at night. Thanks to the sharpness of the shadows, the writing that was chiseled into their surface read clear as noon. Queen Tou had quite a lot of victories to brag about. Memnon wondered how long it would take her tale of the fall of Kemet to join the rest. No doubt, his own small, humbled figure would be carved into the stone as well.

A long reflecting pool marked the end of the avenue. An easy stroll beyond that the palace complex stretched. Hhamoun was larger than Memnon expected: graceful and wide and more than a match for his father's royal precincts.

"We should wash here," Nico suggested. Memnon's second-in-command had refused to leave his prince's safety on this journey in any hands but his. "They will send people soon to meet us, and we don't want to look like this."

Memnon's jaw clenched as he gazed at the beautiful torchlit palace, where in a matter of minutes he would be transformed from prince to possession. His throat felt as rough as the fine gold sand that was coating it.

"No one bathes," he ordered, just as Paneb's pet, Zahi, bent to splash his face. "If the queen doesn't like the honest stink of soldiers, she can damn well send me back."

Nico took one look at Memnon's slitted eyes and thought better of his protest. It was a petty triumph, but for the moment it was all Memnon had.

Their escort appeared soon enough, rendering his small rebellion moot. They were led into a hippostyle courtyard lined with Tou's soldiers and told to wait. Her men stood at attention and uttered not a word, obliging Memnon's to do the same. His guard looked thoroughly unkempt from their journey up the river and across the sand. Memnon had to fight a smile for his own childishness.

And then Tou was coming up the corridor that led into the grand courtyard. Memnon was not the only of his men to jerk a bit straighter. Her form was curved to perfection, her stride as seductive as the handmaiden of a god. Memnon swallowed, his body quickening with lust in spite of himself. The queen was tall, her legs almost as long as his. Their shape was outlined by her tight white gown, the sleek, firm curves drawing the eye. Her golden sandals stopped a few steps away. Wrenching his attention from her strangely erotic toes, Memnon ran his gaze to her face.

When he reached it, his breath punched from him in an unintended gasp. She was lovely. Even up close, even lit by the strong torchlight, she was as dewy as a young maiden. Her lips were full and stained like pomegranates, her eyes black-lashed almonds of honey-brown. Her hair—and it was her hair, rather than a wig—hung past her shoulders as thick and straight as a horse's mane. If she hadn't been wearing her regalia, he'd have sworn she couldn't be the queen. She looked innocent, as impossible as that sounded, as sweet and juicy as a ripe orange.

It seemed whatever age-defying magic the gods had worked on his father, they'd also granted Tou.

"Well," she said, the unexpected richness of her drawl bringing his traitorous cock to full erection. "You must have been eager to greet us to come to us in this state."

It was a royal "us," and it reminded him he ought to be on his knees. He fell to them a little too readily for comfort and bowed his head.

She closed the distance between them, those small, curled toes of hers taunting him again. Painfully aroused, he held his breath for fear of panting. She touched his inclined head like a temple priestess laying on a blessing—except that her thumb swept gently over his sweat-streaked brow.

He was so filthy he wanted to pull away. To his surprise, when he looked up, she was licking the taste of him from her thumb.

Their eyes caught, his black to her honey. Maybe her action had startled her as well. She seemed to shudder through her whole body. He could see her nipples peaking beneath the sheerness of her linen gown, the points as red as her pouting lips. His mouth immediately went dry with a longing to suckle them. The scent of her overwhelmed him, the spicy sweetness of her arousal. His cock swelled fuller against its skin and began to throb like drums were beating inside it. Memnon could hardly believe his own reactions. With a single touch, she'd dragged him to the burning state he only experienced once a moon.

He could have pulled her to the sandstone pavers and thrust into her then and there.

"Come," she said, gesturing him to rise. The huskiness of her voice didn't calm his aching prick one bit. She turned and glanced at him inquiringly over her shoulder, clearly expecting him to follow. He actually trembled with the restraint it took not to reach for her heart-shaped ass, which looked firm enough to have his hands curling into fists. "I'm sure you want to see your soldiers safely ransomed before we move forward."

Right then, this wouldn't have been his first choice, but he had enough pride and self-preservation to pretend it was.

. . .

TOU could tell she'd surprised the prince by touching him, but no more than he'd surprised her. He was filthy, insultingly so, but he smelled like paradise come to earth—a combination of sand and man and Medell oranges. Between her thighs she was wet and clenched, as desperate for possession as she'd ever been.

Considering how the gods had blessed her, that was desperate indeed.

When she'd sucked the taste of him from her thumb, a concussion like a chisel's strike had bolted through the pearl of her pleasure.

The reaction set her off balance. She hadn't been able to look away from him, to stop drinking him in like she was parched. He was a big man, solid and muscular. His black hair was soldier-short, not quite long enough to tie back. Even on his knees, he gave the impression of being poised to attack. He didn't have his father's face, which relieved her more than it should have. Prince Memnon's features were rougher, more masculine. His eyes were nearly black, his mouth a hard, thin slash of bad temper. It made her want to kiss it until it relaxed.

Hardly an appropriate wish for a woman seeking revenge.

He followed behind her now, his unseen presence seeming to have weight and heat. She hoped her strides appeared less self-conscious than they felt, despite which she couldn't help glancing back at him.

Disconcertingly, his dark, sharp eyes were waiting for hers.

"We've kept your father's soldiers safe," she said, pretending this speech was why she'd turned. "I think you'll be satisfied with their condition."

Since their transfer from Kemet, the captives had been housed in a tent prison on her grounds. They'd been treated fairly: their wounds attended, their stomachs filled. While no doubt unhappy with their situation, all were hale.

Her prediction notwithstanding, Prince Memnon seemed less than satisfied when they were led out for his inspection. "This is all of them?"

Tou studied the storm gathering on his brow. "My men fight to kill. You are lucky there are this many."

"You told my father there were only twenty?"

Oho, she thought, sensing a rift between sire and son. "I did," she said. "But perhaps you think he sold you too cheaply?"

His slash of a mouth flattened even more, but then he shook himself. "My freedom is worth whatever my father says it is."

Tou allowed herself a quiet laugh. Prince Memnon didn't like that at all, though he tried to hide how her amusement chafed. For the first time, she realized just how entertaining having her newest husband at her mercy was going to be.

CHAPTER THREE

Memnon stood alone in the chambers that would be his home for the foreseeable future. The space was large, even luxurious, with a separate room for Zahi and a door that opened onto the harem's enclosed courtyard. Sadly, to him the rooms were little better than a prison. He was Tou's husband now, sworn to honor and obey her according to the terms his father had agreed upon.

Memnon's farewells with Nico had been bitter. His second-in-command had wept—angrily, it was true, but the tears could not be denied.

"Your father is a toad's butthole to sell you to that whore this way," he had said. "We fought Queen Tou, lost friends to her in campaigns."

"The chance of capture is a soldier's lot."

"Not like this, it isn't!" Knowing royal walls tended to have ears, Nico dropped his voice. "If ever you wish to supplant that bastard, *ever*, I am your man."

"Peace, old friend. I don't think your looks will be improved by losing your head."

"Mem, your father left Zahi to guard you instead of me. That slinking cat is about as trustworthy as a crocodile."

Memnon agreed, but tried to make light of it. "At least the queen is pretty. Certain aspects of my servitude won't be burdensome."

Nico snorted at that, reluctant to be soothed but understanding Memnon wanted to put the best face he could on this. "If anyone can win that bitch's heart, it's you. You're twice the man your father is."

"That being so," Memnon said with a grin, "you can leave me with an easy spirit."

The rib-cracking force of Nico's last embrace told Memnon his spirit was anything but easy. He was relieved when Nico finally left . . . until the full reality of his situation settled over him.

"Harem boy," he muttered. "And to your country's worst enemy."

"Talking to yourself already. Not a good sign."

Memnon turned toward the interruption. Two of the queen's consorts were leaning lazily on either side of his open door. One had hair the color of winter wheat, and the other's was dark as coal. It seemed the queen wasn't letting her bedmates laze around eating dates. They looked as fit as soldiers, despite being somewhat fussily attired. Though their kilts were simple, their eyes were lined with kohl and painted green with malachite. The coal-haired one had a long gold earring dangling from one lobe, its feathery, jointed leaves brushing his shoulder.

"Bit older than her highness's usual," he observed. "Don't know if you'll be able to keep up."

Memnon snorted. Keeping up was the least of his concerns. Given his response to Tou thus far, keeping himself down was likelier to be a problem.

"I say," said the wheat-haired man. "I think the queen's new consort is insulting us."

Memnon could see these two weren't going to leave him alone until he gave them reason to. With a silent sigh, he strode across the soft carpet to face them both. They straightened as he drew near, their eyes exchanging a quick look of eagerness. The look told Memnon his assumptions had been correct. "My insults aren't what you need to worry about."

"Oooh," quavered the black-haired one with the earring. "Is that a threat, little pr—"

Memnon would never know if he was about to be called a little prince or a little prick, because he cocked his arm and popped his fist into the other's nose. Not wanting to do serious damage, he pulled the punch. Nonetheless, the man—no lightweight—toppled back into the colonnade, like a door burst open by a battering ram.

Zahi ran out from his adjoining chamber at the noise.

"Stay back," Memnon ordered when the servant would have come to his defense. He kept his eyes on the second man, kneeling now beside his unconscious friend.

He bared his teeth at Memnon, a display of aggression rather than a smile. "Not good," he scolded, his eyes glittering with ire. "You broke Abram's nose, little prince, and the queen has rules about damaging her—"

Memnon sent this one flying halfway across the courtyard with a well-planted boot to the chest. That brought the others out of their rooms, more than two dozen men in all. Those housed on the upper level leaned over the ornate stone rail. To Memnon's satisfaction, none appeared interested in trying his patience.

"I could have taken him," Zahi muttered, having stepped to his master's side.

"I'm sure you could, but that wouldn't have accomplished what my taking them did—or didn't you learn that sort of thing while you were playing Paneb's shadow?"

"Your father's eunuch wasn't lord of me." Zahi sniffed haughtily, at which the prince could only shake his head. Zahi's lack of respect for his former master could hardly hearten his present one.

The man he'd punched—Abram, the other had called him—was beginning to come around. He sat up with the help of two others, the back of his hand pressed to the blood dripping from his nose.

"Hell," he said, his gaze on Memnon. "That fist of yours must be made of iron."

Since he sounded reluctantly admiring, Memnon inclined his head.

Naturally, the queen chose then to enter the zenana. She took in the scene with a single glance. "Oh, very nice," she said, her sarcasm plain. "What a fine welcome you boys give." She pinned one of the men with her honeyed eyes. "Where was Deir while this was going on?"

"Otherwise engaged?" the man answered nervously.

"Otherwise engaged, my ass," she said under her breath. But whoever Deir was, his transgressions weren't her priority. Memnon tensed as she came to him, his cock giving a warning twitch. He could smell her again, could see the silken luminosity of her skin. Her pupils swelled slightly larger when she stopped before him, as if she were fighting attraction, too.

That suspicion lifted his kilt considerably.

"You know they were testing you," she said. "They wanted you to lose control."

Memnon crossed his arms, willing her gaze to remain on his. If she looked down, his reaction would be difficult to miss. "I wouldn't call what I did losing control. I'd call it establishing order."

"Establishing order is my master of harem's job."

"Perhaps when he isn't 'otherwise engaged,' I'll let him handle it."

He'd hit the target with his guess. Queen Tou's beautiful eyes narrowed, but Memnon gave her his blandest face. Though his pulse was racing like a stallion scenting a mare, he didn't have to let her know that.

"Call the physician," she ordered the others without turning her head. "Have him splint Abram's nose. Joseph, you may escort this one to my room after you've cleaned the stink off him. I'll choose the rest of tonight's companions when he's gone."

"Your highness!" said Abram's wheat-haired friend. "You can't mean to favor this one after what he did."

Joseph couldn't see the darkness underlying Queen Tou's smile, but Memnon had all too good a view of it. He was pretty sure showing him favor wasn't what she had in mind.

"I believe my newest husband will enjoy a lesson in whose *order* we follow around here."

Joseph sucked a breath of sudden understanding. "You think he'd enjoy your special accommodations, your highness?"

Her dangerous grin broadened, her eyes never leaving his. Memnon fought a shiver that wasn't dread. "Oh, yes, Joseph, I believe the prince will enjoy them inordinately."

. . .

HHAMOUN'S queen knew a thing or two about torturing men. Joseph and three others escorted Memnon to a bathing room where he was doused repeatedly in water and then stripped while he stood spluttering. From there, he was led down stairs and through twisting, narrow hallways to the queen's bedchamber.

Ironically, her room was more prisonlike than his. Though large enough to host a banquet, it was located underground with thick stone walls and no windows. Beautiful furniture and carpets softened the fortresslike impression, but nothing could hide the fact that Tou lived like a ruler with enemies.

Her "special accommodations" proved to be a set of leather wrist and ankle cuffs that were anchored to the granite wall. They were soft from many uses, though he doubted they'd held anyone who could have broken free as easily as he could. Since the restraints provided an excellent view of Tou's capacious bed, he had no trouble guessing why he was being strapped into them.

To make matters worse, his escorts found it hilarious that he was erect, the dousing having failed to discourage him. Memnon gritted his teeth and ignored their words. It was a quirk of his makeup that when he grew particularly aroused, his erection would not subside until he came—and sometimes not until he came many times.

"Oh, you are in for it," Joseph laughed, giving his glans a flick with his fingers that stung too much to be playful. "I wouldn't want to be in your sandals tonight."

Knowing he could have fought off twice their number did not improve Memnon's mood. He'd made an agreement. Short of letting the queen's harem think him an easy mark, he was honor bound to adhere to it. If that meant watching the queen fuck everyone in the room but him, he'd simply have to live with it.

Of course, it didn't help that his cock jerked like a dog the moment Tou walked in. Maybe she was a witch, as his father claimed.

Or maybe—he squirmed in his involuntary spread-eagle pose—maybe she was exactly the sort of woman his god-touched body had been craving.

When she saw him, she widened her eyes at his large erection but made no comment, turning instead to the partners she had chosen. There were five in all, and—like him—they were all naked and aroused. They seemed accustomed to the exposure, but no doubt men in their position had a lot of practice relieving their needs in front of a crowd.

Memnon had never done so, not even with close friends. The nature of his sexual drive was too different, too intense and extravagant. In contrast to his father, Memnon disliked drawing attention to the ways in which he wasn't an ordinary man.

Tou didn't know it, but she couldn't have chosen a better way to punish him.

She lined up her partners, one of whom was the wheat-haired Joseph, on five low stools facing him. Each man grimaced as he sat, their stones being tender from the rigid state of their cocks. Memnon was impressed in spite of himself. The queen hadn't touched them, and they were all so swollen they were shaking. Either making love to Tou was an event worth trembling over, or they didn't get the chance to do it often.

That possibility troubled him; sex was a necessity to a man like him. He wasn't certain what he'd do if he wasn't going to be well used.

"Watch him," the queen said to Joseph, who was last in line on the wooden stools. "If Prince Memnon closes his eyes even for an instant, I want to know."

And then she turned to him herself and unwrapped her gown.

The sheer pleated linen hadn't hidden much, but as she stood there in nothing but her golden jewelry, hers was a beauty bright enough to blind. A sound he didn't mean to make broke in his throat. Her breasts, her curving belly, her exquisitely endless legs, caused his cock to stiffen as if he hadn't spilled in years. When he spied the sheen of aroused moisture on her inner thighs, he almost did close his eyes. To his shock, the thought of not seeing her love-liness was more painful.

Perhaps sensing her advantage, she touched her breast, one fin-gertip lightly circling the jewel-tight peak. Memnon swallowed with a mouth gone as dry as the sands of the Vharzovhin.

"You won't be broken," she said softly. "That's not my way. But you will learn the price of failing to respect what's mine."

"I understand," he said hoarsely, though he knew he couldn't have acted any differently than he had. He wasn't like Nico. He didn't automatically think of Tou as the enemy. She was simply the other side. But that didn't mean he would let anyone think of him as less than he was. Being a prince was more than a role he'd been born into.

"Please," said one of the men behind her, pulling Tou's eyes from the hot lock they had on his. "Let us enjoy each other now."

She didn't scold him for his impatience, perhaps because she shared it herself. Memnon's heart thundered in his chest as she spread her legs around the first man's lap, gripped his muscular shoulders, and lowered herself onto his erection without more ado.

The man cried out as if she'd stabbed him with ecstasy.

"Wait," she ordered, her head falling back with her own plea-sure, her thick, black hair sweeping her spine. "You don't come until I tell you to."

The man groaned but obeyed her, his hands roving her back and hips with a freedom Memnon couldn't help but envy. She brought herself off twice before she gave the man permission to go over, then repeated the process with the other four.

The roll of her hips on them mesmerized him, the graceful tens-ing of her muscles. Each man received a slightly different speed and motion—his personal preference, perhaps—though none were treated with what Memnon would have called gentleness.

The queen needed these releases, every one of them. With each low moan she uttered, the remaining men grew more excited. Evi-dently, being ridden by their queen was extraordinarily enjoyable. When she at last reached Joseph, the man's breath sobbed from him with his thrusts, his knuckles white where they clamped her hips.

He held on for three of the queen's orgasms, some proof of superiority, Memnon supposed. The restraint cost him. When he came, it was with a scream that stood the hairs on Memnon's skin on end.

Despite the strength of his needs, he had never in his life made a sound like that.

But Tou must have inspired such accolades many times. She patted Joseph's cheek and lifted from his body. His penis sagged like a bladder with the air let out.

"You may go," she said to the men. "My thanks to all of you for your care."

They murmured their thanks as they filed somewhat shakily from her room. One of them stumbled as he bent to kiss her hand. Tou had to catch his elbow to steady him.

"Rest," she said with a gentleness that took Memnon by surprise. "You'll want to be strong before you visit me again."

"The gods make it soon," the man replied fervently.

And then he and Tou were alone. Though Memnon doubted she was going to relieve his frustration, their solitude aroused him more than he'd thought possible. The chill of the granite wall he was bound to didn't ease the fire. His skin burned with arousal, his cock a steady, throbbing ache. He realized he'd been straining against the leather cuffs. He had to will his legs and arms to relax before he ripped the bolts from the wall.

Tou gave him time to draw one full breath before she ran her eyes to his groin and smiled. Memnon knew how large he could get, how stiff and reddened by desire, but seeing himself in her eyes was enough to kick his pulse faster.

"You," she purred, "are a better audience than I'd hoped."

"You put on a lovely show, your highness."

She stepped to him, those long, muscled thighs of hers shining with her consorts' seed. The sight made him want to supplant every drop of it with his own. When she touched one finger to his breastbone, it was hard to breathe.

"So polite," she murmured, drawing that spot of fire a few inches up and down. "I wonder if you realize you're mine now, that you'll get no pleasure until I say."

She was testing him, just as her consorts had.

"I'm not too proud to use my own hand," he said as calmly as he could.

"Aren't you?" Her eyes slanted, catlike, with her broadened smile. Both her hands slid up his upraised arms, until she wove her fingers and his together. The grip felt righter than it should have, strangely comforting. Her breasts brushed his chest, warm and silky, the rasp of her hardened nipples forcing a shiver from his tense muscles. "I suppose you haven't heard that my men have forsworn self-pleasuring as a point of honor. Naturally, you must decide for yourself, but if you're the only one who indulges, you'll lose the status you broke Abram's nose to get."

She was on her toes, her mouth hovering an inch from his, her breath as sweet and enticing as the rest of her. Memnon didn't have room enough to lick his lips without touching hers.

"You enjoy their suffering," he said hoarsely. "You like knowing no one but you can relieve them."

"I am a queen. What else would I like? But you, Prince Memnon—" She wriggled agonizingly on his front, her belly whispering over his erection. "Tales of you reach us all the way in Hhamoun. They say you only take a woman once a month, but that you fuck her so long and hard she can scarcely walk when you're done with her."

"You mean like that man who nearly fell to his knees tonight?"

"It's not a complaint, prince. As you may have noted, I value men with strong appetites." She tilted her head to look down his body, to where his cock had begun to weep with longing. Even for him, the flow felt unnaturally copious. "By all appearances, you could be taking women every night. So I'm wondering what your self-control is meant to prove. Perhaps that the son is different from the father?"

The queen seemed to know there was no appropriate response to this. Rather than wait for one, she released his hands, her fingertips skimming the reverse course down his arms. His nerves seemed to have doubled in sensitivity. He shivered again, violently.

Her hands were sweeping down his ribs, toward the muscles of his belly and the tower of pain his prick had become. He had to moan when she clasped him, had to jerk his hips in her too-gentle hold. His balls felt as if they were about to burst with frustration.

"Tell me, prince." Her tongue came out to draw a line of wetness up his chin. "How strong are your needs tonight?"

The tightness of his throat strangled the answer, but he got it out. "You can see how strong they are for yourself."

"But I so want you to tell me."

She licked her tongue over his upper lip, teasing the tip for an instant inside his mouth. She was breathing more unevenly than she had for her men, and that—more than any of her tricks— made him speak honestly.

"I want you very badly, but my desires aren't due to peak for another week."

Her eyes darkened. "That I would like to see."

"You're bound to, whether you pleasure me tonight or not."

She pushed back from him, her laugh of disbelief husky. "You honestly think I'll pleasure you tonight?"

"I think you might. You've had five men already, but you look aroused enough to have had none."

She laughed again and ran her fingers back through her hair. What she didn't do was walk away, and that had his lips curving.

"You'd only need me," he said, knowing a bit about torture himself. "Only me, and you'd be satisfied for quite some time."

. . .

TOU shuddered without meaning to. Was it true, or was this son of her enemy simply arrogant? He was right about her feeling as if she'd had no pleasure, but that was neither here nor there. Men were her slaves, not the other way around.

If she wanted him to know that, she was going to have to control herself. She moved back to him, spread her hands on his broad, warm chest, and leaned in.

"Hold your seed," she said, "and I'll give you a chance to prove what you say."

"Hold my—" He broke off with a gasp as she knelt before him, her mouth breathing fire across his pounding groin. "Lords of Sky and—"

When she took him in her mouth, he groaned, thickly, loudly, with a greedy forward thrust of his hips. Tou could not mind his lack of discipline. He was hot and silky—and larger than she could take whole. Groaning a bit herself, she cupped the weight of his balls in one hand and wrapped the other around his root.

Cream welled inside her when she realized her fingers would not quite meet.

Oh, she was enjoying this! He tasted better than any man she'd had in her mouth, and in all her decades there had been quite a few. It was as if some aphrodisiac were running from his slit. She was hot and achy, dripping with more than her lovers' seed. Despite the many climaxes she'd enjoyed, she wanted Memnon's seed inside her, wanted his long, hard thickness pumping deep and fast. She dragged her tongue across his seeping tip and discovered she was so excited she had to gasp for air.

The momentary pause cleared her head. She narrowed her gaze at him. "What is this spicy, burning fluid that flows from you?"

His knees shifted back and forth, reluctant evidence of his eagerness to continue. "I don't know, my queen. No other woman has mentioned it. Perhaps only you call it forth from me."

He was a flatterer, but possibly an honest one. Chances were he was as god-touched as she—which didn't mean she had to like this heightening of her needs. She took consolation in the fact that his needs seemed demanding, too. The iron screws that held his cuffs to the wall rattled loudly as he tried to lurch back into her mouth.

"How long?" he asked raggedly. "How long do you want me to hold my seed?"

But this wasn't a contest she could afford to let him win, no matter how the ache between her legs urged her to. She resumed her sucking with increased force, massaging him with both fingers and palms. His testicles were heavy—and apparently sensitive.

He began to moan, and then they were like cats singing to each other, his desire setting flame to hers. If she'd had a hand free, she would have jammed it into herself and come a hundred times.

"Oh, gods," he gasped, his shaft swelling dangerously in her mouth. "Please ease up."

Easing up was the last thing she was going to do. She took more of him, nearly all of him, her saliva running down his skin. Her throat was burning but not with pain. She squeezed his balls and that sweet, spicy juice of his shot across her tongue.

More, she thought, lost to reason and swallowing. Her sex constricted so dramatically she almost came.

"It burns," he panted. "Itches. I can't— Oh, gods, go faster."

She gave him what he asked for, all the speed, all the pressure, all the flicking, sucking, cleverness the gods had made her lips and tongue capable of.

He cried out and shoved deeper, exploding with a force that took her by surprise. Those heavy balls must have been stuffed with seed. She had to pull him out, had to finish him with the wrap and rub of her strong fingers.

He groaned at the last hard spurt, sagging against his bonds as if she'd sapped his strength.

Tou had a little trouble getting to her feet herself.

"No one's ever done that to me," he said once they were face-to-face. "No one's ever emptied me out like that."

Tou touched his lower lip, which was bruised where he'd bitten it. His honesty surprised her as much as his climax had. And then he broke into a grin, the expression transforming his hard soldier's face. He looked so boyishly pleased with himself—and so ready to be pleased with her that, for a heartbeat, she wished they weren't enemies.

That was enough to bring her guard up again. This man was not her friend. This man was the means to her revenge, meant to be humbled by her seductive power. Recalled to herself, she ran both thumbs across his smiling mouth.

"I want you to remember how I made you feel," she said. "Every night, when you lay alone in your bed and know that someone else is pleasing me."

. . .

TOU couldn't say how long she huddled in her chamber, trying to will away her uneasiness. She'd bested the prince, proved her control. She was queen of him in much more than name.

Which didn't explain why she'd left his seed spattered on her breasts.

"I burn," she whispered to hear the words. She hugged her knees and rocked on her bed. That's what he'd said while she sucked him . . . right before he'd flooded her with his orgasm.

She wondered if he'd felt what she did now. She wanted to ease herself more than she could remember wanting anything, and yet she couldn't bear the thought of any hands on her but his. Better yet, she wanted his cock inside her, his hips jolting against hers as hard as they could, his slit shooting that strange, fiery fluid into her womb.

She pressed both hands over her tortured groan, then grabbed for a robe when a polite tap sounded on her door. Anyone who saw her naked would guess the state she was in.

"My queen," Deir said with a graceful bow. "I've brought your nightly cup of wine."

Tou tightened the wrap of the silk around her and composed her face. This was a tradition of theirs. She should have been expecting him.

"I'm sorry I'm late," he said, setting down the tray beside her bed. "I found Prince Memnon's body slave wandering the halls. Quite the haughty cat he was to be scolded. Claimed he'd only been looking for a salve to soothe his master's wrists."

"We bound the prince and made him watch," Tou explained with a twinge of guilt and arousal. "Joseph and Abram lured him into a fight."

"Oh," said Deir, his mouth dropping in dismay. "That's why they sent me to the kitchen to check on the progress of Mohinder's farewell banquet."

"So you didn't know what they were planning?"

Her old friend offered a rueful grin. "I'm not that petty, even if I can see how fast this one makes your heart pound."

Tou gnawed her lip, stopping only when Deir noticed. "He won't be easy to control. He's had his own way too long."

Deir shrugged as if to say, what else could one expect from a prince? "I have faith in you, my queen." He set her wine cup on the little burner and dropped the spices in. While they mulled, he slanted a look at her. "Watching you and Prince Memnon makes me wish I were young and just come to you. Then again, you never looked at me like you look at him. Nor sat up sleepless over me, I suspect."

Having no response, Tou straightened the fall of silk that covered her shins. "How is Mohinder's banquet progressing?"

"Very well, though the boy is having trouble pretending he isn't elated about you setting him free."

"I expect Lady Orissa wanting to marry him has a little to do with that."

"Perhaps." Deir's eyes were gentle. "You didn't choose Mohinder very often. He may be looking forward to having his manly skills employed more than once a moon."

Tou sighed and propped her chin on her knees. "I didn't used to neglect any of my harem. I used to employ them all equally."

"Everyone matures, my queen, even you. Perhaps your body is becoming more decided in its preferences. Perhaps it's getting ready to settle on a true consort."

"I don't feel ready," she muttered ill-temperedly.

Deir leaned to her and pressed his lips softly to her hair. When she looked at him, startled by the paternal nature of the gesture, his gaze was bright with unshed tears.

Concerned, she lifted her hand, but he moved away before she could touch him.

"Drink your wine," he said, his voice as light and fond as ever. "The gods watch over your dreams."

"And yours," she murmured, though she had a feeling neither she nor Deir would sleep a wink tonight.

CHAPTER FOUR

The queen was tired, irritable, and felt as if a permanent fever had taken hold of the swollen flesh between her legs.

Other than that, Tou was perfectly fine.

"If he can go a month without taking lovers, so can I."

"My queen!" The exclamation was barely out before Deir pressed a hand over his mouth and glanced warily around. He and Tou were strolling her gardens, which were shaded, lightly at least, by her precious irrigated palms. Bromeliads climbed their trunks, riotous with bloom in this hot season. Her guards formed a loose circle around them, protecting their queen during a much-needed respite from dealing with her advisors. Their broad, sunbaked backs were what faced Tou and her oldest friend, but that didn't mean their ears had stopped working.

Though Tou trusted her men, no purpose could be served by presenting them with too great a temptation to gossip.

When Deir spoke again, it was in a barely audible undertone. "My queen, is that why you've avoided your harem these last five nights?"

"Has it been only five?" She rubbed her face and laughed weakly. "He obsesses me, Deir. This morning, I found myself tracing his name on the tiles while the slave girls gave me my bath. I'm

surprised the water didn't boil off my back." She paced to a beautiful sandstone bench but did not sit. "It's obvious the gods' blessing
has passed to him through his father's blood. If Memnon can fight
this fever, how can I do less?"

"You honestly think the tales of King Ravna's godhead are
true?" Deir wagged his head, his hair pure silver in the bright sunlight. "The gods came to you, my queen. They spoke their blessings
to you when the people of Kemet cast you out."

"I was no one special as a child, Deir, not even close. I've come
to the conclusion that the gods blessed me by chance, a chance that
might as easily have struck Memnon's sire. And, no, I don't believe
Ravna is a god, no more than I believe I'm one." The struggle that
crossed Deir's features was comical. He knew her flaws as well as
anyone. "Better you than him," was all he ended up muttering.

Tou squeezed his shoulders. "In that we agree, though at the
moment I don't think the gods care a whit for my preference."

"If it makes you feel better, I believe Prince Memnon suffers
as well."

"Do you?" she said dryly, doing her best to hide the keenness
of her interest.

"He sleeps no more than you. The others hear him pacing his
rooms at night, and he has—" Deir hesitated until she leveled her
brows at him. "He has been erect since he returned from his first
visit to your highness's room. We have given his slave permission
to go to the kitchens to get him ice from the stores, but it does not
help. One of the men—"

Deir cut his eyes away from her. "Please do not ask me which.
He meant it only as a joke. One of the men gave the prince a flask
of almond oil from Jeruvia, which the males of that country rub
on their staffs when easing their needs. Prince Memnon was so angry, he dangled the man over the upper railing by his ankles, and
said he'd do worse to any whoreson who couldn't leave him
alone."

"And you felt no need to report this?"

Deir pulled himself straighter. "It was an internal matter, between
the men. I have to let them settle some things among themselves."

"And what of the next man Memnon decides to dangle from a height?"

"I don't believe he would have dropped your consort. Prince Memnon is very strong."

"And fair?" Tou suggested. "Even in anger?"

Deir's eyes lowered. "I believe that to be true, your highness."

Tou laid her hand against the base of her throat. She was oddly breathless, her pulse thrumming in her neck as strongly as it did between her legs. The prince was suffering. He had been aroused all this time. What would that feel like? And how powerfully would he take her if she gave him the chance to now?

"Deir," she said, speaking with some effort. "I want you to ask Prince Memnon if he'd like to come to me tonight."

Deir's eyes went rounder than she'd ever seen them. "You want me to *ask*?"

"I cannot order him. It would make me look too needful."

"And who—" Deir cleared his throat. "Who else shall join him in your bed?"

Tou forced herself to meet his gaze. "No one. I shall see the prince tonight or no one at all."

Her master of the harem stared at her, then shut his mouth and bowed. "It shall be as you wish," he promised as he withdrew.

Tou rather doubted that. Her enemy's son was too independent to be fulfilling anyone's wishes.

. . .

MEMNON paced his rooms like a caged tiger. With every stride, his unholy erection bounced beneath his starched white kilt.

His cock was too hard to let him sit or sleep or even think of anything but her. The cresting of his desires had never been this bad. Worse, some of the symptoms were entirely new. For one, his anus was itching like the devil, not an erotic area for him before. For another, two glands in his neck were sore, the skin above them inflamed and pink. Spotting the swelling, Zahi had dosed him with teas from the kitchens—to no avail. Memnon would have thought he was ill, if the rest of his body hadn't been all too hale.

He didn't understand what Tou was up to. Oh, he'd told her the worst of his lust was a week away, and her avoidance suggested she meant to use that against him. But why not take any of her men? Was her abstinence some new, more devious torture?

Thinking of how aroused *she* must be almost made him sorry he'd tossed that almond oil away.

Tou had cast a spell on him. He could remember her mouth on him as if it were there now, her hands, the lightning bolts of bliss as his seed shot from him in huge, hard spurts. She'd been so strong, so skilled. Would he even have to hold back with her? Could she be the woman who'd finally take all of his passion?

Idiot, he thought, his nails scoring his palms. This wasn't some poet's romantic tale. This was politics, pure and simple. Politics and intense physical torment.

Grinding his teeth, he turned at his narrow window to follow the path he'd worn in the carpet the other way. In the last five days, he'd memorized both the pattern on the rug and the one on the pierced stonework that screened the outside window. Although he could see out, strangers weren't permitted to see in. It was forbidden to gaze upon the faces of the queen's consorts.

Despite being neglected the same as he was, his peers were keeping entertained, vying against each other in various games. The stupidest, in Memnon's opinion, involved seeing whose rigid prick could support the heaviest weights without sagging. They'd strung little lead beads on cords that they could hang over the flare of their penis heads. Memnon knew the value of fitting in, but when they'd asked if he wanted to compete, the only answer he could manage was to curl back his lip and growl.

Some of the harem dedicated their victories to the queen. They seemed sincere in this rather than resentful, and Memnon couldn't doubt they admired her. If nothing else, this week from the netherworld had taught him that.

The men were also occupied in planning a farewell banquet for a consort named Mohinder. Unbelievably enough, the queen was releasing him from his vows so he could marry a lady of the court. Memnon had to wonder if *he'd* be cut loose someday. Was that what Tou's unaccustomed absence meant? The possibility should have cheered him, but he was too obsessed with her to want freedom. He couldn't leave Hhamoun. Not until he'd had her and had her and—

The door behind him opened.

Memnon spun, fully prepared to bite Zahi's head off, but the intruder wasn't his servant.

"Forgive the interruption," Tou's master of the harem said. "The queen wishes to know if you'd like to visit her tonight."

Memnon took a moment to close his jaw. "Is this a joke? Because, let me tell you, I am not in the mood for one."

Deir pulled his shoulders back. "I am no prankster, and neither is the queen. She knows of your condition and—"

Memnon moved so fast he shocked them both. He had a grudging respect for the queen's old consort. His job wasn't easy, and he knew how to hold the reins without choking his men. Nonetheless, Memnon's hand was around Deir's neck and slamming him into the wall far sooner than he could think better of doing it.

"She knows?" he growled as he lifted Deir off his feet. "You told her what she's done to me? You think I need her mercy?"

Deir had too much dignity to kick or struggle, though his face was quickly going red. "Prince Memnon," he said, his tone as cool as the ice he'd given Zahi permission to obtain for him. "Please release my neck. It is my job to keep the queen apprised of all her men's well-being. As for mercy, if the queen chooses to honor you with hers, I would advise you to accept. Queens possess no less pride than princes and, should you refuse, the offer may not be extended again."

Memnon's hand would not release the man right away. He blew out one breath and drew in another before his fingers would relax.

"Sorry," he mumbled, massaging his cramped knuckles. "My temper isn't what it ought to be."

Deir nodded curtly, leaving the red marks on his neck untouched—which shamed Memnon even more. "What answer do you wish me to relay?"

Memnon turned away from him. "I can't."

"Pardon, prince, but it seems quite obvious you can."

Memnon's laugh was as hoarse as Deir's throat must have been. His readiness was a bit difficult to hide. "Oh, I'd like to accept the queen's invitation, as anyone with eyes can see. I promise you, though, if I have to watch her take four men besides me, I'm going to rip their fucking hearts out of their chests. But, please, feel free to rephrase that when you relay my regrets."

He'd turned back to give his answer, in time to see a look he couldn't read come over the master of the harem's face. The look might have been part envy, but that wasn't all it was.

"Prince Memnon," Deir said, the softness of his voice close enough to pity that the prince's hands fisted. "I fear I wasn't clear. The queen's invitation was for you alone. She does not wish to see the other men tonight."

His body's response was galvanic, a flood of prickling heat huge enough to drown. She was inviting him and not the others? His toes curled into the silk-wool rug, his cock jerking so forcefully it felt ready to levitate. "You're sure. You didn't misunderstand what she meant."

"The queen's exact words were, 'I shall see the prince tonight or no one at all.'"

That was almost worse than before. His eyes stung with an emotion this woman shouldn't have been able to inspire in him. Embarrassed, he blinked blindly at the screened window.

"I'll need to . . . to bathe and—" He spread his hands helplessly. He wanted to present himself in a more civilized fashion than he had when he arrived, something he wasn't used to worrying about. He was clean, yes, but he'd never doubted he could please a female just as he was.

Again, Deir spoke too gently. "You have time to prepare yourself. The queen will not expect you until sunset."

It took all Memnon's strength not to demand how many hours away that was.

• • •

THE queen was nervous. She knew she didn't look her best, though her worst wasn't anything most men would complain about. They might not even notice the shadows lack of sleep had drawn beneath her eyes.

She donned her best jewelry, then took it off. Memnon wouldn't care about that. He was more warrior than prince from what she'd observed.

My warrior. My lovely, angry-mouthed warrior.

She snapped herself out of her reverie with a curse. What exactly did she think this night was going to be?

And then he was there. She recognized his footfall, his delicious scent. She couldn't turn. The lamps she'd lit and set on every surface did not burn more brightly than her soul.

Her heart felt ready to burst open so he could walk in.

"My queen," he said, the sound so wonderfully broken and breathless she had no choice but to close her eyes.

He came to her, not waiting for permission, simply walking to her as any man might to a woman who wanted him. He brushed her hair around her shoulder onto her breast, then kissed the back of her neck. His hands slid gently up and down her arms.

"What have you done to me," he whispered, "to make me tremble like a virgin boy?"

He undid her. All her guards. All her vengefulness. She felt him tremble, and she let her history dissolve.

She turned in his hold and met his waiting eyes. "I've done nothing you haven't done to me."

He groaned, and an ache as deep as the sound blossomed in her core. "I'm on fire for you, Tou." He shook her, as if only that could make her believe his words. "I can't be kind to you. I can't be gentle."

"I don't want you to."

"Tou—"

"No." She pushed away from him, searching the room for a suitable demonstration tool. A sturdy bronze walking stick hung on one wall, a gift from the chief of a southern tribe. She lifted it, showed him, then bent it with barely an effort into a loop.

"Gods," he breathed.

"You could do the same," she said, tossing it away with a clang. "I know no one chained you to that wall the other night but you. Neither of us has to be careful with the other, because neither of us is going to break."

"We heard stories . . . I wondered . . ."

"You hoped."

His eyes looked black when they fastened on hers again. "I hoped. I didn't know I was doing it, but I hoped."

How could she resist when he answered so honestly? She slid her arms around his warm, strong neck. Something made him wince, a chafed looking redness on either side. He swallowed, licked his lips, and she couldn't care enough to ask what had caused it.

"Will you kiss me then?" she asked. "Or shall I do the—"

He crashed his mouth down and silenced her. His taste flooded her, the same sweet, drugging spice that had flowed from his cock when she'd suckled him. The effect was even stronger with the second taste. Her head spun as his tongue drove deep. He clutched her to him with arms of iron, making a small pained sound, as if the kiss itself was a dire relief. She had seconds to feel the hugeness of his erection before he tore her gown from her. He removed his kilt from himself just as violently.

She flung herself back against his heat, still kissing him wildly. His naked body was perfect beneath her hands, every muscle balanced, every inch of skin smooth and tanned. His hindquarters had to be squeezed, his shoulders stroked and admired. She climbed him with one leg, her mons on fire to rub against him. His cock was a tower of hardness between its lips, shuddering with his heartbeat, welling up with her new favorite wine. Her sexual channel closed convulsively on itself.

"Inside me," she cried, panicked that he would not get there soon enough.

But his haste was as great as hers. He lifted her, speared her, in and in and *in* with that smooth, thick flesh. For a moment, she thought he might be too much; he stretched her so. In the end, though, they fit together like they'd been born to it. He groaned when her legs wrapped around him with all their strength. Fluid shot inside her—not seed, for he hardened even more as it came. It burned like his kiss did, overflowing her pussy, making its tissues itch and swell until she cried out.

When she ground her hips against him, it just increased.

He must have felt the same torment, because he tore away to gulp for air.

"I don't know . . . what's happening to me," he panted. "I don't know what my body's doing."

She didn't either, but she couldn't speak. She grabbed his shoulder-length hair and pulled him back to kiss her again. He gave in to it, gave in to her. He was making noises like he couldn't comprehend how good this felt. Maddened for more, they fell together onto her bed.

"Fuck me," she said, the need for friction on that itching driving her mad. "Gods, do it now."

He did it in long, hard-driving strokes that drew her pleasure from her in keening wails. A dozen were enough to fling her over. She came with a cry she could not hold back, the orgasm clamping down on her like a fist.

"More," she gasped even as she felt him explode. She groaned her dismay, her neck arching up with continued lust. It was all she could do not to pierce his back with her fingernails.

"It's all right," he said, catching his breath and starting up again. "I need more, too."

He did need more. He was grunting with the astounding force of his thrusts, using all his might to get deep inside. The fucking was so good, so hard, like nothing any man had ever done to her. His speed was inhuman, his narrow hips practically a blur. As caught up as she was, he nipped the muscle of her shoulder and sent her over again.

The itch became a pleasure of rare brilliance.

"I'm letting go," he warned. "I'm letting go and giving you all of it."

He pushed her knee up and spread her wider. She couldn't restrain herself, but thankfully neither could he. They were animals, snarling out their enjoyment and clawing each other's backs. She smelled his blood and her own. When the bed collapsed beneath his exertions, all she did was cling harder. She came too many times to count, and he joined her no less than six.

He pulled out, once, long enough to kiss a burning path down her front, long enough to take a firm hold on her thighs, wrest them over his shoulders, and suck her where she felt it most. Her bud of pleasure felt three times its normal size, and his tongue was as swift and forceful as the rest of him.

She screamed at the intensity of that release.

A heartbeat after she spasmed, he had her on his cock again, over his lap and riding him as fast and hard as he could pull her down.

None of these gyrations seemed to ease his need. He emptied into her a seventh time, his hips holding high and hard, after which he finally wrenched himself away from her.

The loss was so sudden and unexpected, Tou had to cup herself between the legs. He, however, did not see that.

"I'm sorry," he said, rolling onto his back with his arm flung across his eyes. "I can't make myself stop. I've never wanted anyone this badly."

"Shh." She stroked his heaving chest, wondering how best to coax him back. He moaned when she kissed his nipples, and louder when she bent to lick a line up his cock. He had not softened, for which she could only be glad. She was hungry still, the throb as strong as ever between her thighs. "I'm not like your other women, Memnon. You can't want this too much for me."

"Tou." His buttocks tightened as she swept her tongue around his tip. "I need—Tou, do you have oil?"

She lifted her head, her hand gripping the thick root of him. Something more was wrong than his ill-placed concern for her. His legs scissored restlessly on the sheets, his face flushed from more than arousal or exertion.

"What is it?" she asked. "What do you wish?"

The flags in his cheeks darkened. "I itch . . . *back there*. I don't think I can take not being rubbed much longer."

She laughed, touched by his delicate choice of words. "There's no need to be shy with me. I've seen everything—more than once."

Her words seemed to arouse him. He squirmed again, more intensely. "You could use a dildo if you don't want to touch me. I just . . . need something."

She kissed his hip and pushed herself from the ruins of the bed, smiling. If he was itching the way she had, she understood perfectly. "I'll be right back, and don't you worry about what I do or don't want to touch."

• • •

HE'D gone to some paradise for the sexually insane. He could hardly endure lying there, waiting, while she searched through a cabinet. When she found the oil, she spun the bottle in the air and grinned at him.

"Roll over," she said, catching the stoppered flask neatly. "I want you on that pretty belly and cock of yours."

"Tou—"

"You will obey me. I am your queen."

He could not match her humor. His skin felt like tiny lightning bolts were streaking over it. He rolled over, careful of his extremely swollen parts. Though he was leery of what she intended, his eagerness would not allow him to call a halt.

She showed no signs of second thoughts. She dripped warm oil between his buttocks, rubbing it into his muscles with those powerful hands of hers. He moaned her name, then simply gasped. Two of her long fingers were sliding into him.

He'd never been stroked there, and the pleasure was shattering, strong tingles of sensation reaching into him more deeply than mere fingers could.

"Relax," she coaxed huskily. "There's a spot in here most men like to have caressed."

He could feel it. It was the epicenter of his torturous itch. "A little farther," he urged, then, "Oh, yes, *there*."

"You're swollen," she said as she probed the perfect, devastating spot. "More than you should be. Are you sure this doesn't hurt?"

Memnon's eyes were threatening to cross.

"It's perfect," he panted. "Perfect. Perfect. Oh, gods." His hips heaved backward, trying to impale himself harder. "Oh, gods, I need to be inside you *now*."

His eyes were hot, tearing up from the suddenly blinding lamps. He actually whimpered when she pulled her hand from him.

"I'm getting the dildo," she said. "I'll need the extra reach if you're inside me."

"I'm sorry," he said once she was back again, though he was already climbing over her. "I shouldn't be making you do this."

When she laughed, he was too crazed to take offense.

"You promised," she reminded him. "You said if I took you, I wouldn't need another man for a long, long time. Do you really think my needs are near exhausted?"

It was the perfect thing to say, the perfect thing to free him— especially since she was sliding the ivory dildo into him in synchrony with him sliding into her. Her sheath was hot enough to burn, her inner muscles rippling over him greedily. His itch increased as her cream flowed and painted him.

Despite how much he wanted to grind into motion, he couldn't quell one last worry at hurting her.

"Take me," she said, her voice breathy with desire, her fingers tightening on his hips. "However you need to. You can't want this more than I do."

He hadn't thought their lust could build, hadn't known any living being could need so much. The earth should have shaken with the force of his thrusts, and still he couldn't get enough. The way she worked the ivory phallus made him want to scream. It hit that magic spot with every motion, the pleasure of it radiating from back to front in increasing waves.

More, was all he could think. *More and more and more.*

What was happening was tied together by a dreamlike logic: his swollen glands, the fluid that had poured from his throat and cock, the heightening of their desires. Climax after climax wracked their bodies without satiating them. They were drunk on each other and starving for another sip. When the crest of his cock seemed to split open and try to reach farther, some corner of his mind could only say, *of course.*

Of course he had to bind her to him. Of course he had to lock the source of his maleness into her womb. No matter that it felt like fire was searing his penis, whatever unknown appendage was uncoiling from his glans was doing exactly what it needed to. It stretched into her, probing, reaching, each brush against her velvet sheath a small climax. The snakelike thing was jangling like one raw nerve . . . and then it found a spot inside her to snug onto that had both their eyes squeezing shut with unutterable bliss.

He'd been waiting all his life to feel this without even knowing it.

"Mem," she gasped, shuddering around him. "The gods have blessed you as strangely as they did me."

His throat was too tight to speak. He kissed her, his shaft locked deep inside her. He couldn't move, didn't want to, and neither did she. They strained closer, closer while the slender length of flesh that bound them began to vibrate like a plucked sistrum. That pleasure was so sharp, it seemed impossible for human bodies to contain.

They could not make a noise when they exploded into ecstasy; they didn't have the breath for it. Memnon's balls convulsed like they'd been slapped, propelling the last of his seed in one hot, thick rush. Tou came a second later, her amazing inner muscles sucking in every drop.

They shook long enough for the world to destroy itself and reform.

When the wild glory finished, when it melted golden and sweet, they could breathe again. Then their clinging limbs could relax. Memnon had no strength left. He dissolved on her, her hair a tangled silk pillow. He must have been heavy, but one of her hands slid to the back of his neck, limply holding him where he was. He kissed her ear, murmured her name. Sleep rolled up him in a long, inexorable wave.

I'm keeping her, he thought as it swallowed him. *From this night forward, Hhamoun's queen is mine.*

CHAPTER FIVE

Tou hated the memories of what had been done to her as a girl as much as she'd hated the acts themselves. It galled her that no matter how many decades passed, nightmares could grip her sleep in their cold, dark fist. Nightmares were all they were, but she loathed the weakness they implied. The chance that she might have one was the reason she never let her harem spend the night with her. She was their queen. If they thought her in need of comfort, much of the awe in which they held her would be undercut. She wouldn't have that. Couldn't.

Which meant she'd have to live with the dream's refusal to let go tonight.

Her body tried to shudder her out of it, but her demons kept coming. She struck at them, screamed for them to die . . . and then two big, warm hands closed on her shoulders, lifted her off the mattress, and shook her awake.

"Tou," he said. "Love, wake up."

She blinked at Memnon's worried face, cold sweat from the nightmare trickling down her back. One alabaster lamp still glowed in her belowground chamber, the one on the inlaid table nearest her bed. The rest of the room was dark enough to make the jackal-headed

Lord of Darkness feel at home. *Like a sarcophagus*, she thought, then pressed a palm to her stinging cheek.

"You slapped me," she said, amazed.

"I couldn't wake you. You were thrashing and crying out—like a soldier who returns in his mind to an old battle. Tell me, love, what battle troubles your sleep?"

That was the second time he'd called her "love" since he'd woken her. As uneasy with the endearment as she was with the dream, she pulled her knees to her chest. She was still naked, still sticky from their lovemaking. Her womb nearly purred as *those* memories flooded back. She wanted him with a strength that had another ribbon of unease uncurling in her breast.

"You may not want to hear of this particular battle."

He squeezed her knee, one more liberty to add to the rest. "Sometimes you can purge the memories by sharing them."

"Would that I could." She raked back her hair, regarding him regarding her. His rugged face was patient . . . and so confident that she was tempted to slap him. She doubted he knew the kind of viper he'd sprung from, but maybe he should.

Maybe she needed him to.

"I was born in Kemet," she said, deciding. "My parents were poor and not well liked. I don't know why, though I once heard someone call them oath breakers. When they died, no one in the village wanted to take me in."

Memnon shifted cautiously. "Many who wear a crown have humble origins. How old were you when they died?"

"Eight or so. Every meal I ate after I was orphaned was charity, and every bite came with an insult or a kick. The wives of Kemet grew more grudging as my years increased. I suppose they feared their husbands might show me mercy of another sort. I had the prettiness that comes to girls around fifteen—not much of it, but enough."

"It's hard for me to imagine you as anything but beautiful."

Tou felt compelled to turn her eyes from him. His compliment meant more to her than it should. "Beauty has its uses, but other traits are more valuable. Do you wish to hear the rest?"

If he heard the dare in her question, he pretended not to. "I do," he said simply.

"One day—It was a famine year, as I recall. The tribes of Upper Southland were not organized beneath one ruler then, and those who hadn't laid up stores did not fare well. Kemet was neither starving nor fat, but her larders were as closed to me as if she hadn't one grain of wheat to spare. I stole to live that year, whenever I dared, until at last I was caught with my hand upon a loaf of bread.

"I was dragged to the council tent, where I was given a speedy trial. The sentence was clear enough, and stealing food was a serious crime. Rightfully, the village elders should have cut off my hand, but they were men, and—as their wives had feared—they decided to show mercy. I was to be banished. If I survived, I could start anew. If not . . ."

Her voice was steady, but Memnon pressed the fingers she would have lost. "That wasn't all they did."

"No," she agreed. "It wasn't. They tied the tent flaps closed—so their wives wouldn't interrupt, I later realized. Then, to make sure I'd never be tempted to steal again, every one of them raped me. Ten men, all old enough to be my father, taught me a lesson I would not forget."

She let out her breath, lifted her gaze to hold Memnon's. His eyes shone with something stronger than pity—anger, she thought, and maybe even the knowledge that none of this had weakened her. Part of her was reluctant to tell the rest, but in truth, the rest was the only part that mattered.

"Your father watched them do it."

He flinched, a small, sharp movement, but a telling one. His hand drew back from holding hers. "My father."

"They called him the King's Justice then. He was touring the province for your grandsire. When the other men finished, Ravna sent them away. He helped me sit up, gave me a drink of water, even wiped my tears on his royal cloak. I was in shock, but I thought he would help me. He was young, and a prince, both of which I thought meant something. I lost my naïveté when he began taking me himself."

"My father raped you." His voice was rough with his reluctance to believe and his dread that it was true.

"There was no mistaking it." She twisted her mouth at the memory. "When I realized what he meant to do, I fought him hardest of all. He claimed he couldn't help himself. Mewled that it was my fault. I hear he calls me witch-whore after all these years. The encounter must have been memorable for him."

"Perhaps he secretly regrets it."

Tou had to laugh, if only bitterly. "I expect he most regrets I didn't die in my trek across the Vharzovhin."

"The gods had—"Memnon swallowed and began again. "The gods had touched him by then. If his needs were heightened as ours are now . . ."

"Have you ever raped a woman, Memnon? Ever hurt one physically?"

She had spoken softly, but he stiffened. "Of course I haven't."

"And are your needs less than his? Could they *ever* drive you to force yourself on anyone?"

She knew she'd made a mockery of his argument. He wagged his head, trying perhaps to shake out the point she'd made. When that failed, he stood and paced away from her.

"You are right," he said, finally stopping. "There is no excuse for what he did to you. I told myself that side of my father's life wasn't my business. If he treated women callously, I told myself— But such things aren't right, even if done by a god-touched king." He looked at her, his expression tightly controlled. "I will leave. You cannot find it a pleasure to be with his son."

"Can't I?" she murmured to them both. Then she shook her head almost as he'd done. Her pleasure in his company changed nothing. "Your father will fall before me. Not because I hate him, or because it would be just, but because these people I have pulled together beneath my rule have made me stronger than he is. Southland will be united, and it will be united under me. That is my destiny."

He nodded. "I can see you believe that."

"It is not a *belief*, Memnon. It is what I know. The question is, whose side will you stand on when that day comes?"

His mouth closed in a hard, thin line, the answer not so easy to make. Tou suspected the difficulty unnerved them both.

. . .

THE prince returned to the harem wing unescorted, feeling like a sandstorm had swept through his soul. Despite the turmoil of his emotions, for the first time in his life, his body was at peace. Always he had fought it, either denying it what it wanted or holding back for fear of hurting his partner. The queen had ended that—at least for now.

She can humble you any time she wants, he told himself. Denial would be twice as hard now that he'd known its opposite.

Except . . . humbling him didn't seem to be what Tou wanted. What she did want he didn't feel ready to draw conclusions about. She might be playing a deeper game than he thought.

When Memnon reached his rooms, dawn was breaking outside his single window's *jali* screen. His servant, Zahi, sat on his broad low bed, his torso decorated by the lacework of pale gold light. Catlike as ever, his weight was propped on his elbows, his long legs sprawled. He followed Memnon's entrance as intently as if his master were a long-awaited mouse.

The sight caused Memnon to regret that, with the exception of the master of the harem's chambers, none of the consorts' doors could be locked.

"What are you doing here?" he asked. "I didn't tell you to wait up for me."

Zahi stretched his toes, then sat up straighter. "The other men say the queen never keeps a partner throughout the night. In all the years of her reign, you are the first."

Memnon kicked off his sandals, turning to the washstand to splash his face. Among other things, he didn't think he liked Zahi's tone. "Are you accusing me of something?"

"Not at all, master. Merely congratulating you on your coup. I trust you both enjoyed yourselves."

"I wore her out," Memnon said flatly. "We fell asleep."

He dried his face on the towel and watched Zahi over it. Paneb's protégé was definitely fishing for something, though the servant was working to keep his expression uninformative.

"Your father hoped you'd call to the queen's affections."

Memnon snorted. "But not call to them too much, I wager."

"Do you think she's falling in love with you?"

A flash of heat ran through him. Could she be? Was that why she'd shared the damning story about his father? To win Memnon to her side? That the tale was true, he had little doubt. It fit too well with what he already knew of King Ravna.

Fearing his thoughts might show, Memnon turned away to toss the towel onto a light, carved chair. Its feet were fashioned in the shape of gazelles. "I spent one night with her, Zahi. Your apprenticeship with a eunuch no doubt prevented you from learning this, but no man is that good in bed."

Zahi's awareness of the implied insult betrayed itself in a darkening of his cheeks. "What I'm wondering," he said, his gaze narrow, "is if any woman is."

Memnon feigned a weary sigh. "If you were a bit more seasoned, you'd know a man of my experience is as unlikely of succumbing as the queen."

"Many men have fallen to her charms."

"Many men aren't me."

"You dislike her then."

"Zahi, I am true to my people and to my king—as I have always been. When you send your report to Paneb, be sure to include that."

"What report?" Zahi said sourly. "The queen's spies read every message that leaves this place."

"If you've managed to ascertain that, you've made good use of all that running back and forth to the kitchens on my behalf."

A twitch beside Zahi's left eye confirmed his guess.

"Look," Memnon said. "I can imagine why my father assigned you to me and, frankly, I don't care. I simply advise you to keep an important truth in mind. I am here, and Paneb is not. In fact, I am the only person even vaguely resembling an ally that you have in this place. You're in the lion's den now. Keep me happy, and you're liable to remain safe. Cross me . . ." He spread his hands. "Let's just say anything could happen to you, anything at all, and no one would shed a tear."

"Least of all you?" Zahi asked softly.

Memnon didn't bother to deny his conjecture. "I am a fair man. If you haven't learned that, you are no judge of character at all. And now I think you should return to your room. Your master has sleep to catch up on."

Zahi bowed to him respectfully enough, despite which Memnon did not turn his back on him until he was gone.

If he believed even half of what Tou had told him, his father—and, by association, his father's tools—had far less conscience and far less loyalty to Memnon than he had presumed.

"And what might you be?" he murmured, spotting something on his covers where Zahi's weight had rumpled them.

He picked up what turned out to be a feather. His curiosity piqued, he squinted at the screened window. The wind could not have blown this through the tiny holes in the stone. It must have been stuck to Zahi and fallen off.

Memnon turned the feather musingly in his hand. It was the same rich brown color as his father's homing hawks. Maybe Paneb's slinking cat had found a way to get a message out, after all.

• • •

FOR the next five days running, Memnon received an invitation to spend the night with Tou alone, each delivered personally by Deir. Given Memnon's last exchange with the queen, he hadn't expected to be shown this partiality. He accepted the invitations gravely for the eyes that watched. Inside, however, where none could see, he could not deny his jubilance.

Being with Tou was such a pleasure. His desires would rise whenever she was near, but they were never as difficult to satisfy as that initial time. When the first fierce rush of need was over, they were free to enjoy each other more leisurely. Tou taught him bed tricks that stole his breath, while he offered her a strength she seemed to have been longing for all her life.

Sometimes, as they waited for their well-used bodies to recover, they simply held each other and talked. They were shy with each other then, but that was sweet as well. When they laughed together, Memnon thought it felt like the sun rising.

"Tell me," she said one night as they lay together in her restored bed, her finger lightly circling his rosy glans. "What do you suppose that extra part of your manhood was?"

He grabbed her teasing finger and nipped it. "You liked that, did you?"

"I did," she said without a blush. "But I am wondering what it is for, and why it has not emerged again since that night."

He slid his knee between her silken thighs, not to rouse her—though of course it did—but simply to tangle them more intimately. "I suspect it will not emerge again until my cycle peaks. It has never done so for other women. Because it searched inside you until it found your womb, I think, perhaps, it is supposed to help make babies."

"Babies."

"I am the only child my father has, and neither you nor I have any. Perhaps this extra part provides some needed advantage."

"Does your father—" She stopped, but he understood what she meant as clearly as he understood her aversion to continuing.

"I haven't heard that his organ is different from other men's, and, no, I don't know why we wouldn't be the same. Maybe the gods are as capricious as our priests like to claim."

She grimaced, obviously ready to let this line of questioning drop. Her eyes shifted to the loll of his penis against his thigh. The length of him was relaxed but slowly thickening. She licked the pad of her thumb, cradled him in her palm, then used the wetness to rub the spot where the little whip of flesh had come out. Tonight it was no more than a faint red seam, but Memnon jerked at the sharpness of the sensation.

Tou's lips curved slightly. "I wouldn't mind having babies."

"Would you mind having them with me?"

She was a queen, and this was more than a romantic question, but it came out as hoarsely as if his heart were all it concerned. Her eyes fired gold as they rose to his. "I would love having them with you, would love *making* them with you."

Moved, he leaned to kiss her, but the hand she pressed to his breastbone caused him to pause.

"Memnon," she whispered. "A child is the only thing your father has that I do not, the only blessing the gods have given him and not me."

Something in him chilled at her words, even as his shaft jerked and began to rise. It knew how to respond to talk of children. He cupped one of her breasts and gently squeezed its curve. Her nipples were dusky, tightening with arousal. What would it be like to see his son or daughter suckling here?

"Is having a child the only use you have for me?"

She stroked his chest, the brush of her fingers enough to make his groin vibrate. When her answer came, it was throaty. "Never. I have too many uses for you to count."

She rolled herself beneath him, and his mind went blank, the submissive posture as unexpected as it was enticing. She was hot and ready—thighs spread, torso writhing—and all he could focus on was sliding into her tight, wet sheath. She met him with full strength, which drove him wilder yet. They coupled as ferociously as they had their first night, groaning out their peaks and clutching each other as if their lives depended on holding on.

The breathless aftermath was broken by Deir's arrival with the nightly wine. The master of the harem brought two cups now, his extreme politeness the only thing that suggested this change in tradition was hard for him.

"He doesn't taste your wine," Memnon commented as he sipped his own. "Don't you take precautions against poison?"

Tou's honey-brown gaze slanted at him from beneath her lashes. Like him, she seemed to be struggling with awkwardness. "No one handles those supplies but him. He keeps them locked in his room. I don't ask him to taste it first, because I wish to keep that sign of trust between us."

"He loves you," Memnon said softly. "Enough that seeing you with me is breaking his heart."

Tears sparkled without warning in her lovely eyes. "I cannot help that," she whispered. "I love him, too, but I can't help that."

He felt his own heart threaten to crack, or maybe it was just opening at long last. The possibility frightened him more than physical danger could. If Tou loved him, if none of this was about revenge . . .

Overcome, he said her name because he had to and touched her cheek because he could.

"Hold me," she said, her face hidden in his shoulder. "I want to sleep in your arms tonight."

CHAPTER SIX

The flurry of preparations reached a crescendo the night Mohinder's farewell banquet arrived.

The event was being held in the palace gardens, beneath a white silk tent to shield the royal consorts from curious eyes. Extra soldiers were ranged around it, because the queen would be attending, too. The guards stood outside the ring of torches, so as not to compromise their night vision. Out of habit, Memnon studied them. They appeared competent: alert, calm, communicating among each other with near-silent efficiency.

One caught him watching and nodded. Memnon assumed he'd been recognized from his trips to the queen's chambers. With an odd start, he realized that wasn't it at all. He'd faced this man on a battlefield. He was a captain, just like Memnon was.

Impulse had him leaving the other consorts to speak to him, which—obviously—was more of a response than the man had meant his nod to invite.

"Your highness," he said, drawing himself up stiffly. "You should go into the tent. You are not veiled."

He wasn't, and by all rights he should have been. Memnon's face wasn't his to flaunt the way this soldier's was.

"I will," he said, though for now some indefinable wrongness in the atmosphere held him where he was. He was taller than the captain by an inch or two. Thicker as well. Tou trained her soldiers lean. Memnon squinted at the black, starry sky. "It's a quiet night, and after a bloody sunset."

In spite of his discomfort at having to caution a prince, the captain grinned. "I haven't heard that old soldier's superstition since my father died."

"It is an old one." Memnon rubbed the tightened back of his neck. "Never hurts to keep a sharp eye out, though."

"Yes, sir," said the soldier, snapping out a bow he might not have meant to make. "Enjoy your evening."

Memnon took pity on his position and rejoined his fellow harem slaves.

Inside, the tent was decorated with hanging blankets and elaborate camel regalia, doubtless meant to resemble those of Mohinder's home. Memnon had learned, much to his surprise, that the departing consort hailed from Kemet and was the son of a chief. A dozen Kemish cooks had been brought in to prepare the feast, which was going to be odd from the smell of it.

Sour goat milk, Memnon thought, shuddering privately in disgust. No wonder the back of his neck was tight.

He found a seat among the heaps of cushions on the carpeted floor. Dinner would be served on the colorful drumlike tables that stood between. Abram, whose nose was plastered and healing, handed him a cup of wine.

"Better drink up," he said, lifting his own cup in salute. His single feathery earring twinkled merrily with the motion. "I know this is Mohinder's night, but I'm not sure any of us are going to choke down that meal unless we're skunked."

Memnon laughed, pleased to be welcomed in this simple male fashion. Before he could respond in kind, the sight of a number of the consorts bowing near the entrance drew his eyes away. He couldn't see her yet, but Tou must have arrived.

"And there she is," Abram murmured. "Our one and only

sweet goddess." He raised his hands, palms out, when Memnon glanced at him. "Don't mind me, prince. I'm not bitter. Best man wins and so on. We all knew she might find the other half of her heart someday. We each just hoped it would be us."

Memnon felt a flush sweep up his face, one he could not force back for all the tea in Yskut. "The queen hasn't— She and I aren't—"

Abram cut off his stammering. "Yes, she has, and, yes, you are. We see the way you look at each other. We can tell how happy she is."

As if a chain were connected to his eyes, Memnon had to look at her. She was laughing with the other consorts, kissing some on the cheeks. Tou wasn't just their queen, she was their friend—a bond he suspected few among the harem had experienced with other females. He struggled to sigh silently. She was so lovely, so brave and clever and passionate. The rest of his life would fade to paleness if he couldn't spend it with her.

Watching him, Abram chuckled into his wine. "See."

Tou turned then and spotted him. Pierced brass lamps hung from the tent poles, and her smile flashed in their golden light. Memnon's heart jolted in his chest like a lovesick boy's.

Yes, he thought. *Yes, I am.*

. . .

TO judge by the men's delighted reactions, Tou's decision to hire a nearly naked female dancing troupe to entertain them had been brilliant.

The soon-to-be-bridegroom had drunk too much to pretend not to be happy. Mohinder was on the little platform with the dancers, doing his best to imitate the snakelike undulations of their bare bodies. Tou could only smile at his antics. Lady Orissa was a good woman, a widow and head of her house. Mohinder was a softer man than Tou would have chosen to stand beside herself, but she thought the pair would suit.

And, really, if she wasn't going to take full advantage of her men, someone had to.

She wouldn't miss Mohinder, she realized. She had no feelings of possessiveness toward the boy. Nor had she missed the others while with Memnon. She was fond of her harem and enjoyed their company, but she didn't feel the need to own them anymore.

Her eyes slid to Memnon's profile. He sat beside her, tall and still, his folded leg touching hers. He smiled at Mohinder's performance, but didn't shout encouragement like the others. He was quieter in company than when he was alone with her. Tou liked what that said about his ease with her.

As if he felt her watching, his fingers closed warmly over her hand. His attention did not follow. He was too busy scanning the shadows of the room.

"You watch the dark like one of my guards."

He started at her observation and turned to her. "Sorry. Old habit."

Now that he faced her, she stroked a finger down the crease beside his mouth. Only she knew how appealing it looked when he smiled. He was serious now, his gaze holding hers as if he never meant to look away. Tou found herself wishing he never would.

"I didn't know," he said, "until tonight."

"Didn't know what?"

"That Mohinder was from Kemet. You knock me over, Tou, as surely as a catapult."

"It's only a banquet. And everyone who harmed me as a girl is dead by now."

Memnon took her face between his hands, his dark eyes glittering as if filled with stars. "Love, if what had happened to you had been done to my father, he would have burned Kemet to the ground and salted the earth."

"I wanted to," Tou admitted, her shoulders hunched in embarrassment. "For many years, I could have done just that." Then a crooked smile broke from her. "Kemet was lucky I hadn't amassed the power to do evil deeds back then."

Memnon kissed the tip of her nose. "They are lucky, but not for that reason."

What she saw deep in his eyes had both emotion and desire pooling in her body. She was ready for him in an instant, throbbing and growing wet. He must have smelled her reaction, because his nostrils flared.

"Would you mind if we left?" she asked a little breathlessly. "I'd like to be alone with you."

His hands slid to her shoulders, tightening as if they wished to hold other things.

"Yes," he said, rough as gravel. "I think that's a fine idea."

• • •

RESIGNATION knotted in Deir's chest as he watched them leave. They looked like lovers, their eyes as hungry for each other as the rest of them. He slipped from the tent himself, in no mood for celebration now that she was gone.

The corridors were silent as he sought his chambers, the harem as still as an abandoned tomb. His door was unlocked, which shouldn't have been the case, but he must have forgotten to secure it with all his other distractions. Sighing to himself, he went to prepare the tray for her wine. Maybe, tonight, he could catch her and the prince before they grew sweaty and sleepy-eyed from lovemaking.

As ever, he poured a sip into the golden cup for himself. Deir treasured Tou's trust, but he always tested it anyway. His queen didn't have to know he protected her.

He put his mouth where hers would go, just above the emerald cabochon. The wine was sweet and clear, exactly as she liked it.

One last kiss, he thought as he wiped away the residue. *One last kiss for lips that might never meet again.*

• • •

THIS had to be the sweetest kiss of Memnon's life.

Tou's arms hugged him greedily close, while he cradled her head and clamped her strong, round bottom tightly enough to lift her to her toes. They were plastered to each other, not a breath of space between them as they kissed and kissed and dared the world to make them notice it.

He was drunk on her, aroused and hot and thoroughly home.

"I love you," he murmured against her mouth, not caring how many men had said it before. He meant it. With all his heart and soul, he meant it.

Tou drew back, her eyes wide and wondering. "Mem."

He smiled and touched the lips his hunger had turned red. "I like when you call me that." He hitched her groin more perfectly to his. "It makes me hard."

She laughed softly. "Everything makes you hard. Memnon, I—"

And then Deir's knock sounded on her door.

Memnon cursed, but she touched his arm. "We were so quiet, he must have thought it was safe to knock."

They'd been quiet because their tongues had been busy with other things, because they hadn't immediately gotten naked and started thumping the furniture. Memnon told her with his eyes that she would pay for this delay. When hers sparked back at him over her shoulder, they told him she wouldn't mind.

"Just serve it cool," she said to Deir as he came in with the mulling tray. "I've had enough complicated tastes in my mouth tonight." She laughed and touched the base of her throat. "Hunger must have lent the food of Kemet savor when I was a girl. I swear, I don't remember it being that atrocious."

Some of the strain left Deir's face as he smiled at her. "It was rather unique." He knelt when he placed the tray beside her bed, a graceful, practiced motion. He lifted the wineskin to pour, then—inexplicably—set it down and stood jerkily.

"Excuse me, my queen," he said, white as chalk. "I don't feel—"

Memnon was already stepping toward him when he rushed to a corner and vomited.

"Don't touch the wine," Memnon snapped at Tou. He caught Deir's shoulder, hoping against hope, but it was too late. Some part of him had known that the moment the man went pale.

"What's wrong with him?" Tou asked, her voice as small as a girl's.

He didn't answer, and probably didn't need to. Deir was convulsing in his lap, his eyes beginning to roll. Memnon held him, able to control the violence of the spasms but not the cause. He stroked Deir's hair from his clammy brow.

"Take . . . care—" Deir managed to choke out.

"I will," Memnon soothed. "I promise."

Deir's body relaxed as suddenly as it had convulsed. His eyes were wide and staring, his chest no longer moving with his breath.

Tou let out a keening wail.

"He wouldn't," she said through the fingers of her shaking hands. "Deir wouldn't poison himself. He wouldn't poison us. He isn't a man who loves that way."

Memnon eased the former consort's body gently to the floor.

"Shh," he said, rising and going to her. "I don't think he did."

"But who could have?" Her tears slowed as she pushed back from his embrace. "Deir isn't careless. He keeps all these things locked up."

Memnon didn't have to think twice. "Zahi," he said, the answer a growl. "He wasn't at the banquet tonight."

"Your body slave?"

"My father's choice, not mine. I imagine he could get through any lock he wanted with sufficient time."

"But . . . the wine was for both of us. You must have been a target, too. Lords of Sky and Darkness, Ravna must not ever want to give up his throne."

Memnon was grateful beyond measure that she wasn't thinking what others would: that Memnon could have known what would happen and simply refused to drink.

"No," she said, reading his expression. "I know your character better than that. If you wanted to kill me, you'd do it face-to-face and stick me through the heart."

He barked out a laugh that just as quickly stilled. A prickling dread was rolling across his scalp. "Tou, this can't be all. My father had to be planning more than killing us. He'd want to press his advantage as fast and hard as he could." He squeezed his pounding temples between his palms. "If you were dead, it would throw your guards into confusion, which would be the perfect cover for an attack. He must be hoping to take Hhamoun."

"His troops would never make it inside the palace."

"But if there were someone to sneak them in . . ."

"Memnon, I don't care how clever your Zahi is. One slave can't manage all of that."

"Unless he had help. Unless he'd gotten word to his handlers how a dozen agents could be invited in by the queen herself."

Tou's mouth dropped in horror. "The Kemish cooks!"

Memnon shook his head grimly. "I think you'll find the real cooks from Kemet were intercepted and killed on their journey here. Those who prepared that banquet are my father's men."

Tou took four paces back and forth across her floor, her tears mere tracks drying on her cheeks. "We have to alert the guards. Coordinate a defense. The cooks are inside the building already . . ." Her eyes met his. "They'll have found ways to let others in. We may have to fight through the corridors."

He strode to her wall and pulled a pair of short swords and daggers from their display hooks. Tou handily caught the pair he tossed her, slinging the belt that held both around her shoulder. Decorative or not, the blades were working weapons, as worthy of respect as the chiefs who'd sent them to her as gifts.

"You used to lead your men into battle, as I recall."

She looked behind her, toward Deir's lifeless form. When her eyes returned, they burned with the cold, hard rage of the witch-whore his father feared.

"I did lead them," she said, testing the short sword against her thumb. "And I assure you, I haven't forgotten how."

. . .

HE followed her lead. She didn't have to argue, he just did it.

"These are your men," he said, running full out with her. "Your home. You know its ins and outs."

They engaged the first invaders near the kitchens. Tou's captain hadn't liked letting her risk herself, but with Memnon and his god-touched strength to guard her back, the plan was the best they had. The bulk of Tou's forces were in Kemet protecting the fort. They'd have to be cunning if they were going to win this without great losses.

"Don't kill them all," Memnon had warned her. "We want them calling for reinforcements, and we want as many as possible chasing us. They won't be able to resist. We're the targets they came here for."

She knew he was right, though it was difficult to rein in her rage over Deir.

"Back!" she cried to Memnon now, parrying the six who came hard at her.

She was glad now for the practices she'd taken with her harem men. They'd kept her reflexes sharp. More attackers joined the ones they were already fighting as she and Memnon retreated into the bowels of her lower floor. They'd seen dozens of the enemy now and had killed perhaps half of those. Memnon had predicted at least a hundred would make up the attacking force.

It's what I asked for, he'd said, *when I offered to take back Kemet.*

Her brows had risen at the smallness of the number. She was fortunate he fought for her and that the invaders weren't men he'd trained—probably because Ravna hadn't trusted them to betray his son. Tou was glad Memnon didn't have to kill friends, or watch her do so. As to that, she suspected men he'd trained would have been harder to trick than these.

Not that tricking them was all fun and games.

"Shit," he said as another group came at them at the meeting of two narrow passageways. They were back-to-back now, a pair of heroes out of a tale, circling and slashing to keep their enemies at bay. There was a bitter joy in knowing they'd defend each other to the death, in knowing she had at last found her match. Tou's muscles sang with effort, but she was not tired.

For Deir's sake, she could have slaughtered these men all night.

"I count forty," she said, jumping back to avoid the sweeping swing of a bloodied blade. It was her blood, as it happened, though the injury from which it flowed was numb.

"All right," said Memnon. "Forty will have to do. You take out the torches on the right."

Tou let out an ululating cry and ran, extinguishing the torches with the neat expedient of slicing off their heads. Memnon bolted after her, as did the attackers. They shouted excitedly, obviously believing they had their prey running scared. By the end of fifty paces, the hall was black as a cave. As one, she and Memnon increased their speed, much too fast for ordinary men to catch up.

Being blessed by the gods did have its advantages.

"Here," hissed a voice, guiding them into a side chamber.

Stone rumbled far behind them, a giant grindstone that would block the enemy's retreat.

"We're ready," said the captain of her guard.

When he opened his lamp, revealing his fresh and well-armed force, the forty bedraggled invaders skidded to a halt.

CHAPTER SEVEN

Their victory was violent and swift. King Ravna had sent two hundred men, but thanks to losing the element of surprise, that hadn't been enough. Ravna's soldiers were no match for hers. Even her harem had killed a substantial number—despite their inebriated states. The treacherous body slave, Zahi, had fallen to Abram and Joseph, a loss no one appeared to mourn.

To Tou's relief, she had wounded among her people but no slain.

Except for Deir, she thought, her grief welling up anew. He had loved her better than she'd ever loved him, and had lost his life for hers as a reward.

She pressed her hands to her eyes, willing the endless tears to ebb. Bad enough she hadn't been able to face returning to her chamber. Rather than watch her men remove the body, she'd escaped to the palace roof, now under the discreet protection of a dozen guards. In the grounds below, hundreds of torches flared, their dancing flames twinned by her long reflecting pool. Extra patrols slipped like shadows between the palms, on the lookout for more attacks. Tou didn't expect one. She was safe for the night, she judged, or as safe as any queen at war could be.

She wondered if Ravna had realized his failure to take Hhamoun would guarantee she'd be that. Maybe he hadn't cared. A man who'd try to assassinate his only son wouldn't quibble over starting up a war again.

Quiet masculine footsteps had her twisting around. It was Memnon, returned from speaking to the wounded and victorious. No one had batted an eyelash when she'd ceded that task to him. He had slipped into the role of leader as smoothly as if it were his skin. Now he gazed at her with so much understanding her heart couldn't help but turn over.

"Tou," he said, pulling her into his arms.

Though she'd been crying for what felt like hours, she broke down again.

"I'm sorry," she said between gasps for air. "I hate being weak."

"You lost your oldest friend, the only one who knew you from your early reign. If I'd lost a friend as dear as that, I'd be crying, too."

"You wouldn't be abandoning your responsibilities to someone else. You wouldn't be hiding on a roof."

He eased her face away from his warm shoulder, gently tipping up her chin. "If I weren't here to help, if you didn't trust me to stand in for you, you'd be doing everything you think you're hiding from."

She sniffed and wiped her arm across her tear-wet cheeks. "I love you," she said, trying to be steady, "but after this attack, our people are going to be more at odds than ever."

His thumbs caught the tears she'd missed. She wished she could make out his expression, but the glitter of starlight was all she read in his guarded eyes.

"Do you want me to stand at your side?"

"Of course I do."

"Then that's where I'll be. It's time for peace, Tou. Time for your people to enjoy the fruits you've won for them. Time for mine to trust their king again. Southland can be united under both of us."

"You'd go against your father?"

His laugh was like the rattle of river reeds. "I believe my father decided that question himself tonight. He never meant for me to woo you. He only wanted to use me as a Trojan horse, one he could kill when he was done with it. The thing is, I have supporters, Tou. I never courted them, but they exist. I think we could overthrow him with minimal bloodshed."

In spite of everything, her heart beat faster.

"Oh, gods," she said. "I think the idea of more fighting actually excites me."

"You are a queen," he said, and she could hear the smile in it. "A warrior. I'd be surprised if you felt otherwise. I do have one condition. Some people will expect it, but I don't want to sit on your throne. You've earned your crown, maybe more than I'll earn mine. I want us to rule as equals, each over our separate realms."

He struck her dumb. Of all the respect she'd earned, his meant the most to her. And what other man in the world would offer what he was? She had to clear her throat before she could speak. "If ever I were to take a king . . ."

"Yes." He pressed his lips to her forehead. "That I would be the king you'd choose is all I need to know."

"My harem—"

"Will live without you," he finished for her, his warmth abruptly cooled. "I will not give you a chance to crave them. That much I promise you."

It was a promise he could keep. She bit her lip against her amusement. Here was the pure male arrogance he hadn't shown before. She enjoyed it more than she cared to have him know. "My harem has served me well. They even killed for me tonight."

The growl that rumbled in his chest made her knees secretly go weak.

He lowered his head and kissed her, the delving of his tongue sufficiently explicit to have arousal welling inside her. His reaction was equally fervent, perhaps because the most primitive drive in life was pushing at them both. They'd faced death tonight, and they'd survived. Holding her tighter, he nipped her lower lip and groaned in her ear. His cock bumped thick and hard against her, rising fiercely beneath his fresh white kilt.

The way he could grow so big so quickly was a marvel she'd never weary of.

"The scent of you . . ." he murmured. His hands roamed restlessly down her back, squeezing her bottom in a brief caress. "I swear, it's enough to drive a grown man mad."

Tou nuzzled the prickly tightness of his jaw. To her, his sweat smelled as alluring as her arousal. "I smell this way because I want you, because that cock of yours is the most impressive I've ever known."

"If your guards weren't all around us, I'd remind you how impressive my cock can be."

She tipped her head to let his voracious kisses trail down her throat. His arms had locked her hips tight against him, the throb of his erection an astounding thing. She thought the ridge was as big as when he'd hit his cycle's peak a week ago.

A sticking plaster clung to her side where she'd been injured, but she wasn't feeling it now.

"The guards won't stop us," she said. "They'll understand if I can't wait."

He stared at her, a muscle ticking in his jaw. "Tou—"

"You're wet," she said, her nails digging into his bare shoulders with her need to convince him. "I can feel you dampening your kilt."

His gaze lasted one heartbeat longer, time enough for his pupils to jump larger. Then he kissed her, deep and desperate, and she knew she was about to get what she wanted.

"Here," he said, lifting her off her feet. "At least we'll go as far as here."

He carried her to the wall around the stairwell he'd come up from, pressing her spine to the plaster with a throttled moan. The sound was enough to draw a fresh rush of fluid burning from her core.

"Spread your legs," he said, already kicking her feet apart. "If they see us, they'll only think we're kissing."

Tou doubted that, but she let him gather up the front of her gown. His fingers found her cream-drenched folds and parted them: a quick, but pleasurable prelude, during which he also fumbled with the wrap of his kilt. Soon his shaft slid huge and hot between her sexual lips, rubbing, teasing, then finally tilting for the drive inside.

She gasped at the feel of him slowly filling her. Her head shook back and forth helplessly. "You're so big, Mem. Oh, gods—"

He grunted and pushed harder, his hands like iron at her hips. "Take me, Tou. Take it all."

She wriggled and spread her legs wider. "I want to wrap my thighs around your waist."

"Leave them where they are."

She groaned. "I need to."

"Leave them."

"The guards won't care."

"I'll—" He shoved one more inch and sucked in air. "I'll care. I'm not . . . a performer. Oh, gods, Tou, you feel so good."

He was all the way inside her, hot as noon and shaking with pleasure. His breathing was loud in the hushed, dark night, and Tou was as stretched and eager as she could get. His cock felt like a heart beating in her sheath, each hard pulse a tormenting tease. She could hardly bear to restrain herself. She was used to letting go with him, used to being taken hard and fast.

"Don't you want this?" she pleaded, her need swelling inside her until it hurt. "Don't you want me to ride you?"

She knew he did, but he shook his head stubbornly. "You can do things with your sheath, can't you? You can move your muscles in ways other women can't. Move them now, Tou. Make this pleasure strong for both of us."

She nearly killed him when she did it. The sensation of her undulating over his hardness was sharp and sweet, like velvet fingers on the rigid pole. The taste of blood tinged his mouth. He'd come so close to climax, he'd bit his cheek.

She grew wetter around him, letting him slide a fraction deeper into her heat.

"Does that feel good to you?" he demanded once he'd caught his breath. "When you tighten yourself around me?"

"It feels too good," she panted, her hands pulling streaks of fire up his sweating back. "Too good and not good enough."

"Do you want me to touch you? To rub your bud?"

He drew his cock out to tease them both, to run the bulging, silky tip across her swollen pleasure spot. Her nails broke his skin as he strafed it, her curse of frustration a heady compliment. This attraction between them was the best thing he'd ever known— a blessing without question. He pressed his cock back inside before she could grow violent, sinking in with a sigh he could not contain.

"Maybe you'd prefer my fingers?" he suggested.

She glared at him, but his fingers were already closing over her ripeness, and she came with a sudden cry. Her contractions felt so delicious, he worked his fingers harder and pushed her up again.

"Not fair," she gasped after the third time he'd sent her over. "I can't reach your trigger spots from here."

Giving in, he hitched her thigh around his hip, immediately groaning at the change in pressure on his suffering cock. Its head was bumped against the rear of her passage, its sensitive nerves singing now with bliss. Remembering what she wanted, he took her hand from where it clutched his back, pushed it down between their bodies, and wrapped it around his balls.

They were sore from being kept waiting, warning him how very much he needed this.

"There," he said somewhat hoarsely. "Now you can reach one."

"Are you going to come with me this time?"

"I like to wait sometimes. It deepens my ejacu—" He jerked as she squeezed him inside and out.

"I said, are you going to come with me this time?"

"If you keep massaging me like that, I won't be able to stop myself."

"Good," she said. "I don't want you holding back with me."

He couldn't then. He had to thrust, *really* thrust, no matter how it put them on display for the guards. His strokes grew longer, faster, his shaft thickening so much she started to cry out. He couldn't doubt she enjoyed it. She was thrusting just as hard as he was, and there was only her for him, heat and cream and a desire to come so frantic it felt like pain. Blind with need, he shoved up inside her, her body coming off the ground with the force of it. Again he surged up inside her, again and again, grunting with effort as his pleasure rose dizzyingly.

He didn't think he needed to be concerned about his ejaculation being less than full. His seed felt like it was boiling inside his balls, a sea of semen striving to break free. Her heel dug into his backside, reminding him a bit too strongly of the ivory dildo she'd used on him. Sensation spiked powerfully inside him. He had an instant to wonder what this would have done to him, to *them*, had his desires been at their peak, and then the orgasm burst.

He came with the strength of a dam breaking, came with a shout that should have seared his throat, claiming her, joined by her, flooding her with seed as she arched against him in ecstasy.

Afterward, her gorgeous leg slid down his side, as if all its muscles had gone limp.

They hadn't been close to silent for their climax—and he'd arguably screamed—but it was too late to worry about that. For the moment, the best he could do was clasp her tight and pray his knees would hold.

"There," she said, stroking the breadth of his shoulders and smiling creamily. "Now the whole palace knows there's more than politics between us."

He laughed with what remained of his exhausted breath. "Is that what you were aiming for by seducing me in public?"

She ducked her head shyly. "Maybe in part."

"And the other parts?"

Her grin flashed like dawn breaking in his heart. "I'll reacquaint you with those, love, after you carry me inside."

In a Wolf's Embrace

Lora Leigh

FOREWORD

They were created, they weren't born.
They were trained, they weren't raised.

They were taught to kill, and now they'll use their training to ensure their freedom.

They are Breeds. Genetically altered with the DNA of the predators of the earth. The wolf, the lion, the cougar, the Bengal; the killers of the world. They were to be the army of a fanatical society intent on building their own personal army.

Until the world learned of their existence. Until the council lost control of their creations, and their creations began to change the world.

Now, they're loose. Banding together, creating their own communities, their own society, and their own safety, and fighting to hide the one secret that could see them destroyed.

The secret of mating heat. The chemical, biological, the emotional reaction of one Breed to the man or woman meant to be his or hers forever. A reaction that binds physically. A reaction that alters more than just the physical responses or heightens the sensuality. Nature has turned mating heat into the Breeds' Achilles Heel. It's their strength, and yet their weakness. And Mother Nature isn't finished playing yet.

Man has attempted to mess with her creations. Now, she's going to show man exactly how she can refine them.

Killers will become lovers, lawyers, statesmen, and heroes. And through it all, they will cleave to one mate, one heart, and create a dynasty.

I dreamed of a man, lost, broken, and alone.
I dreamed of a woman, disillusioned, weeping,
and forced to roam.
I dreamed of a child, cold, hungry, and without a home.
A wolf cried out.
A lion roared.
And the lonely eagle screamed upon the winds,
where he soared.
And in a dream, a story was born.
Thank God for the dreams.

CHAPTER ONE

New York City
Dubbree Suites Hotel
2023

Two assassinations in one month, each tied to known or suspected Genetics Council members. It was going to be a public relations nightmare for the Feline Breed contingent of the species.

First General Cyrus Tallant. Of course, his assassination had been laid at the feet of the Genetics Council upper-level members. As would this one be. After all, Dr. Benedikt Adolf Albrecht was under just as much, if not more, suspicion of being aligned with the shadowy twelve-member directorate of the council.

Matthias Slaughter knew Albrecht was more than just aligned. Albrecht was an actual member of the council directorate. He was also the director of training. It was his, his father's, and his father's before him, legacy to the hellish existence the Breeds had endured in the labs.

The Breed species hadn't been lucky enough to be born. No, nature hadn't, in all her insight and mercy, thrown a genetic kink in the works of an everyday human. Quite the contrary. In one of her rare fits of humor, she had decided instead to work with what man had created. What monsters such as Albrecht had pieced together. With their genius in genetic engineering and the past atrocities of their forefathers, the council had managed to create the human and animal species they had envisioned as their own personal army. An army that would be the muscle behind their quest for power.

How nature must have chuckled over that one.

Matthias imagined over the years that he had heard a giggle or two from her as well.

Physically, mentally, genetically, the Breeds were everything the council had hoped for, paid for, killed for. Psychologically, they fell far short of the mark. Like their natural cousins, the predators of the earth, the Breeds worshipped freedom, and they worshipped their own honor.

Many had died remaining true to that inner code, an ideal rather than a set of rules. An instinctive hunger and drive to attain the freedom their wild cousins knew.

They were animals in men's bodies. Primal, savage, predatory. And intelligent.

That intelligence had been the downfall of the council's plans. And it found him here now, more than a century after the first Breed had drawn his first breath.

The technical wizardry of another Breed enforcer was ensuring that the security cameras didn't record Matthias's entrance or later his exit. It was ensuring that the council itself was blamed for this death, as well as the generals before him.

The council must be cleaning house.

Matthias grinned at the headlines he imagined. The grin was quickly gone, as the sound of the penthouse's double doors opening had him waiting expectantly.

He didn't tense. Not so much as breath disturbed the air, as he inhaled carefully. Albrecht was known to travel with several bodyguards, though tonight, as they had every night during this short stay in New York, Albrecht's bodyguards were heard entering their separate room farther down the hall.

Excellent. Albrecht was known to depend on the Dubbree Hotel's security. Arrogant bastard. He thought his position protected him. That his genius in genetics and his fortune in pharmaceuticals could possibly shield him from retribution. But he had always flaunted security. Just for the hell of it. After all, who would dare attempt to harm him?

"Cretins." The heavy German accent had Matthias's lip curling to reveal the wicked canines at the side of his mouth.

Benedikt Adolf Albrecht wasn't well known for his respect toward his bodyguards.

Lights flared in the entryway, the doors closed, Matthias waited.

His prey was a creature of organized habits. Albrecht believed an organized mind was a stable mind. That could explain the accusations Matthias regularly received in regards to his own sanity. Or lack thereof.

He waited patiently in the darkened living room. The bar sat across from him. Albrecht would go there first.

And just like clockwork, the low lamps flared to life, all but the two that sat near Matthias, and Albrecht moved slowly toward the bar.

Albrecht looked like a cadaver. Tall, skinny, thin gray hair lying close to his scalp, and pale, almost bleached flesh. He stalked to the bar, as Matthias lifted his weapon from his lap.

Ice clinked in the glass, liquor splashed into it. Matthias aimed, pulled the trigger, and watched the back of Albrecht's head crack from the bullet. A second later the council member fell over the bar. Crystal carafes rolled, broke, scattering glass and the scent of liquor. But even that couldn't drown out the sound of horror from the entrance.

A woman's shocked gasp, the scent of fear—and of recognition. For the first time in his thirty years of life, Matthias felt regret, and a tinge of sadness. Because he knew his own fate had just been decided.

Matthias turned to his side, a snarl on his face, a growl in his voice.

"Goddamnit, Grace."

Static crackled in the communications link at Matthias's ear.

"Get her out of there, Matthias. I can control the security monitors for five minutes, tops. Use the stairs, proceed to the ground floor. Lawe will be waiting with the van at the exit."

Matthias was moving, even as Jonas barked the orders into the receiver at his ear. He was across the room before the slender, doe-like figure of Dubbree's assistant manager, Grace Anderson, could run.

Her lips were opening, her lungs filling. Before the scream could leave her throat, his hand was over her lips and nose, his other arm jerking her against his chest, compressing her lungs and causing instant unconsciousness.

He slung her over his shoulder and strode quickly from the suite, pausing a precious second to make certain her prints didn't show anywhere on the doors, and securing the locks before moving down the hall.

He picked up the sounds of the bodyguards in the next room, the television they were watching, someone was showering. He strode by the door, slipped down the stairwell, and began taking the steps at a quick run.

Grace's weight was slight, her scent wrapping around him like silken regret. She shouldn't have been here. He had watched her get into her car and move into the traffic that congested Manhattan that afternoon. She was supposed to be on her way out of town, on vacation, leaving the city for the peace and relaxation of the mountains.

She wasn't supposed to be here. And she wasn't supposed to be anywhere near Albrecht.

The assistant manager of the exclusive hotel had earned herself a well-deserved break from the city. She had laughed with him about it and invited him to join her when his business in town was completed. Sun and fun, clear streams and lots of trees, she had teased. And he had promised her, first thing in the morning, he would follow her.

Dammit to hell, why had she come back?

"Lawe's in position, you have three minutes," Jonas spoke in his ear. "You have to clear that exit and be in the van before the cameras go to normal operation again."

The scheduling of the security upgrades was top secret, even the floor security personnel had no idea when it happened. Jonas, miracle worker that he was, had managed to find out not only when it would happen, but how to ensure how long it would take.

"I'll have ten seconds to spare," he muttered, racing down the stairs, his steps silent, his movements sure despite his burden. "Have the doors open."

"Open and ready," Law reported. "Get a move on big boy, this area won't stay secure the full time."

Get a move on. He grunted at the order. As though he wasn't going fast enough.

"Break the girl's damned neck and dump her." Another voice came across the line. "She's a liability."

A growl rumbled from Matthias's throat, though his pace never faltered.

"Shut up, Simon," Jonas ordered. "Two minutes, Matthias."

He would make it in plenty of time if Sleeping Beauty didn't decide to wake up and pitch a fit. And she could pitch a fit. He'd met her during the mugging Jonas had staged for Matthias to save her from. If he hadn't moved in when he had, Simon might have been charging the Breeds extra for hazardous-duty pay.

Thankfully, she stayed quiet. He hit the exit, ducked, and disappeared into the interior of the van, with two seconds to spare. The door slammed shut, barely missing Grace's head. The van was accelerating away from the exit less than a second later.

"Security system active. All monitors showing normal operational status. The Monarch Suite is locked and secured. Good going, Matthias," Jonas congratulated him.

Matthias placed his hand protectively against Grace's head, shifted her from his shoulder, and laid her on the tarp-covered floor of the van.

Simon watched him, smirking. The blond haired mercenary with the smooth southern drawl was a pain in the ass under normal circumstances. A blue-eyed ladies man and self-professed rogue, the mercenary was also a tactical genius.

Beside him, Jonas, the director of the Bureau of Breed Affairs, sat in the secured chair in front of a bank of monitors and finessed a keyboard like it was a lover. The military cut of his black hair revealed an imposing profile, though his eerie silver eyes were damned odd for a Lion Breed.

Breed Enforcement agent, Lawe Justice, drove, and Rule Breaker (hell of a set of names for cats) watched him expectantly from the front passenger seat.

"He didn't kill her," Simon stared down at Grace almost mournfully, as he tipped his cowboy hat back and flicked a glance at Matthias. "What the fuck are you going to do with her, wolf?"

"My problem." Matthias moved to peer over Jonas's shoulder at the monitors that recorded the hotel's security, tracked personnel, and alarms.

"No alarms." Jonas moved between the monitors using keyboard commands. "Your entrance or exit wasn't recorded or seen. We're in the clear."

Jonas turned in his chair, and Matthias retreated to rest his back against the wall of the van, as Jonas stared down at Grace's unconscious form.

"Why didn't you kill her?" Jonas repeated Simon's question dispassionately. "If she was in Albrecht's suite this late, then she was a part of him."

Matthias stared back at him coldly. "I won't reward her help by snapping her neck."

"Then I will," Jonas decided, moving as though to do just that.

Matthias lifted his lip in a growl, causing Jonas to pause.

"Matthias, she's a risk. She can identify you and place the weapon in your hand. What other choice do you have?" Slashing quicksilver eyes clashed with Matthias's gaze.

"I'll take care of the situation."

"And when she's reported missing? I managed to have her vehicle picked up by one of my enforcers, but she only had a week's vacation. What then?"

Matthias shifted his gaze from Jonas's to Grace's face. Her features were relaxed, her dove gray eyes closed. Rosebud lips were softened, and her creamy flesh was pale.

He had terrified her, but there hadn't been time for gentleness.

"I'll take responsibility for her," he stated firmly.

IN A WOLF'S EMBRACE   263

"And when she reports what she saw?" Jonas asked, his voice hard. "When she reports that a Breed, a known associate of the Bureau of Breed Affairs, killed Dr. Albrecht. What then, Matthias? You're risking the whole community, not just yourself."

"Touch her, and I'll kill you next," Mathias growled, a hard rumble of violence that had the tension in the van spiking to heated levels. "Think about harming her, and I'll kill you."

"Then hide her." Jonas shrugged. "And hide her well, wolf, because if she even breathes the truth of tonight's events, I'll make sure she never takes another breath."

. . .

JONAS watched, several hours later, as Matthias loaded his conscious, bound and gagged little burden into the folded-back front seat, secured her into place, and drove away.

He leaned against the outside of the van and grinned, hell if he could help it. Sometimes, his people just amazed him, especially those who hadn't yet heard the truth of the mating heat, or the first signs of it.

Common sense was the first casualty to the heat, and he almost regretted letting the Wolf Breed drive away to parts unknown. It would have been fun as hell to watch.

"He's gonna mate her," Simon drawled from inside the van. "That look in his eye was impossible to mistake. I thought he was going to rip my throat out when I suggested breaking her neck."

"He came close." Jonas smirked.

"You should have warned him," Lawe sighed.

"You should have had him dragged back to Sanctuary for those stupid tests," Rule snarled. "If they don't find a cure for that shit, I'm never going to fuck again. It's starting to give me the jeebies."

Jonas chuckled. "We need to understand it, you can forget about curing it. Besides, Ely and the Wolf Breed scientists have enough victims. No sense in adding a new pair to the mix."

"And if he can't convince her to keep her mouth shut?" Simon voiced the question rolling around in Jonas's head. He grimaced at the thought of the answer to it.

"Track him," he ordered the other man. "If he can't convince her not to talk, then we'll have to."

Permanently if necessary. He'd hate it. It would sicken his soul, but he had done worse to see to the Breeds' survival, and he was certain he would do so again. Shedding innocent blood would add to the nightmares, though, and that he wasn't anticipating. As far as Jonas was concerned, he had enough nightmares to fight.

CHAPTER TWO

She should have changed out of the short black skirt and white blouse she wore to work. She should have worn jeans. Pants, anything but the leg-flattering little skirt she was so fond of. Because it was now around her thighs. So indecently around her thighs that Grace felt herself flushing.

And while she was considering her recent mistakes, she should have let someone know she had returned. Checked in. Put off dealing with Albrecht's complaints. Anything but what she had ended up doing.

But she just had to come back for that stupid little bathing suit she had stuffed in the pocket of her jacket. And when she had, Mr. Albrecht's message had been flashing on her machine. Irate. Demanding action over some slight by the staff.

She had listened to the message, erased it, because she was anal about stuff like that, and then had gone to Albrecht's suite. That had been her biggest mistake.

The door had been slightly open, but Albrecht was known for that kind of absentmindedness. He was so arrogantly certain no one would dare attack him under the eagle eye of the security cameras that he ignored every precaution. Security had warned him repeatedly that they could not ensure his safety if he didn't stop leaving the suite door open. Normally, one of the security personnel contacted his bodyguards in the other room and had them do it. Tonight, security hadn't taken care of it. Which meant they were updating the security system. Which meant the damned system, as well as the backup, was off-line. *Which meant no one knew what the fuck had happened to her!*

Ten minutes. The system had been off-line for ten freaking stupid minutes, and one of their most influential residents was dead.

It didn't matter that he was an asshole. He was still dead. And Matthias had killed him.

Her breath hitched as she battled the tears filling her eyes. The man she had fallen in love with was a killer.

She glanced over at him.

His expression was imposing in the low lights from the dash. The wicked scar that slashed over his forehead, across his eye, then to the center of his cheek was hidden from her view. His profile revealed only the dark curve and slash of arrogant bones, the arch of black brows. Thick, coarse black hair, as dark as night, flowed down his neck and was caught at the nape of his neck with some sort of elastic band.

Broad shoulders and a body so tight and hard it gave a girl damp panties. He was dressed in his customary black leather pants, shit-kicker boots, a T-shirt, and black leather jacket.

The gloves he had worn on his hands had been black as well. They were gone now.

And to top it all off, he was a Wolf Breed. Powerful, charismatic, scarred, and dangerous. All the things that made a girl's heart go thump in the night.

And he was a killer.

She flinched as his hand moved, then drew in a shaky breath as the gag was removed from her mouth. He didn't stop to untie her, or to release the restraints holding her to the lowered seat. But at least she could speak now.

"Just how damned stupid are you?" The words broke past her lips before she could think. "You should have killed me back at the hotel, because I swear to God I'm going to watch you fry."

She tried to tear herself loose, jerking and writhing against the bonds furiously.

"Keep it up, and I'm going to see more than just those pretty thighs, Grace." His husky voice had her stilling, her gaze jerking to where he was glancing at her thighs before looking down her body.

"Oh yeah, as if you haven't already made certain you could see more," she yelled, flushing at the knowledge that her skirt had ridden to the crotch of her panties. Her damp panties. "What are you going to do now, rape me before you kill me?"

He stared down at her with whiskey colored eyes. Those eyes almost mesmerized her.

"If I intended to kill you, I wouldn't rape you first," he promised her mockingly. "Somehow, that just reeks of foul play."

"And murder doesn't?" She gasped in outrage.

"Albrecht was a member of the Genetics Council." The sound of his voice, low, husky, nearing another of those dangerous growls she had heard just before he grabbed her, had her flinching. "That wasn't a murder, Grace, it was an act of mercy."

She stared back at him in shock.

"He was a mean old man," she admitted in disbelief. "But he couldn't have been part of the Genetics Council any longer. He was so absentminded he forgot to close his stupid doors. If he *had* been a member, he had likely forgotten it by now. Which makes it murder."

She hated liars.

"You were using me all along." Fury filled her at the thought. "Was the mugging a setup, too? A way to get on the stupid manager's good side? Is that what it was? And here I didn't even get a mercy fuck for my trouble."

He hadn't wanted to be seen with her, she had thought it was because of her plain looks. He said it was because he was a Breed, he didn't want to see her hurt. It hadn't been. It had been because right there in her living room, shoved into her little bookcase, was all the information he would have needed to get to Albrecht.

But how had they known when the security would be off-line? And was it just Matthias, or were there others?

"I have your luggage in the back," he told her, obviously gritting his teeth. "Your car has been taken care of."

"Should I thank you?"

He ignored her again.

"I liked the thought of joining you at the cabin. I checked the place out last week. It's a nice little place. I thought I'd escort you up there, maybe stay a while. Discuss some things with you."

Her breath stilled in her lungs. The cabin was by a lake. He could drown her there, and no one would ever know what had happened to her.

He was going to kill her. She had been falling in love with the man who was going to murder her. Now this was just a hellacious ending to a perfectly fucked up love life.

Her father had been right all along. Grace had finally jumped into something that was going to get her killed. He had been predicting it since she was four and she climbed her first tree. Now, it seemed it was going to happen.

"I'm not going to hurt you, Grace."

"Oh yeah, that's why I'm trussed up like a Christmas turkey and heading to a conveniently out-of-the-way cabin." She had to fight pack her tears. "Does that mean you're going to just kill me fast?"

Oh man, she had really stepped into it this time. Wasn't she the one wishing for adventure, just a few months ago? Surely she wasn't the one that had taken one look at Matthias after he rescued her from a mugging and thought he was some kind of dark, sexy knight. He wasn't a knight, he was a monster.

Yeah. He wasn't going to hurt her. He was just going to let her waltz right into the police department and identify him as Albrecht's assassin and wish her good luck with the future. Uh huh. She could see that happening.

"Damn, you're melodramatic, do you know that?" He slanted her a look from the corner of those sexy, exotic eyes of his, and her stomach clutched at the look.

He looked at her like that a lot. Like a man with sex on his mind, but he had yet to touch her, to kiss her. That look was as much a lie as everything else about him had ever been.

"I tend to get that way when I see harmless old men assassinated and I get kidnapped. It has a decidedly melodramatic effect on my life, Matthias."

He glanced at her again. But not at her face. Once more, his gaze slid to her thighs.

"Yeah, I can see where that would be upsetting." His gaze finally slid to her face. "But I said I wouldn't hurt you."

"Like you said my mugger was gutter trash," she retorted. "Tell me Matthias, was that a setup?"

He jerked his head to face forward, his expression tightening, as she stomped her feet into the floor of the vehicle.

"Damn you. Damn you. Damn you." The curses were throttled screams, as she then slammed her head back against her seat. "Let me go! Just let me go, so I can kill you myself."

She had been terrified. Terrified and so damned grateful to the man who had saved her that she had overlooked every sign that he was trouble. And the signs were there. The diamond glittering in his left ear. The scar on his face. The tattoo she had glimpsed on his bicep, the nipple ring, the faint outline of which she had seen beneath his T-shirt.

He looked like a thug, but he carried himself with such supreme confidence, such arrogance, that every stupid feminine instinct she had possessed had been drawn to him.

"Your mugger *is* gutter trash," he finally muttered.

"So you didn't set that up?"

"I didn't set it up."

Her gaze narrowed. "Was it set up for you?"

"I had to find a way to make you trust me, quickly," he admitted. "That was the only way."

Anger vied with fear. Damn him, there wasn't a chance he could let her live. She might as well go down letting him know exactly what she thought of him. She'd already watched him blow another man's head off. It wasn't like it could get much worse.

"You lied to me." She gritted her teeth in fury, surprised at how much it hurt.

"I didn't lie to you, Grace," he finally sighed. "I stretched a few truths and didn't tell you exactly why I was there."

"You used me to kill a man."

"I rid the world of a monster, and I'll prove it to you," he said. "What you do after that, is up to you."

"And if I go straight to the police?" Of course she would go straight to the police. Was there any question of it?

"Then I'll do everything in my power to protect you." The regret that shimmered in his voice had her chest tightening. "But once I'm behind bars, others will kill you. I won't be able to save you then."

He was lying to her again, of course.

"Grace. Give me a chance." His hand lowered from the steering wheel to her knee. The shock of his calloused, scarred hand against her bare flesh for the first time sent a riot of sensation cascading through her.

It was his *hand*, for God's sake. On her *knee*. It wasn't like it was tucked between her thighs.

"I gave you a chance." She tried to jerk away from him, but his hand only tightened, holding her bound legs in place. "And look where it got me. More lies. And more threats. No thank you, Matthias, I think I've trusted you too much already."

CHAPTER THREE

Matthias felt his fingers tighten on the fragile width of her knee and forced himself to relax. He wouldn't hurt her, and he didn't want to frighten her further.

Already the scent of her fear was nearly overpowering the soft, subtle scent of the arousal that filled her each time he was near her.

It was one of the reasons he had rarely touched her over the past weeks. He had kept his distance as much as possible, knowing that until he had dealt with Albrecht, he didn't have the time to deal with what he knew was coming with Grace.

Jonas thought it was such a closely guarded secret that Wolfe Gunnar, the leader of the Wolf Packs, adhered to the strict order of silence on the subject of mating heat. But Wolfe wasn't a fool. He knew his enforcers were a danger to themselves if they weren't aware of what could happen at the most unlikely moment.

Matthias knew what mating heat was, just as he knew that Grace was his mate.

The glands beneath his tongue had been sensitive for weeks, and he could feel them becoming swollen tonight. Those glands were filling with a mating aphrodisiac, a hormone that would push sensuality, sexuality, into the bounds of extremity.

It would affect Grace worse than it would affect him. She would be unable to deny her natural response to him, unable to hide from it. She would be as helpless within it as he would be once he began touching her.

The fine, almost imperceptible little hairs along his body were prickling with another hormone, one more subtle, but no less intense. His cock was rock hard. His balls were drawn tight. And he had learned in the past week that jacking off only made it worse. There would be no satisfaction until he found his release within the snug depths of Grace's body.

And there the problems would truly begin. If what Wolfe, Jacob, and Aiden had explained to their enforcers months ago were true, then during his mating with Grace, he would become more of an animal than he could have ever imagined.

Even now, as his fingers lingered on the flesh of her knee, he found a pleasure in that small touch that he had never known before. Even in the midst of the most sexual acts he had performed during his sexual training in the labs, he hadn't felt such pleasure as he did now in simply touching.

He was one of the younger Breeds. Barely thirty, but he hadn't escaped that phase of training. Not that the scientists had included sexual training for any pleasurable benefits. As in everything else, even that phase of training had held more sinister purposes.

When entranced by their lover, a man or a woman could be convinced to trade their soul for the love of the one capable of giving them such extreme pleasure. Powerful figures could be blackmailed, the sons and daughters of such figures could be used for information. Wives could be seduced, husbands could be tempted. It was all the same to the council. Every weakness could be exploited.

In the years since his release, Matthias had never used the talent he had found to please a woman, to betray one. Until Grace, he had refused to involve any woman in the dangerous, bloody life he led.

He was an assassin. The council had taught him how to be an assassin. He carried the scars from his failed attempts during training, and he carried the marks of his successes since his escape.

He didn't kill for money, and he didn't kill from hatred or greed. He killed for mercy. He killed to make the world a safer place, not just for his own species, but for the humans as well.

Council members, scientists, trainers, and soldiers—many had been released once they were revealed. If they were smart, they lived the rest of their lives without picking up their old ties. If they weren't, then Matthias or one of his kind made house calls. And there were many who eagerly, if more secretly, renewed those old ties.

He had gotten lucky with Albrecht, though. He was impossible to forget. And Matthias just happened to have been at the right place at the right time, before the Breed rescues ten years before. He had seen Albrecht with several scientists, heard the scientists refer to him as "director." Only council members were given that distinction.

Matthias had remembered, and he had given the bastard a chance. A chance Albrecht had deliberately ignored. The proof of that was in the bloody, broken bodies of the mated Breed pairs he had managed to capture over the past years. Young Breeds, independent. Rather than seeking the Wolf or Lion Breed compounds when mating heat overtook them, they had tried to figure it out on their own. And they had died in the effort.

The horrifying evidence that Albrecht was once again experimenting with Breeds was too much to ignore, and Matthias had been called in.

He had used Grace to make his house call, and gaining her forgiveness wouldn't be easy.

"Where are we?" she finally asked wearily, staring up at the ceiling of the SUV, trying to hide her response to his touch.

"We're about two hours from your cabin," he told her softly, enjoying the feel of her satiny knee and the flesh in the curve of her leg against his fingertips.

"You researched me well then," she said, fighting to control her breathing.

The scent of her arousal was growing. The glands in his tongue were thickening. He should stop touching her, he should place both hands on the steering wheel and concentrate on driving the vehicle rather than driving them both crazy with lust.

"I researched you for months," he admitted. "I followed you at night when you jogged and tracked your movements otherwise. You were under surveillance for nearly six months."

He hurt her. He could smell the scent of her inner pain, and he hated it.

"Why did you choose me? Why not the head of security? Or the head manager? Why a lowly assistant manager with limited power?"

He snorted at that. "You mean the lazy manager who has shifted all the work, responsibility, and information to your shoulders, while claiming the fruits of your labor?" He asked. "I didn't have to smell the laziness on that woman to know the truth of her. All I had to do was read the file that had been prepared on her."

"How did you know Albrecht would be here during the security upgrade?"

"I have my sources." He shrugged.

"How many of you are working together?"

Matthias flashed her a grin. "How many of us did you see?"

"You had help," she bit out. "How else did you manage to get my luggage or have my car moved? You couldn't have done this alone."

"I kill alone and this is all that matters." He wouldn't tell her different. There was always a chance she wasn't the person he thought she was, and he didn't dare betray the others. "Stop asking me questions, Grace. We'll talk when we get to the cabin."

"Stop touching me then. And I swear to God, if your fingers go any higher, the first chance I get I'm cutting them off your hand."

His hand had slid higher, inches above her knee, and despite the vehemence of her order, she was enjoying it. The smell of her arousal was now covering that of her fear. The air around him was indolent with the scent of a wicked storm. He could feel the wild pulse of her blood beneath her flesh, and he knew it matched his own.

"I've been dying to touch you, Grace," he finally admitted. "Holding back these past weeks has been hell on my control."

"Well isn't that just too damned bad," she snapped, though he could hear the breathlessness, the hunger inside her. "Because you don't have a chance in hell now. Unless it's rape you're after, big boy, you fucked up when you pulled that trigger. I wouldn't sleep with you now if all that mating heat crap the tabloids printed were true."

He almost winced. Those tabloids had no clue. And neither did she. Because he would have her, and by the time the mating heat was finished with them, they would both be begging for it.

• • •

SHE couldn't believe this mess. She couldn't believe Matthias had actually killed, in cold blood. He hadn't even given Dr. Albrecht a warning.

She shuddered at the memory of it. The memory of his face, so dispassionate. There had been no anger, no fury, it hadn't even been emotionless really. Just unconcerned. What he had done had caused not so much as a flinch of remorse.

How many others had he killed? Would he kill her the same way?

Grace turned her face away from him and stared at the door of the SUV. The seat was reclined fully: that, in combination with the dark night and the rural area they were driving through, left her completely out of sight.

She was stretched out, bound, helpless. Most women would have been begging for their lives, screaming, crying. She was trying to think instead. To wait. To steal a chance to escape. If one came.

She had a feeling one wouldn't come. And begging would do her no good. It wouldn't have done Albrecht any good, either.

She had been falling in love with Matthias, and perhaps that was the part that hurt the most. They had spent most of her breaks sharing coffee in her small office, and the evenings enjoying quiet dinners together, or long walks in the park.

He fascinated her. Drew her. Knowing what he was, the horrors he had experienced had pricked at her heart, and her woman's heart had wanted to erase those horrors with softness.

She had even told her family about him. About the Wolf Breed whose eyes were so filled with loneliness. Who smiled as though he hadn't known he could do so. Who watched her in a way no other man ever had. Her father had wanted to meet him. Her mother wanted to cook for him. Her brothers offered to teach him to play football.

She blinked back her tears at the loss. At both their losses. He had no idea what he was missing out on when he lost *her* family.

She liked to say she was fully a part of reality, and reality demanded that she accept that Matthias wasn't just going to let her go. He couldn't afford to. The whole Breed community would suffer for what he had done tonight, if the authorities ever learned of it. And Grace was well aware of his loyalty to not just the pack he claimed as his own, but to the Breeds in general.

She closed her eyes as she felt his fingertips stroking her leg again. His palms were horribly scarred, the faint ridges from those past wounds rasped over her flesh, and her soul. They brought pleasure and pain. Pleasure from his touch, pain at the knowledge of all he had endured.

She thought she had gotten to know him. She knew he *could* kill. He'd told her of some of the assignments he had been sent on during his time in the labs. She'd known he had killed since then in the confines of the investigative work he did. She hadn't imagined he could kill in cold blood, though. Shooting a man from behind, without warning, somehow seemed worse than killing one face-to-face.

She knew there were rumors that Albrecht had been part of the Genetics Council. Rumors that he had ordered deaths, worked on the genetic alterations, and perhaps even been a part of what the press called the twelve-member directorate. He had been the head of the Genetics Council—the shadowy figures that financed, directed, and oversaw each stage of the Breed development.

All Grace had ever seen was a mean, disillusioned old man, though. One who didn't even have the common sense to close the door to his suite and was constantly searching for his appointment journal.

If the rumors were true, he should have been arrested rather than released after the inquest into the Breed atrocities. He shouldn't have been killed the way he was.

"Grace, the smell of your fear is killing me." His voice was soft, gentle. "I promise, I'm not going to hurt you."

"And I'm supposed to believe that?" She turned her head to stare back at him, seeing the flash of somber regret in his gaze before he turned back to look at the road.

"You will believe it," he said, his voice as heavy with regret now as his gaze had been. "But you won't die. Not by my hand, or by any others, as long as I can protect you."

"What? You think you can make me forget what I saw?" She hated the tears in her voice, but even more, she hated the damned disillusionment. She hated looking at him and fighting herself to believe what she had seen with her own eyes.

"Not forget it," he admitted. "I'm hoping, though, that you'll understand it enough to keep the knowledge of it to yourself."

He was crazy. That was all there was to it.

"Oh, well, if that's all you want, then I'm all for it." Living was worth lying for. "Let me go now, and mum's the word. I promise."

He flashed her a chiding smile.

"I can smell your lie as easily as I can smell your arousal, Grace. Have you forgotten that?"

Her eyes widened. Cream flooded her pussy and wept to her labial folds, rushing to surround her clit. That little bundle of nerves was pulsing now, engorged and swollen. The sound of his voice was rasping, filled with male lust and determined aggression.

"You never mentioned the arousal part," she gasped.

"I didn't, did I?" His fingers slid higher on her thigh, and, traitorously weak, her legs trembled, her breathing became rougher, and her juices thicker.

His fingers grazed the damp crotch of her panties, and Grace heard the low, weak moan that betrayed her slip past her lips.

"The scent of your arousal has made me crazy." His voice deepened, as a growl rumbled in his chest. The sound should have frightened her; it turned her on instead.

Sensation was humming through her body, tingling in her clit and her nipples, making her gaze heavy as his fingers continued to brush lightly against the damp cotton of her panties. That slow, deliberate caress held her spellbound.

He was using the hand that had held the gun that killed Albrecht. But it wasn't death she felt. And it wasn't disgust. It was pleasure. A hot, insidious pleasure that held her mesmerized.

"Matthias, this is wrong." She wanted to tell him to stop, but the words wouldn't push past her lips. "Don't do this to me. Please."

"You do it to me, Grace," he accused her darkly. "Each touch you've given me, no matter how innocent, made me weak. Made me hard. I've been so damned distracted by you, my head so filled with the memory of your scent that I didn't know when you entered that suite. I should have known. I should have sensed you and been able to pull back. To hide until you were gone. But you were already so much a part of me, that I carry you with me, whether you're actually there or not."

The SUV slowed. It didn't stop, but it was definitely slowing as he glanced at her. A second later he jerked his gaze back to the road, but his hand didn't leave her, his fingers didn't pause in their caresses.

The implications of his declaration seared her mind. There were rumors, tabloid tales and obscure reports of Breed mates. Mates that were rarely photographed, rarely seen by journalists. It was said that in the ten years since the Breeds had been revealed, that the mates to those Breeds hadn't aged. Tabloids ran stories almost weekly of a sexual frenzy during what they called "mating heat." And then there were the wild tales of orgies and animalistic behavior.

There were also stories of other animalistic occurrences. Reports that the Breeds' sexuality was closer to that of their animal cousins than that of humans. Feline Breed males were said to lock inside their females during ejaculation, with a penile extension just beneath the head of the cock, referred to as a barb. And as for the Wolves . . .

Grace stared at Matthias's taut profile. Wolves were supposed to lock within a female with a heavy swelling known as the knot.

It couldn't be true. She'd scoffed at the stories then, and she refused to believe them now.

But she couldn't refuse to believe the heavy, lethargic arousal overcoming her. He was barely stroking her, his fingers were but a slight pressure against the covering of her panties, and still, it made her too weak to protest. And the cotton covering was becoming damper by the second with her juices.

"You need to stop," she whispered, her lashes fluttering with sharply rising need. "Please, Matthias . . ."

CHAPTER FOUR

Grace's family cabin sat in the Catskill Mountains northwest of New York City. The heavily forested area called to the wildness of Matthias's spirit. The sounds of the night wrapped around him, but the scent of Grace filled his mind.

The two-story cabin sat next to a small, unpolluted lake. The crisp scent of the water was refreshing, the sound of a waterfall played somewhere in the distance. It should have been relaxing. It would have been, if the fever to take his mate weren't filling his insides with a burning hunger.

He sat his restrained captive in a wide, padded porch chair and dug the keys from her purse. She glared at him, her tapered, dark blonde hair falling over her brow and shadowing her eyes.

The door opened easily. Matthias inhaled deeply, searching for any scent other than that of an empty cabin. Satisfied that they were alone, he picked her up, carried her to the heavily cushioned couch, and left the cabin again.

He carried her luggage and his bag to the large downstairs bedroom then checked the well-stocked cabinets and refrigerator. Once he had assured himself of the security of the cabin, he disconnected the phone lines, locked the front door, and turned back to her.

Grace remained silent. And she was still aroused. He could smell the arousal, and it was killing him. But he could also smell her fear and her anger. She had judged him the moment she saw him pull that trigger, and if she had her way, he'd be locked up forever.

It was a heavy burden, to understand the event from her viewpoint. Her innocence couldn't understand the conditions under which the Breeds had been trained, the forces that had shaped their lives from conception to escape. The nightmares were nearly as brutal as the reality of it had been. Even now, ten years later, Matthias could feel the agony of those years.

"Why did you do it, Matthias?" When she spoke, her voice was agonized, filled with tears and disillusionment. She had already tried him and found him guilty.

Matthias knelt in front of the couch, his hands moving to the restraints that bound her hands and feet, his fingers massaging the slight welts on her flesh as he frowned down at them.

The beatings, the hours of mental torture, and the deaths. Imprisoned behind bars and forced to watch as friends and littermates were murdered with such brutal means, that even now, Matthias had trouble sleeping for the horrific memories.

All in the name of training. Of numbing the Breeds to the sight of pain, cruelty, and death. Turning them into emotionless machines that responded at the councilmembers' beckoning.

"I was created in Albrecht's lab," he finally answered her, lifting his head to stare back at her. "I know his cruelties. I know the monster he was." He lifted his hands from her flesh and stared at the palms. The scars that crisscrossed them had been put there by Albrecht's knife. A punishment for a failed mission.

"He was released after the hearings about Breed atrocities. You had no right to kill him after that."

His gaze jerked back to hers. "He was released on his oath that he was not a part of the council directorate, which I know was a lie. He was released on his oath that he would never again attempt to create or imprison Breeds. Ten years ago, he was released. And he never stopped. We found the bodies, his scent covered them as well as the marks of his abuse. He never stopped."

To know they hadn't found all the Breeds, even in the ten years of searching, was like a poison in Matthias's soul. The council scientists and soldiers who had escaped had taken the young with them and turned them over to the Council, to be hidden in other, even more secret labs. And now those children, ten years older, were turning up dead, horribly tortured. The experimentation that had been done on them was brutal. But even worse were the mated pairs, those that had known freedom for but a short time, recaptured, and tortured to death.

"We were the test models. The first generation of Breeds to actually survive the first few years of life are barely older than forty. They had their first success nearly a century ago—Lion Breed who managed to escape with one of their scientists. But it took them another several decades to get it right again, because the first Leo destroyed everything in that hellhole of a lab as he escaped. We were the disposable models." Fury twisted his expression. "Imagine watching your friends, your brothers and sisters being dissected, live. Being beaten until they died, broken and still trying to fight. Or so drugged they were no more than the animals whose genes they carried. I watched Albrecht do this. For years. For so many years." He pushed his fingers through his hair and moved away from her.

The blood. He could still smell the blood and death.

"Had he finished, I would have walked away from him, as I was ordered to do." He turned back to her, his eyes narrowing on the tense set of her expression. "I would not have killed him, Grace, had he not continued those atrocities."

"You should have gone to the authorities."

"The authorities had their chance. I took care of it. He will never rape another young Breed. He will never dissect another while they scream in agony, and he will never, ever attempt to prolong his own misbegotten life because he lucked out and found a mated Breed pair."

That had been the final nail in his coffin. They had found the bodies. The two young mates, so horribly mutilated, the signs of experimentation so monstrous, that even he and Jonas had thrown up.

"That doesn't make sense. What would two lovers have to do with prolonging his life? You're lying to me, Matthias. Don't do that."

Matthias shook his head. It would do no good to argue it with her—until she experienced the mating, she would never believe it.

"One of these days, you'll know the truth," he said heavily. "Are you hungry? I could fix us something to eat."

Grace stared back at him in disbelief. One moment he was talking of death, the next he was willing to cook? She shook her head as she moved, tugging her skirt farther over her thighs, before shrugging her restrictive jacket off.

"What are you going to do with me?" she asked. "You promised not to hurt me."

He nodded. "I won't hurt you."

"Even knowing I have every intention of telling the police what I saw?" She couldn't lie to him. He would smell it.

The hurt that flashed in his eyes shouldn't have bothered her, but it did.

"Even knowing that," he answered. "I'm going to spend this week with you. Let you come to know me better. Try to make you understand . . ."

"Why?" She crossed her arms over her chest and glared at him. "What does it matter if I understand or not? You murdered a man, Matthias."

"And if you report it, and I'm arrested, then I can't protect you. Other Breeds will come for you, and they will kill you before you ever have the chance to testify. Is that what you want? Do you want to die?"

"The authorities will protect me."

"Don't be so fucking naive, Grace," he snarled, causing her to flinch. "Don't be stupid. You know better than that."

Yes, she did know better. She knew she didn't have a chance at living if she ever breathed a word of what she had seen. Perhaps, in some small way, she could even understand why he had done it.

Now that the shock had worn off and her mind had accepted the fact that he had done it, it was her own anger driving her instead.

"Just leave then." She rose to her feet and breathed out roughly. "I'm smart enough to know the rules, Matthias. That doesn't mean I ever want to see you again. Just get out."

"It doesn't work that way." He shook his head, his whiskey gaze remote.

"Why not? You can smell a lie, then fine, you know I'm not lying. Albrecht may have deserved every agony you could have possibly given him, but I can't accept it. We have laws in this country for a reason."

His bark of laughter shocked her. "Do you, now?" He crossed his powerful arms over his chest and watched her, mocking. "Let me tell you about your laws, little girl. Laws that allowed all your fine politicians to stick their dirty little fingers into the Breed pie before the world learned of us. How they sent their special-forces teams after the small pride that was hiding in Kentucky. How they turned a blind eye to the tortures that were inflicted on us. Until the world learned of us and drew a horrified breath. Those same fucking bastards faked their outrage and had no choice but to back us. Back us or be revealed as the lying sons of bitches they were."

Throttled rage filled his voice and glowed in his eyes. Grace had never seen such fury, such banked violence in any one, in her life.

There were reports of this. News articles and documentaries, but until now, Grace hadn't been certain what was the truth and what were lies told to enhance the popularity of the Breeds' right-to-life laws.

She licked her lips, knowing he wasn't lying. Her chest ached for him, ached about the pain he had endured. But he had killed an unarmed man. Without remorse.

She nodded, swallowing tightly as she let his furious gaze capture hers.

"I won't report it," she whispered. "But I won't condone it. Whatever was growing between us, Matthias, if anything other than your need to use me was there, is over. Please, just leave."

"It's not going to happen."

Grace watched his expression harden, his eyes darken in determination.

"What do you mean, 'it's not going to happen?'" She watched him warily.

Had he been lying to her? Did he mean to kill her after all?

A tight smile curled his lips. "I already smell your distrust," he growled. "I don't lie, Grace. I'm not going to kill you. And I won't torture you."

"Then why stay?"

"Because you own me now. You're my mate."

CHAPTER FIVE

Grace stared back at the wild man standing in the middle of the cabin's living room. Dressed in black leather and facing her with an arrogant determination that had once appeared sexy. Now it was downright scary.

"What do you mean, I'm your mate?" The tabloid stories were rocking through her head, and she really didn't have time right now for the perversions they had reported.

She should have known better than to read that trash. But, like most Americans, she had been fascinated with the discovery of the Breeds. Fascinated and outraged by their creation and the horrifying abuses they had endured.

But, did he answer her? Hell no. He shook his head slowly, his lips curling at one corner, as he continued to watch her with those dark golden eyes. And he kept inhaling slowly, reminding her that she was still wet. So wet from his earlier play that her panties were literally clinging to her pussy.

"Matthias, right now is really not a good time to pull the silent Breed act on me," she snapped. "I'm about two minutes from a nervous breakdown. This has not been a good night for me."

Instantly his expression altered. From arrogance to sensual delight. His facial features softened as he moved toward her, his arms dropping from his chest, his shoulders flexing as he drew the black leather jacket from them. He tossed it to the couch as he neared her.

Grace took a step back. The sensuality in his gaze made her even more wary than the earlier anger had.

"Don't touch me," she ordered him roughly.

"Poor Grace," he crooned, a hint of a rumble in his voice sending a shiver racing down her spine as he moved behind her. "Yes love, it's been a very hard night for you. Seeing your mate for what he is, for who he is, hasn't been easy." She felt his breath on her hair, then his hand as he smoothed it over her shoulder. "I had hoped to ease you into it."

"Ease me into what?" She tried to jerk away, but the hand that suddenly gripped her hip wasn't allowing that to happen. "Into murder? Not going to happen."

"Into this."

Her knees nearly buckled as his lips brushed across the nape of her neck, a hint of the damp warmth of his tongue stroking along it.

"Stop it, Matthias. You can't seduce me into approving what you've done."

"I don't care if you approve of me, Grace. I only care that you accept me."

Oh my God. His teeth raked over her neck.

Grace blinked, fought to clear her vision and to remain on her feet. Because that little scrape of his extended canines did nothing to return her common sense. On the contrary, it only dampened her panties further.

"Get away from me." She tore from his clasp, turning to face him furiously, fighting her arousal and the drugging pleasure his touch brought. "I don't want you to touch me."

"Your body is begging for my touch." He grinned as he sat down on the couch and began removing his boots.

"What are you doing? Put those back on." Shock dumbfounded her. He had murdered a man in front of her, and now he was undressing? As though it were normal?

"Come on, Grace." He flashed her a seductive smile. "I'm tired, and you're snarling. Let's take tonight to rest, and tomorrow we'll revisit this little disagreement."

"Little disagreement? You *killed* a man."

"He wasn't a man." Matthias shrugged as he set his boots to the side. "He was a monster."

"That doesn't make it right."

"And it doesn't make it wrong, either," he sighed, his expression flickering with regret. "It doesn't make the need for it any less. I don't have to like what I do to realize the fact that it has to be done. Now, let's go find the bed and try to rest."

He gripped her wrist and began drawing her through the house.

"I'm not sleeping with you."

"Fine, I'll sleep with you."

He tugged her behind him like a recalcitrant child, tugging at her arm and drawing her into the bedroom before locking the door behind them.

"Matthias, stop this." Frustration, fear, and arousal converged inside her as he finally released her. "You can't believe there's any way to fix this. Surely you can't."

She couldn't let him believe it could be fixed. The past weeks were over. They were gone. She would never forget the look on his face as he killed, and she couldn't forget how easily he had done it.

He pulled her suitcase from the bed and laid it on the nearby chair. Her frilly, girly bedroom had never held a man as intensely sexual and powerful as this one. He filled it with testosterone and stubbornness to the point that she was nearly choking on it.

"I'll find a way to fix it." He opened the suitcase and drew out the plain white, long summer gown and robe she had packed.

"Matthias." She stared back at him in confusion. "You're more logical than this." How could any one man be so stubborn? "You know you can't fix this."

"I know I don't have a choice." The gown and robe were flung at her, causing her to catch them in surprise as he stared back at her with furious intent. "What I found with you is too important, Grace. I won't let this destroy it."

She shook her head slowly. "It was destroyed the minute you pulled that trigger."

"The minute I made certain another Breed never died. The minute I ended the agony for untold mates in the future that he would have captured. The minute I fucking destroyed a nightmare," he snarled. "I should do as you ask and fucking walk away from you now, because by God, you have to be the most judgmental, self-righteous creature I have ever known."

Grace's lips parted in shock. "That's not true."

"Isn't it?" He flicked her a hard, heated look, his lips curling in a little half sneer. "What did you do when you learned of the lives the Breeds led? When you read your little news report on your PDA and went about your life? Did you think, *Oh, poor creatures*? Did you even download the pictures of those labs they found? Did you even take the time to see what those sons of a bitches did?"

She hadn't. The reports alone had given her nightmares. She couldn't bear to see the pictures. And now, she felt ashamed of that.

"Live through it, then tell me how wrong I was," he snapped. "Watch your baby sister die beneath the rutting of soldiers. See your friends, those you call family, die screaming in agony, and then tell me you wouldn't have done the same."

She could see it in his face, in his eyes, and it broke her heart. She had to blink back her tears, force her lips not to tremble as she thought of the horror he had faced in ways she never had.

The scars he carried, the shadowed horror that sometimes reflected in his eyes, the bleak, hollow sound of his voice.

"I'm so sorry, Matthias," she whispered huskily, clutching the gown to her chest. "What you endured was hell. But you are not a judge and jury."

"No, I'm the executioner." He stood before her without remorse. "He had already been judged and his sentence was passed. I merely carried it out. Now get that fucking gown on and get your ass into bed before I lose what little control I have tonight."

With that, he stalked from the bedroom. Even in bare feet he seemed to stomp, his steps heavy, fury pulsing in every line of his body before the door slammed behind him.

Grace sat on the bed slowly, staring at the closed panel, knowing, somehow, she had managed to do more than merely hurt him.

She stared at the gown, pushed her fingers through her hair wearily, then rose to her feet and did as he had ordered. She was exhausted. So tired she could barely think straight. Maybe tomorrow she could find a way to make sense of it. Maybe she would realize it had all been a horrible nightmare that would just go away.

The thought of escaping Matthias flitted through her mind. She should at least try. After all, she had seen him kill, he could still kill her.

As she drew the blankets over her shoulders and stared at the bedroom window, she knew she had at least a chance of escape. And yet here she lay, and she didn't know why.

All she knew was that as she stared into the darkness, all she could think about was the horror his life must have been. Never having anyone. Never being able to care for anyone. How alone he must have felt.

She had seen that loneliness in his eyes the night she thought he had saved her, during that stupid staged mugging. She had dragged him into the hotel with her and made him drink coffee with her. He had watched her as others might watch a snake, expecting her to strike at any time.

He had touched her heart that night, with the scar slashing across his forehead, over his eyelid, and onto his cheek. With his sexy, sensual lips and whiskey brown eyes, his obvious discomfort with a smile.

But she had made him smile that night. Not a whole, unbridled smile. A tentative smile, as though he were trying it out first, waiting to see if it was going to hurt.

Three weeks. He had come into her life just three weeks before, and he had become such a part of it that now she wondered how she was going to do without him.

She looked at the window again. She really should run from him.

A tear slid down her cheek instead, because she couldn't run from him. But she could never have him, either.

CHAPTER SIX

It wasn't a nightmare. The next morning Grace awoke to the knowledge that she couldn't just escape the events from the night before any more than she could escape Matthias, and she couldn't run from them.

She brushed her hair and teeth, stared at her pale reflection, then grimaced and headed to the kitchen. She could smell coffee, and she was dying for it. The need for caffeine was crawling through her system, with the same craving that desire for Matthias was clenching between her thighs.

Dreams had tormented her through the night. Dreams, nothing, she had been tormented with visions of sexual delights that had her blushing at the thought of them. She should have had nightmares of blood and death, not dreams about what that bulge beneath those black leather pants could do to her.

"Good morning." He came to his feet from the kitchen table, another pair of leather pants covering his muscular legs. His feet and chest were bare.

Grace stared at the broad, hairless chest, as she came to a sudden stop. She'd been wanting to see that nipple ring she had glimpsed under his T-shirt. Now that she was seeing it, her mouth watered, her lips tingled with the need to capture it, to tug on it.

But as sexy as the sight of it was, nothing could detract from the thin white scars that crisscrossed his chest and abdomen.

He pulled a shirt from the back of the chair and shrugged it on, covering the horrific scars. They weren't thick and ridged, but they crisscrossed his flesh like a road map.

"Sorry about that." He turned away from her, walking across the cheerful, bright kitchen, buttoning the black shirt. "I made coffee."

She couldn't help it. Grace moved quickly across the room, facing him as he turned back to her.

"I have to see it," she whispered, her fingers going to the buttons of his shirt. "All of it, Matthias. You don't have the right to hide it from me now."

His hard, sharply defined features tightened, as her fingers undid the buttons of his shirt. She pushed the cotton shirt from his wide shoulders, and tossed it over a chair.

"Did *he* do this?" she whispered, her fingertips touching the evidence of the cruelty he had experienced.

Some of the scars were older, almost invisible. Tough, darkly tinted flesh rippled under her touch, as he glared down at her.

"He enjoyed using the whip. The scientists needed to know under what conditions we couldn't fight or complete our objectives. We were put through a variety of simulations. Torture being the favorite of them all. If we didn't succeed in the objective given us, we died."

Her breath hitched in her throat, as tears flooded her eyes. She followed the scars on his chest, his side, then moved around him to stare at his back.

"Oh, God, Matthias." The scarring was worse on his back.

She leaned her forehead against his back, clenching her eyes tight at the incredible pain he must have endured.

"It doesn't hurt any longer, Grace," he assured her.

Grace lifted her head, her gaze going to his shoulders. On his left shoulder was the Breed marker. A genetic shadow of a paw print. Within that print, four blood-red teardrops had been tattooed into his flesh. Around the paw, a precise tattoo of what appeared to be dark smoke had been drawn, a single feather, tipped with blood, caught within it.

"Why this one?" She touched the bloodstained feather wrapped in wire.

"The price of submission," he growled.

"And this one?" A line of carefully disguised bones, wrapped in the same barbed wire, the wire twisting from the base of his spine to the middle of it.

"Friends who died for their freedom," he answered.

"And this?" She touched the blood-red teardrops encased by smoke.

"The tattoo was made by a tribal medicine man. It's a protection symbol, to hold the evil within it from marking my soul." His voice was heavy, filled with pain.

"The teardrops are the evil?" She asked. "Why?"

"They mark each Council member I've killed."

Grace froze, her fingers trembling over the four markers.

"The larger one denotes a directorate member. The two medium-sized ones are scientists, the smallest are trainers. I don't bother to list the coyote soldiers, they aren't worth the need for protection." Disgust for those Breeds colored his voice.

"And Albrecht will add to it," she whispered. "What happens when you run out of room?"

"Then I return for another protected circle and begin again." His back tightened, as rage thrummed in his voice.

"And does it help the nightmares?" she asked, "or make them worse?"

Matthias stared over the room, his soul bleak at the sound of her voice. He could hear the pain and compassion in her voice, the need to understand. And despite the blood that stained his hands, all he could think about was touching her.

"Sometimes, it stills the nightmares," he answered, as he turned to her. "And sometimes, they only grow worse."

His hands gripped her shoulders, the softness of the cotton hiding the warmth of her flesh from him.

"Would you stop?" she asked.

Matthias could see the hope in her eyes, the innocence. That innocence alternately lightened his soul and weighed it down. He had never meant for her to know what he was, he had thought he could keep that part of what he did hidden after he claimed her.

Because he couldn't stop.

"We have other things to discuss," he said, rather than answering her. "We need to discuss *us*."

"There's no *us*, Matthias." The regret in her voice tore at him. "I won't report what I saw, but whatever we had is over."

She tried to move away from his touch. Despite the arousal he knew she felt, the tender feelings he knew hadn't died, still, she moved away from him.

Once she had come to him with a smile, her pretty eyes lighting up in pleasure. Now, her dove-gray eyes were dark and shadowed, knowing the truth of what he was.

"It doesn't work that way." He had to tell her the truth. He couldn't force her into the mating, as much as he wanted to. He couldn't pull her into it without her knowledge.

"Of course it works that way." Her lips turned down in a sad smile. "I decide who I sleep with."

"The mating changes that." He kept his voice low, gentle. "You can never just walk away now."

"Watch me." She tried to pull away again.

"How many nights can you handle the arousal without me in your bed?" He asked as his grip tightened on her shoulders. "Without my touch? It's been building since the night we met, the need to touch, to kiss, to lie beneath me. Admit it."

"Once you're gone, I'll get over it." The confidence in her eyes was overshadowed by her arousal.

Matthias continued to touch her, his hands moving over her arms, sliding the robe past her shoulders, touching her bare skin, his fingertips lingering to relish the feel of warm silk.

"It won't go away, it will be there. It will become worse some nights, easier others, because we've never kissed. Because my lips haven't touched your flesh. But you'll never be free of it."

He watched the suspicion grow in her eyes.

"You're trying to frighten me," she chided, her lips trembling now.

"No, I'm trying to be honest," he said. "You laughed about the tabloid stories, the Breed community sneers at them, but there's truth to some of them, Grace. There's a bond, a hormonal, biological bond once a Breed comes in contact with his mate. It doesn't go away. It doesn't lessen . . ."

"No." She shook her head desperately. "That's not possible."

"There are small glands at the side of my tongue. They fill with a very powerful hormone once the mating begins. It takes no more than a lick on your flesh to make you burn. A kiss will turn you inside out with the need to be fucked. Eventually, the fires burn so hot and so desperate, that nothing matters but easing the hunger twisting inside you. How long it lasts depends on each couple. But it never completely goes away. In each case, though, there is love. There is emotion to make the bonds created endurable. It only occurs between a couple that would have loved, despite the heat."

He watched her pale. Her small hands flattened on his sweat-dampened chest. He was already burning for her. The glands in his tongue had become fully engorged the night before, and already the hormone was spilling into his system.

"Let me go, Matthias."

"Listen to me, Grace. You were loving me, I know you were, before last night."

"Last night changes everything," she cried out, her expression fraught with fear. "Let me go."

He released her, feeling the damning sorrow that weighed at his soul, as she put the length of the room between them.

She stared at the palms of her hands before wiping them on her gown, staring back at him in disbelief. Her gaze flickered from his face to his thighs, then back again.

"How long have you known about this reaction? That it could happen between us?" she asked.

"Since the beginning," he answered her honestly. "The night of the mugging, when I touched you, when I wiped the tears from beneath your eyes, I could feel something inside me shifting, changing. Within a week, I could feel the itch in my tongue, the arousal that wouldn't abate. I knew then."

He had known even before then that she would hold his heart. Months he had spent watching her, investigating her, learning things about her that softened him toward her. She was a good woman. Loyal. Honest. She worked hard, she had friends, and she often went out of her way to do good things for them. Taking them soup when they were ill, visiting them in the hospital. Late nights on the phone, when one of them lost a lover.

"God, you infected me with something." She was staring back at him in horror.

Hell, he should have just kissed her and let nature take care of it.

"Not fully." He finally shrugged. "But I will, before this week is out." His muscles tightened in determination. "You are my mate, Grace. I won't let you just walk away from me. No other woman will ever be as important to my soul. No other woman will ever bring me the pleasure you do, with just your smile. And you know you will never forget how I make you feel. You know it."

She was shaking her head desperately. "You can't do this to me! I won't let you."

"I can't control it," he said. "Tell your body it can't happen. Tell your heart you don't care. By God, Grace, fix it and then tell me how you've done it, and I'll let you go. Until then, I can't walk away, because it would rip my soul from my body to do so."

"You don't love me," she cried.

"I cherish you," he growled. "But even more than that, for once in my misbegotten life, I have a chance at real freedom, and you're it. The chance to be more than the animal I was created to be. With my mate, I can be a husband, a father . . ."

Grace flinched at the sound of his voice when he said the words *husband* and *father*. He softened, a sense of wonder flashing in his eyes. He stared at her as though she meant something, as though she were important, as though she held his soul.

That look overrode her horror at what he was telling her. It diluted her anger. And nothing should have been able to dilute her anger.

"You knew all along. That's why you made me fall in love with you," she accused him, trying to hang on to the fury. "You deliberately made me care for you."

He pulled his shirt back on, though he didn't button it.

"Only because I cared as well," he stated, his voice rough. "All my life I've had to hold back. I've had to force myself to care for no one, because I knew they would suffer for my emotions. Once I escaped the labs, that restraint was so much a part of me that even forming friendships has been difficult. Until you." He shook his head, his dark gold eyes locked on her. "You gave me a chance to know what I've been missing all my life, Grace. You still the fury inside me, and you made me hope there was more to my life than the constant battle for freedom. You made me love you. Why shouldn't I respond in kind?"

She had hoped he would love her. She had teased him, she had tempted him, she had done everything to draw him into a touch, a kiss. She had laughed with him, and knowing he was a Breed, tried to show him a softer, gentler side of life. She had set out to bind him to her, believing this scarred, shadowed wolf she was coming to love needed her.

And maybe he did, in more ways than she knew. But he was a killer, wasn't he? He had taken Albrecht's life without remorse, hadn't he? Or had he?

The blood-red teardrops on his shoulder told another story. Teardrops, a sign of pain and regret. They told a story she knew he would never admit to. Teardrops denoted sorrow, blood-red teardrops, grief. She wondered if he even realized the grief that lurked in his gaze, and in his soul?

God, he was killing her. He stared at her with such longing, with such hunger, that it broke her heart.

"I would give my life to touch you and not have you pull away from me now," he whispered, moving slowly toward her. "If I swear not to kiss you, would you let me touch you?"

Wild, unquenched hunger rose inside her.

"Matthias, that's not fair to you." She shook her head desperately as she backed against the door of the refrigerator.

"Not fair to me?" His lips quirked mockingly. "It's far more than I deserve. I need it, Grace. Just this once, let me touch you."

CHAPTER SEVEN

She wasn't a virgin. Grace liked to consider herself a well-rounded, experienced woman, but even for her, the way Matthias touched her made her feel almost innocent. She felt unable to deny him, unable to reassert her common sense and run like hell.

It was one thing to know the ways of the world, and in some cases, the ways of men. But with Matthias she was finding out that everything she had learned over the years was just wrong.

Matthias didn't act like other men. He didn't react as other men, and he sure as hell didn't go after what he wanted as other men did. If he had argued, gone dominant, arrogant, and stubborn, she could have walked away, she told herself.

But he stared at her with such hunger. A hunger he didn't attempt to hide or push away. She wasn't a threat to his independence. The way he watched her, she was imperative to his survival.

"You're so pretty," he whispered, as he stopped before her, causing her to ache as she stared up at the wonderment of his expression. "I look at you, and sometimes, I'm afraid of touching you. Of giving you the power to destroy me. Most people have a little healthy fear of Breeds, but you stand before me, knowing in your soul, I'd never harm you."

The backs of his fingers smoothed over her cheek, sending curious tingles racing through her body.

"I'd die before I ever harmed you, before I'd ever see you harmed. Do you know that, Grace?"

She could feel it, see it in his expression and in his eyes. This wasn't stalker material, nor was it an edge of desperation. This was a man, a strong, powerful man, stating his intent, nothing more. It wasn't tinted with fanaticism or with a threat. It was a clear statement.

"Matthias, you need someone—"

"No." His fingers covered her lips, stopping the words. "I need whatever you'll give me, right here and right now. Nothing more. Just my hands on you, Grace. Let me touch you."

His thumb smoothed over her lips as she leaned her head against the refrigerator and stared back at him, torn, uncertain.

"I touched silk three months after our rescue from the labs," he whispered, as his fingertips moved over her jaw. "I swore there was nothing softer in all the world, until I touched your hand."

His hand smoothed down her arm, lifted her wrist and brought her palm to his stubbled jaw. "Your hands were warm and so soft. As soft as innocence itself."

His eyes closed, and he held her hand against him as he worked his cheek over it. She let her fingers touch his cheeks, smooth over them, and his expression shifted to one of bliss.

"I'm not innocent," she told him, but she meant the reminder for herself. Because he made her feel innocent. He made her feel nervous, excited, uncertain, but without the fears of virginity. He made her feel so much a woman that it was frightening.

"But you are innocent." He laid his cheek against hers, his lips at her ear, as he pushed her robe over her shoulders. "Innocent of deceit and corruption. When I smell your scent, I smell summer. I feel warmth. All the things I wondered if I would ever know."

Grace shivered with excitement at the guttural sound of his voice, the latent growl that bordered it. He was breathing hard and deep, his chest rasping over her gown-covered nipples and sending shafts of pleasure to tighten around them.

"Matthias, what are you doing to me?" Her head fell to the side, as his chin stroked over her neck.

"Just touching sunshine," he said softly. "Heat and magic. Warm me, Grace. Just for a minute."

At this rate, she was going to forget all that pertinent information he had just given her on what sex with him would be. Hormonal aphrodisiacs, mating heat, and biological bindings be damned. Her clit was screaming a silent demand for touch, and her sex was clenching in need.

And he hadn't even kissed her. His rough cheek and jaw were doing no more than smoothing over her neck, her shoulders, as his hands slowly did away with her gown.

Her gown.

Grace gasped as the material pooled at her feet, leaving her naked but for the high-cut cotton and lace thong she wore.

"Shh. Easy, Grace," he whispered. "I'm just touching you. That's all. No kisses. No demands. Ah God, just a little touch."

His hands cupped her breasts.

"Matthias. It's more . . ." she sucked in a hard breath as his thumbs raked over her nipples. "More than little touches."

"It warms me, Grace." He pressed his forehead into her shoulder, his black hair falling to the side, covering the swollen mounds of her breasts. It was cool and heavy, another sensual stroke against her flesh.

Suddenly, nothing mattered but warming Matthias. She knew the hell he had lived through, had triumphed against. She knew the pain and blood his life had been filled with.

So he had killed the bastard who had caused it, her dazed mind pondered. Would she have done any less? Her life had been filled with laughter and love, with acceptance. Things Matthias still fought for. Things she had dreamed of giving him.

• • •

MATTHIAS fought to control the shaking of his body, the need to lick and taste her flesh as he stroked her. He could smell the sweet heat of her pussy, drawing him, making his mouth water for the rich syrup he knew flowed from her.

His hands were filled with her swollen breasts, her pebble-hard nipples poking against his thumbs. But he had promised. He had promised not to let the aphrodisiac filling his mouth touch her.

It was killing him. The glands were pumping the hormonal fluid into his mouth, filling his system, burning him alive with the need to fuck her. His cock was so hard, throbbing so viciously he had to fight to hold back his growls.

He let his cheek touch her, his forehead, praying the sweat gathering on his skin didn't have the aphrodisiac effect. He moved along her neck, her shoulders, bending to her to allow his cheek to caress her upper chest, then the hard mound of a breast.

His hand slid to her waist as he panted, his lips a breath from her hard nipple, her little whimpers of pleasures causing him to clench his teeth to hold back.

"Matthias, you're killing us both like this." She trembled in his arms. "Don't do this."

"Are you asking me to stop, Grace?" Please, God, no! He couldn't bear it. He had to touch her, if he didn't touch her, he was going to die.

"Matthias," the soft protest dragged an unwilling growl from his lips.

"I dream of holding you." He rushed his cheek over her nipple and moved lower.

He went slowly to his knees, his hands and face alone touching her, stroking skin so soft he knew it couldn't be real. This had to be a dream. God had been merciful. Somehow he had died, and God had given him an angel to love. It had to be. Because she was so warm and soft, all the things he had dreamed of with none of the scent of death surrounding her.

When he reached the elastic and lace band of her panties, he felt a hard spurt of pre-cum erupt from his cock. He jerked at the pleasure of the small ejaculation, his fingers tightening on the band, as he forced himself to go slowly.

"I can smell you," he sighed against her hip. "Like hot cream and sweet syrup. Have I mentioned, I have a weakness for cream and syrup?"

Her hands were on his shoulders, her fingers kneading them beneath the shirt he wore, as wicked little cries left her throat.

He pulled at the band of her panties, sliding them slowly from her hips, then along her rounded thighs. The little swell of her belly drew him. He wanted to lick it, longed to taste it, but contented himself with pressing his cheek against it instead.

"Matthias, I don't think I can stand this," she gasped.

"Sweet Heaven, just a few more minutes, Grace." His eyes had opened, and he was treated to the prettiest sight of his life.

Sweet honey gold curls beaded with her female cream. Luscious little drops of it clung to the soft curls that shielded her pussy, glistening with arousal and heat.

"Oh God, Grace." His hand was shaking, as he touched a single droplet with one finger, easing it from the curl before rubbing it against his lips.

His eyes closed, his nostrils flared, and the growl that tore from his chest was animalistic, hungry, almost violent.

He licked the taste of her from his lip, drowning in the need for more and relishing even that smallest hint of passion.

"I've dreamed of going down on you." He clenched his teeth desperately, as he fought for control. Maintaining it was iffy. "Licking your flesh, seeing these pretty curls wet with your need for me. Breeds don't have body hair, you know?"

"I know." Her voice was thin, her breath panting as he parted her legs further.

"I've never taken a woman like this," he told her softly. "With just my hands, just this touch." His hand slid up her thighs, his fingers parting the curl-shrouded folds with a reverent touch.

God help him. She was hot. So liquid hot his dick was burning for it. Another hard ejaculation of pre-cum jerked the engorged flesh, warning him, that for him, the mating heat was progressing too quickly. That wasn't just pre-cum. It was a slick hormone-filled lubrication that eased the tender flesh of the vagina, preparing it for his penetration.

Wolf Breeds were thickly endowed. Most women, even female Wolf Breeds struggled to accept the girth. But during mating heat, a Wolf Breed's hormonal responses prepared the female. The pre-seminal fluid aided that, but only during the mating heat. It helped relax the tender muscles, built the arousal, ensured that the sexual act progressed without undue pain, and prepared the feminine sheath for what would come later.

Mother nature was a bitch. Breed mating was wickedly sexual and sometimes, for the females, it could be terrifying.

"Matthias, you're making me weak," Grace moaned, dragging him back from the sight of his index finger piercing the swollen lips and gathering her moisture to it.

He had to taste her again. He couldn't put his lips to her, but maybe, like this.

He looked up at her, brought the sweet juice to his lower lip and smeared it there. When his finger had eased back, he licked.

He moaned at that rich taste. She cried out, her nails piercing his shoulder, as her hips jerked forward, almost slamming her pussy into his lips.

"Stop. Grace. Easy, sweetheart."

"Damn you!" She cried out. "This is killing me."

It was the expression on his face that was killing her. Absorbed, intent, so filled with pleasure it humbled her. His face was flushed, his eyes glittering with rich, golden browns, almost a fire inside the dark orbs.

He was staring at her pussy as though it contained all the secrets of his pleasure. His fingers slid through the slick folds again, parting them, easing inside her.

Easing inside her, when she needed more. Her hips jerked, her pussy convulsing around the single finger as it rubbed against the sensitive tissue.

"Matthias, please. Please. I need more." She was shaking, sweating. God, she had never before perspired like this in the height of sex, let alone foreplay.

Her muscles were tightening, pleasure was streaming through her bloodstream, her clit was on fire, engorged and needy.

"Easy baby. I have you." Two fingers slid inside her as his thumb slid against her clit, circled it, rasped along the bundle of nerves and sent her exploding into a cascade of pleasure.

Violent, white hot, blistering in its intensity, the orgasm that tore through her had her crying out his name. Her nails dug into his shoulders as she lifted on her tiptoes, tightened on his fingers, and felt her juices rushing around them.

She felt one arm surround her hips, his head digging into her belly, and she wasn't certain, but she could have sworn she heard an animalistic snarl.

Nothing had ever been so good. No pleasure she had experienced, or had imagined, could prepare her for something so perfect, so intense, or mind shattering.

Nothing could have prepared her for Matthias.

CHAPTER EIGHT

Matthias needed to give Grace time to accept him on her own, without the mating heat clouding the issue or making her feel that she had been forced into something she didn't want. But the next day, he was beginning to wonder if that would happen.

After he had driven her to climax, she had escaped to the shower, and for the rest of the day, and now into the next morning, she watched him with a wariness that tore at his soul.

He had never been forced to see himself from another's eyes, especially one who had never known the horrors of those labs, or the price of Breed freedom. He had accepted his part in the scheme of preserving Breed independence and establishing their position on earth. It wasn't as though there were another planet they could escape to.

He had been trained by his creators to kill. He now used that training to make certain that those who created them could never repeat the horrors of the past. At least, not for long.

Until Grace, he had never considered how the non-Breed population of the world would view this, how they would view him.

He stood beside the lake outside the cabin, as the sun rose high in the sky, resting on his heels, as he looked out over the water and frowned at the thought.

The blood of monsters shouldn't stain a man's soul. He had saved countless lives, both Breed and non-Breed alike, by the actions he had taken, and he had never given it much thought, until now.

He marked the kills within the smoke circle and gave their souls up to a higher being to judge. He didn't consider himself judge and jury. He was merely the means to stop the atrocities they committed.

Or was he just making excuses for himself?

Bending his head, he picked up a smooth rock from the sandy ground and rubbed his thumb over it, frowning as his thoughts held him captive.

He considered himself neither a good man, nor a bad man, but he was questioning his own actions now, because of one small woman. She saw blood on his hands, whereas he saw peace from the fact that one less monster existed. She saw an injustice, where he saw justice. And he now found himself in conflict with his very beliefs and his perceived place in the world.

He was a Breed. There was no changing that, and he had just as much right to exist in this world as any other creature did. He had the right to laughter, the right to dream, and the right to love. But did he have the right to kill?

A part of him howled *yes*. A part of him questioned that belief. Could he ever do his job again, now that he had seen the look of horror and betrayal in Grace's eyes?

And he knew he wouldn't. Whether she accepted the mating between them or left at the end of the week to resume her life alone, Matthias knew that this part of his life was over.

The smoke assassin would exist no more. He would drift out of men's minds with the same ease that he had slipped into their most secured areas and destroyed the monsters. All because of a woman.

His lips quirked at the thought of that woman.

She was the softest creature on the face of the earth, as far as he was concerned. Gently rounded and tender of flesh as well as emotions. Stubborn. He could see the stubbornness in the sharply rounded chin, but he saw her compassion in her pert little nose and rosebud lips.

Her gray eyes were always soft, even when she was angry, and when she was aroused, they were like a storm. Dark, shifting with color, and firing with hunger.

She moved him. She made him wish for things he had never believed he would want. Made him dream of things he had never believed he would dream of. Things like a home, perhaps children, but at the very least, her soft smile filling his heart before he slept each night, the warmth of her body curled against his.

He wanted to protect her, he wanted to laugh with her, as he had done before she had seen him take a life. She had kept a smile on his face with her gentle teasing and her determination to make certain he knew what the finer things in life were.

Such as a pillow fight. She had whacked him over the head with a couch pillow one evening in her apartment and informed him that even Breeds needed to learn the rules of a pillow fight.

He had nearly kissed her that night. She had dusted him in the pillow fight, but he had retaliated by wrestling her to the floor and stealing her pillow.

He smiled at the memory. Her need for the kiss had filled the air, and only the thought of what would come had kept him in control.

She needed the choice. He wouldn't surprise her with it, he wasn't going to force it on her.

She had cooked him dinner many nights then made him help her wash the dishes rather than using the dishwasher. Another evening she had made him help her cook. He doubted she would repeat that exercise very soon. They had ended up eating from room service, but they had laughed.

They had taken long walks through Central Park, holding hands.

He had gone shoe shopping with her. She had helped him pick out a new pair of boots. He'd talked her into a leather miniskirt, she'd made him buy a pair of jeans, and then they wore their new clothes in the privacy of her apartment, as they ate popcorn and watched a comedy movie she'd been wanting to see.

She could bust his ass playing poker, but he had her on Monopoly. They had fit. Despite the sexual tension that had steadily grown between them, there had been something about being with her that fit him, all the way to his soul.

And he couldn't help but think that finally he belonged to someone.

Breeds weren't born, they were created. They belonged to the labs. They were no more than expensive tools and experiments, until their escapes. After that, they belonged to no one. They were without family, in many cases they were without friends. They were part of the pack they had trained in, but true belonging went deeper. It went to the soul. And his soul belonged to Grace.

But he was beginning to realize that perhaps Grace really didn't want to belong to him. He stared at the rock in his hand, then, feeling the bite of that knowledge as it tore at his heart.

Walking away from her would destroy him. It would mean that there truly was no place in the world that he would fit, and he didn't want that to be true.

He had fought for ten years to make the world safe for Breed mates. With each year, the knowledge of the mating might not be publicized, but the knowledge of the danger to them was. The world was standing behind them, and in several cases where Breed mates would have been kidnapped, regular citizens had raised the alarm.

The Council Directorate was finding it harder with each successive year to strike against known, registered Breeds. They were too well known in the communities they had come into. They were well liked and considered members of the community. Even the pure blood societies were reportedly finding it harder to gain members outside the fanatical few.

There was still a long road to travel in making peace with society at large. And there were still too many Breeds dying needlessly. But inroads were being made.

Now, if only Matthias could make his own inroads.

Straightening, he turned his head to the cabin, eyes narrowing, as Grace stepped out onto the porch. She hadn't tried to run yet, and he had given her every chance to do just that.

She stood just outside the door, staring at him across the clearing. She wore a stretchy, snug top with thin straps and a pair of cutoff jeans. Her silky hair fell around her face to her shoulders in several natural shades of blonde. Even from here he could see the somber reflection in her soft eyes.

Breakfast and lunch had been so silent between them that it weighed in the air like a heavy fog. He had left the cabin to escape it, to escape the pain he knew he was causing her.

Matthias felt his body tighten as she stepped from the porch and moved down the steps before coming toward him. Her steps were slow, the air of reluctance that hovered around her had his teeth clenching.

He dropped the rock he held back to the ground, shoved his hands in his pockets, and waited for her. He felt as though he had waited for her all his life, only to watch her slip from his life once he found her.

"You're not a very conscientious kidnapper," she informed him, as she stepped up to him and brushed the hair back from her face. "You don't even watch me properly."

His lips twitched, as amusement flooded him for a brief second.

"I'm new at this," he bantered back. "You'll have to forgive me my mistakes."

She sniffed in apparent disdain. "I think I'd drop it, if I were you. It's one of those things you either have a talent for, or you don't."

"Perhaps you're right. I'll give it some thought."

Silence descended between them once again. Matthias was forced to curl his fingers into fists to keep them in his pockets, to keep from touching her. She had no idea about the forces that were beating inside him. The hormonal changes in his body were ripping him apart, the taste of the aphrodisiac filling his mouth reminding him by the second that she was his mate.

It would take so little to ensure she never left him, he thought. So little. A lick to her neck as she slept, perhaps. The scrape of his canines against her skin. A kiss. Just the softest kiss, and he would have her forever.

Her body anyway. But it wasn't just her body he wanted, it was her heart, her woman's spirit, and her capacity to love. He didn't want more of her condemnation, or her hatred. And she would hate him, if he stole the choice from her—she would never forgive him. And he would never forgive himself. Prison would be preferable to that. Or death.

"Why did you target me to get to Albrecht?" she finally asked, though now her voice was devoid of anger.

"It gave me an excuse to get close to you," he admitted. "I had been watching several of the hotel's employees. You were just one of them. But you were the one that fascinated me."

Being honest with this woman about such things would never be easy.

She looked out toward the lake for long seconds, following his stance and shoving her hands into the pockets of her cutoffs.

How forlorn she looked. He would give anything, everything to go back and change that moment that she had seen him kill.

"I was falling in love with you, Matthias," she finally whispered.

"I know." He nodded. "I already love you, Grace."

And he did. He loved her so much it was ripping his guts to pieces.

"I've never loved before," he told her quietly. "It wasn't hard to realize what you meant to me. You made me laugh, you lightened my soul."

"And you set out to destroy it." Anger flashed in her gaze.

Matthias sighed bleakly. Perhaps he should just leave, give her a chance to think, to consider being without him. But God help him, he was terrified to do that.

"I won't explain my actions again." He shook his head before staring up at the deep blue of the sky. When he looked back at her, she was watching him somberly once again.

"Go back into the cabin, Grace," he finally told her. "Or work in your flowers or whatever it is you do on vacation. You're straining my control."

A frown snapped between her brow, and her eyes darkened in anger. "I can't relax. I can't do that while you're kidnapping me. Maybe someone will return the favor on your next vacation."

"I would first have to experience such a thing," he growled.

He had never had a vacation. There was still too much to do. There were ten council directors still free, funding the pure-blood societies and training them to kill Breeds. There were trainers still at large and coyote soldiers still lurking. Who had time for a vacation?

"You've never had a vacation?" Disbelief colored her voice. As though it were yet another crime that she marked against him.

"I wasn't taught vacations in the lab," he snarled. "Remember?"

"As though that's an excuse." She sniffed with such ladylike disdain that she fascinated him.

"Grace, I'm going to warn you one last time," he ground out between clenched teeth. "Remove yourself from me, or you are going to regret it."

"It's my property. You remove yourself from *me*." Her hands went to her hips, as her little chin tilted stubbornly. "I did not kidnap you, Matthias. It was the other way around."

"Fine!" He knew he flashed the sharp canines at the side of his mouth as he snarled the word out, because her gaze narrowed, and her lips tightened. "Then you can accept the consequences if you stand there so defiantly, much longer."

"What consequences? Are you going to tie me up again and re-strain me to my seat? Oh wait, why don't you just re-kidnap me, that was scary enough."

"Why don't I kiss you?" he suggested ferally. "Why don't I cover your lips with mine, shove my tongue in your mouth, and force this be-damned hormone into your system, to torture you as well? Why don't I make your pussy so wet, so hot, that you would use your own fingers to tempt me to fuck you? That you would beg me to be inside you? Why don't I do that, Grace?"

He could feel the blood pumping harder, faster inside him now. Adrenaline was mixing with the hormone, and that wasn't a good thing, pumping the effects through his body, straight to his cock. He was so ready to fuck, his cock was about to rupture.

His hands had torn from his pockets and gripped her shoulders now, as he glared down at her.

"My dick is so hard it's agony. I think of nothing but being inside you. Of feeling you, hot and melting around my cock, as you did my fingers. Perhaps you should remember exactly what will happen if I do that."

Grace pressed her hands into Matthias's chest, feeling the thundering of his heart beneath her hands, the tension in his body. She stared into his eyes, feeling as though she were drowning in them as he snarled down at her. What was she supposed to remember? Oh yeah, uncontrolled nympho-sex. Needing him so badly it hurt.

Hell, it hurt now.

"What, Matthias, all that incredible control you've had over the last three weeks is finally fraying? Poor baby. So much for all that Breed training to control your baser impulses."

Had she really said that? Obviously she had, because he was staring at her as though she were crazy.

"Have you lost your mind?" He asked her slowly. "Do you think that now in any way resembles the last three weeks? Sorry, baby, I hadn't tasted that hot little pussy then. I have now, and trust me, the need for more is wearing my control thin."

"It was a decision *you* made, not me." Her finger poked into his chest. "How many low-cut blouses did I wear? Would you like to know how many times I didn't wear panties under my skirt or took my bra off after we came to my apartment? It didn't bother you then, why should it bother you now?"

And he was right, she was crazy. She was aroused, and she was mad. This was her damned vacation, and he was messing it up. What was worse, he had been messing her life up for three weeks, and now she found out that she couldn't even have a hot one-night stand with him without committing for life.

She would be damned if that was fair. Because she knew he was right. Sex with another man would never satisfy her, because he held her heart. She was in love with a killer, and she wanted to kill him for it.

"Do you think I didn't know what you were doing?" His head lowered, his lips only inches from hers as he scowled down at her.

"Do you think it was easy to try to be one of the good guys? To not take advantage of you and force you into this heat?"

"One of the *good guys*?" Her eyes widened, as her voice rose. "Where in the hell do you see yourself as a good guy? You are so fucking *bad*, you give the word a new meaning."

CHAPTER NINE

Grace stared at Matthias in shock, as the words slipped past her lips. Amazingly, he didn't become angry. He didn't take her accusation in the worst light, and that wasn't how she had meant it.

Though, she wasn't certain how she had meant it. She just hadn't meant it in the sense of the killing she had witnessed. The thought of that had her sobering further.

His eyes crinkled at the corners. "You like bad boys," he accused her. "You told me you did."

"That's beside the point," she huffed. "And stop making me crazy. You *are* making me crazy, you know."

"Because you love me." There was so much confidence in his voice that she grit her teeth in agitation.

"Don't tell me how I feel, Matthias. I don't like it." She glared back at him. "You have to be the lousiest kidnapper in history."

"Should I tie you to your bed?" he mused, his expression strained, despite the amusement in his eyes.

"You'd enjoy that too much," she finally sighed before turning away and moving a few paces along the finely ground dirt that bordered the lake. "Would you give it up?" she finally asked, turning back to him.

"Give what up?" he asked, but she saw in his eyes that he knew what she was talking about.

"What you do." The killing. The bloodshed. The danger.

He pushed his fingers through his long black hair. The moment he released it, an errant wind blew it back around his face, giving him a savage, warrior appearance.

He breathed in deeply, stared out over the lake, then turned back to her. "For you. As long as no danger threatens you."

She felt herself trembling, hope surging through her, burning through her mind, as he stared back at her, his expression stoic.

"You wouldn't hate me for it?"

"Grace, dammit, I love you," he snarled. "Do you think I'm unaware that things have to change if you accept me? That what is acceptable as an unmated male would be unacceptable as a mated one? For God's sake!" He glowered down at her. "Do you think I was born stupid?"

She shook her head slowly, a smile trembling on her lips. "No. You weren't born stupid, Matthias."

"What about you?" he growled. "Could you forget Albrecht? Could you forgive what you saw for a life with me?"

She licked her lips slowly. "I understand why you did it. Why you feel you had to do it. Because of what he did to you and to those you knew, you would have had no choice."

But she couldn't face a life with him, never knowing who he would kill next, or why, or living with the fear that the day would come when he would make a mistake. That he would take an innocent life. No man was perfect, and eventually she feared, he would shed innocent blood. That she found too hard to accept.

"So I make this promise to give it up. It doesn't mean I won't continue to fight for Breed rights. I won't sit back and watch my people die without working to help them."

"I understand that."

"The least I can do is be an enforcer, an agent for the Bureau of Breed Affairs."

"I can handle that." She knew about the bureau and their work.

He nodded slowly. "Then come here, mate, take me."

Instantly, Matthias's expression transformed from pure self-assurance, to wicked, carnal arrogance. His lips became fuller, his gaze darker, his thick black lashes lowering as a hard flush stained his cheekbones.

The sensuality he had kept locked inside was finally free. It glittered in his eyes, turned them to dark, whiskey fire, as he watched, waited for her to come to him, for her to accept him.

Grace cleared her throat. "An aphrodisiac in your tongue, huh?"

His lips quirked with a decidedly anticipatory grin.

"Hot, uncontrolled sex?"

A growl rumbled in his throat.

"Well, in for a penny, in for a pound." She stepped to him, her hands sliding from his chest to his shoulders, as his head bent and her lips touched his.

There was no drugging sensation, only sweet, hot pleasure. His lips moved slowly over hers. They both learned the shape and texture of each other, held back, and relished this first touch.

Grace lifted one hand from his shoulder, her lashes lifting, so she could stare into his face with dazed fascination, as she touched his whiskered cheek.

He looked disreputable. Wild and bold. And he was all those things. But his gaze, though burning with arousal, was tender, his hands gentle as one threaded through her hair and the other gripped her hip.

"Like sunshine," he whispered against her lips. "That's how you taste, Grace."

Her lips parted, accepting his again, her tongue reaching out to lick at the harder curves of his. He jerked, his hands tightening on her, as he pulled back.

"Come on." He gripped her wrist and began striding quickly to the cabin.

"Wait." She stumbled along behind him. "What happened? What are you doing?"

"I refuse to take you outside," he snarled, moving up the steps to the porch. "We're going to the bedroom."

"Well, you could have kissed me properly, just once," she argued a bit peevishly. She had been waiting for that kiss.

"Once I get my tongue in your mouth we're both goners." He slammed the door behind them, set the security alarm on the doors and windows, and continued toward the bedroom.

As the bedroom door slammed behind him, he turned, wrapped his arm around her hips, and jerked her to him.

"Now," he groaned. "Sweet God in Heaven. Now!"

His lips descended on hers, parting them, making way for the stroke of his tongue and the spicy, heated taste of lust.

Grace had never imagined that lust had a taste, but it did. It was spicy hot, a hint of jalapeño and the taste of a tropical breeze. It was fine whiskey with an undertone of honey, and it was addictive. Once she had the first taste of him, she knew why he had hesitated to kiss her. Because she could never get enough. She wanted his kiss inside her forever.

Her lips surrounded his tongue, hers battled with his and suckled at it with delirious demand, arching in his arms. She moaned into his lips, felt his groan and his hands. Hands that pulled her clothes from her body. Hands that moved her fingers to the band of his pants.

She tore at the metal closures, releasing the band quickly, before sliding her hands inside to test the muscular contours of his sexy male ass.

"You taste good," she moaned, as his lips lifted from hers to lower her to the bed. "I need more."

"More is what you'll get."

He sat on the bed, jerked his boots off, then straightened and removed his leather pants. Of course, he went commando. No underwear. She wished he had worn underwear, she might have been better prepared for exactly how well endowed he was.

It wasn't so much the length, which was impressive, but he was thick, thicker than she had expected. Thicker than any other man she had ever taken.

Fascinated, she sat up on the bed, reaching out with a single fingertip to touch the throbbing head of his cock. Of course, it was pierced. A silver bar pierced the ridge of its head, the locking balls at each end glittering in the sunlight that slanted through the window. It matched the piercings in his left nipple and ear.

"Any reason for this?" she touched the curved silver lightly. Then her gaze was caught by the two rune tattoos inside his thighs. She knew those. Strength and wisdom. He was both.

"Later," he growled. "I'll explain it later."

Shadows flashed in his eyes, and she didn't want them there. She wanted the flaming arousal back in full force. She wanted all his attention on her.

Grace lowered her head, parted her lips, and let her tongue swipe over the damp crest, pausing to pay particular attention to the silver piercing. She rolled her tongue over it, gripped the small locking ball with her teeth, and tugged at it gently.

Matthias froze. But the shadows were gone. His expression was watchful now, dark with sensuality. Grace parted her lips further and slowly lowered her mouth onto the straining, engorged crest of his cock.

"Ah, fuck!" His groan was followed by a hard, powerful clench of his abdomen. A second later, it was Grace's turn to freeze.

That wasn't just pre-cum that spurted into her mouth, and it wasn't the consistency of semen. The taste was like that of his kiss, honey and spice, pure lust.

She stared up at him, her tongue licking over the thick head and the piercing, as she tried to analyze it. Tabloid rumors, fanatical accusations of perversions and animalistic characteristics flitted through her mind.

Maybe they weren't all lies. Maybe the past ten years of accusations against the Breeds' sexuality was more than just supposition. If it were, it gave a whole new meaning to the idea of wild sex acts.

She eased back, her lashes drooping over her eyes, as he watched her carefully.

"What's next?" She breathed over the head of his cock, watching his cheekbones flush from arousal, as carnal knowledge lit his gaze.

"It's a surprise," he growled, the fingers of one hand curling around his thick shaft. "If I tell you, it would spoil it."

Oh, he was bad.

"Could I convince you to tell me?" She lowered her mouth over the straining crest again and sucked it deep. She watched his face, as she worked his flesh with her tongue, with the suckling heat surrounding him. She gripped the silver that pierced his flesh with her lips, tongued it, then sank her mouth over his cock head once again.

His lashes drifted closed, as his body tightened further. A ragged growl rumbled in his chest. She loved that sound. The hotter he became, the more aroused, the deeper it became.

She knew what was coming, she could sense it. She could feel it. Her hand brushed his away, stroking the thick flesh slowly. She could feel the tension in the middle of the heavy length, a harder pulse of blood, the flesh more heated.

Another spurt of the pre-cum filled her mouth, as a groan ripped from his throat. His cock throbbed, the blood beating furiously through the heavy veins.

"Enough." He drew back, ignoring her frantic attempt to hold him in her mouth.

She could feel the back of her throat tingling, a deeper hunger rushing through her.

"You'll wait," he snarled, pushing her back. "You'll not destroy my control this time."

"You have control left?" Her arms curled around his shoulders, as his lips moved down her neck. "I don't think that's fair. Mine's gone."

She could feel the burn now. It was racing through her, licking over her nipples, her clit. She arched to Matthias, rubbing the hot tips of her breasts against his chest, feeling the fine, silken body hair that was almost invisible to the naked eye. Damn, it felt good, though. Like rough silk rasping over her nipples.

"Do you feel it, Grace?" He whispered as his lips moved lower, his canines rasping over her collarbone. "Do you feel the need building? Burning inside you like its been burning inside me?"

She felt it. Her eyes closed in delirious pleasure with it. The sensations were nearly painful, the arousal building inside her until her womb was rippling with it.

"I'm going to make it burn hotter." His voice was guttural now, hoarse with his own arousal just before his tongue licked over a nipple.

"Oh, God, yes. Suck it." She arched, driving the tight peak against his lips. "Suck my nipples, Matthias."

Another growl. But his lips parted, and he sucked the tender tip inside.

Wet liquid fire wrapped around her nipple. He sucked her deep, his mouth hungry, his tongue stroking and licking, as her nails bit into his shoulders.

"Oh, that's so good," she moaned, her hips arching to grind her pussy against one hard, lean thigh, as he held himself above her. "It's so good, Matthias. I love your mouth. I love your tongue."

He caught the peak between his teeth, his tongue lashing it as she writhed beneath him. Tingles of electric sensation tore from the tip to her womb then struck with brilliant heat to the heart of her pussy.

She jerked in his arms, arched, cried his name.

"Sweet, Grace," he whispered, kissing the swollen slope of her breast reverently, before pressing more kisses between the two mounds and easing slowly down her body. "I can smell your pussy. Sunlight and syrup and sweet cream. I'm going to eat my fill now. I'm going to lick that pretty pussy so slow and easy."

"Oh yes," she moaned, writhing beneath him, her legs falling farther apart as he neared the agonized flesh there.

Her hips lifted, as his lips grazed her hipbone. Her hand tangled into his hair, holding him to her as he whispered over the curls at the top of her pussy.

"Matthias, please." Her heels dug into the bed as she lifted to him. "Now. Touch me now."

His hands slid beneath the cheeks of her rear to hold her in place. Locking his gaze with hers, his tongue distended, sliding through the saturated slit with a long, slow lick.

Spikes of sensation shot through her. Tingles and flares and fingers of electricity arcing from nerve ending to nerve ending as the breath caught in Grace's throat.

Sheer pleasure.

Her eyes closed, and her head tipped back as a keening cry spilled from her lips.

CHAPTER TEN

Matthias licked at delicate, creamy flesh, humming his pleasure in a long, low rumble. She tasted better than honey, better than sweet cream. The luscious juices spilling from her pussy were tinged with spice and spiked with pure sweet fire.

His hands kneaded her ass. Sweet delicate curves that clenched beneath his fingers as she lifted to him without reservation. And he accepted. He ate her with a greed he didn't believe was possible, terrified he couldn't get enough of the sweet, addictive juices spilling to his lips and tongue.

Stretching out along the bed between her thighs, he lifted her closer, staring up at her absorbed expression as slowly, so slowly he pushed his tongue into the gripping, spasming channel he had dreamed of.

Her pussy was like silk. It flexed around his tongue as she cried out again, her hands clenching in his hair, pulling him closer.

Matthias could feel the hormone spilling from his tongue into the sweet depths of her cunt. The potency of the taste was diluted by the sweet juices he sipped from her. He rimmed the opening, lapped at it like the favored treat it would now become. He could eat her for hours and never get enough. Lick her forever and die with the hunger beating at his soul.

"Oh yes," her trembling voice speared through his senses. "Oh, Matthias, it's so good." She stretched beneath him, arching closer, as her hips worked her pussy onto his tongue.

His cock throbbed, the pre-cum spurting from it to the blankets beneath him. He wasn't ready to fuck her yet, he thought desperately. Not yet. He had waited his entire life for this moment. For that one perfect moment, when touch, taste, moans, and whispered passions came into sync.

Everything melded together with Grace. Her taste was perfect. There was no scent of promiscuity, no taste of another who had gone before him. The Breed sense of smell and taste was often too good. But with Grace, there was only the sweet, heated taste of her woman's passion.

Slick, silken, her juices clung to his lips, to his tongue, as he slowly drew back from her.

Swollen glistening folds of flesh drew his gaze. Silken damp curls, ruby red, passion flushed, her pussy lured him. He licked again, hearing her cry, then drew back to gaze at the slickness again.

Had any woman ever been so wet for him? He knew there hadn't been. Only Grace. Farther up, her clit was swollen, fully exposed and flushed with need. He reached out with his tongue, curling around it and groaning at the taste of it.

Grace jerked, and more of her juices spilled from her.

He needed more. A rumbled growl fell from his lips, as his tongue pierced her core again, and he allowed the tip of his nose to caress the hard nub of her clit.

"Oh, God, Matthias." She never called him Matt. He liked that. He wasn't a Matt. He was Matthias. It was the name he had chosen for himself, the name he preferred, and she never used anything else.

"Yes." She stretched beneath him again, her hips rolling, pressing his tongue deeper inside the clenching muscles of her cunt. "Lick me there. Right there."

She was vocal. He liked the sounds of her passion, the feel of it. And he liked knowing she enjoyed his tongue. He licked as she pleaded, caressing into tender tissue as she gasped then cried out for more.

"Your taste," he groaned as he pulled back, licked the outer folds once again, and then caught the spill of sweet liquid from the opening of her pussy. "So sweet, Grace. Your pussy is like nectar. Soft and sweet and addictive."

He lifted his head again, his tongue curling around her clit, as he pressed two fingers inside the grasping depths of her pussy.

She was shaking in his arms, shuddering. Each muscle of her body was drawn tight, and her pussy was so snug he was suddenly thankful for the unique hormones that would prepare her for him. He couldn't hurt her, the thought of hurting her destroyed him.

"Matthias. Oh God, Matthias, what you do to me," she cried out hoarsely, as he drew her clit into his mouth.

She was close to orgasm. He could feel it pounding in her clit, in the tender muscles of her pussy and knew within seconds she would explode beneath him. He wanted it. He needed it. Sex had never been like this. This hot, this desperate. The need for *her* pleasure overriding the need even for his own.

When it came, growls tore from his own chest. Her clitoris, that delicate little nub of flesh expanded, swelled further, and the sweetest taste fell from it, as he felt her vagina tighten and pulse forth more of her slick juices.

The taste of her clitoral response was incredible. Slight. Fresh. New. As though no other man had drawn it forth before.

She was screaming his name. He could hear it, distantly, feel it vibrating through his soul, as this unique taste tempted his tongue. And Matthias knew he would never be satisfied, never be tempted to taste another woman again. Because nothing could ever be this good again.

• • •

GRACE couldn't breathe, she couldn't draw enough oxygen into her lungs, couldn't seem to find the instinct to force it in, as everything, conscious and subconscious, centered on the orgasm imploding inside her.

She shook her head desperately, fighting for air, but she couldn't get enough. Her eyes opened wide, her chest straining as the resulting panic caused the breath to still in her chest. She had warned him. Overexcitement. It happened every time.

"Easy, Grace." Matthias came over her, holding himself above her, one hand easing from her stomach to between her breasts with a gentle, caressing movement. "It's okay, my love. Slow and easy."

"Matthias," she gasped, feeling his fingers lower to massage her diaphragm.

"It's okay, Grace," he soothed her tenderly, his lips lowering to her neck and pressing against the flesh there in a soft, heated kiss. "Relax, love. It will ease."

Her hands were clenched in his hair, tight. It had to be hurting, but there was no strain in his voice, no attempt to loosen them.

"You're so sweet, so responsive," he whispered deeply. "I won't let you come to harm. I swear it."

His palm eased the horrible tightness, relaxing her, making breathing easier. As she drew sweet, clear air into her lungs, her breath caught again.

Oh God. His cock was poised at the entrance to her vagina, parting her folds, thick and hard. The shudders that raced through his body coincided with each, deep spurt of heated fluid that erupted from it.

She could feel it heating her inner flesh, doing something so odd, relaxing it, yet sensitizing it further.

"What . . . ?" She stared back at him in shock.

"It's preseminal fluid," he groaned in her ear. "Hormonal. It eases the tender flesh inside, makes penetration easier. Sweet God, Grace." He shuddered. "I need you now. *Now*."

His lips lowered to her shoulder, as he began to ease inside her.

The pressure, the heat, was incredible. White hot tingles filled her pussy, causing her to lift to him, desperate to still the little fingers of sensation that dug into her muscles.

He stretched her. Then stretched her more. She could feel her flesh parting, burning with a pleasure so intense it bordered on pain. Or was it pain so intense it merged with pleasure?

"Matthias," she gasped his name as he worked his engorged crest slowly inside her.

"It's okay, Grace." The hand that had been stroking below her chest now moved to enclose a swollen breast. "Slow and easy. I promise. I'll take you slow and easy."

She heard the desperation in his voice, the need to ease into her rather than ravish her. But she heard the hunger as well. He was burning as hot as she, his body shuddering with the same force that was trembling through hers.

He was thick, hard, and heavy, and she needed more. Grace lifted to him, working her hips closer, rolling them, taking the shaft deeper, as a groan ripped from his throat and his hand clamped on her hip.

"Easy," he snarled.

"You go easy," she panted, lowering her head to nip his neck demandingly. "I don't want easy."

His hips jerked, burying another hard inch inside her and stretching her with burning intensity.

"God yes." Her neck arched, her hips rolling again. "Fuck me, Matthias. Like I dream."

"Can't hurt you." He was the one fighting to breathe now. "Easy, Grace."

She twisted, digging her heels into the bed and lifted closer again. Her eyes went wide, and the blood thundering through her system went wild. Another hard blast of the pre-cum, and the sensations burning inside her increased. Her pussy rippled around his cock, flexed, spasmed.

"Hell's fire, woman," he bit out. "Don't do that."

It happened again. His hips jerked, and with a snarl he buried inside her, full length, the thick shaft overfilling her, the engorged head pressing demandingly against her cervix.

And it wasn't enough. She needed strokes. She needed taking. She needed . . .

"Fuck me." She nipped at his neck. "Now, Matthias. Fuck me now."

She felt it coming before he moved. The muscles of his back flexed beneath her hands. His thighs tightened, then with another hard growl, he began to move.

It wasn't easy. It wasn't a slow, peaceful loving. It was as wild as Matthias, as hot as her most wicked fantasies, and Grace knew she would never be the same.

"Like this." His hands lifted her legs around his hips, and he sank in farther.

She could feel his balls slapping against her rear, hear the hot, wet slap of flesh against flesh, and feel the hot burn of a possession so intensely carnal it would be branded into her very being forever.

His lips were everywhere. Kisses on her neck, her shoulder. He bent and suckled her nipples with deep hard draws of his mouth, lashed them with his tongue. His hips drove his erection inside her with furious thrusts, and she accepted him with hoarse cries for more.

"So hot and sweet." He nipped at her ear. "So giving. God yes, Grace, give to me. Take me."

The tension was gathering in her womb again. It flexed and spasmed with the power of the pleasure racing through her now. Sensations that tore through her, stripped her control, and left her racing toward an edge of ecstasy that should have been terrifying.

Matthias groaned against her breast, his body bowed over her, his cock moving hard and heavy inside her. The fierce strokes stretched and burned and sent fiery fingers of absolute pleasure tearing through her. He fucked her with wild hunger, his cock shafting into her with desperate strokes, as her legs tightened around his hips.

He pumped inside her demandingly, stroking and igniting flames of devouring lust. It rippled and burned through her body, left her gasping, begging for release.

Her nails dug into his back, as his lips returned to her shoulder. Sweat coated them, their moans blended, mingled until Grace's turned to screams.

This orgasm didn't just implode inside her. It exploded through her, tore past her body and lit her soul with fireworks. Her pussy tightened on his shuttling cock to the point of pain, as she felt the release of her juices wetting her further. Then something else happened.

She should have been prepared. He hadn't hidden it from her. He had warned her.

She felt his release build, heard his throttled male groan at her shoulder a second before she felt his canines bite into her flesh.

There should have been pain. There should have been a rending of flesh. There wasn't.

There was a sharp, fiery blast of sensation, as she felt the first spurt of semen, then the sudden thickening of his cock.

It thickened. And thickened. And thickened. Just in one place. Burning through the thick, heavy muscles that gripped him so tightly, exposing nerve endings she couldn't have known existed, stretching her, secured inside her, as he shot his seed straight to the opening of her cervix.

He was locked inside her. Pulsing violently, stroking her pussy, even though he was still inside her. It throbbed with his release, the feel of the blood pounding through it, throwing her into another orgasm so violent that she didn't have to worry about breathing, because she knew she must have died.

Nothing could be so incredible and still allow life afterward. This was the pinnacle. This was ecstasy, and she would never survive.

CHAPTER ELEVEN

Matthias found himself gently massaging Grace's diaphragm after the explosion that tore through her body. She was trying to laugh and gasp for breath at the same time, her face flushing with an edge of embarrassment.

He was still locked inside her, his muscles tight and rippling with the final spurts of his own release. His long black hair fell over his face and hid her expression, like a dark cocoon, insulating them from the world.

Tenderness filled him, as her soft gray eyes watched him with a pleasure reflected in her gaze. Her hands stroked his shoulders so gently, as his palm pressed beneath her ribcage, easing the tightness.

"That's so embarrassing," she finally whispered, stroking his hair back from his face, as he kept his gaze locked on her.

God he loved her. Loved her until he could think of nothing but her.

"Overexcitement," he whispered, kissing her cheek tenderly, as he felt his cock finally, blessedly, ease in its stiffness. "And a bit of fear, perhaps?"

Her lips tilted teasingly. "You have a few aspects that are a little overwhelming," she admitted. "But it's not totally your fault. Sometimes, I panic a little."

A little? Her diaphragm was relaxed now, and her breathing, though a little quick, was coming easier.

"Has it happened often since you were a child?" he questioned, easing from her, shuddering at the snug grip of her pussy as he slid out.

"Oh." She breathed out hard at his movement. "That still feels good."

Her hands slid over his shoulders and stroked down his chest, as he moved to lay beside her. She was a gentle weight against his chest now, one slender leg tucked between his, as she pushed his hair back from his face once again.

"It doesn't happen a lot," she finally answered him. "It used to happen all the time when I was little. New situations or if I got scared or excited. My dad was in the army. Every time we heard of a new battle near his area, or if he was late coming home on leave, it would happen."

Stress perhaps, Matthias thought as he tucked her closer to him.

"It hasn't happened since I hit my twenties. But then again, I've never been so excited in my life," she laughed, pulling her head back to stare up at him.

"Or perhaps so frightened?" he asked.

She shrugged, a wry smile on her face. "But it didn't happen when I saw you in Albrecht's suite. Or when you kidnapped me."

"Because you trusted me." He cupped her face in his hand, feeling his chest tighten at the knowledge of how much she had trusted him without even knowing it. "You knew I wouldn't kill without reason, Grace. Just, I think, as you knew that Albrecht was all he was accused of being."

She didn't turn away from him now, nor did she avoid his look. "I knew," she finally whispered. "Inside. But you still scared the life out of me."

"Not enough to steal your breath," he reminded her.

A soft smile from remembered pleasure shaped her well-kissed lips, this time as she shifted against him, her hand stroking down his arm. "No, it's your touch that steals my breath, Matthias. Maybe, if we practice a whole lot, I'll learn how to control it."

"Hmmm, perhaps that's the answer." He leaned down, allowing his lips to rub against hers, to feel the passion and desire in her acceptance of him.

He hadn't expected this. The price of keeping her wasn't so very bad, though. No more assassinations. He could live with that. Jonas could use him at the Bureau of Breed Affairs. He had requested his help there on a full-time basis many times, and Matthias had refused. Maybe he could talk to the director about that now, see what was needed.

There were very few Wolf Breeds in the bureau. The pack leader, Wolf Gunnar, was now on the Breed Ruling Cabinet and met often with the human and feline sections of the Breed community. The separate Breed races were slowly coming together, adapting and learning how to ensure their place in the world. Matthias could help with that. Grace could help with that. He had seen her at the hotel managing the staff. She was like a little general directing the running of the establishment.

"I think I'm hungry," she finally sighed, as his head lifted. "Starving, actually."

Matthias touched her cheek with the backs of his fingers. "Then I better get you fed," he said. "Because the heat will build again, Grace. And soon."

Grace stared back at him in surprise, as he moved from the bed, then helped her rise as well. The surprise quickly changed to admiration. He was hard from head to toe. His body was lean, his muscles flexed with power without being ungainly.

She could understand now why her childhood panic had returned. Her difficulty breathing was due to stress, to emotional overloads, as the doctors had coined it. That was Grace, too damned emotional sometimes. She could handle watching her lover kill a suspected monster, but she couldn't handle the knowledge that he was imperative to her happiness.

Just as her father had been. Just as the knowledge of the danger he had faced had brought on the emotional attacks.

She had thought she was over them. Her father had just retired from the army a few years before, but she hadn't had an attack in more than six years. Until Matthias.

Because she loved him.

She shook her head as she followed him to the shower. They washed quickly, hunger of a different sort driving them now.

Showering with Matthias was a unique experience, though. He loved the water, and he hogged it. She had to push him back several times to get her share, and a wrestling match ensued for possession of the stream of water. She lost, of course, but he did hold her close enough to make certain she was both washed and rinsed from head to toe.

Then he made certain she was dry as well. By time he finished, Grace was ready to head back to the bed rather than to the kitchen.

"Food first. I need my energy." He inhaled slowly, his lashes lowering, as sensuality filled his expression. "Then we'll go to bed. Perhaps we'll even sleep sometime tonight."

He backed her against the bathroom wall, the heavy length of his cock burning against her lower stomach, as her hard nipples raked his chest.

Grace ran her palms over his biceps, then his shoulders, as his head lowered, and he licked the small spot where he had bitten her earlier. Sensation sang through the small wound, a clenching pleasure so deep and hot she rose to her tiptoes to prolong it.

He was definitely a bad boy. Tattooed, pierced, and arrogant as hell. She had seen that arrogance more than once over the past weeks. But he was gentle with her. He touched her like a dream, and he kissed her like fire.

"Food," he whispered regretfully against her lips, drawing back and staring down at her somberly. "Are you sure you're okay?"

"I'm fine." She was so damned horny now she thought she might melt in a puddle at his feet.

They dressed in the bedroom and headed through the cabin to the kitchen.

The refrigerator was filled with cold cuts, vegetables, and cold water that the caretaker had stocked before her arrival. The freezer held a variety of packaged steaks and other frozen goodies.

She grabbed the meat from the refrigerator and some lettuce and tomatoes. Thick, fresh bread was wrapped and stored in the cabinet. She removed it and set it on the counter.

Matthias was unusually quiet as he moved through the kitchen, the living room, then back to the kitchen. His expression was somber, the way he watched her finally grating on her nerves.

"Is there a problem?" She laid the bread knife down and watched him closely. "If you're still considering killing me, I should point out that has to be against the rules, or something."

His lips quirked as he shook his head. "That would be worse than suicide."

"Then what's bothering you?" She set the bread on plates and began heaping them with meat, cheese, and veggies.

"I just thought of something." He slid his hand into the pockets of his leather pants as he faced her. "What were you doing in Albrecht's suite?"

"He left a message on my machine, demanding my presence. I thought I would see what his problem was before I left."

"Why did you come back?" He was frowning curiously.

Grace waggled her brows. "My bikini. I forgot it. It was new, and I wanted to wear it while I was on vacation. I love swimming in the lake."

The frown eased away, as his whiskey eyes lit with arousal.

Grace snickered at the look, as she picked up the plates and moved them to the kitchen table, before grabbing two bottles of water from the fridge.

"A bikini, huh?" he asked, taking his seat across from her. "What kind of bikini?"

"A little black bikini." She clenched her thighs, the burning in her clit was becoming a bit irksome. Surely to God she could get through a meal without attacking him?

"I'd like to see it," he murmured, picking up his sandwich and biting into it with strong, white teeth.

Teeth that had bitten her. She could feel the mark at her shoulder throbbing and irrationally wished he would lick it again.

She ate her sandwich with more determination than actual hunger now. After they finished, she quickly cleaned the dishes. And Matthias was still quiet.

He had moved from the kitchen to the living room, where he stood in front of the wide picture window, staring out at the lake.

He looked almost regretful.

Maybe Breeds didn't like women with a weakness, she thought morosely, remembering how her breathing had seized up. It was a stress reaction, it wasn't like she was terminally ill or anything. To be honest, her climaxes had terrified her. She had never come so hard, never felt such pleasure ripping through her. It was no wonder she had panicked a little, especially when his cock had thickened, spreading her further and sending her into another, sharper series of orgasms.

"The panic attacks aren't a big deal," she finally said as she stepped into the living room. "They go away eventually."

He turned to stare at her, his eyes narrowing, flicking to her breasts. Her nipples were poking against the soft material of her dark blue shirt, and her pussy was clenching in need.

Violent need.

It didn't make sense. Before, she hadn't ached like this, not to the point that it was physically painful.

"I'm not worried about the panic attacks. If you were ill, I'd detect the scent of it."

Okay. That told her.

She pushed her fingers through her hair and glared at him.

"Then why are you moping around like it's the end of the world? Did I do something wrong?"

Maybe she hadn't pleased him sexually. A man could get a little out of sorts when a woman failed to pick up on something he was wanting but was too stupid to ask for it.

His jaw clenched as he inhaled roughly. "You didn't do anything wrong."

She nodded sharply. "You know, I understand that being a Breed could make you more testosterone-impaired than most men tend to be. But I can't read your thoughts any more than I can read other men's. If something is wrong, I'd prefer you just get it out in the open rather than making me miserable by pulling the silent treatment. Trust me, I have several brothers, I can handle your delicate sensibilities."

His brow lifted, as amusement glittered briefly in his eyes. Amusement, arousal, and something undefined. Anger, perhaps.

"My male sensibilities are functioning fine," he assured her, the corner of his lips tilting wryly.

Grace crossed her arms over her breasts, almost gasping at the feel of the material of her shirt raking over her hard nipples.

"Then what's your problem?"

"You're in pain," he said softly. "Aren't you?"

Grace shifted uncomfortably. "Not really."

"I wanted to hide from you exactly what the mating would do to you," he finally sighed. "There's still so much we don't know about it, or its effects. I should have waited."

"Now, you're starting to frighten me, Matthias."

"Do you know that only two of our wolf mates have produced children? In one of those, the wolf's genetics were so recessed that the scientists theorize that it made conception easier for his mate. The other was so brutally experimented on that she still has nightmares."

Grace flinched at the thought of such pain. "The Felines seem to have no problem."

"More than you know," he sighed. "It's true, the original pride initially had success in conception, but after that, the heat continued during the females' ovulation periods, and no other babies were conceived. It's been ten years. Scheme Tallant, the mate to the felines' head of public relations, is now carrying twins. One child has been born to Merinus and Callan, one to Veronica Andrews, and one to Kane Tyler's mate, Sherra. There is one child born to Dash Sinclair and his mate, and to Aiden's mate, Charity. For the Wolves, conception has proved extremely difficult, and the heat extremely severe."

His voice was heavy, his expression dark, remorseful.

"I tried to be honest with you, Grace." He shook his head, his lips tightening with what she now knew was self-anger. "But I hungered for you." A frown creased his brow, as he stared back at her as though that hunger still confused him. "Even now, my control is less than it should be." His frown deepened. "I tried to tell myself it would be different between us, but I knew better."

Her sex clenched as slick juices spilled between her thighs.

"Do you think explaining it any further to me would have made a difference?" she asked "I'm not a child, and I'm not completely ignorant. Once you told me what you had, I remembered the tabloid stories, I knew I could be looking at more than you were telling me. Evidently, I didn't care."

His head tilted as he watched her with confusion. "How could you not care, Grace? It will change your life forever. Place you in danger. It will restrict your life and will turn you into a target for the scientists out there, who are determined to destroy us."

"And that's what bothers you the most," she said softly. "That danger. Admit it, Matthias. You're frightened."

His lips tightened. "I will protect you."

"No matter the cost," she guessed. "You're afraid that your attempts to protect me will cause me to hate you."

He growled. That sound sent rapid little bursts of near-ecstasy to explode through her vagina, as it tightened her clit further.

"That isn't all," he admitted. "They want our mates." He stared back at her, tortured, desperate. "The mating causes a decrease in aging. The couples who have mated are aging only one year per every five to ten years. You will live far longer than you ever imagined, and it's because of this that the rogue scientists are so desperate to get their hands on mated pairs."

Okay, now that was shocking. Grace stared back at him, her lips parting in disbelief.

"How much longer?" she asked.

He swallowed tightly. "We aren't certain, but there's rumors that the first Lion Breed created more than a century ago still lives, and that he and his mate are still in their prime."

"Whoa!" She breathed out, moving to the chair beside her and sitting down heavily. "That's definitely a decrease in aging." Her hand pressed against her lower stomach. "Does it stop after conception?"

He shook his head sharply. "Not that we've seen. Conception is so difficult that our doctors and scientists believe this is nature's way of ensuring the species. Until the babes have grown and we see how this aging affects them, we can't be certain of anything."

"Well, this definitely throws a little kink into things," she breathed out roughly. "You said Merinus and Callan have only one child? The reports state three. I remember that."

He shook his head. "There are three pride children. The press mistakenly reported the children as all belonging to the pride leader and his mate, and they didn't bother to correct it. They keep their mates closely guarded while they're pregnant, and out of the public eye. It's the only way to ensure their safety."

"And the wolf mates?"

His jaw flexed, a muscle ticking violently just under the flesh.

"No one knows where Dash Sinclair hides his family. Aiden and Charity stay on the Wolf Breed compound in Colorado and never leave it. Their child will be born under as much restriction as we were created in."

"And if I conceive?" she whispered.

"We'll have no choice but to return to Colorado. If it happens."

CHAPTER TWELVE

Grace rubbed at her bare arms as she stared back at Matthias, the irritating pinpoints of sensation racing over her flesh were driving her insane. She needed him to touch her, not stand there trying to explain things neither of them could change at this point.

"So, you're regretting not telling me all this before?" She leaned back in the chair and licked her lips, watching as his eyes darkened, his dark cheeks flushing a brick red, as his lips became fuller, his expression darker with lust.

"I should have told you." His nostrils flared as she lifted her hand and stroked it over her collarbone. Every inch of her body was tingling now, begging for him.

"Consider me told," she stated.

"What?" He was staring at her, almost dazed now, his hands slowly pulling from the pockets of his black leather pants. Pants that did nothing to hide the straining length of his arousal beneath them. He was thick and hard. She was wet and wild, and she needed him now.

"Look, this is all very interesting, and I'm sure I'm going to have questions eventually. You know, once the ramifications of the whole mating thing hits me? Sometime after you get your wolfie ass over here and fuck me."

His eyes narrowed, as his hands went to the black shirt he wore, his fingers sliding buttons from their holes, and his gaze gleaming now with pure lust.

"My wolfie ass?" he asked her softly, his voice dark, rough.

Grace slid her shorts from her body, leaving only the silk panties she wore, as his shirt was tossed to the floor. Her own shirt came off easily, as he sat down and pulled his boots and socks off.

She rose to her feet, and before he could rise from the wide, padded stool he had sat on, she was in front of him.

"You're slow." She knelt before him, pushing him back against the chair behind the stool, her fingers moving for the metal closures on his pants.

"So I am," he growled, his tight abs flexing as she parted the edges of the pants and revealed the straining length of his cock.

The piercing gleamed against the dark flesh.

"Why the piercing?" she asked, lowering her head to let her tongue worry the little ball at one end of the bar.

His hands slid into her hair, a tight groan leaving his throat.

"A reminder," he panted.

"What does it remind you of?" She held the hard shaft, turned her head, and sucked the upper side of the crest between her lips to allow her tongue to stroke around the jewelry with flickering movements.

"Freedom," he bit out. "It reminds me of freedom."

"Why?"

He tightened further as her teeth gripped the bar.

"We weren't allowed piercings or tattoos in the labs. Nothing that would identify us. Nothing that would make us individuals. It reminds me. I'm free."

Her heart clenched, and her soul bled for the pain that resonated in his voice. His freedom came down to his choice to be pierced and marked. His ability to be an individual.

She sank her mouth over the engorged head of his erection and sucked him in deep. She wanted the memory of that place wiped from his mind. She wanted it replaced with need, with hunger. For her.

He belonged to her.

He growled her name as he leaned back against the chair, sprawling across the stool and the chair cushion behind him. Her fingers stroked the thick shaft as his hands clenched in her hair, guiding her movements, showing her how to please him best.

He liked to feel her teeth raking gently along the crest. The way her tongue played with the bar piercing his flesh.

As she sucked his cock head, her hands pushed at his pants, sliding them over his thighs, and pushing them down his legs.

There, now she could explore flesh she had been dying to touch. His scrotum was silky and smooth, only the faintest hint of silky hairs covering it. It tightened as she cupped it in her palm then slid her nails over it.

"Grace," the growl in his voice was warning. "Leave me control, sweetheart. Don't push this."

Oh, a dare.

She opened her eyes, lifting them to meet his as her lips lifted from the throbbing crest and began to slide down the straining shaft.

He was breathing hard now, his hands gripping the arms of the chair rather than her hair.

"What control?" she whispered. "I don't have any, why should you?"

She wanted that loss of control. She wanted the wild man she glimpsed in his eyes, the bad boy she knew he was. Her lips moved lower, her tongue licking until she came to the tight, silky flesh of the sac below.

"Dammit. Grace," he cursed, but he arched to her, allowing her the freedom to lick over the tight flesh, to feel the straining tension there.

As she watched, a small spurt of pre-cum spilled from the slit on his cock head. He growled again, a thick rumbling sound of hunger that had her heart racing in excitement.

She used the slick fluid to ease the stroking of her hand along the shaft, feeling it flex beneath her fingers as her lips investigated his balls and her tongue flickered over the silken, tight flesh.

"You don't know what you're doing," Matthias snarled. "What you'll cause."

The fingers of her other hand moved lower, beneath the tense flesh of his scrotum and found the ultra-sensitive flesh beneath. She couldn't have anticipated his reaction.

She was only stroking the flesh between his balls and his anus, but he jerked, his hands gripping her shoulders and pulling her back as he jackknifed from the chair.

"I warned you," he bit out, his voice tight and hard, wicked with a sensual threat. "You want to play games, mate. Let me show you what happens when you do."

She had somehow released more than she had bargained for. Within seconds she found herself bent over the stool, Matthias behind her, and before she could stop him, his lips and tongue were moving along the cleft of her rear.

She should have been frightened, terrified. She had never been touched there, refusing to allow any previous lovers that freedom.

But Matthias wasn't asking for anything. His tongue was ravenous, licking and stroking, as his hands parted the full curves and he delved lower.

"Matthias!" She cried out his name, trying to lift herself from the wickedness of the caress, the stroke of his tongue over the entrance to her rear. Another stroke, then an entrance so shocking she began to shudder.

"I've been dying for this," he groaned behind her, his hands caressing over her ass as he rose, his cock tucking against the entrance.

"It's not going to fit," she gasped.

At the same time, she felt the first blast of the preseminal fluid explode from the tip of his cock and his cock sinking into the tight orifice.

Grace tried to writhe beneath him, but his hands held her in place, his cock parting her flesh marginally as the forbidden channel began to burn.

Sweet God, what was he doing to her? What was in the silky fluid that both lubricated and eased the passage she knew he was preparing to take?

With each spurt, he was able to sink deeper inside her, stretching the unbreached entrance, burning it with a pleasure/pain that had her screaming beneath him.

"I love your ass." His hands kneaded the curves. "I would watch you when you walk, my cock so damned hard I thought I would die, imagining this. Imagining taking you here, feeling you accept me. Submit to me."

Submit.

That was it. Grace could feel it in him. The dominance and power he had kept hidden from her. He had let her make nearly every decision in their relationship until now. He was ensuring his dominance now. Reinforcing the fact that he might give up a few things for her, but he still controlled this. He controlled her response. He controlled her sexuality.

She arched before him now, feeling another heated spurt of the fluid that relaxed and eased, even as it intensified sensation. She could feel the burn inside her anus, demanding more, demanding the hard stretching, the submission required to take him in.

"You're mine!" The declaration was made with a rough demand. "Say it, Grace. Mine."

"Yours," she panted. She wasn't about to argue. Not now. Not when he could stop and take the incredible sensations away from her.

He was thick and hard, hot and demanding, and with the aid of the slick, forceful jets of heated fluid, he was taking her, stretching her, forging inside her until his scrotum was pressed into the wet heat of her pussy, and his cock was fully embedded in her rear.

Then he was moving. He didn't pause. He didn't wait for her to make sense of the pleasure that mixed with the pain or the burning need and heated resistance.

His hands gripped her hips, and he began fucking her with slow, forceful thrusts. Each time he slid back another spurt of heated fluid sensitized her inner flesh further. Each forceful thrust was taken with slick ease and with a desperate cry.

He moved one hand from her hip, sliding between her thighs, his fingers surrounding her clit, stroking and milking it as his thrusts increased.

She could feel the drag of the bar that pierced his cock, an added sensation that dragged a desperate breath from her lungs. His thighs braced hers, his balls slapped against sensitive flesh, and within seconds Grace felt her release racing through her.

She bucked beneath him at the hard explosions that began to shudder through her. Pleasure became an agony of ecstasy. Sensation became waves of desperate, clenching release that she was certain she would never survive. As one would recede, another would build. As the thickening of his cock filled her ass and his spurts of release began to burn inside her, another took her, shook her, and had her fighting to scream.

She was writhing, jerking beneath him, held still by his body as he came over her, his lips covering the mark he had made on her shoulder earlier, his tongue stroking it as his sharp teeth held her in position.

She was lost. Lost in the orgasms pouring over her, and the mental and physical submission racing through her. She belonged to Matthias, just as he belonged to her. And the knowledge wasn't scary. It was right. For the first time in her life, belonging to someone was just right.

CHAPTER THIRTEEN

The horrible craving for Matthias's touch had finally eased as the day gave way to night. He forced her into the shower again, chuckling as she leaned against his chest and tried to doze while he bathed her. It was a good thing he still had some strength in his legs, because hers was shot.

She was limp, physically and mentally sated, and sleepier than she could ever remember being in her life. When he finally carried her to the bed and tucked her in close to his chest, a satisfied little sigh left her lips.

Her lips smoothed over the curved bar, secured at both ends by small silver balls that pierced his nipple. The metal was warm from the warmth of his flesh and reminded her of what he had said about his reasons for getting the piercings. To remind him of his freedom, his individuality. He was pierced and tattooed, scarred inside and out, and he was the most beautiful creation on the face of the earth, as far as she was concerned.

The thin scar that ran from his brow, across his eyelid, and halfway down his cheek was barely noticeable to her, though she ached often at the thought of the pain he must have felt when he was wounded.

He was a bad boy. There was no doubt about that. Wicked, carnal, intense, and arrogant. But when he held her, his arms were gentle, his hands tender as he soothed her closer to sleep.

"My dad would like you." She yawned as she snuggled closer to him. "My brothers would, too."

She felt his hand still on her back where he had been stroking her spine.

"Do you think they would?" His voice might sound unconcerned, but Grace knew him now, and she knew that strained edge to his tone was one of hope.

"I know they would." She was confident of it.

"Why would they like me?" he asked her. "I don't look like any man's vision of a son-in-law, Grace." Stark, almost bleak, his regret washed over her, forcing her to blink tears from her eyes.

"You're strong, honest. You stare people in the eye when you speak to them, and I love you. Trust me, Dad won't be able to resist you. And of course, Mom is just going to be in heaven. She'll think you need to be fattened up. She'll bake you homemade pies and bread and spoil you every chance she gets with her best dishes."

"Why would she do that?" Confusion lingered in his tone.

Grace moved her head back, staring up at him in the dark. "Because she'll love you, Matthias. That's what mothers do. My brothers will teach you how to play touch football, and their wives will ogle your ass when they aren't looking. My sisters-in-law are exceptionally intelligent. They know a fine male form when they see one."

Matthias stared down at her, frowning. She was talking as though his acceptance within her family was a done deal, without him having to make concessions or scrape for it. That couldn't be true. Nothing had ever come so easily to him. He had to fight for everything. It was accepted.

"Your father and your brothers will see me for what I am, Grace," he warned her, hating that fact. "They'll want you to choose another man. Accept that now."

He felt her surprise, then her amusement at the soft laugh that wrapped around him. "Oh, Matthias, you just don't understand families," she whispered into the darkness. "Daddy will take one look at you, and he'll take you out to his shed where he tried to fool us into believing he's building something. He'll give you a beer and interrogate you for hours as he puts you to work sanding this or that, or using a hammer. That's his form of acceptance. Trust me. He's going to love you."

"I don't know how to sand or hammer." For the first time in his life Matthias wondered if he was feeling an edge of fear.

"My brothers will follow along, of course," she informed him, as he felt a curl of trepidation. "They'll grin and smirk, as Daddy questions you, throw out a few questions of their own, then grab the football and rescue you."

"I don't know how to play football." He cleared his throat nervously.

"That's okay, they don't either," she assured him drowsily, confusing him further. "And while the neighborhood guys gather around in the back lot to teach you how not to play football, Mom will be cooking up a storm, and me and the sisters-in-law will be admiring your manly butt and broad shoulders. But don't wear leather to play football in. You need jeans."

"I always wear leather." It was slicker, harder to grip. It didn't make as much sound when one moved, and he had grown accustomed to it.

"You wear jeans to meet Mom and Dad, so you can play ball with the boys." She yawned again, as though compliance with her little demands were a foregone conclusion. "And remember, Mom makes the best cherry pie in the world. And she still makes homemade vanilla ice cream. You'll love it."

He was certain he would, but that wasn't the point.

"Grace, don't get your hopes up," he whispered, pressing his cheek to the top of her head, as his eyes closed in despair.

She wasn't like him, she had a family, interaction, a life outside of him. He only had her.

"You'll see." She sighed, her body relaxing against him. "You'll see, my family is going to love you."

Her father and brothers would likely warn him away from her with a weapon. When that didn't work, they would complain to the Bureau of Breed Affairs. When that didn't work, they would attempt to turn Grace against him.

He hadn't considered this, the reaction of her family. Hell, he hadn't considered her family at all, and that had been a mistake. He could hear her love for them in her voice. They were important to her. She would hate losing them. She would hate him, if she lost them because she was bound to him by the mating heat.

Matthias could feel sweat beading on his brow. What the hell would he do when that happened? Grace didn't know, she had no concept of how important she was to him. She was his life. She was every dream he had ever dreamed in the hell of the labs. And after his release, the thought of the woman who would eventually fill his life had been his every hope for the future. The first time he had seen her, he had known she would carry his soul through eternity. Life or death, it wouldn't matter, he belonged to Grace Anderson.

And she belonged to her family.

There had to be a way to ensure her family's compliance, he thought. He had money. He could make certain they had no legal difficulties. He could kill their enemies.

No, no killing. Grace wouldn't like that. Okay, he could make their enemies wish they were dead. He had a few resources he could draw on. Men understood such matters. At least, the non-Breed men he knew understood such matters. Were fathers and brothers somehow different?

Surely they couldn't be. They were still men. He might not be good enough for Grace, but he could find a way to ensure that they didn't hurt her by turning their backs on her when she refused to toss him free of her life, like she should the mutt he was certain they would believe he was.

He resumed stroking her back, using just his fingertips, relishing the feel of her satiny flesh. He knew she longed to live closer to her parents. He could buy her a home near them, that would surely earn him a few good points.

Damn. He would have to make plans to deal with this one. Research her family before he went to meet them. He would have to research them extensively. Perhaps he'd get lucky, and if worse came to worse, he could find something to hold over their heads to ensure that Grace wasn't hurt.

Because there wasn't a doubt in his mind that they would want him out of her life. He was a Breed. Part animal. He wasn't a man, he was a creation. A freak of science. No man who loved his daughter would want such a mate for her. Hell, he wouldn't want it for his own daughter, why would her father want such a thing?

And he was a killer. Or, he had been a killer.

A smile quirked at the corners of his lips. He had a feeling that before it was over with, many of his habits would be changing. But, that was okay. He was looking forward to it. She was soft and gentle, and as long as he could forestall the problems he knew would come with her family, then he could ensure she stayed soft and gentle with him.

Losing her would kill him, he knew that. Even without the mating heat, his soul was already bound to her in a way that he knew he would never be free of.

He kissed her head, loving the feel of her against his chest, a delicate weight that warmed him to his core.

He would figure out this family thing, for her. He wasn't so certain about the football, though. He had never touched a football in his life, though he had watched other Breeds attempting to learn during his stay on Wolf Mountain in Colorado.

Dealing with her family's hatred of him would be a small price to pay to have her in his life. He would pretend not to notice it, make himself as unobtrusive as possible, and should they need any help in anything, he would take care of the matter.

He nodded with a barely discernible movement. That should work. And if worse came to worse . . . he sighed. If worse came to worse, he would deal with it. She was worth it to him.

"I love you, Grace," he whispered against her hair.

He loved her laughter, her smile. The way her nose wrinkled when he teased her, the way her ears twitched when he kissed them.

She shifted against him as though trying to burrow deeper into his chest, and he let a smile tilt his lips and gathered her closer to him. His arms surrounded her, his head bent over hers, and he let her legs tangle with his.

His body was now as bound by her as his soul was. Silken limbs encased him, and soft breaths fell against his chest.

For the first time in his life, Matthias closed his eyes and slept while a woman lay tangled with his own body. He had never before been able to relax with a lover. But damn if he could help it. She had worn him out. She was as enthusiastic in their sex play as she was at everything else she did. Maybe a bit more so, he thought, as he remembered her nails raking his back and her demands for *harder, faster, now,* echoing in his head.

Yeah, definitely more enthusiastic in their love play was his last, distant thought as he breathed out in exhaustion and let sleep throw its final web across his senses.

CHAPTER FOURTEEN

Dawn wasn't far from making its first appearance over the horizon when Matthias came awake with a start. The scent of diseased perversions and hatred filled his senses, as he pressed his hand over Grace's lips and brought her quickly awake.

"Danger," he growled softly at her ear, while he pressed the panic button at the side of his watch. Jonas was their only hope. "Dress quickly."

He moved out of the bed, pulling her with him and tossing her the clothes he had insisted she keep by the bed, just in case. Jeans, a T-shirt, and light jacket. Thick socks and hiking boots.

He jerked his leather pants on, a black shirt, socks, and boots. Within seconds he was dressed and pulling his duffel bag away from the wall.

His weapons were there. The tools of his trade. He strapped the pistol to his thigh, knives against the underside of his arms. He tucked a backup pistol in one boot, a dagger in the other. He grabbed the shorter model automatic rifle he used for warfare.

"Matthias?" Grace whispered in fear, as he grabbed her wrist and moved her quickly from the bedroom.

They didn't have much time. He could feel the coyote soldiers moving in, could smell their blood-drenched souls, but they hadn't surrounded the house yet.

"It's okay. Just do as I say, and we'll be fine."

He prayed. Oh God he prayed, as he quickly unlocked the window on the far side of the living room and lifted it soundlessly.

He dropped to the ground, then lifted Grace from the ledge, as she attempted to follow him. She was shaking, but stayed silent. Silent was good. It could have been their ticket out of there, if it weren't for the smell of her heat.

The soft scent of mating arousal was unmistakable. There was no way to hide it. That meant their asses were in a sling, if Jonas didn't get here fast.

Matthias made certain they were downwind of the coyote soldiers, who had attempted to come in downwind themselves. But the winds in the mountains were capricious. At some point they had shifted, betraying the coyotes' advance while hiding his escape with Grace, for the time being.

He didn't dare use the vehicle they had driven up in. The sound of a motor would betray them instantly. That left their feet. He only prayed he could get her far enough away to ensure a fighting chance at saving his mate's life.

What the hell had made him think he could have this time with her? That he could possibly steal just a few days of peace?

Somehow, he must have missed the signs that he was being watched. Only a coyote could have scented the mating heat building between him and Grace before he kidnapped her. But how had he missed a coyote trailing him?

Matthias kept Grace close to his side, as he moved from the house to the sheltering trees that ran along the rough track leading into the cabin. He kept to the far side, knowing the coyotes were moving up along the upper side.

The breeze drifted around him, bringing the smell of them to him and causing his lip to lift in a snarl of hatred. If he were alone, he would have gone hunting. He would have killed every fucking mongrel that thought he could blindside Matthias this way.

But he wasn't alone. At his side, his mate was struggling to keep up with him, trying not to breathe too hard, to stay as quiet as possible.

As a twig crunched under her feet, he throttled a curse and wrapped his arm around her waist, lifting her off the ground. Her arms wrapped around his neck, and he felt her tears against his shoulder. Tears he wished he could shed.

There was no time for tears now. He had to get her as far away from danger as possible. There were a few other cabins farther down the mountain; there had been vehicles there as they drove in. If he could steal one and get a head start . . .

That wasn't going to happen.

He caught the scent of the coyotes' change of direction and knew he was fucked. Somehow, they had figured out that he and Grace had left the cabin, and now they were on his ass.

"Leave me," she whispered in his ear, as he found a faint animal path and began to move faster along it. "You can get away on your own."

"It's you they want, Grace."

She shuddered at his words and pressed her face tighter into his shoulder.

"It doesn't matter." Her voice trembled at the words. "I know how to hide. You can get away and go for help."

He would have howled then, if he could have. She honestly thought he would allow her to sacrifice herself? For him?

"You're wasting your time," he growled. "I won't leave you."

Even in death, he would follow by her side. But he didn't intend to die. If ever there had been a time when he intended to live, then it was now.

"Four. I have you."

Matthias slid to a stop at the sound of the number he had been known by in the labs. Not a name, by all means they shouldn't believe they had the rights that even pets had. No, they were known by numbers. He had been the fourth Breed created in the Albrecht lab in the German mountains.

Matthias stared at the six coyote soldiers that stepped from the surrounding trees. Behind them stood Vidal Velasco, the Spanish directorate of genetic protocols.

It was this bastard who had chosen the women who were kidnapped for the European labs and used for their ovum and life-giving wombs. It was he who had decided which woman would be released and which woman would be bred to death. It was this bastard who had slit the throat of the surrogate that had birthed Matthias.

Matthias had been five when Vidal had gathered three of the Breed children in that lab together, called this woman their mother, then slid his blade over the weakened female's throat. Even then Matthias had recognized the thankfulness in the woman's eyes at her realization that the horrors she had been suffering were over.

"I hear you have chosen a name for yourself, Four," Vidal's mocking, aquiline features were illuminated by the glow of the full moon, as it peeked from the clouds above.

Vidal was much older now, nearing his seventies, Matthias knew, but he moved like a much younger man, his black eyes glowing in the night, his short gray hair gleaming.

Even now, he wore a dark gray suit. His black shirt was dull against his swarthy flesh, his gray tie cinched snug at his neck. Matthias bet he was wearing the overly expensive leather shoes he was partial to, as well.

Vidal was nothing if not precise and neat in appearance and action. Even when he was killing.

Matthias lowered Grace to her feet, keeping his arm wrapped snugly around her, as he checked the position of each coyote. He held his rifle in one arm, his finger on the responsive trigger, as the coyotes began to spread out behind him.

"You picked the wrong night, Vidal," Matthias growled. "I'm not in the mood for you."

Inside, he was praying. He needed the coyotes closer together, not farther apart. He needed just one chance to catch them in a spray of bullets and to keep them from shooting Grace.

If he died, he would die knowing he left his mate to these monsters. He couldn't allow that to happen. Grace must survive.

"Is she breeding yet, Four?" Vidal asked him in his precise, flawless English. "I hear wolves are having a difficult time transitioning from animal to man when they take their mates. Have you managed that yet?"

Matthias watched Vidal carefully. He stood just behind two of the protective coyotes whose weapons were aimed, not at Matthias, but at Grace.

"When the shooting starts, I'm taking you out first, Vidal," Matthias said. "My bullets will tear right through your coyote pets and enter your chest. I won't miss."

Vidal frowned. "Now, Four, we don't have to be antisocial about this," he chastised Matthias. "Just give us your pretty girlfriend, and we'll let you run for a while longer."

Matthias lifted his lip in a mocking snarl. "I think you know that's not going to happen. I'm well aware of the experiments the council scientists are running. I'd kill her before I'd let you get your hands on her."

Vidal crossed his arms over his chest, as Matthias tracked each soldier with his eyes and with his senses. He would have one chance to get Grace out of this alive. If the coyotes continued to surround him, he would have just enough room to drop and roll Grace to the small, rocky crevice next to them. It would provide the barest cover, but perhaps enough for him to cover her body with his own, as he tried to take the coyotes out.

"I can't believe you allowed yourself to be caught so easily." Vidal's teeth flashed in the darkness. "You had a coyote on your ass the whole time you were courting Miss Anderson and never realized it. Have you grown soft, Four?"

Matthias shook his head. He had wondered about that.

"There was no coyote tracking me. You got lucky, nothing more. Seems fate shines on the diseased and soulless at odd times after all."

The scent of Vidal's anger began to pour around him. It made the coyotes nervous, as well it should. Vidal never could handle a Breed who dared talk back. It was one of his failings.

"Why did the directorate decide to send you on this little mission anyway?" Matthias shifted closer to the shadowed natural indention in the earth, as he watched Vidal. "Did they decide they didn't like you after all?"

"I am part of the directorate, you ignorant mutt," Vidal snapped.

"But not the head of it," Matthias pointed out, knowing well the ego that filled the bastard. "Are you certain they didn't send you on a suicide mission, Vidal? Every assassin you've sent after me has failed. What makes you think you could succeed?"

"I tracked you. I trapped you. With your mate," the other man gloated.

"Everyone gets lucky sometimes." He turned to glance around him, shifting ever closer to the rocky ledge that dropped into a four-foot ditch that water and erosion had created. "I think you just got lucky this time." He turned back to Vidal once more, giving him a cool smile. "Will your luck hold out?"

"Give me the woman, or the coyotes will fill her with holes, Four. My patience is wearing quite thin with your taunting."

Grace was shaking in his arms, but for each move he made, she slid into place with him. Her hands gripped the arm wrapped around her waist, and her body was tense, prepared. He could smell her fear, but he could also smell her determination to live.

Unfortunately, for them to live, their enemies had to die. The thought of shedding more blood in front of her was abhorrent to him. He had promised her the killing would stop. He had promised himself that for her, he would no longer kill. And yet, the cycle the council had began couldn't be stopped. Not for Matthias, not for any of them.

"I'll just have a bullet put in your head," Vidal sneered. "And I'll take your woman from your lifeless body. I hear it's quite painful for a woman after having been mated by you creatures, to be touched by another. Perhaps I'll get lucky, and my coyote was right when he sensed the possibility of her fertility. Is she carrying your pup?"

"Perhaps." He felt Grace's start of surprise. She wasn't carrying his child, he would know it if she were. But the thought of that could keep the coyotes from directing their bullets at her. "But you'll never know one way or the other," Matthias assured him. "Because you'll be dead."

"I will listen to her screams, just as Benedikt and I listened to the last bitch we dissected to get the brat she carried," Vidal sneered. "Her mate begged for her life, Matthias. Will you beg for your mate's life?"

And what of the child? Sweet God, what were those monsters doing now? Matthias remembered the sight of the female mate. She had been cut in so many places, sliced to ribbons. There had been no way to tell exactly what the scientists were looking for. If they had successfully removed a fetus from her body, though . . . His stomach twisted at the thought.

He lowered his head just enough to whisper, "I love you."

Her fingers tightened on his arm.

"Whispering your good-byes?" Vidal sneered.

Matthias moved.

His fingers tightened on the trigger, fire erupting into the night, as he threw Grace into the shallow ditch, then twisted and jumped in behind her, his gunfire still lighting the night, as he pushed her to move.

He could smell the blood behind him, but he could also hear Vidal's enraged screams. Matthias pulled Grace up the small gorge rather than running down it. Just ahead was a stand of boulders. If he could reach it, he might be able to hold them off long enough for Jonas to make it.

He had felt the answering vibration at the back of his watch against his wrist moments before. Jonas was on his way, and he wouldn't be too far off. The locator on the watch only sent out a short-range signal. He wouldn't have been able to detect Jonas's reply unless he was within range of the watch's tracker.

He pushed Grace behind the boulders, cursing as bullets rained around them. He pushed her to the rocky ground, moving to a crack between the boulders, and began shooting back.

A slender hand jerked the Glock remake from the holster at his thigh. Sensing her intent, Matthias quickly shrugged the ammo pack from his back and prayed she knew how to use the weapon.

"Grace, if anything happens to me . . . ," he growled back at her.

"Shut up and keep shooting. Nothing's going to happen to you." Her voice was shaking, terrified.

Matthias sighted a coyote soldier moving in closer, using the trees for cover. He gave the bastard one last chance to stay in place, and when he moved, Matthias fired.

One down, but there were more. And they were smarter about keeping cover.

"Jonas is on his way," he told her. "We just have to stay in place and stay alive. We'll be fine."

"Of course we will." Her voice was weak, thready.

The smell of gunfire filled the air, as Matthias continued to fire into the darkness, praying he would get lucky.

"Four, you're making me angry," Vidal called out. "You know I'll punish the woman for this."

Amazingly enough, Grace was the one that fired. She was kneeling at his feet, aiming low. A scream of coyote rage echoed in the night. She had obviously hit what she had aimed at.

"Stay put, and stay down," he ordered her, as he glimpsed a flash of gray moving through the underbrush. Vidal was trying to move into sight of the only weak point of their cover.

"I've got your back." Fear seemed to be making her voice tremble.

Matthias moved to the opening behind them, slipped past it, and waited. Behind him, Grace was firing. Occasionally a grunt or curse could be heard from the darkness. The smell of blood was thick in the air, but the smell of Vidal's treachery was thicker.

He moved closer. Closer.

Matthias lifted the rifle and watched, waited. Just a little to the right, he thought. He almost had him.

Vidal's graying head peeked from the tree that had been sheltering him, and Matthias fired. The bullet zipped through the night, struck Vidal's forehead, and the bastard went down.

Enforcers filled the area at the same time. Dozens of them were falling from the sky, sliding down black nylon ropes suspended from the night-black, silent heli-jet that had moved in overhead.

Matthias shook his head at Jonas's timing and slid back into the shelter to collect his mate.

CHAPTER FIFTEEN

Grace had never given much thought to death. Her thoughts since meeting Matthias had been filled with dreams for the future and plans to show him all the little intricacies of being part of a family. But when she felt the bullet tear into her chest, death was uppermost in her mind.

Strangely, it wasn't pain she felt. It was cold, not hot. It seemed to fill her body with ice rather than the burning pain she would have imagined. She was numb, yet able to move.

She had to move. She had to help Matthias. Just this one last time, she had to do something for him.

She managed to get his gun out of his holster and help hold the coyote soldiers back, determined to at least take a few with her if she did die. Matthias couldn't help her until this was dealt with, so she fought to hold back the ragged cries that tore at her chest.

Not from pain. She was numb to the pain, just aware of it. She wanted to cry because of what she was losing. As she felt herself growing weaker, felt the haze of blood loss engulfing her mind, she thought of leaving Matthias forever. She thought of the pain he would feel when she was gone.

It had taken her weeks to get a smile out of him, and she remembered the thrill the sound of his first laugh had brought her. She had a feeling Matthias hadn't often had occasion to laugh.

As Grace lay on the ground staring into the crack between the boulders, the gun dropped from her hand, and a whimper of agony left her lips.

She didn't want to leave him. She wanted to watch him play football with her brothers. She wanted to see her mother fuss over him and realize her father's approval of him.

"Matthias," she whispered, finally feeling him beside her again.

The gunfire had abated. Were the coyotes all dead? She hoped they were. She wanted them all dead.

"Grace. *Grace!*" She heard the panic in his voice, felt his hands as he turned her over, and knew he saw the blood.

She blinked up at him.

Shock, rage, agony creased his face, filled his dark eyes, and sent pain raging through her. She hated seeing the pain in his face.

Dawn was moving in, lighting the shelter they hid in, shadowing his scarred face, his incredible whiskey eyes.

He was screaming. She could hear him screaming, though what he said didn't make sense.

She lifted her hand to touch him. Just one last touch. Oh God, she didn't want to leave him. She wanted to lie with him one more time, she wanted his kiss again, to feel his touch.

"Matthias," she whispered. She loved his name, loved his face, and his heart.

"Don't you leave me, Grace." He was pressing something to her chest. "Do you hear me? Don't you leave me."

He was so arrogant. He was glaring at her, as though his refusal to let her go was all that was needed.

"Grace I swear to God, if you die, I'll never wear jeans. I'll never eat pie. I'll shoot fucking football players. Don't you die on me!"

She smiled. She was so glad it didn't hurt. That was so strange, the pain should have been agonizing.

"I love you, Matthias," she told him softly. "Like the earth loves the rain, like the flowers love the sun."

She was so tired. So tired and so frightened. She didn't want to leave him.

Her breathing hitched as the tears she couldn't hold back any longer began to fall from her eyes.

"Grace!" He was screaming at her, as her lashes fluttered. "Ah God, Grace, stay with me! Stay with me!"

She was so tired. She touched his face, feeling his hand clasp her fingers to his rough cheeks, and she fought to smile back at him.

Like a flower loves the sun . . . that thought drifted through her mind again. He warmed her like that. The sun warmed the flowers. "I love you."

She couldn't stay with him any longer. She tried. She tried until a silent scream was echoing in her head, because she could feel herself drifting away from him, and she couldn't stop it.

As her eyes drifted closed and rich darkness engulfed her, she could have sworn she heard a wolf cry.

Matthias . . .

. . .

"LET the medic work on her, Matthias!" Jonas was screaming in his face, as Matthias fought the hands pulling him away from Grace.

She was so weak. The smell of her blood was in his brain, and agony beat at him with blows harsher than any he had received in the labs.

Matthias fought like the beast he was to tear away from the Breeds restraining him. To get to Grace. To hold her to him.

"You mangy fucking wolf, listen to me." Jonas's forearm slammed into Matthias's throat, driving his head back against the boulder.

Matthias let out another bloodcurdling howl of agony.

"She's alive, Matthias, but if you don't fucking calm down, we won't be able to help her. Do you understand me? We won't be able to help her."

Silver eyes flashed in the dawn light, the savage expression of the Lion Breed who was helping to restrain him finally took shape.

"Jonas! Grace . . ."

"Help us, Matthias, don't go wild on me," Jonas snarled, his canines flashing dangerously. "She's alive. If we're going to keep her alive, we have to move fast, and you have to keep your head."

The forearm across his throat flexed powerfully, as Matthias struggled against him again.

"Can you keep your fucking head, Matthias?" Jonas yelled in his face.

"As long as she breathes," he screamed back.

"Good! Let's get going." Jonas released him, and only then did Matthias see the basket that Grace had been strapped into and the medic working furiously to keep her alive.

"Jump in." Jonas pushed him to the wide metal basket used to transport the wounded from the ground to the hovering heli-jet above. "You and the medic. The hospital has been notified, and doctors Armani and Morrey are en route."

Matthias clutched the side of the basket, as he knelt on one side of Grace, the medic on the other. An IV was strapped to her arm, a compress on her chest.

Sweet God, they had shot her in the chest. He felt the grief raging inside him now, the knowledge he could lose her, and he knew he would never bear the pain of it.

She had to live. Without her, he would never be warm again.

As the Breeds waiting in the transport heli-jet secured the basket, the hum of the craft grew louder.

He heard the report the medic was transmitting to the hospital in New York City. Her vitals, the site of her wound and its depth. She was on oxygen and had an IV. Surgeons were waiting, and the Breed doctors were on their way.

Within minutes the heli-jet was landing, and they were taking Grace away from him. She was loaded onto a stretcher and rushed across the roof as a second heli-jet landed and deposited the two doctors, who had been redirected from a flight to Virginia just minutes behind Jonas.

Doctors Armani and Morrey rushed across the landing area and followed the gurney. Within seconds, the heli-jets lifted off and left Matthias alone.

He stood on the hospital roof, staring around at the blinking lights, the buildings that rose like sentinels around them, and felt a striking loneliness fill his soul.

They had taken Grace away from him. Because of him, she was hurt, possibly dying. Alone.

Matthias stared down at his scarred hands and saw her blood, heard the ragged growl that tore from his throat. He was lost.

He stared around the rooftop again and realized that clear to his soul, without Grace, he was simply lost.

CHAPTER SIXTEEN

Joe Anderson entered the surgery waiting room, his wife, sons, and their families closing in behind him. He knew him the moment he saw the young man Jonas Wyatt had told him to look for.

Wearing black leather, streaked with blood, his face resting in his broad hands, as long, night-black hair flowed around them.

He sat alone. The other families awaiting word on their loved ones were gathered at the other side of the room, casting wary looks his way.

Matthias Slaughter.

Grace had told him about Matthias, of course. Not what he looked like, or about the air of danger that surrounded him. She told him things only a woman would think of. Things like his sadness, his wariness, and how he made her feel.

Joe sighed heavily. This man made his daughter feel alive. Grace had said, "As though there's adventure around every corner, Daddy." And she had laughed. But he had heard the love in that laughter.

This was his daughter's man. That made him family. No matter what.

Matthias's head lifted, and the scarred face looked around, as he swiped the overly long black hair back from his face. He was an imposing figure. Standing to his feet, Matthias paced over to the windows, looked out, paced back to the small table, sat down, and tried to blend into the shadows of the room.

Joe could see the man's attempts to become invisible, and it bothered him. Jonas hadn't said much about this Wolf Breed enforcer, but Joe had learned years ago how to read between the lines. And what he had sensed rather than heard, made him ache for the young man.

Joe fought back his own fear, his own anger at the thought of his daughter lying in surgery, a bullet in her chest, her life hanging on the line.

Daddy, I love you like the flowers love the sunshine. And you know they love it, 'cause they open right up and spread their petals like arms. Have you noticed that, Daddy? They hug the sun, because it keeps them safe and warm. That's why I love hugging you, Daddy. You keep me safe and warm.

He had to blink back his tears at the memory of her, barely ten, trying to wheedle her way out of some trouble she had gotten into at school. Grace had been his wild child. She had fought and scrapped, climbed trees, and jumped into water that was invariably over her head. Just as she had this time.

And just as he had always known she would, she had picked a man strong enough to follow her into adventure. Grace loved adventure. She restrained it now, worked hard, and never got into trouble. But she still liked to climb trees, and she still liked the deeper waters.

"There he is. Joe, why are you just standing here?" His wife, Janet, moved around him, her still-shapely figure drawn tight with fear for her daughter and worry for this Breed that their daughter spoke so highly of.

Matthias Slaughter was streaked with dirt and their daughter's blood, and his expression was haggard, bordering on savage. The sight of him broke Joe's heart.

As Joe stood there, Janet and his three daughters-in-law left him alone with his silent sons. Grace's older brothers were a lot like Joe. They watched and assessed.

Joe looked back and saw their eyes, and knew the boys saw the same thing he did. A man almost broken. The Breeds had lived horrifying lives. If that Jonas Wyatt's expression was anything to go by, then this Breed had known hell as few others had.

If he loved Grace as Wyatt said this man did, then the fear he would be feeling right now would be staggering.

He watched as Janet, with her mussed, shoulder-length gray hair and petite figure, fearlessly walked right up to that Breed.

The man's head lifted, and his eyes were alive with rage and agony, as he stared up at Janet. Joe knew the moment Matthias realized who she was. His expression clenched, his reddened eyes turned moist, and he whispered in a rough, growling voice, "She's my sunshine . . ."

Joe knew in that moment, Matthias Slaughter was family.

. . .

MATTHIAS wasn't ready for Grace's family. They would be angry, enraged at the danger he had brought to their daughter. There would be no buying or threatening their acceptance now. If she lived, they would demand his immediate removal from her life, and by God, he couldn't blame them.

He stared at his hands. He couldn't wash Grace's blood from them, it was all he had left to hold on to, her blood covering his flesh, reminding him that her love hadn't been a dream. It had been real. As real as the fight she was waging for her life right now.

When he looked up at the figure that moved to stand beside the table, he had immediately been snared by Grace's eyes. Soft, gray, tear-filled eyes in a lined face.

"Matthias, I'm Grace's mother." Her voice was soft, like a whisper of acceptance, and his heart clenched at the pain of it.

"I love her like the sun," he whispered, needing them to know before they accused him, before they raged at him. "She's my sunlight," he repeated.

And he could have never expected what happened next. Tears fell from those soft gray eyes, as she wrapped her arms around him and laid her head on his shoulder.

His arms gripped her, as she began to cry. His eyes lifted to the other women surrounding him, and to the men who watched him silently.

There was no condemnation. They all looked at him with compassion, especially the older man, the father, whose eyes reddened from the tears he held inside.

"I'm sorry." He was, to the bottom of his soul, so bleakly sorry that she had taken that bullet instead of him. He would give his life to trade places with her. He had offered his life to God to take him instead. He had prayed, bargained, raged, and begged the Almighty not to take his sunlight.

The father nodded once. He moved forward then, drew his wife from Matthias's embrace, pulled chairs back from the table for both of them, and introduced Grace's family to him. As though he weren't the enemy. As though it was important he know who they were.

"Not the first time she's been in surgery." Joe cleared his throat, as he sat beside his wife and wrapped his arm around her. "Remember when she was six, Janet?" He cleared his throat as Matthias stared back at him in confusion. "She fell out of that tree and started bleeding internally. I thought we were going to lose her then."

The three sons nodded, the women smiled watery smiles.

Matthias stared at them. "I have money." He clenched his hands on the table. "I have some small connections." They stared back at him questioningly. "I know I didn't protect her well this time." He stared at the blood on his hands. "I'll do better." He lifted his gaze to the father. "I'll make certain I do better in the future." His teeth clenched. He had sworn he would beg if he had to. "Don't take her from me."

Joe blinked, lowered his head, and shook it.

"I won't let it happen again."

Joe lifted his eyes once again. "Matthias . . ."

"I can't live without her." He meant to beg, but it came out as a growl of fury. "She would be torn between us. I don't want this . . ."

"Matthias." It was Janet that reached out to him. She placed her hand on his, over Grace's blood, and caught his eyes with hers.

"We all love Grace. And if she loves you, then you're family. You don't buy acceptance, son. You don't bargain for it. It's there or it's not. You love her, and we accept you because of that. But, she loves you. Because of that, you're family."

"You don't know me." He shook his head, terrified and confused, certain they had to hate him. They had to be hiding it, for Grace's sake.

"We'll get to know you." Joe's voice was a warning.

Matthias latched onto that. A warning. He knew how to handle that.

He stared back at the father, whose lips suddenly quirked with hidden knowledge. "Trust me, we'll all get to know each other. Grace will make certain of it."

He could handle that. Matthias nodded sharply before sliding his hand back from Grace's mother's touch. He breathed out roughly, stared around the room, then froze as Dr. Armani, the head Wolf Breed doctor and scientist, entered the room with her feline counterpart, Elyiana Morrey.

He jerked to his feet. Their expressions were pale, their lab coats wrinkled, and exhaustion marred their features.

"Nikki." He took a step toward her, then froze again.

They were watching him quietly, their gazes flickering over the family, who finally also came to their feet.

He had prayed over the past hours. He had bargained with God. He had begged for just one more chance and offered his life for hers. He had pleaded with a being that hadn't created him, but one Matthias prayed would bless him.

"It was close," Nikki finally said, a smile creasing her dark, exotic features. "But she's alive, Matthias . . ."

Two months later

"I TOLD you to wear jeans." Grace was laughing at him, her gray eyes shining with happiness, as tears of mirth rolled down her cheeks. "Didn't I warn you to wear jeans?"

"Shut up, Grace," he growled, attempting to peel the wet leather from his legs as he stood in the middle of their bedroom, dripping from sweat and the pain. "Those brothers of yours are fucking insane," he snarled violently. "Have I ever mentioned they are fucking crazy?" His voice rose at the accusation.

She was laughing. She was standing in the middle of the floor, her arms across her stomach, and she bent over, struggling to breathe as she laughed at him.

She was barely healed from the wound she had taken the night the coyotes attacked them. It had been slow progress, until Dr. Armani had given her a transfusion of Matthias's blood. After that, her recovery had moved quickly. Although the blood they had given her in surgery saved her life, her body had attempted to reject it. The unique qualities of the hormones in her body had fought it, and fought her recovery, until Matthias's blood had been added to it.

It shouldn't have worked. Their blood types didn't match, and his Breed blood should have been an instant poison to her system. Instead, from the moment it was introduced, she had begun to heal.

Now, two months later, she was standing here laughing her ass off at him because he was coated with mud and grime and struggling to get his damned pants off.

"I told you, jeans," she reminded him, finally straightening. "Geeze, Matthias, you need a shower." Another peal of laughter left her, as a mud-sodden hunk of hair fell over his face.

He swiped it back and glared at her.

"Poor little wolfie," she crooned, as he kicked his pants free and stood before her, naked. And aroused. Horribly aroused. He had felt the mating heat returning in the past week, tormenting him with the need to possess her. To taste and touch her.

In the weeks since her surgery, as though her body recognized its need to heal, the heat had only been a slow simmer inside them both. Now it was blazing inside him, and the scent of her heat filled his head.

His lashes lowered, as he flicked a look over the shorts and T-shirt she wore.

"Shower with me." He moved toward her, his body tightening with hunger. He had been like this for days, and it was killing him. If he didn't touch her, take her, he would go insane.

Her tongue swiped over her lips, as she pushed her hair back from her face, sensuality marking her features.

Grace hadn't forgotten for a second what she had almost been taken from. Over the past two months she had made certain Matthias became an integral part of her family, so that, should the worst ever happen, he wouldn't be alone.

He fought her, of course. He knew what she was doing. But when she awoke in that hospital room, saw his pale, haggard features and his agonized whiskey eyes, she had known. Had she died, Matthias wouldn't have been long behind her. His soul was a part of hers. She wondered, even now, if either of them could survive without the other.

God she loved him.

She leaned against his damp, muddy chest, her eyes closing, as she felt the warmth of him surrounding her. She loved him like flowers loved the sunshine. They embraced it, drew in its heat, and basked in its approval. That's what she did with Matthias.

Her hands slid over his powerful forearms, as they enclosed her, his hands gripping the hem of her shirt and drawing it away from her body.

Tossing the material aside, his lips went instantly to the mark throbbing on her shoulder.

"Like the flowers love the sun," he whispered at her ear, echoing her thoughts. "That's how I love you, too, Grace. I can't survive without your warmth. Without your love."

She turned to him, her head tilting back, her lips accepting his, as his tongue swept into her mouth. Honey and spice. That was his taste, and she gloried in it. Her tongue wrapped around his, drew the hormone from the swollen glands beneath it, and she let the fire have her.

Kissing her, touching her, Matthias lifted her into his arms and carried her to the shower. He didn't take his lips from hers as he adjusted the water. He sipped at them, licked at them, shared his taste with her, then lifted her beneath the spray of the dual showerheads.

The glass doors closed behind them, wrapping them in steamy intimacy, as his hands coasted over her body. His lips moved down her neck, to her chest. Just beneath her collarbone, he licked the scars the bullet and subsequent surgery had left. They were still a little tender, but the stroke of his tongue was like the sunlight.

Grace lifted herself against him, her head tipping back, as water ran over her head, soaking her hair, running in rivulets over her face, down her neck, to his lips. Lips that were moving from the scar to her nipples.

He sucked the hard points inside his mouth, drew on them deeply, growled in pleasure as she rubbed her leg along his thigh. The tiny, nearly invisible hairs that grew there, soft as a whisper of silk, caressed her.

Her hands weren't still, and neither were his lips. As he sucked at her nipple, scraped it with his teeth, her head lifted to allow her lips to touch his brow. Her hands smoothed over his shoulders, over the bulge of his arms.

Warmth and pleasure filled her. Wicked, sharp pleasure that clenched her womb and had her breath catching with an overload of sensations.

She had missed this. She had missed his touch, his kiss, the heat of him flowing over her and through her, until she didn't know where he ended and she began. He was her dreams, her adventures. Her sunlight.

"Poor Grace," he whispered against her breast. "I can smell how hot you are, how sweet."

"So fix it," she demanded breathlessly, leaning back against the shower wall, as his tongue swiped between her breasts, followed by a hungry growl.

She loved that growl. A bit of a rumble, a latent vibration of pleasure. She could distinguish between the sounds. Matthias growled a lot. Especially when he reached the saturated, slick folds of her pussy.

"Oh, God." He shuddered beneath her hands. He did that a lot, too. "I could eat you for hours. For days." His tongue licked through the narrow slit, circled her clit, and had her shuddering.

She was supposed to stand when he did this? When his tongue licked and stroked, and sent fingers of electric heat whipping through her?

"I don't think I can hold out that long," she panted, feeling the excess juices that gathered and built between her thighs.

She ached for him. Ached with a need that went beyond the heat that seared their hungers, one that went to her soul. She wanted him inside her again. She wanted that affirmation, that proof that they were alive.

"You don't have to hold out long, Grace," he groaned, his fingers parting the tender flesh as he tongued her clitoris.

Sensation raced from the bundle of nerves, struck her womb, clenched it, and sent her arching, tilting her hips closer, as the need for orgasm began to thunder through her. She was desperate. Didn't he know she was crazy for this now?

"It's been too long," she cried out, as she felt his fingers fill her rather than the thick length of his cock.

It was good. It was wickedly good, the feel of his fingers caressing her inside, parting her pussy and rubbing against sensitive nerve endings. But it wasn't enough. It wasn't what she hungered for.

Even as his fingers slid deep inside her sex, flexed and stroked the tender tissue, she was begging for more. His tongue licked around her clit, tightening it with agonizing need, as the nerve endings pounded with the need for release.

He nuzzled his lips against it, drew it inside his mouth, and suckled her with firm heat and disastrous results. Grace exploded in pleasure, the clitoral orgasm whipping through her, jerking her muscles tighter, and causing her nails to bite into his shoulders, as he rose before her.

The violent contractions of release were still thundering through her body, when he gripped the backs of her thighs and lifted her.

Grace curled her legs around his hips on instinct, forcing her eyes open to watch him in drowsy pleasure, as he tucked the head of his cock against the mouth of her vagina.

"I love you," he groaned raggedly, as he began to press inside her, the silky preseminal fluid filling her, sensitizing her further. "Like the flower loves the sun, the earth loves the rain. You're my life, Grace Anderson Slaughter."

She felt her heart melt for him all over again. That happened at least a dozen times a day, and it was always fresh, always new.

"I love you," she gasped, as he continued to slide inside her, stretching her, parting her, burning her. "You're my soul, Matthias. My sun and my rain." Her back arched, as he seated his erection fully inside her.

Grace felt her muscles flexing, tightening around the width of his cock, and sending brilliant shards of exquisite pleasure racing through her. They raked her nerve endings, embedded her soul, and whipped through every cell of her body.

Words weren't needed now, only gasping cries of pleasure and the hard thrusts and acceptance of the heat burning through them. His cock shuttled inside her hard and deep in luscious strokes. Grace twisted in his grip, taking him, stroking him, tightening on the hard, heavy length of his cock, as she began to tremble in his arms.

She could feel her orgasm coming now. It was tightening in her womb, through her muscles. Her clit was distended, her nipples hard and aching, as they raked against his chest. She was on fire. Burning. Sweating, despite the water rolling over them, and exploding in his arms as she screamed out his name.

His release followed. The thickening in the center of his cock spread across her sensitive pelvic floor muscle, causing it to spasm and contract, to milk tighter at his flesh, as a snarl of pleasure left his lips. The additional swelling didn't affect the entire length of his cock, just that one portion, the section that aligned just above the delicate vaginal muscle, effectively locking him inside her.

The blast of his semen inside her triggered another orgasm, not as fierce or as hard. This one was gentler, easing through her rather than exploding over her nerve endings.

As it ended, Grace found herself still pressed against the shower wall, as Matthias trembled against her. Cool water sprayed over their overheated bodies, washing away the perspiration that would have coated them, but doing little to still the heat that had raged through their bodies.

Her hands stroked his shoulders, her lips pressed against his neck. Grace held him to her, absorbing the hard spasms that gripped his muscles with each spurt of his release.

With each eruption, the hard swelling inside her throbbed, pulsed, and sent tremors of response racing through her. Like mini-orgasms clenching her womb. With each spasm, she tightened on that thick swelling, causing another pulse of his release to blast inside her. Causing him to shudder and groan in her arms.

"This . . . this is ecstasy," he whispered at her ear. "This, Grace, is home."

She felt tears fill her eyes. *Home.* Matthias finally had a home, and it was her. She buried her head against his broad shoulder and thanked God for the Breed that had found her.

"That was worth waiting for," she panted minutes later, as the swelling of his cock receded and he slid out of her, groaning.

"I couldn't handle having to wait like that again," he informed her, his breathing hard and heavy, as he lifted his hand and touched the scar on her chest. "Never again, Grace."

Her hand covered his. "I'll always be a part of you, Matthias. No matter what. Just as you'll always be a part of me."

He shook his head. "I took a job at the hotel. I'm head of security. You're assistant manager, and I have every assurance you'll be promoted to manager before much longer. We're going to live nice, sedate lives from now on. Do you understand me?"

He looked so arrogant. So dominant.

Grace grinned. "I still get to climb trees."